Don't you ever wonder about the future, Andy?
Sure, Lucy. I wonder if we'll have lunch, and what we'll hunt for dinner, and if there'll be leftovers for breakfast, and...

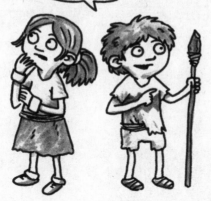

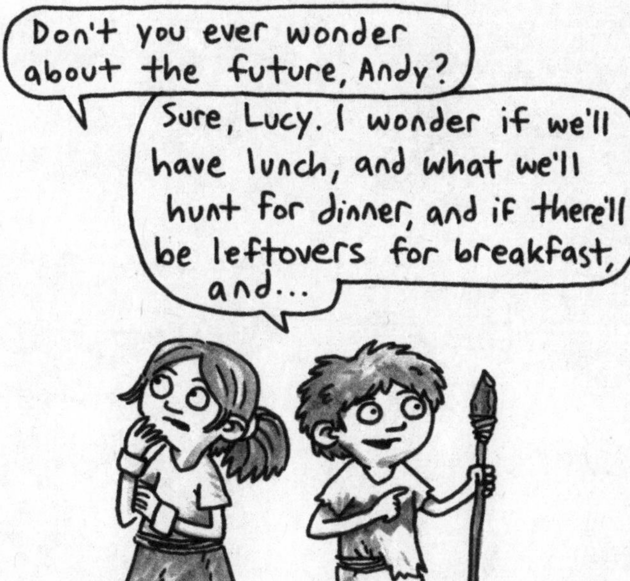

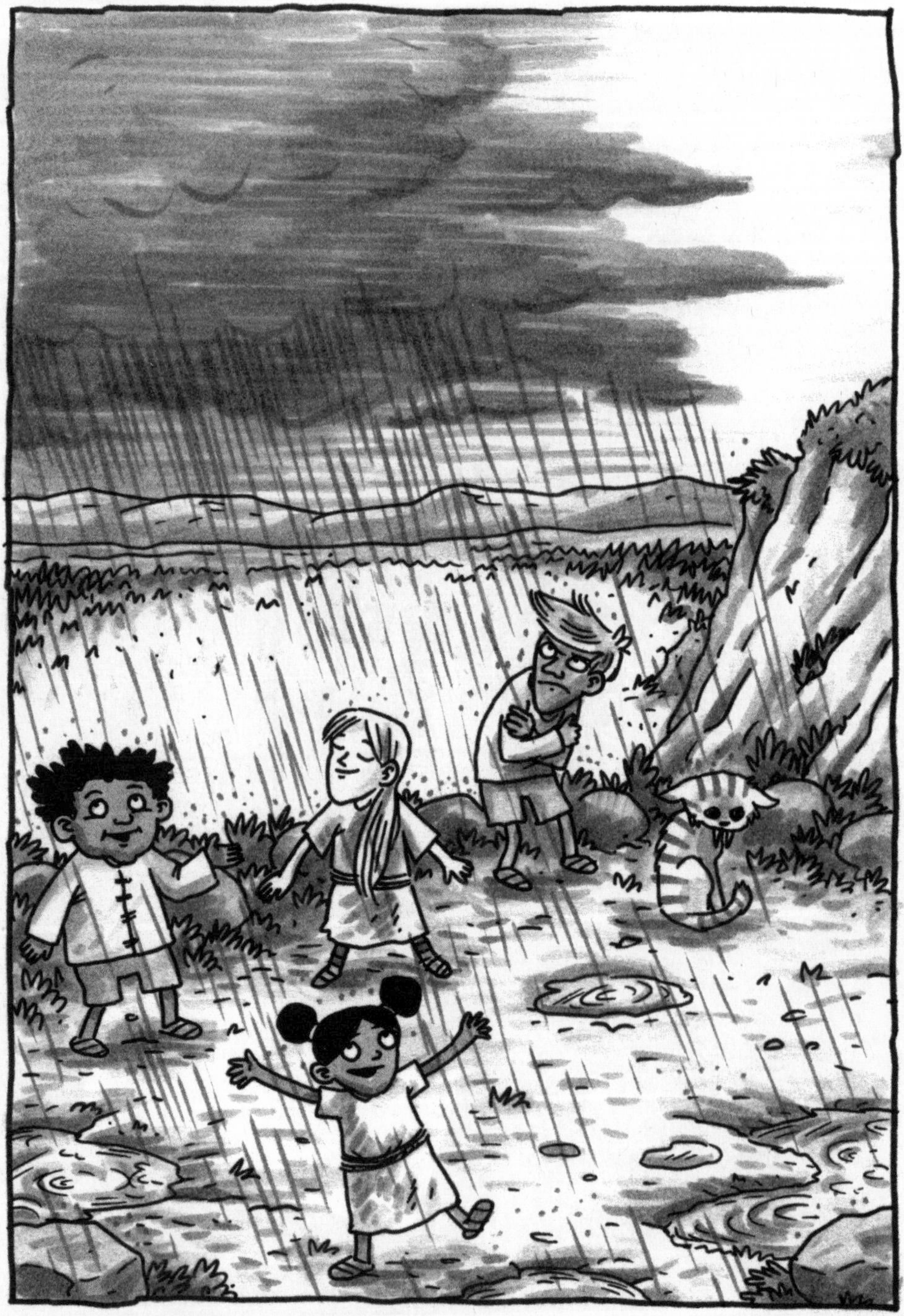

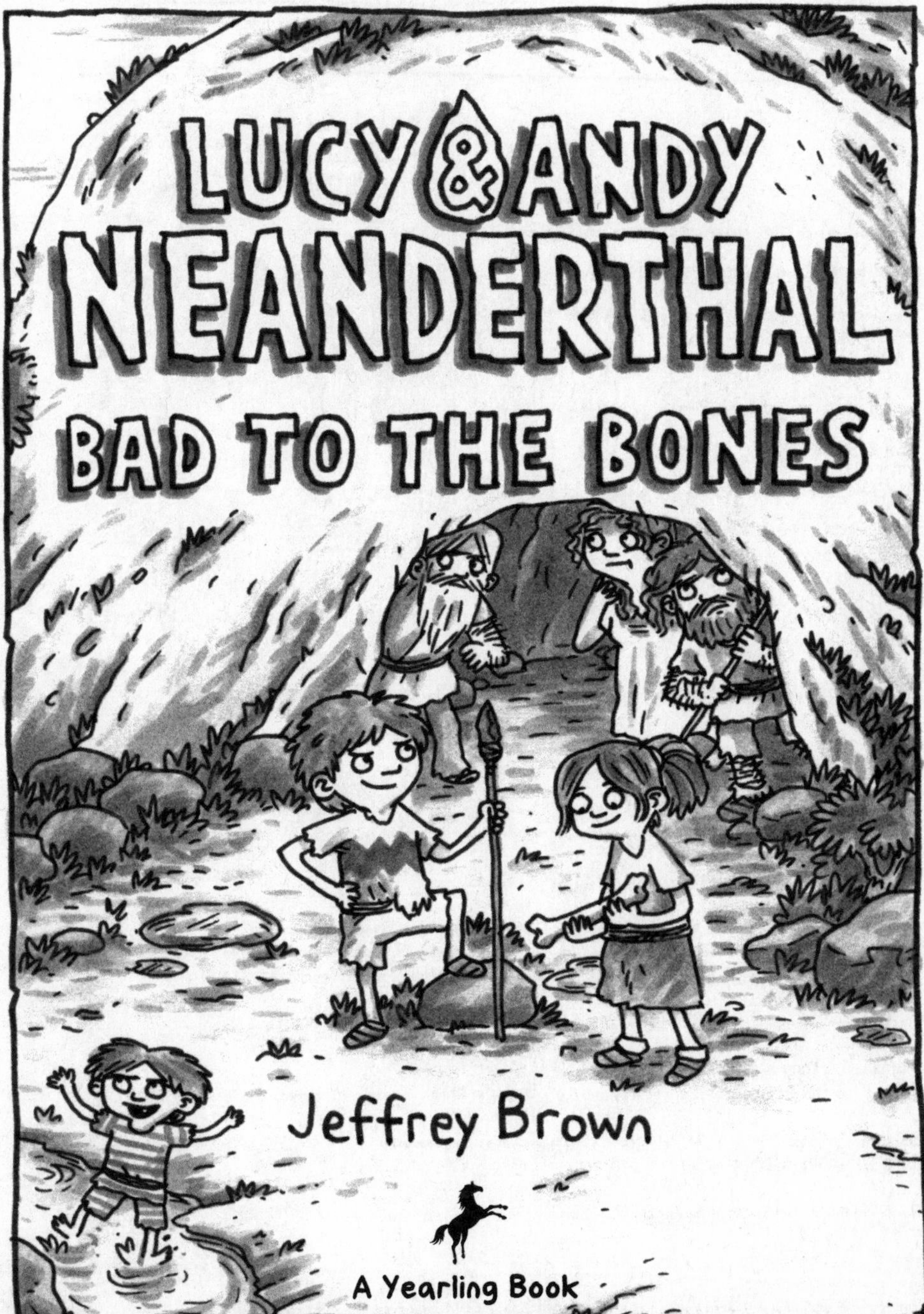
LUCY & ANDY
NEANDERTHAL
BAD TO THE BONES
Jeffrey Brown
A Yearling Book

Did you figure out the deal with these words yet, Eric?

I have some theories, Pam, but I need to read more books to figure it out!

Thank you to my family, friends, publishers, and readers for all of their support. Thanks also to Marc, Phoebe, and everyone at RH for making this book happen. And special thanks to Kevin Lee for giving me the nudge that led to the idea for this book.

For his expert assistance, grateful acknowledgment to Jonathan S. Mitchell, PhD, Evolutionary Biology, and member of the Geological Society of America, Society of Vertebrate Paleontology, and Society for the Study of Evolution.

All rights reserved. Published in the United States by Yearling, an imprint of Random House Children's Books, a division of Penguin Random House LLC, New York. Originally published in hardcover in the United States by Crown Books for Young Readers, an imprint of Random House Children's Books, New York, in 2018.

Yearling and the jumping horse design are registered trademarks of Penguin Random House LLC.

Visit us on the Web! rhcbooks.com
Educators and librarians, for a variety of teaching tools, visit us at RHTeachersLibrarians.com

Library of Congress Cataloging-in-Publication Data is available upon request.
ISBN 978-0-525-64399-9 (pbk.)

Printed in the United States of America
10 9 8 7 6 5 4 3 2 1
First Yearling Edition 2019

Random House Children's Books supports the First Amendment and celebrates the right to read.

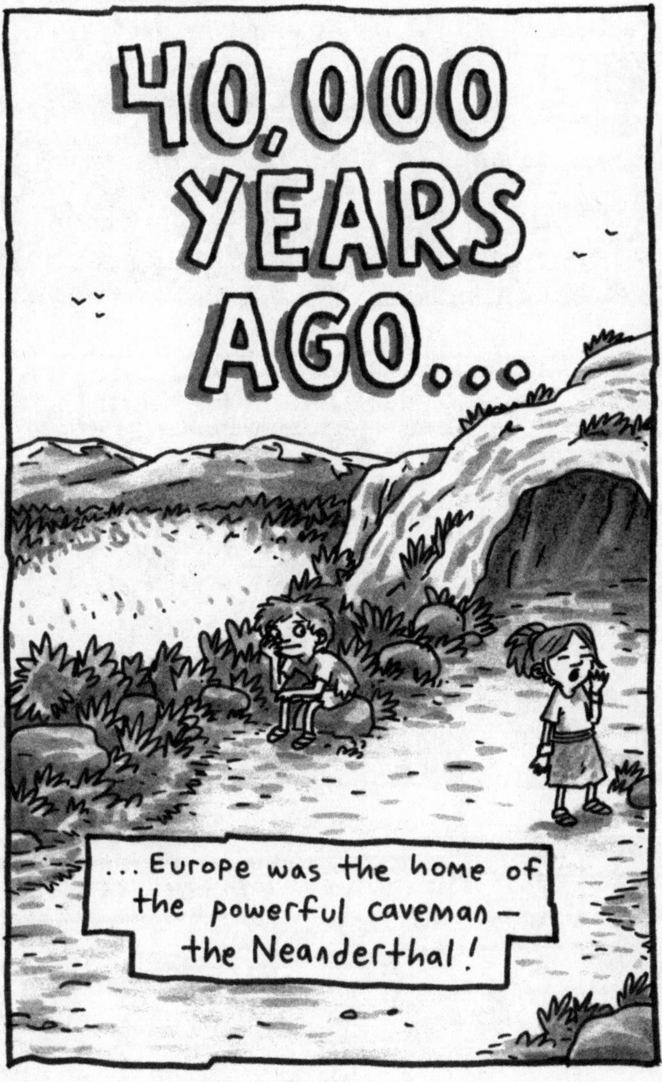
40,000 YEARS AGO...
...Europe was the home of the powerful caveman— the Neanderthal!

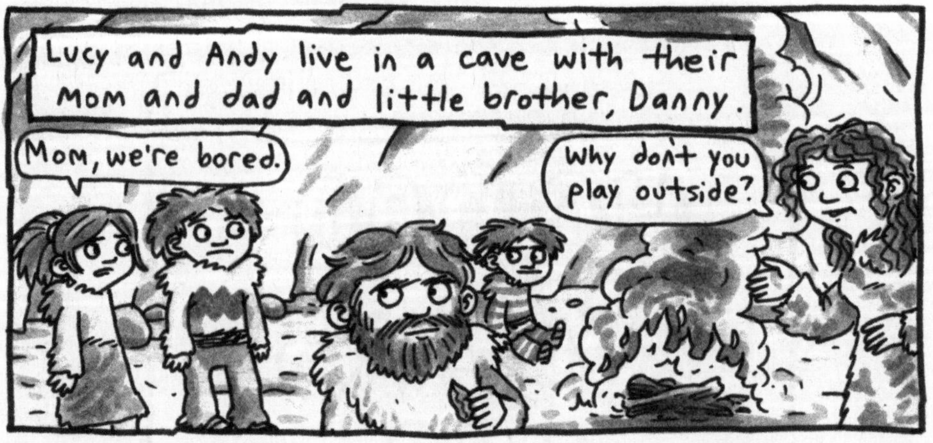
Lucy and Andy live in a cave with their Mom and dad and little brother, Danny.
Mom, we're bored.
Why don't you play outside?

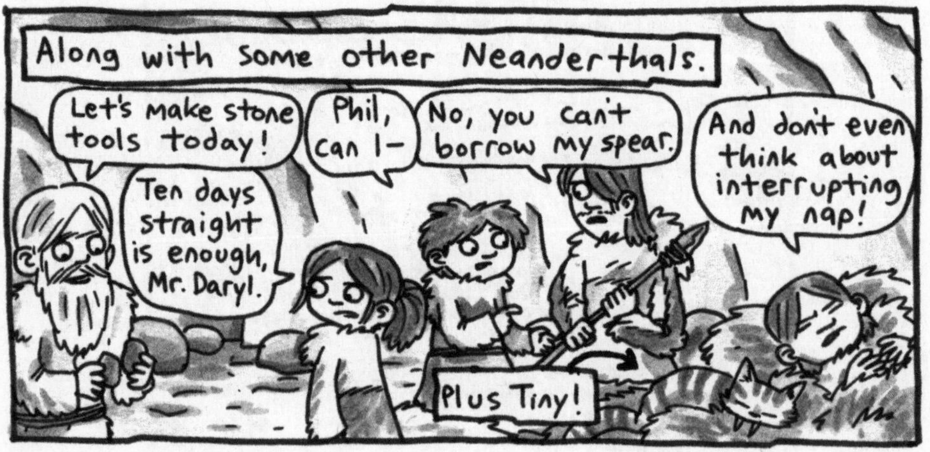
Along with some other Neanderthals.
Let's make stone tools today!
Ten days straight is enough, Mr. Daryl.
Phil, can I-
No, you can't borrow my spear.
And don't even think about interrupting my nap!
Plus Tiny!

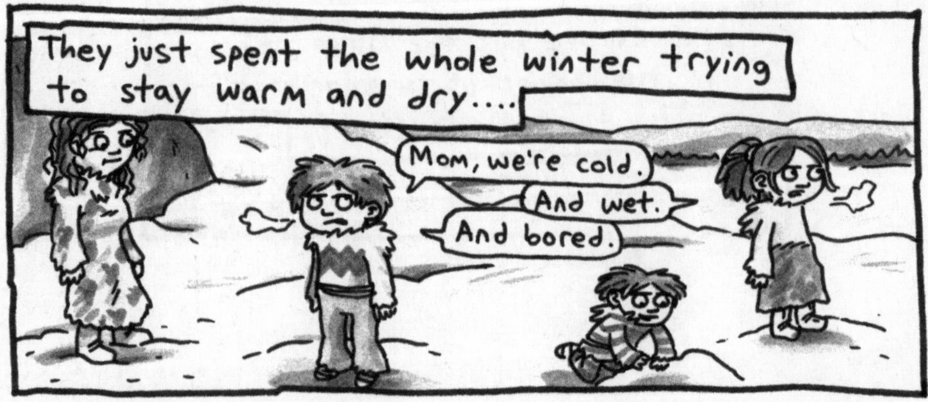
They just spent the whole winter trying to stay warm and dry....
Mom, we're cold.
And wet.
And bored.

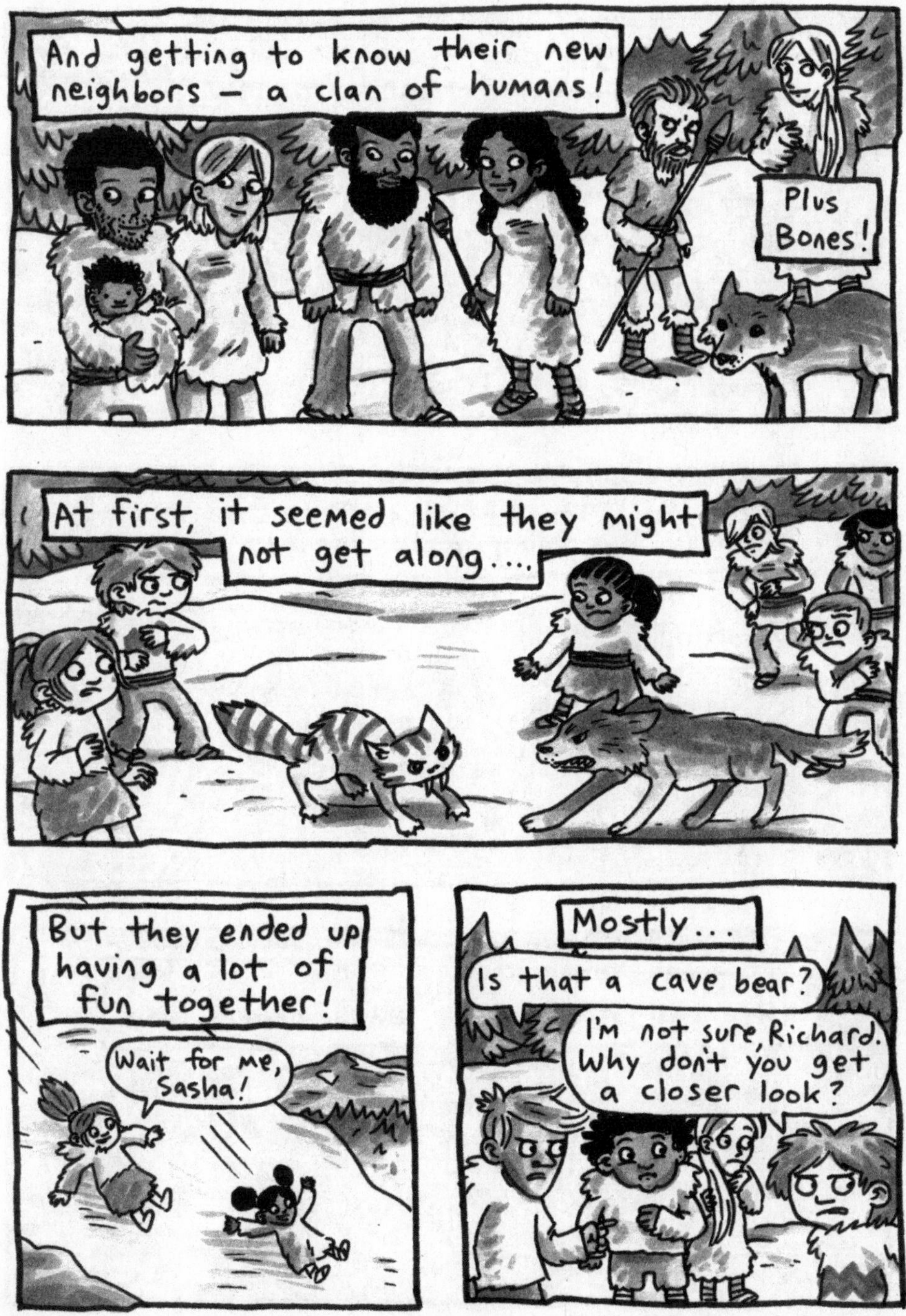
And getting to know their new neighbors – a clan of humans!
Plus Bones!
At first, it seemed like they might not get along....
But they ended up having a lot of fun together!
Wait for me, Sasha!
Mostly...
Is that a cave bear?
I'm not sure, Richard. Why don't you get a closer look?

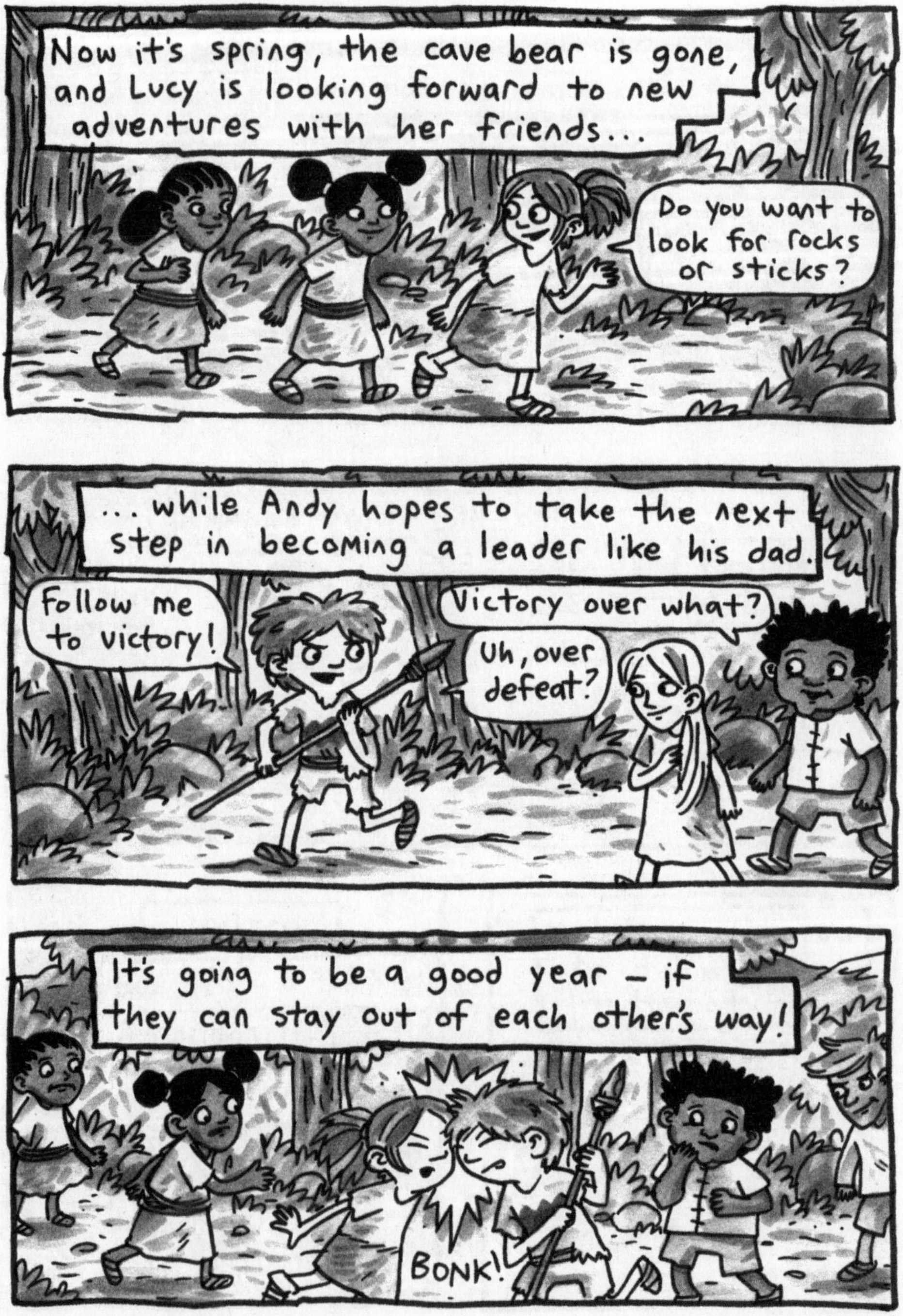
Now it's spring, the cave bear is gone, and Lucy is looking forward to new adventures with her friends...
Do you want to look for rocks or sticks?
...while Andy hopes to take the next step in becoming a leader like his dad.
Follow me to victory!
Victory over what?
Uh, over defeat?
It's going to be a good year – if they can stay out of each other's way!
BONK!

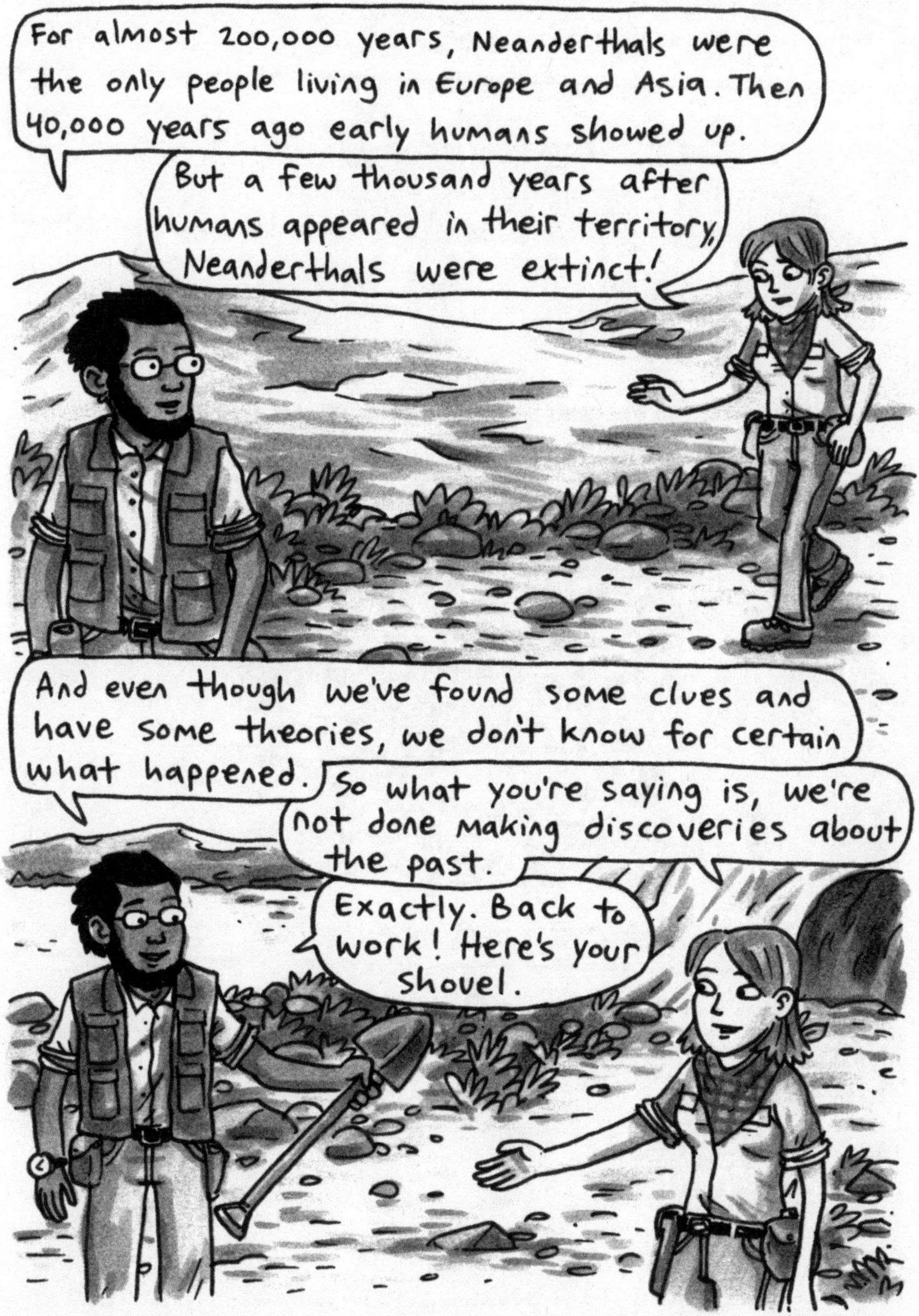
For almost 200,000 years, Neanderthals were the only people living in Europe and Asia. Then 40,000 years ago early humans showed up.
But a few thousand years after humans appeared in their territory, Neanderthals were extinct!
And even though we've found some clues and have some theories, we don't know for certain what happened.
So what you're saying is, we're not done making discoveries about the past.
Exactly. Back to work! Here's your shovel.

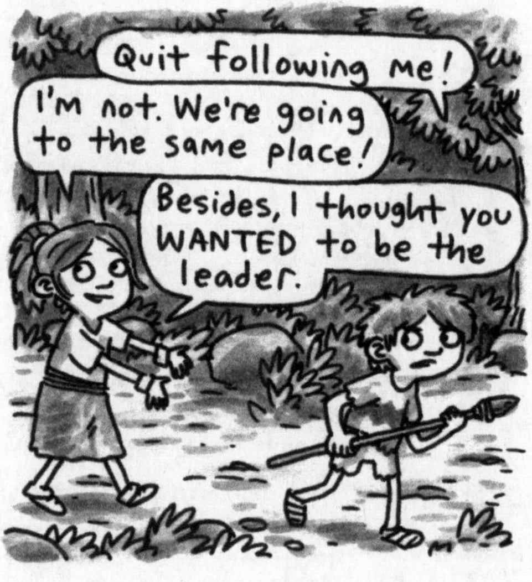
Quit following me!
I'm not. We're going to the same place!
Besides, I thought you WANTED to be the leader.

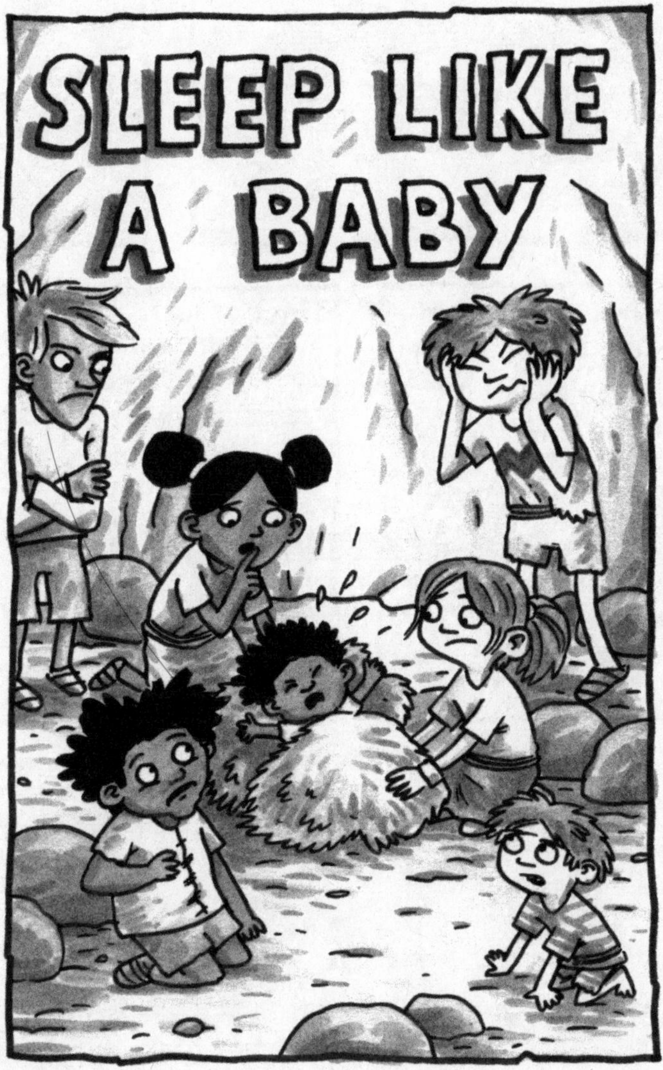
SLEEP LIKE
A BABY

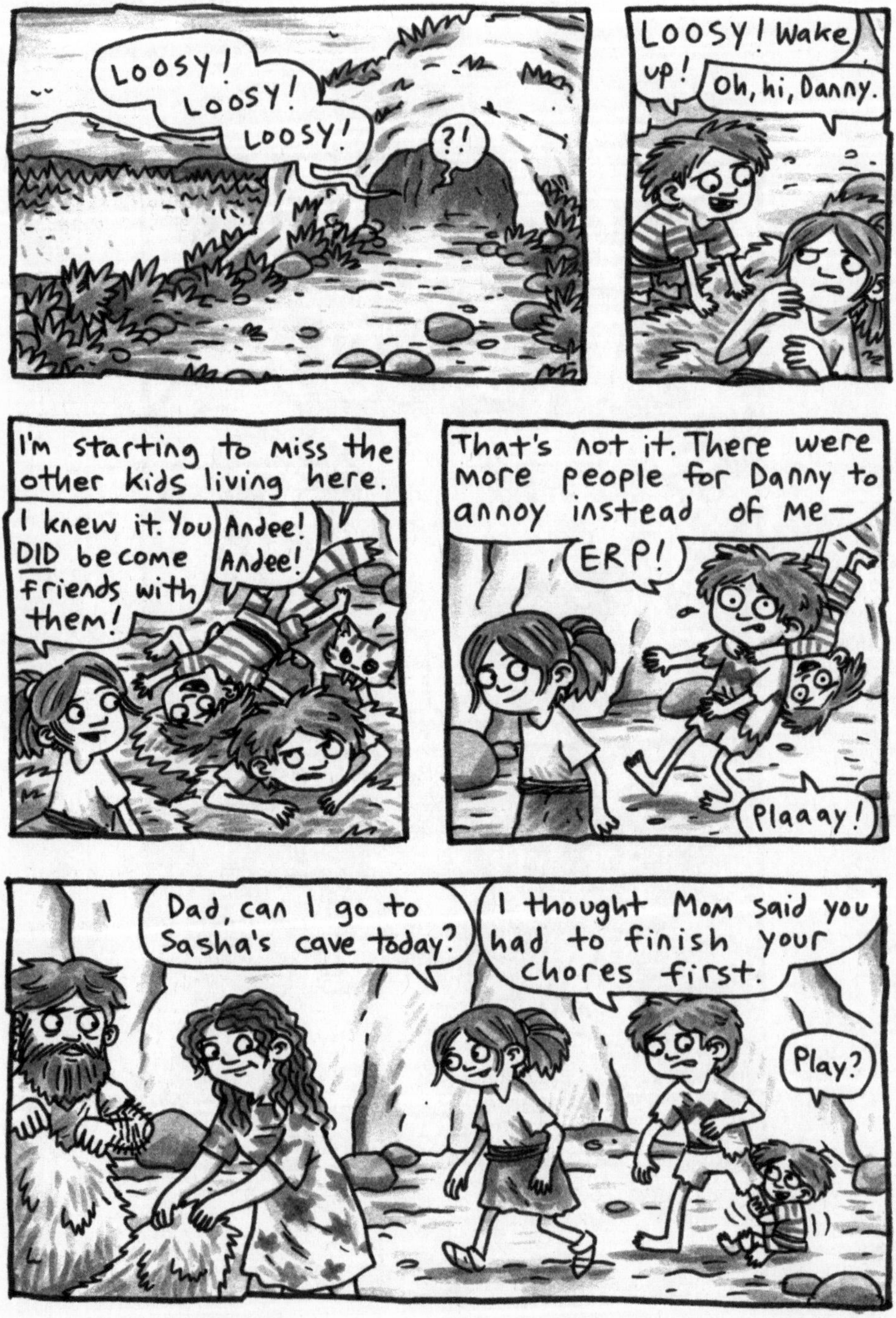
LOOSY!
LOOSY!
LOOSY!
?!
LOOSY! Wake up!
Oh, hi, Danny.
I'm starting to miss the other kids living here.
I knew it. You DID become friends with them!
Andee! Andee!
That's not it. There were more people for Danny to annoy instead of me—
ERP!
Plaaay!
Dad, can I go to Sasha's cave today?
I thought Mom said you had to finish your chores first.
Play?

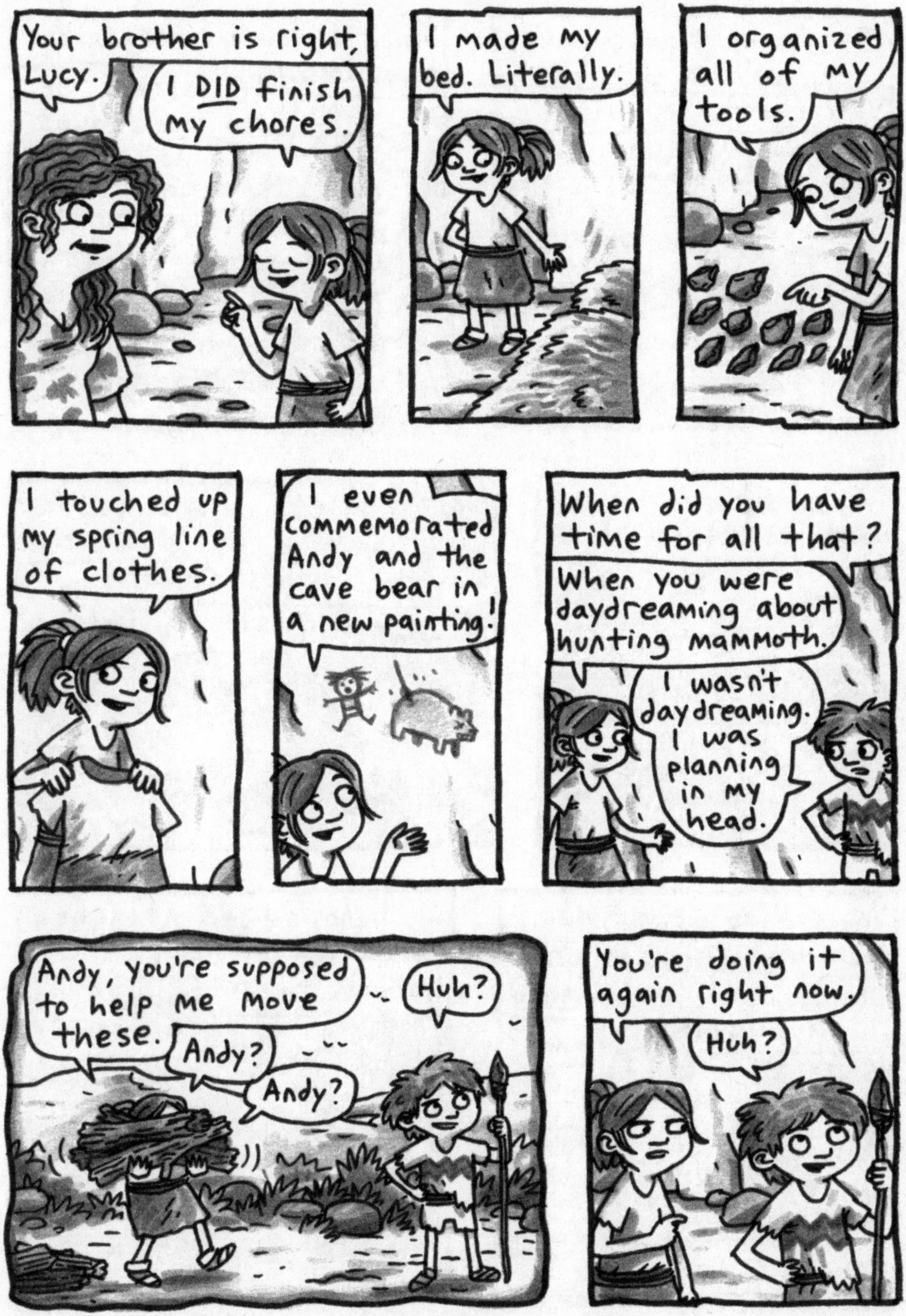
Your brother is right, Lucy.
I DID finish my chores.
I made my bed. Literally.
I organized all of my tools.
I touched up my spring line of clothes.
I even commemorated Andy and the cave bear in a new painting!
When did you have time for all that?
When you were daydreaming about hunting mammoth.
I wasn't daydreaming. I was planning in my head.
Andy, you're supposed to help me move these.
Huh?
Andy?
Andy?
You're doing it again right now.
Huh?

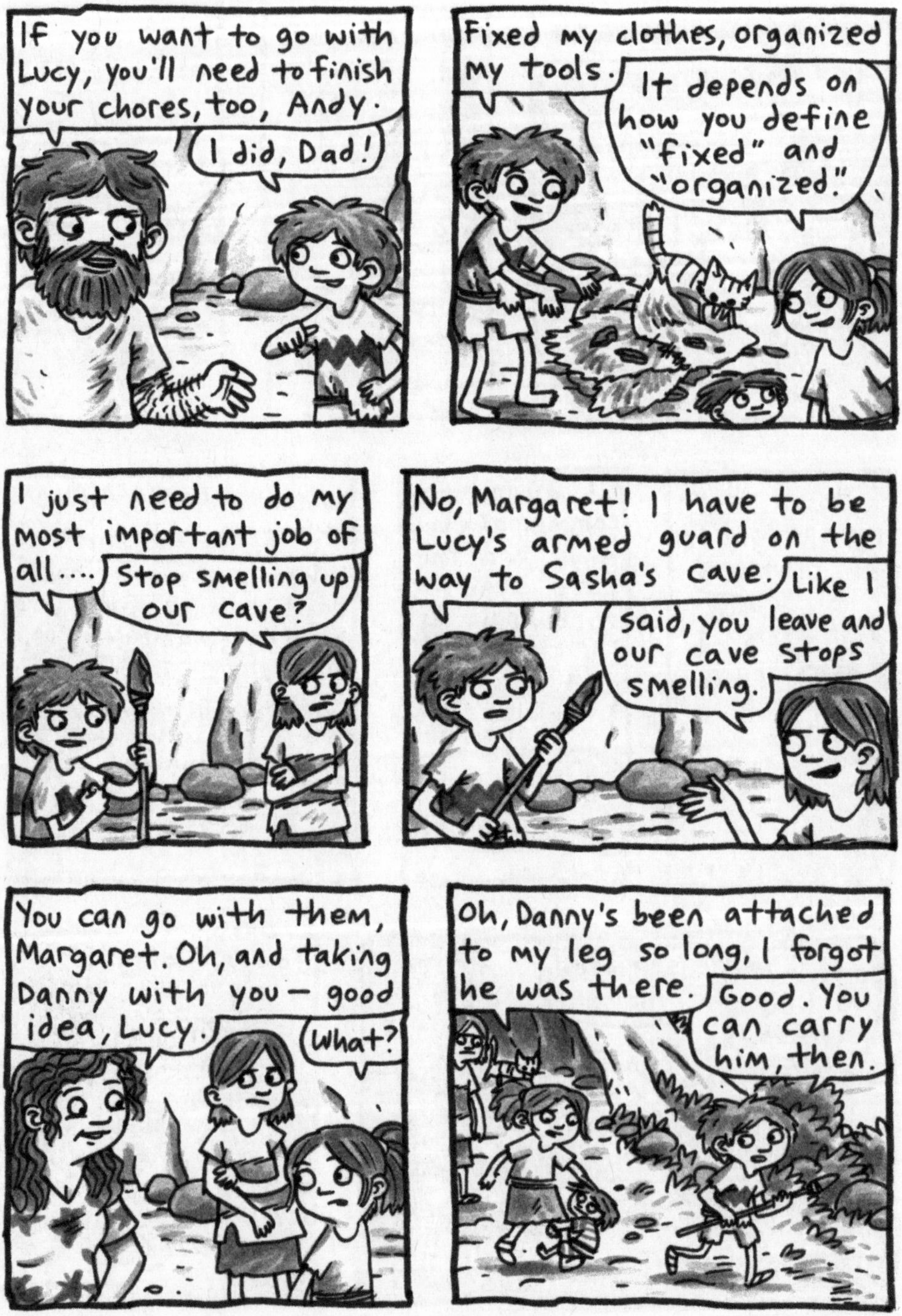
If you want to go with Lucy, you'll need to finish your chores, too, Andy.
I did, Dad!
Fixed my clothes, organized my tools.
It depends on how you define "fixed" and "organized."
I just need to do my most important job of all....
Stop smelling up our cave?
No, Margaret! I have to be Lucy's armed guard on the way to Sasha's cave.
Like I said, you leave and our cave stops smelling.
You can go with them, Margaret. Oh, and taking Danny with you— good idea, Lucy.
What?
Oh, Danny's been attached to my leg so long, I forgot he was there.
Good. You can carry him, then.

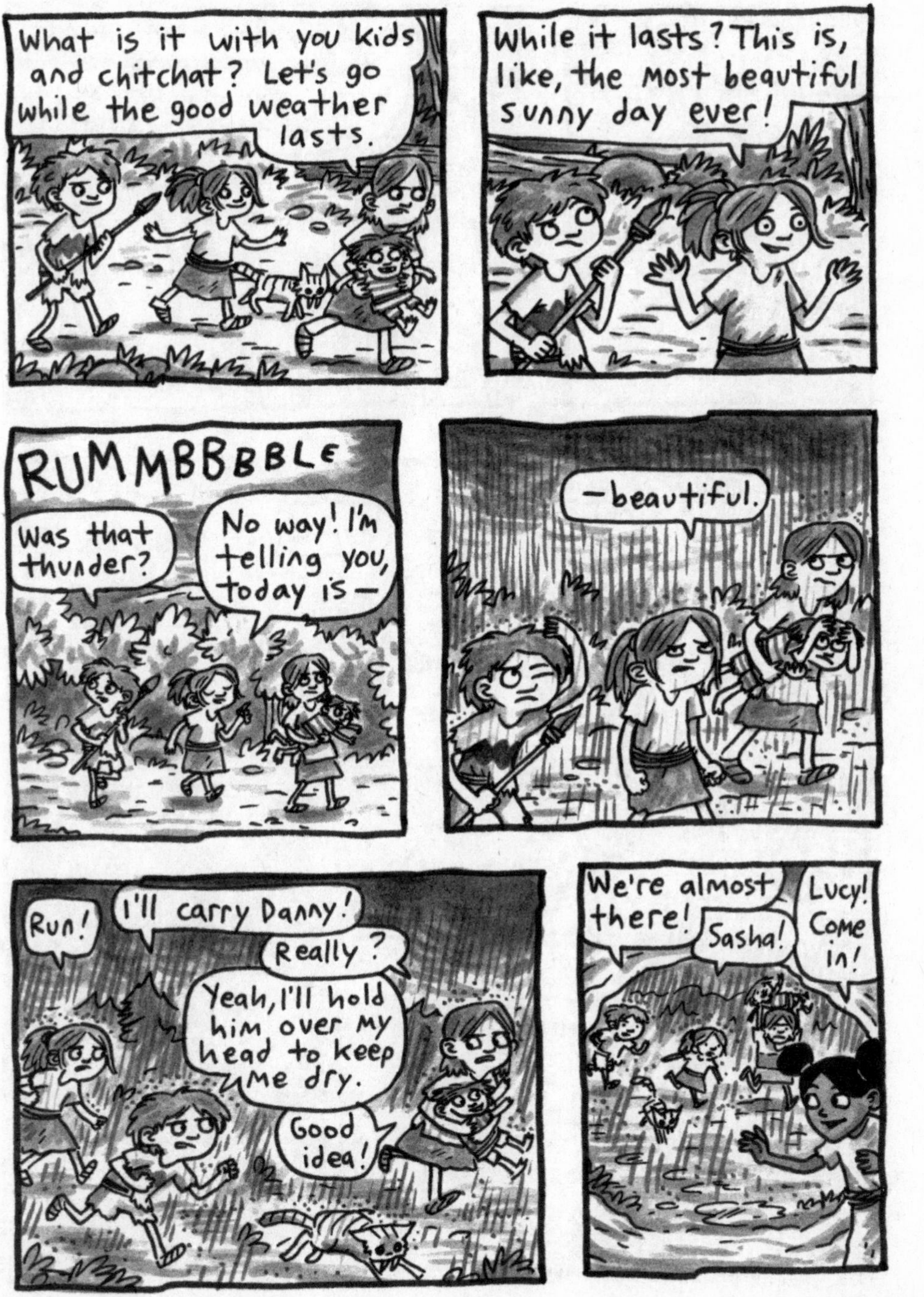
What is it with you kids and chitchat? Let's go while the good weather lasts.
While it lasts? This is, like, the most beautiful sunny day ever!
RUMMBBBBLE
Was that thunder?
No way! I'm telling you, today is—
—beautiful.
Run!
I'll carry Danny!
Really?
Yeah, I'll hold him over my head to keep me dry.
Good idea!
We're almost there!
Sasha!
Lucy! Come in!

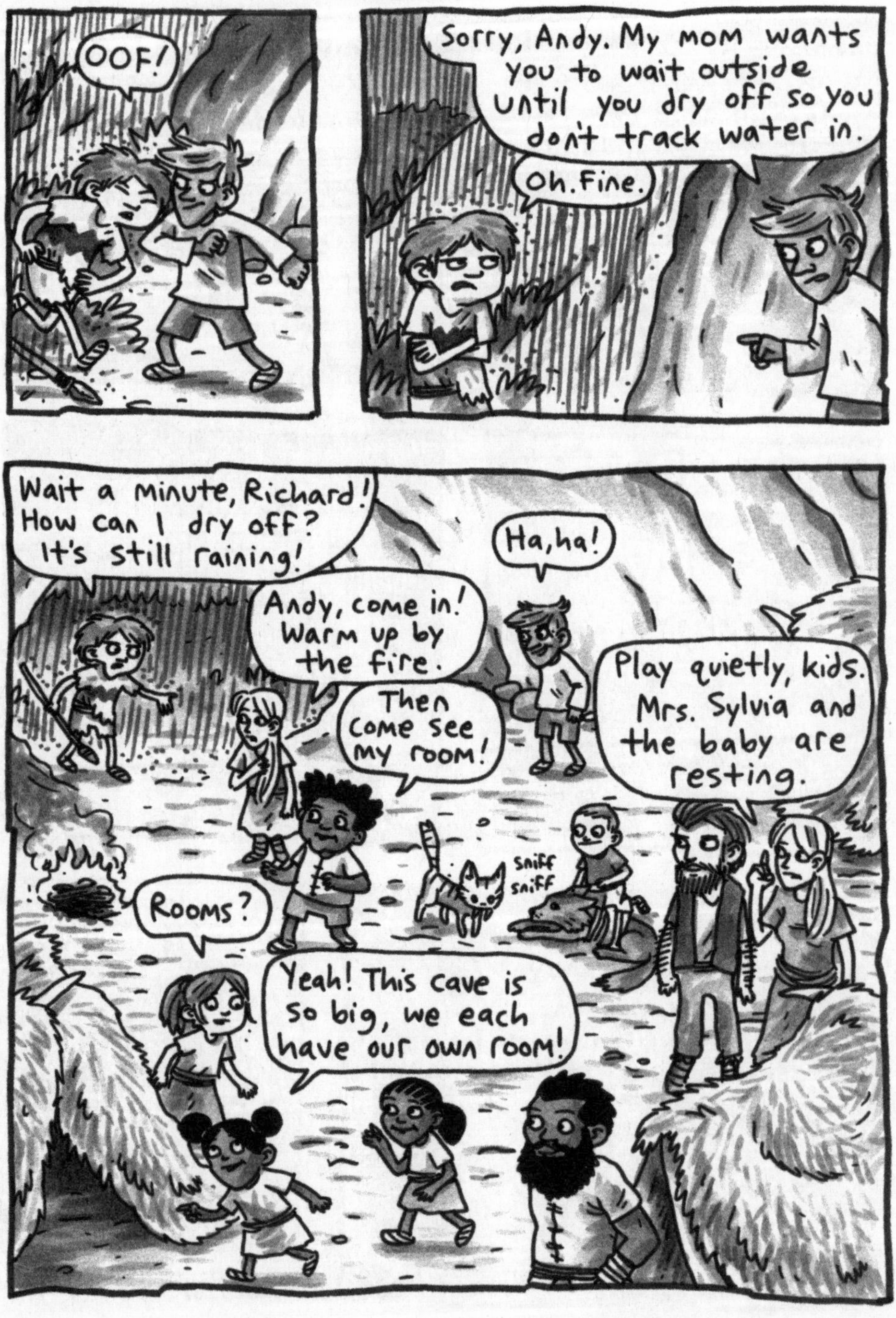

OOF!
Sorry, Andy. My mom wants you to wait outside until you dry off so you don't track water in.
Oh. Fine.
Wait a minute, Richard! How can I dry off? It's still raining!
Ha, ha!
Andy, come in! Warm up by the fire.
Then come see my room!
Play quietly, kids. Mrs. Sylvia and the baby are resting.
sniff sniff
Rooms?
Yeah! This cave is so big, we each have our own room!

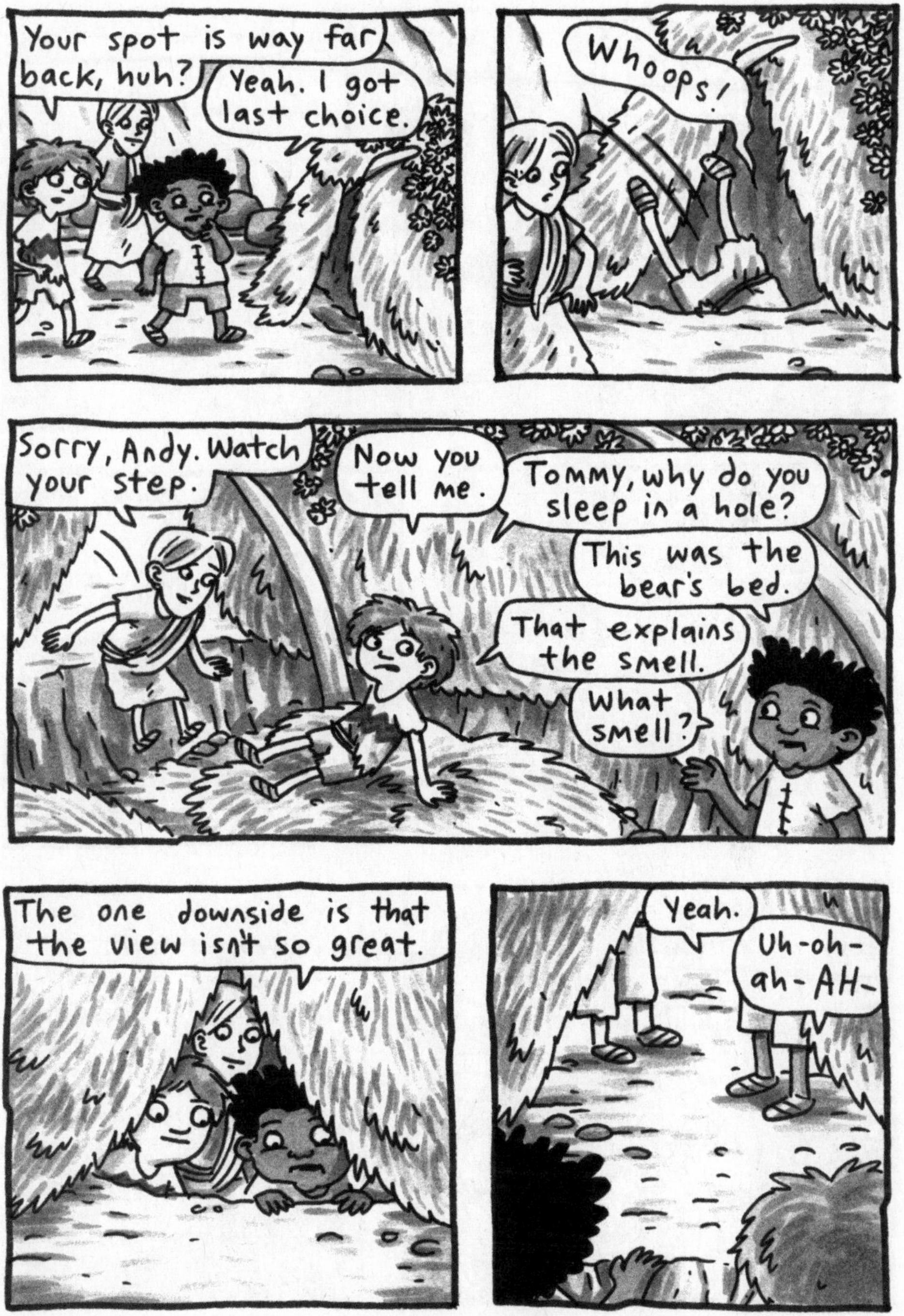
Your spot is way far back, huh?
Yeah. I got last choice.
Whoops!
Sorry, Andy. Watch your step.
Now you tell me.
Tommy, why do you sleep in a hole?
This was the bear's bed.
That explains the smell.
What smell?
The one downside is that the view isn't so great.
Yeah.
Uh-oh-ah-AH-

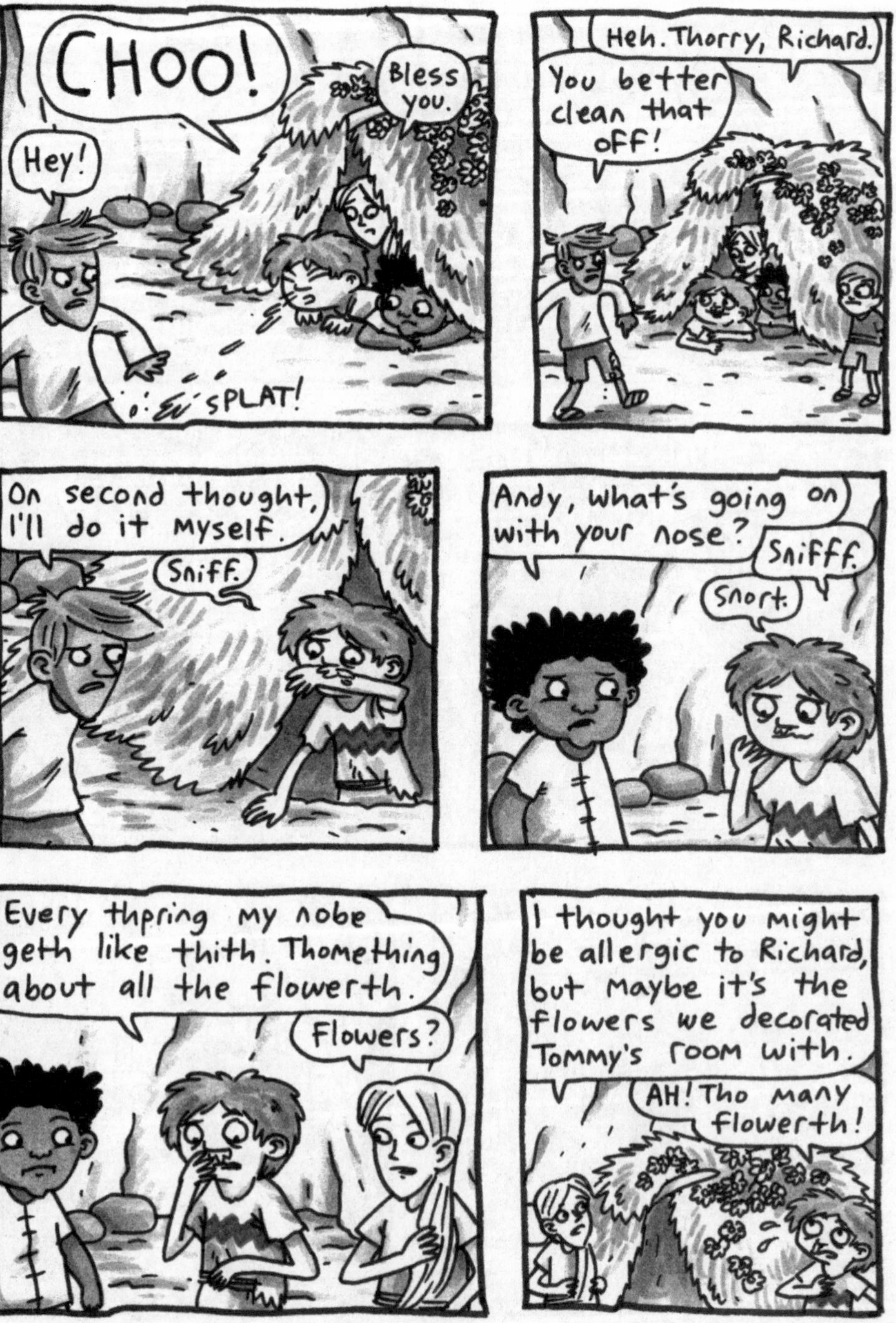
CHOO!
Hey!
Bless you.
SPLAT!
Heh. Thorry, Richard.
You better clean that off!
On second thought, I'll do it myself.
Sniff.
Andy, what's going on with your nose?
Snifff.
Snort.
Every thpring my nobe geth like thith. Thomething about all the flowerth.
Flowers?
I thought you might be allergic to Richard, but maybe it's the flowers we decorated Tommy's room with.
AH! Tho many flowerth!

In modern humans, hay fever is a seasonal allergy that causes runny noses and watery eyes.

Research shows that Neanderthals had allergies very much like ours.

There are no studies on how much Neanderthals wiped their noses on their sleeves!

AH-CHOO!

DODGE!

Wahhhhh!

Andy! You woke up Sasha's sister!

No, Tara was already up. Andy just surprised her.

She's surprised someone can have a snottier nose than she does.

Sniff.

Maybe I AM allergic to Rithard... Ah-AH—

Heh, heh!

I would high-five you, but I'm afraid your hand is slimy.

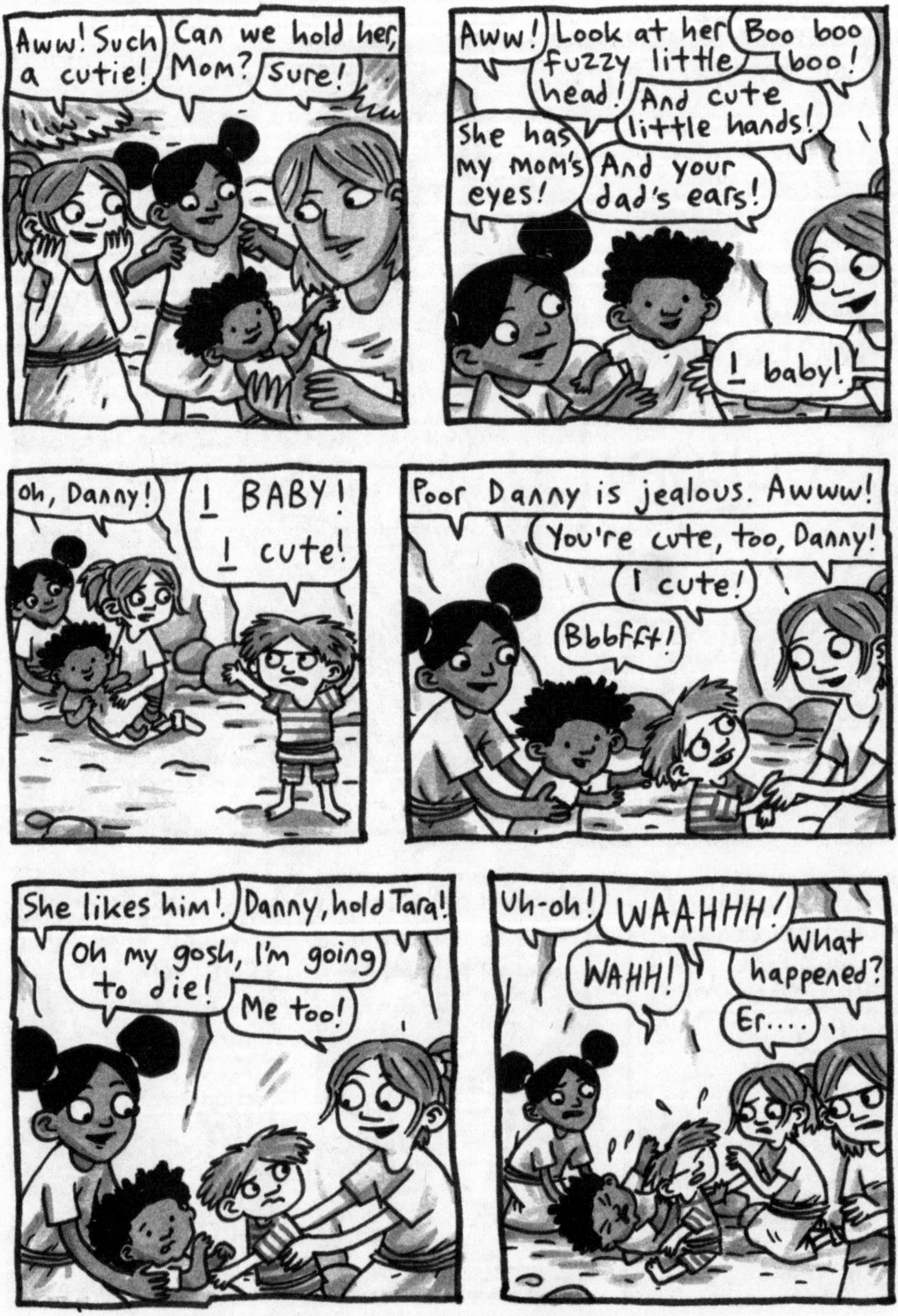
Aww! Such a cutie!
Can we hold her, Mom?
Sure!
Aww!
Look at her fuzzy little head!
Boo boo boo!
And cute little hands!
She has my mom's eyes!
And your dad's ears!
I baby!
Oh, Danny!
I BABY!
I cute!
Poor Danny is jealous. Awww!
You're cute, too, Danny!
I cute!
Bbbffft!
She likes him!
Danny, hold Tara!
Oh my gosh, I'm going to die!
Me too!
Uh-oh!
WAAHHH!
WAHH!
What happened?
Er....

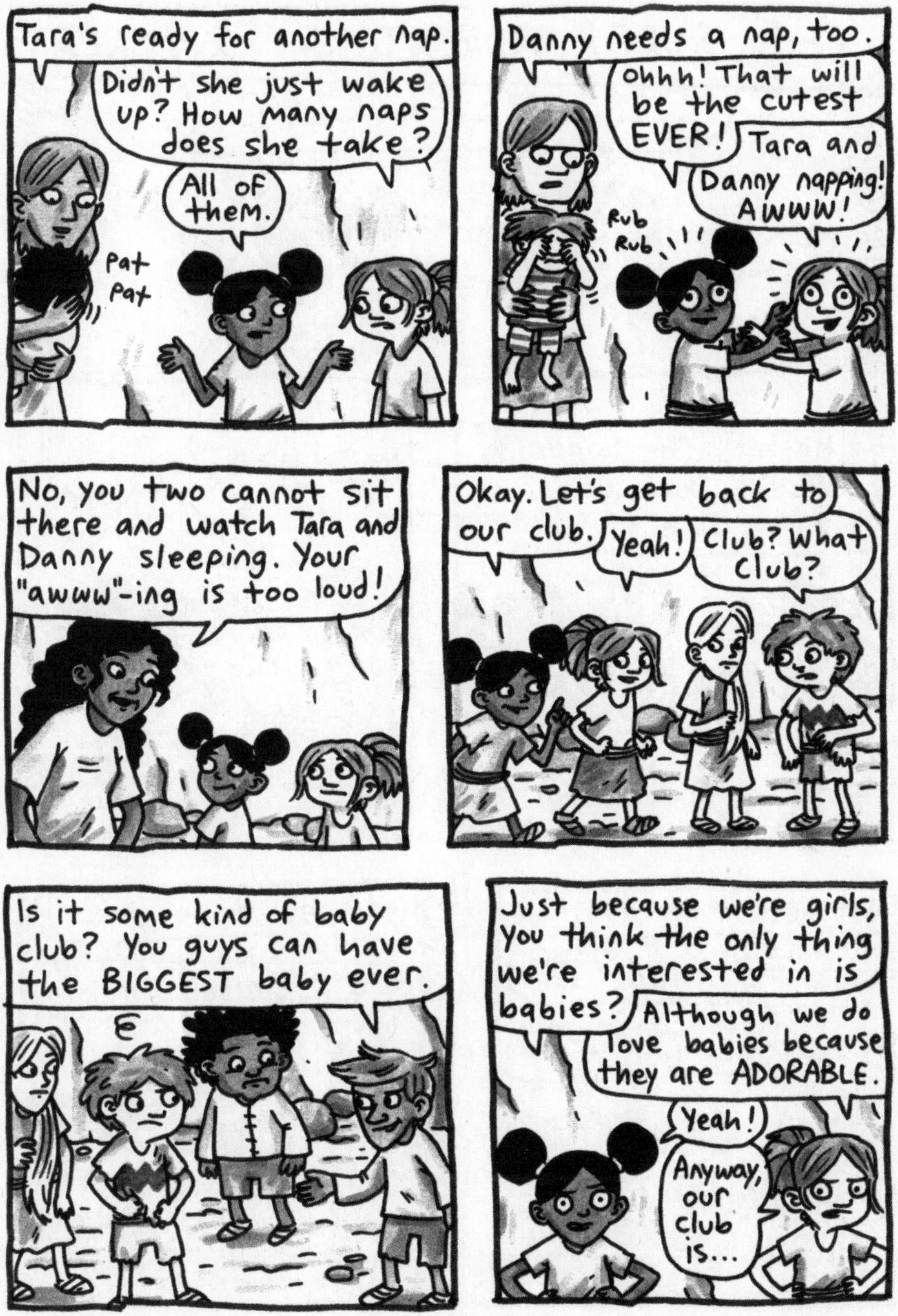
Tara's ready for another nap.
Didn't she just wake up? How many naps does she take?
All of them.
Pat pat
Danny needs a nap, too.
Ohhh! That will be the cutest EVER!
Tara and Danny napping! AWWW!
Rub Rub
No, you two cannot sit there and watch Tara and Danny sleeping. Your "awww"-ing is too loud!
Okay. Let's get back to our club.
Yeah!
Club? What Club?
Is it some kind of baby club? You guys can have the BIGGEST baby ever.
Just because we're girls, you think the only thing we're interested in is babies?
Although we do love babies because they are ADORABLE.
Yeah!
Anyway, our club is...

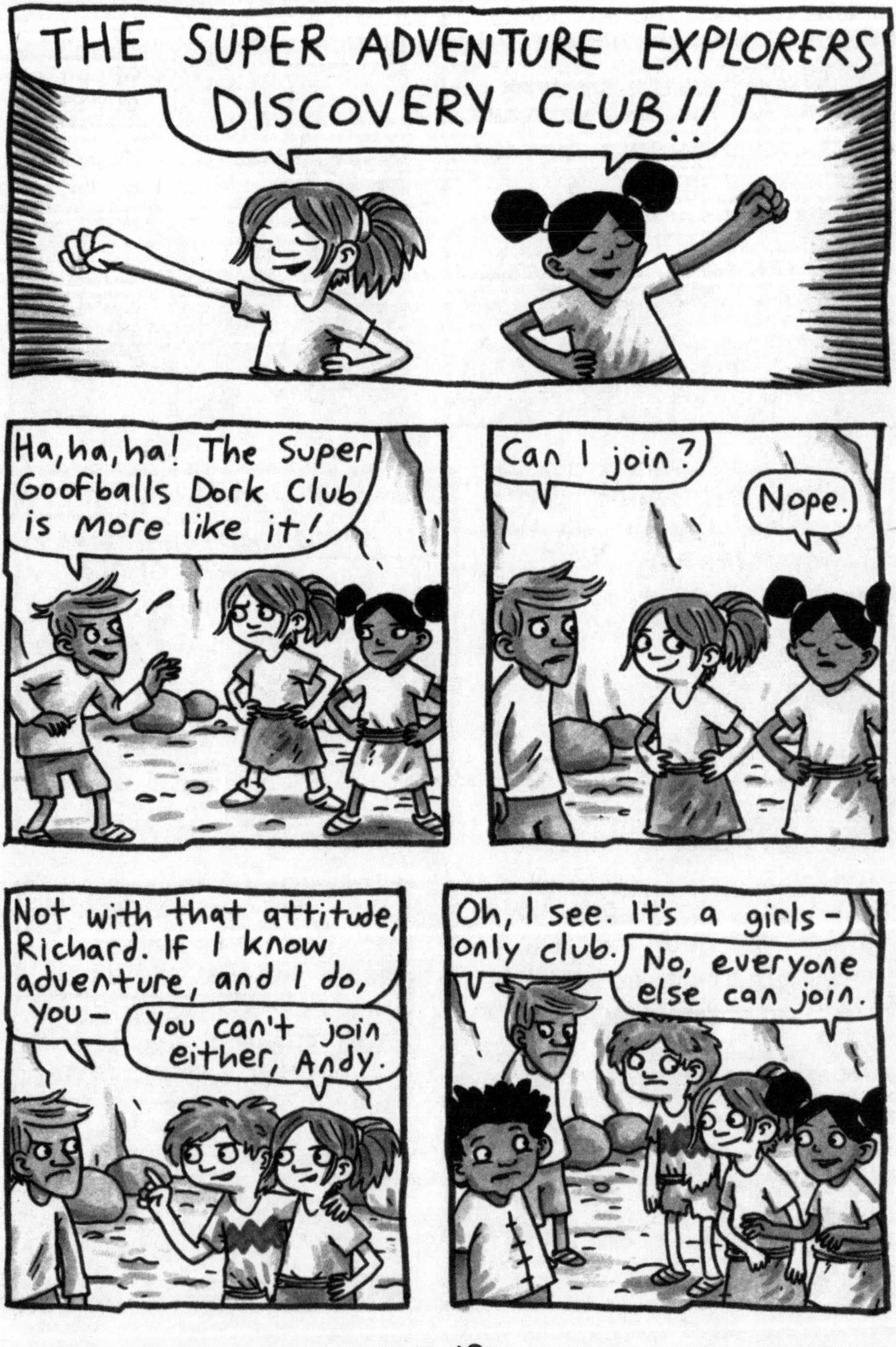
THE SUPER ADVENTURE EXPLORERS DISCOVERY CLUB!!
Ha, ha, ha! The Super Goofballs Dork Club is more like it!
Can I join?
Nope.
Not with that attitude, Richard. If I know adventure, and I do, you–
You can't join either, Andy.
Oh, I see. It's a girls-only club.
No, everyone else can join.

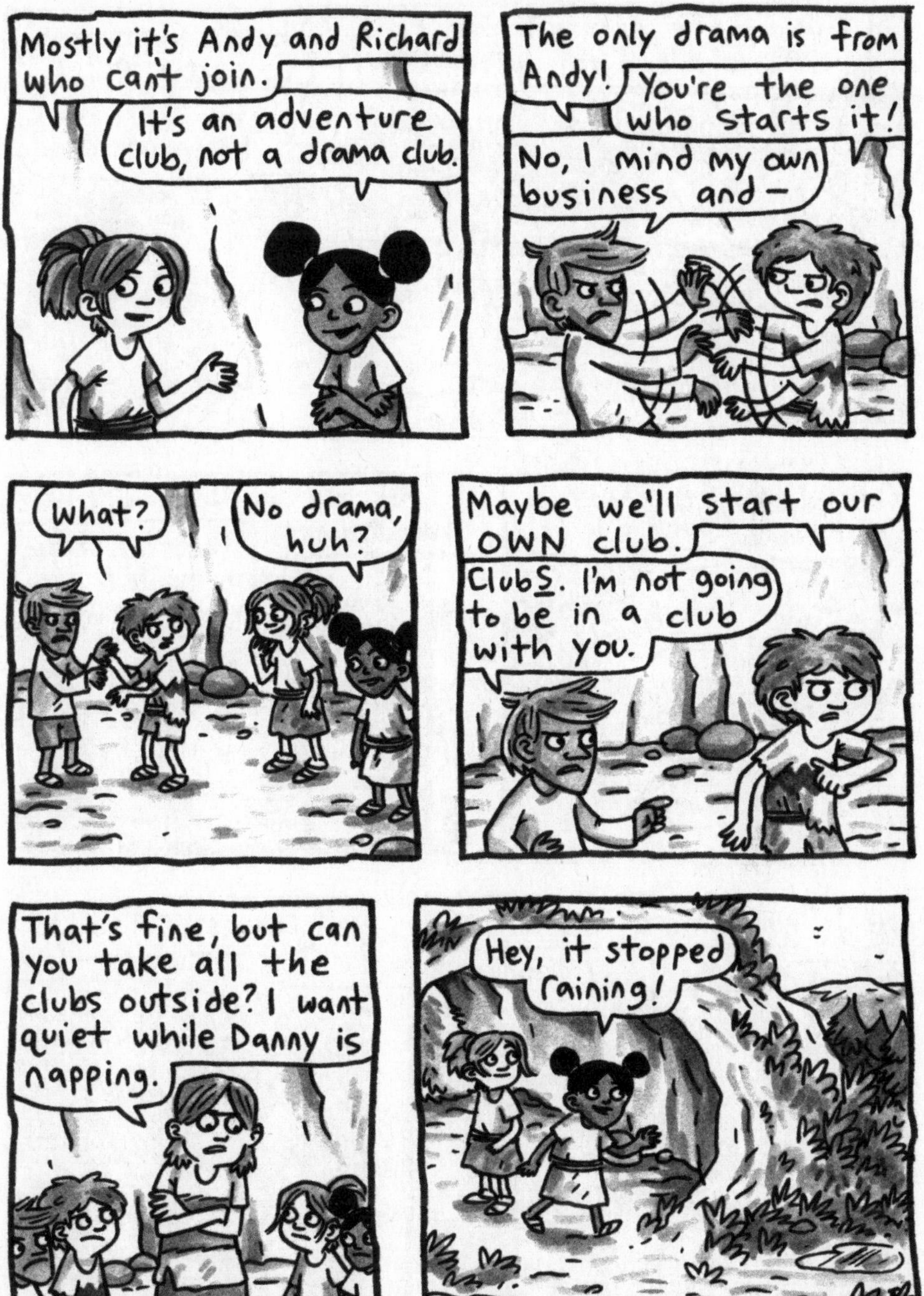
Mostly it's Andy and Richard who can't join.
It's an adventure club, not a drama club.
The only drama is from Andy!
You're the one who starts it!
No, I mind my own business and—
What?
No drama, huh?
Maybe we'll start our OWN club.
ClubS. I'm not going to be in a club with you.
That's fine, but can you take all the clubs outside? I want quiet while Danny is napping.
Hey, it stopped raining!

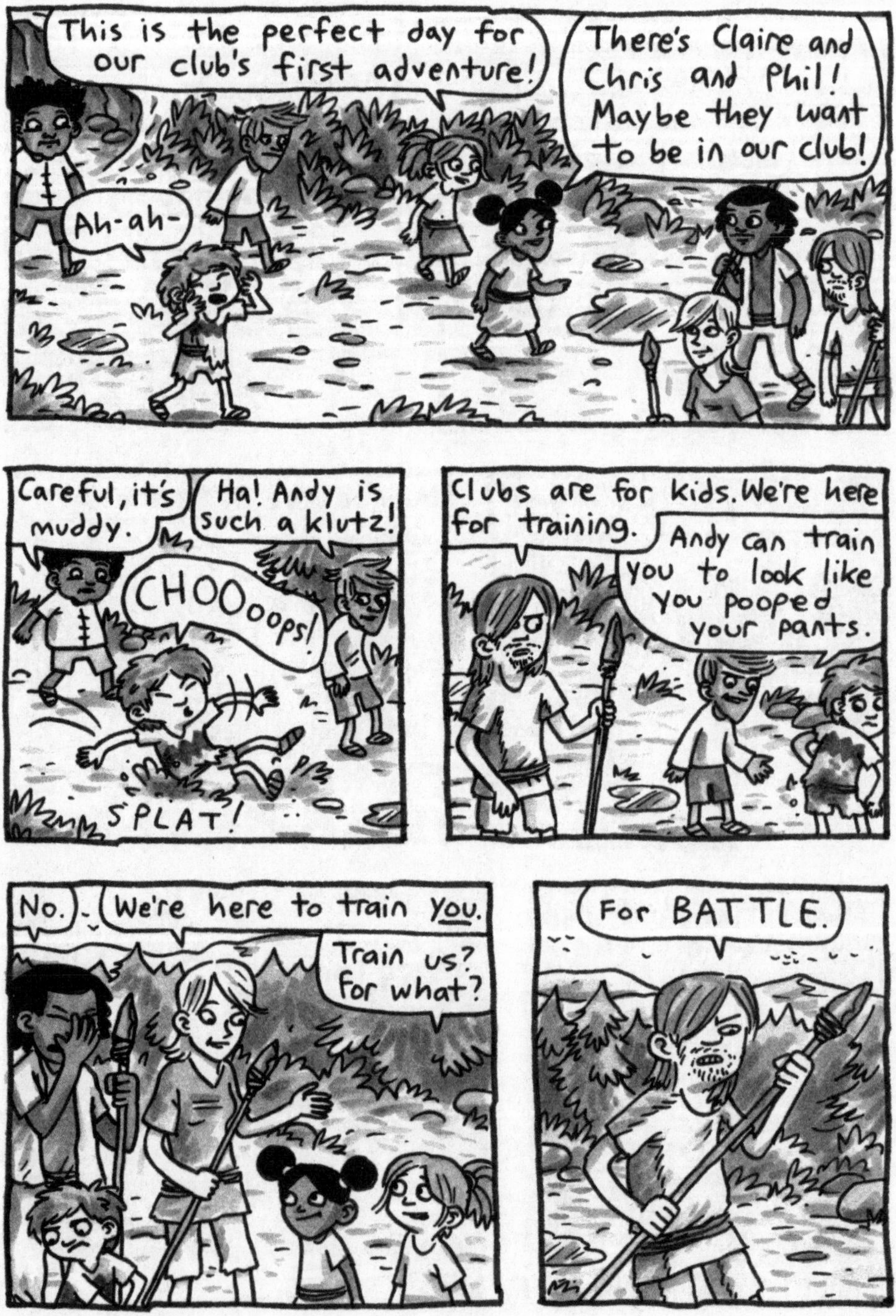

This is the perfect day for our club's first adventure!
There's Claire and Chris and Phil! Maybe they want to be in our club!
Ah-ah-
Careful, it's muddy.
Ha! Andy is such a klutz!
CHOOoops!
SPLAT!
Clubs are for kids. We're here for training.
Andy can train you to look like you pooped your pants.
No.
We're here to train YOU.
Train us? For what?
For BATTLE.

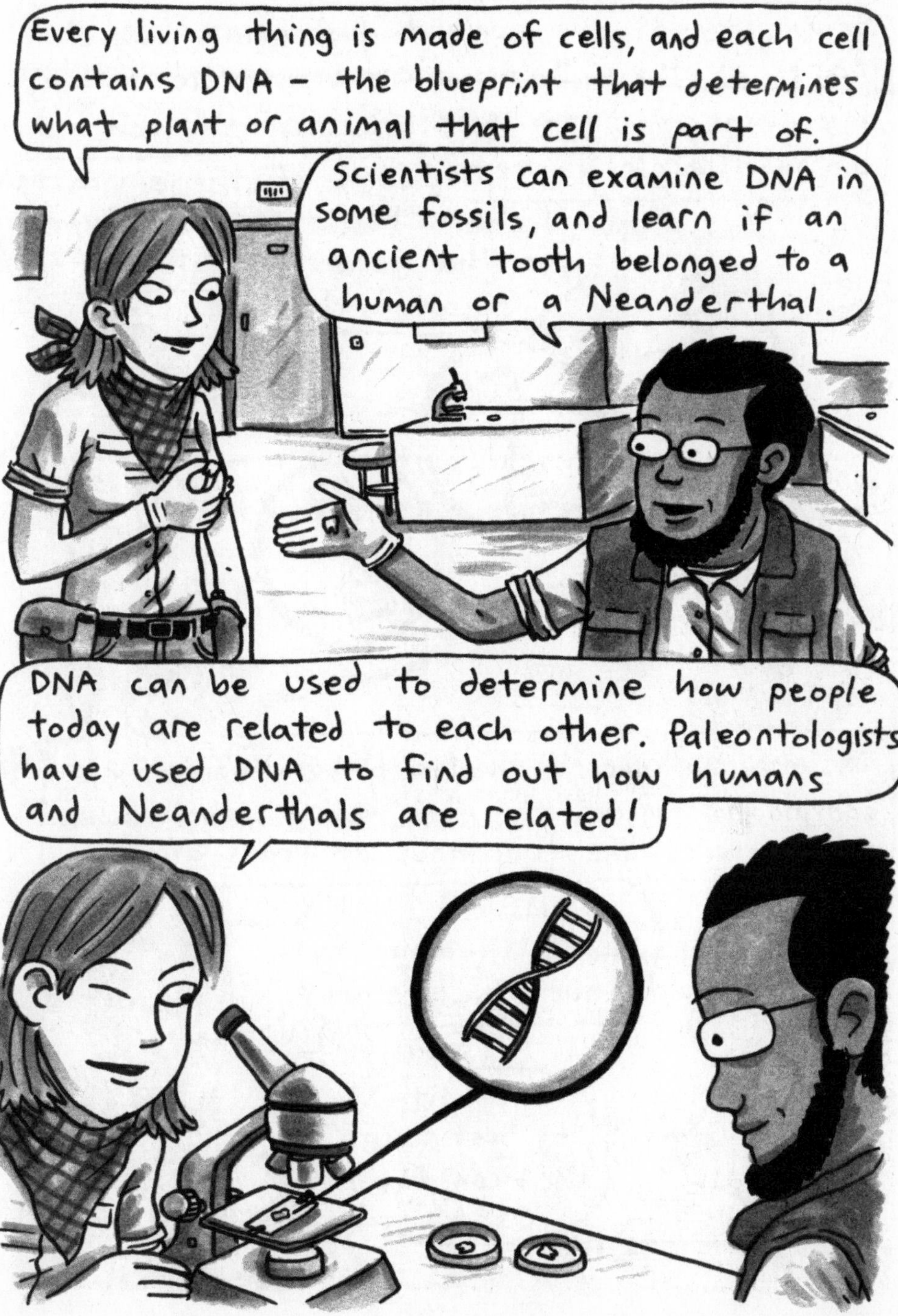
Every living thing is made of cells, and each cell contains DNA - the blueprint that determines what plant or animal that cell is part of.
Scientists can examine DNA in some fossils, and learn if an ancient tooth belonged to a human or a Neanderthal.
DNA can be used to determine how people today are related to each other. Paleontologists have used DNA to find out how humans and Neanderthals are related!

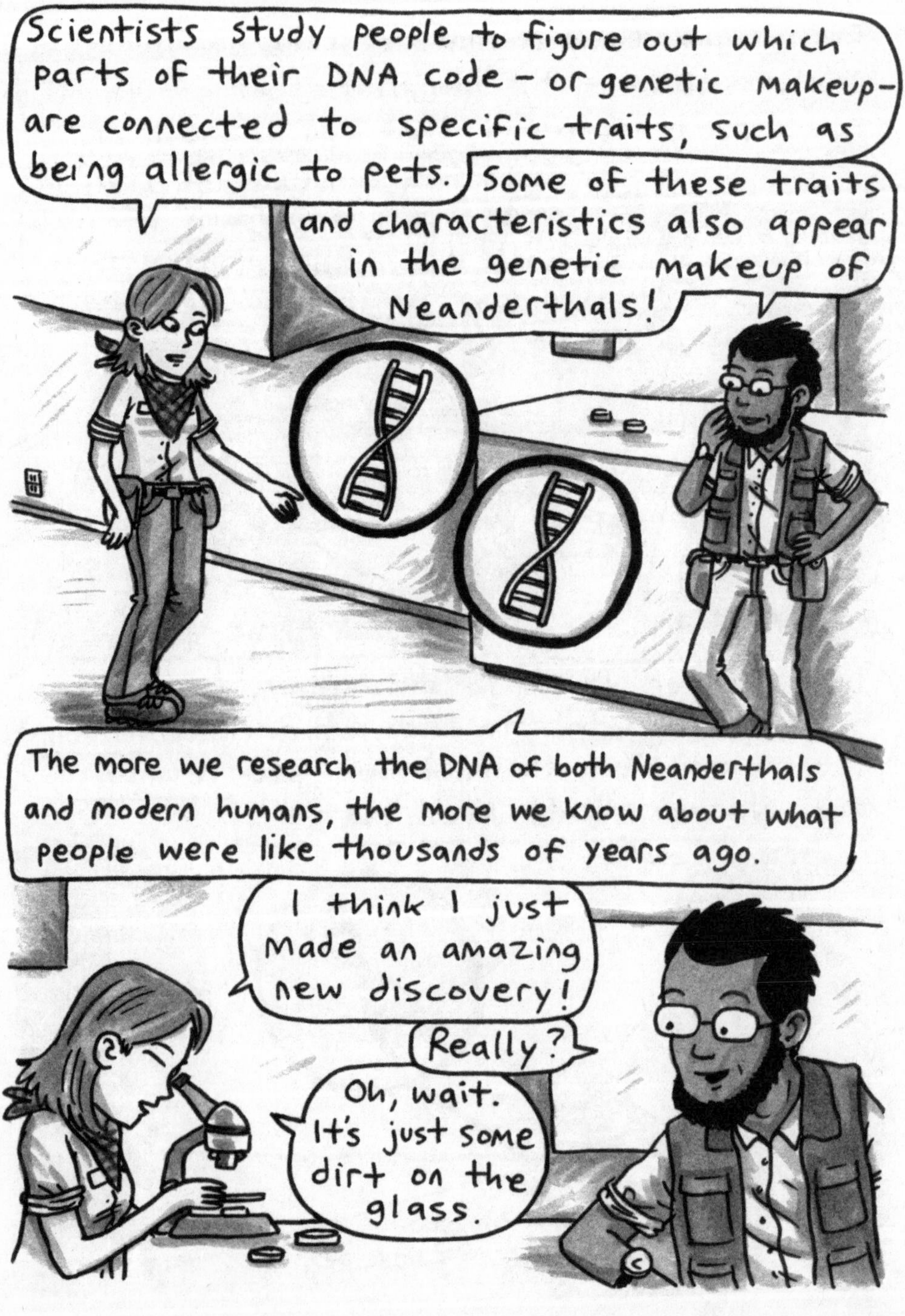

Scientists study people to figure out which parts of their DNA code - or genetic makeup - are connected to specific traits, such as being allergic to pets.
Some of these traits and characteristics also appear in the genetic makeup of Neanderthals!
The more we research the DNA of both Neanderthals and modern humans, the more we know about what people were like thousands of years ago.
I think I just made an amazing new discovery!
Really?
Oh, wait. It's just some dirt on the glass.

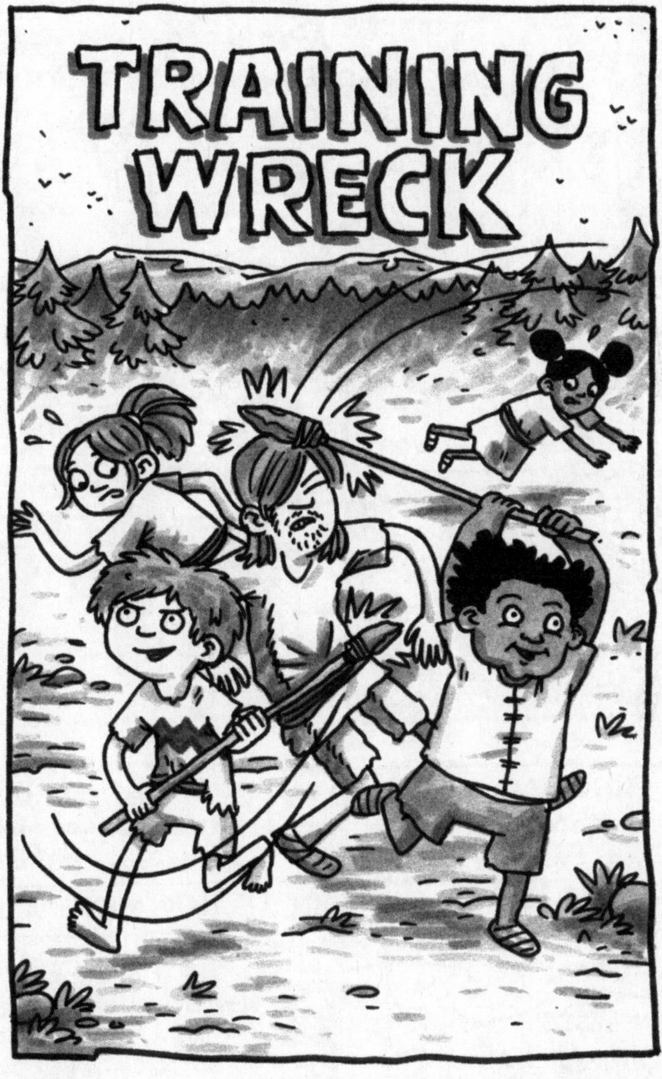
TRAINING
WRECK

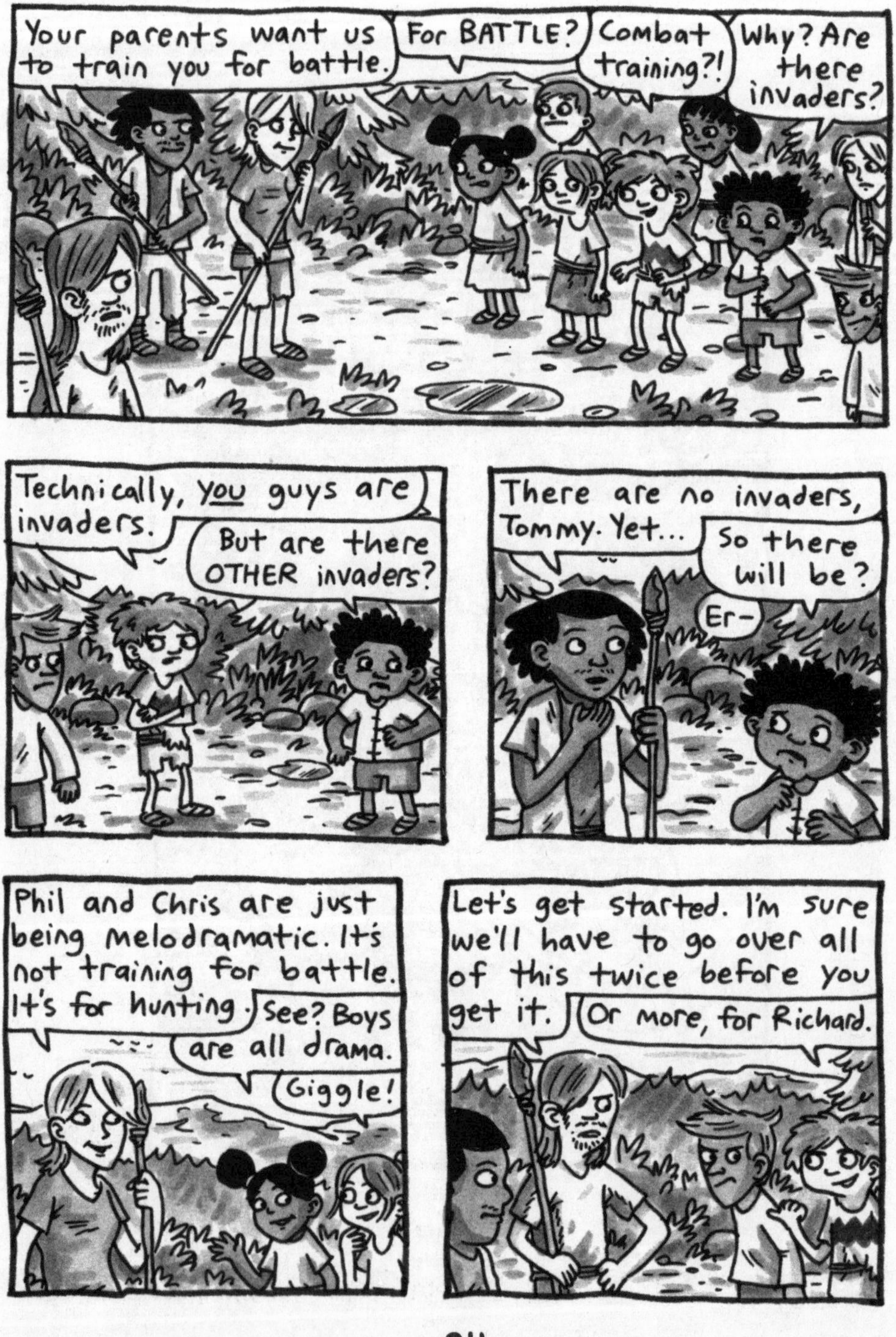
Your parents want us to train you for battle.
For BATTLE?
Combat training?!
Why? Are there invaders?
Technically, YOU guys are invaders.
But are there OTHER invaders?
There are no invaders, Tommy. Yet...
So there will be?
Er-
Phil and Chris are just being melodramatic. It's not training for battle. It's for hunting.
See? Boys are all drama.
Giggle!
Let's get started. I'm sure we'll have to go over all of this twice before you get it.
Or more, for Richard.

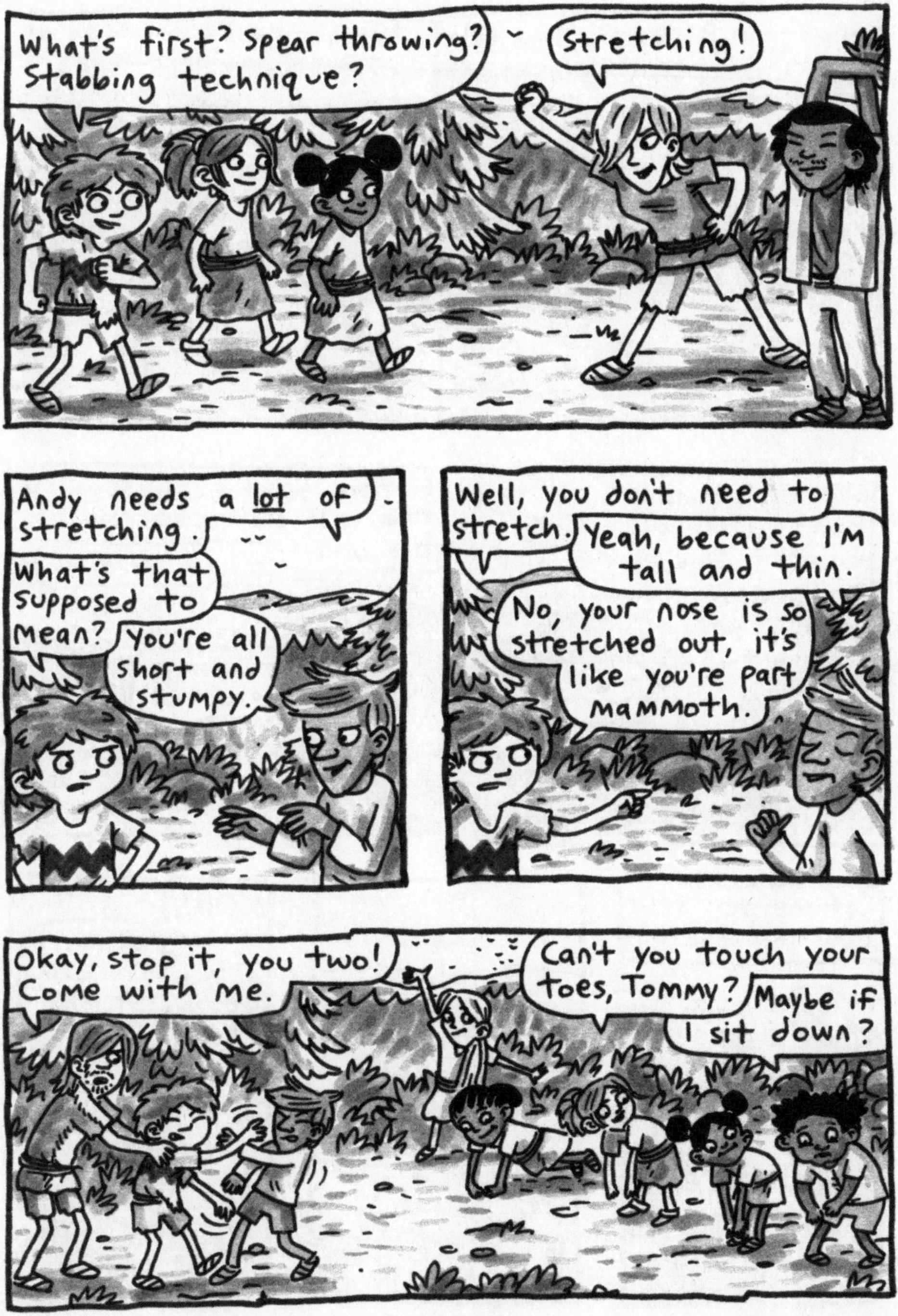
What's first? Spear throwing? Stabbing technique?
Stretching!
Andy needs a lot of stretching.
What's that supposed to mean?
You're all short and stumpy.
Well, you don't need to stretch.
Yeah, because I'M tall and thin.
No, your nose is so stretched out, it's like you're part mammoth.
Okay, stop it, you two! Come with me.
Can't you touch your toes, Tommy?
Maybe if I sit down?

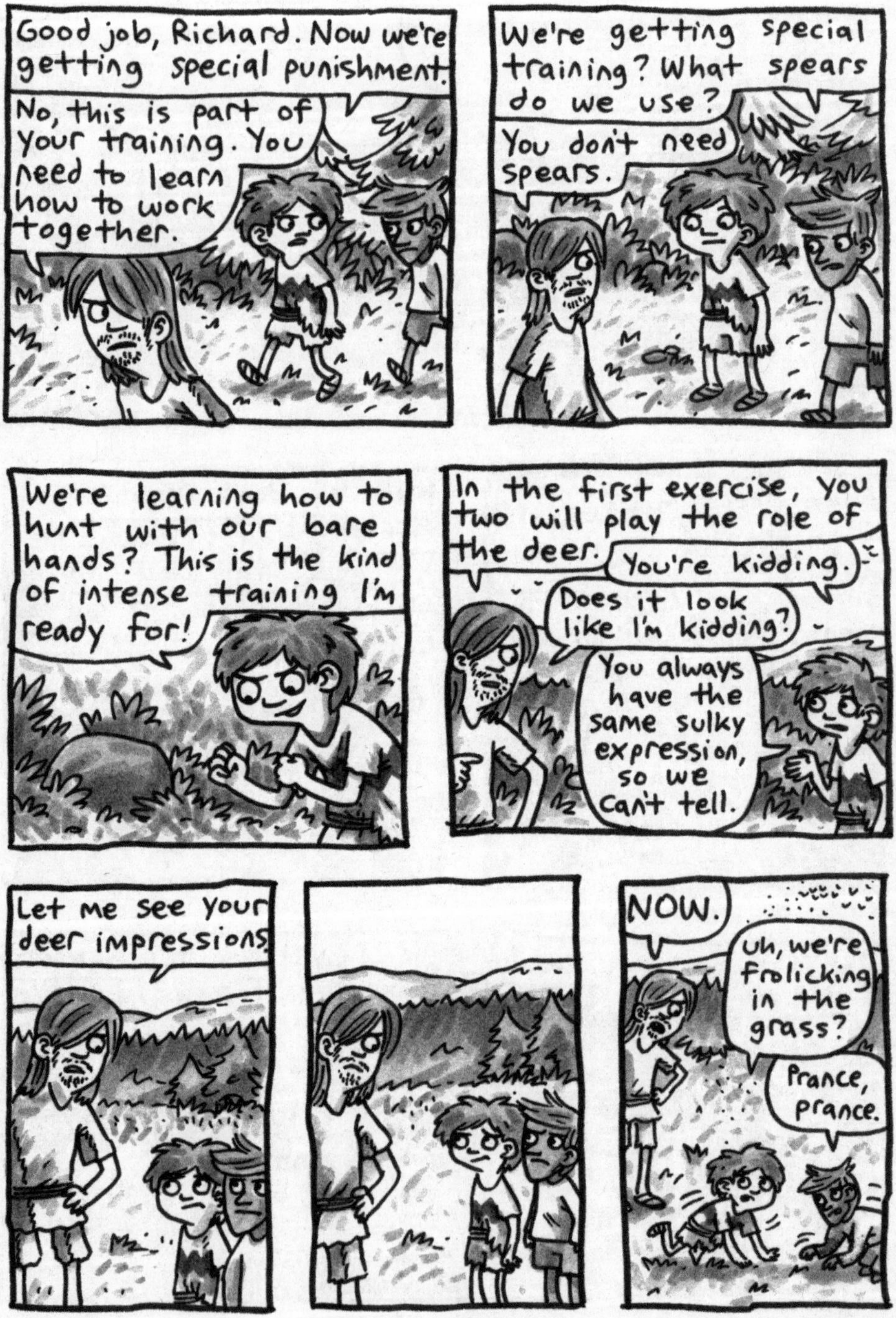
Good job, Richard. Now we're getting special punishment.
No, this is part of your training. You need to learn how to work together.
We're getting special training? What spears do we use?
You don't need spears.
We're learning how to hunt with our bare hands? This is the kind of intense training I'm ready for!
In the first exercise, you two will play the role of the deer.
You're kidding.
Does it look like I'm kidding?
You always have the same sulky expression, so we can't tell.
Let me see your deer impressions.
NOW.
Uh, we're frolicking in the grass?
Prance, prance.

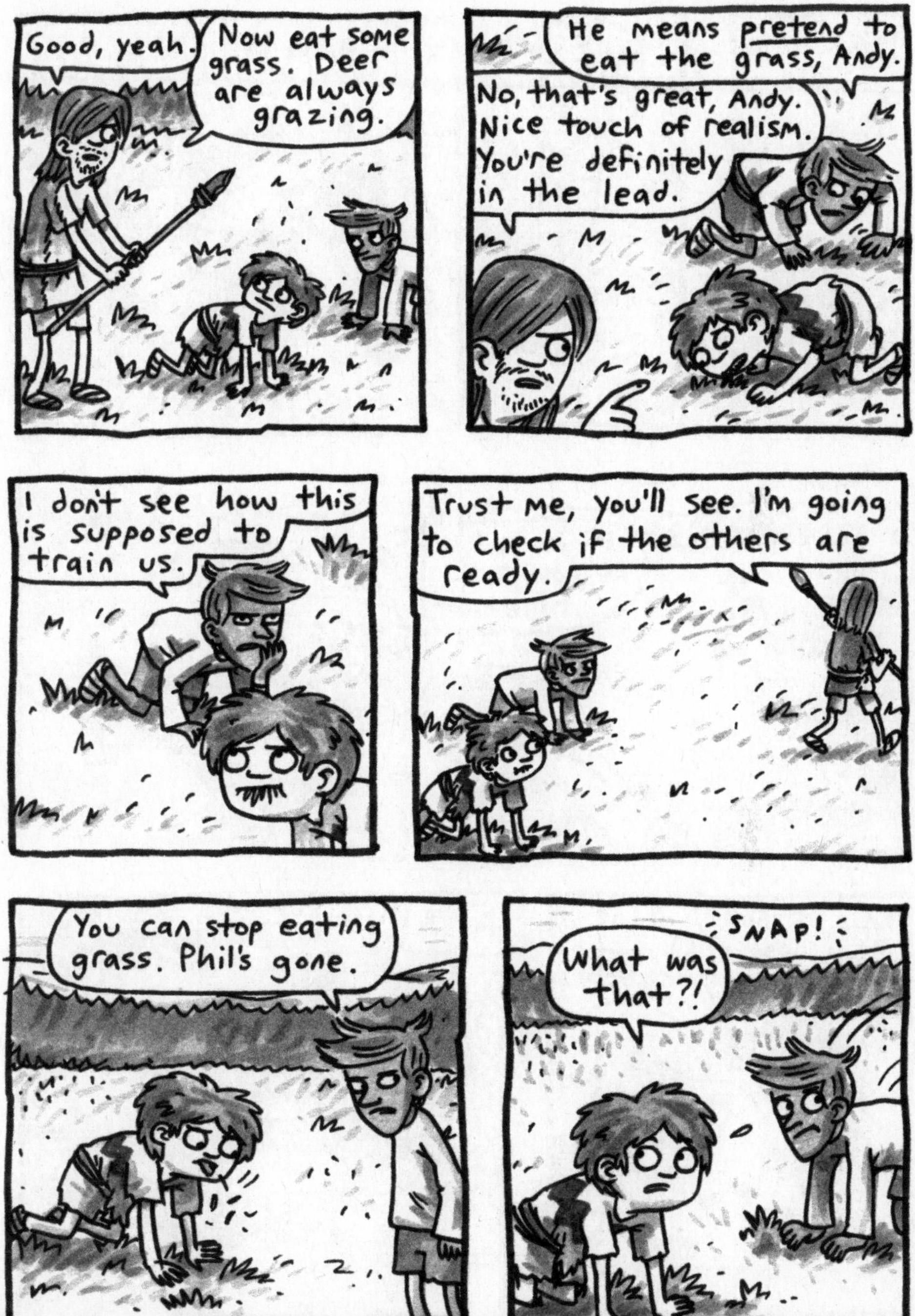
Good, yeah.
Now eat some grass. Deer are always grazing.
He means pretend to eat the grass, Andy.
No, that's great, Andy. Nice touch of realism. You're definitely in the lead.
I don't see how this is supposed to train us.
Trust me, you'll see. I'm going to check if the others are ready.
You can stop eating grass. Phil's gone.
SNAP!
What was that?!

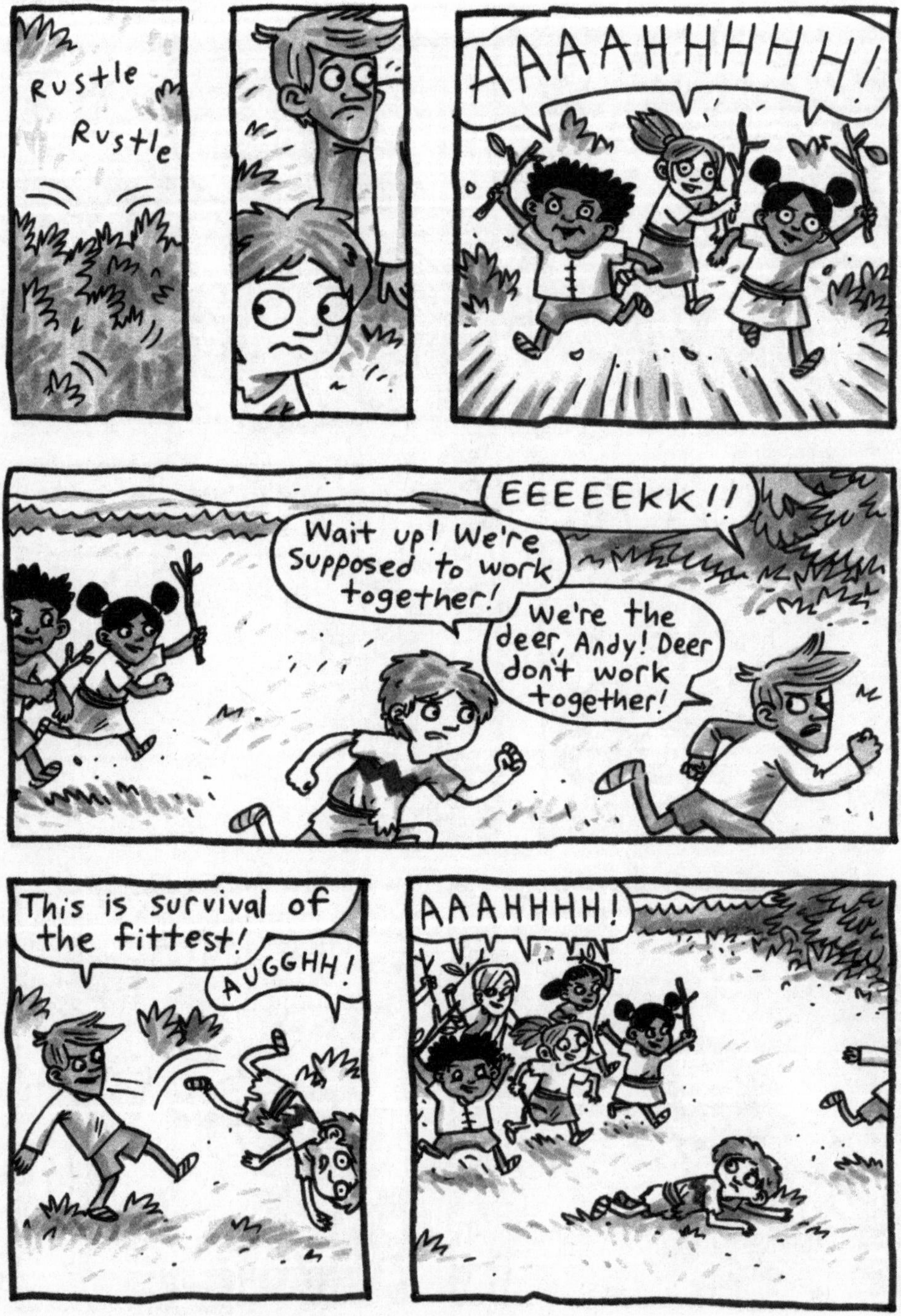
Rustle
Rustle
AAAAHHHHH!
EEEEEKK!!
Wait up! We're supposed to work together!
We're the deer, Andy! Deer don't work together!
This is survival of the fittest!
AUGGHH!
AAAHHHH!

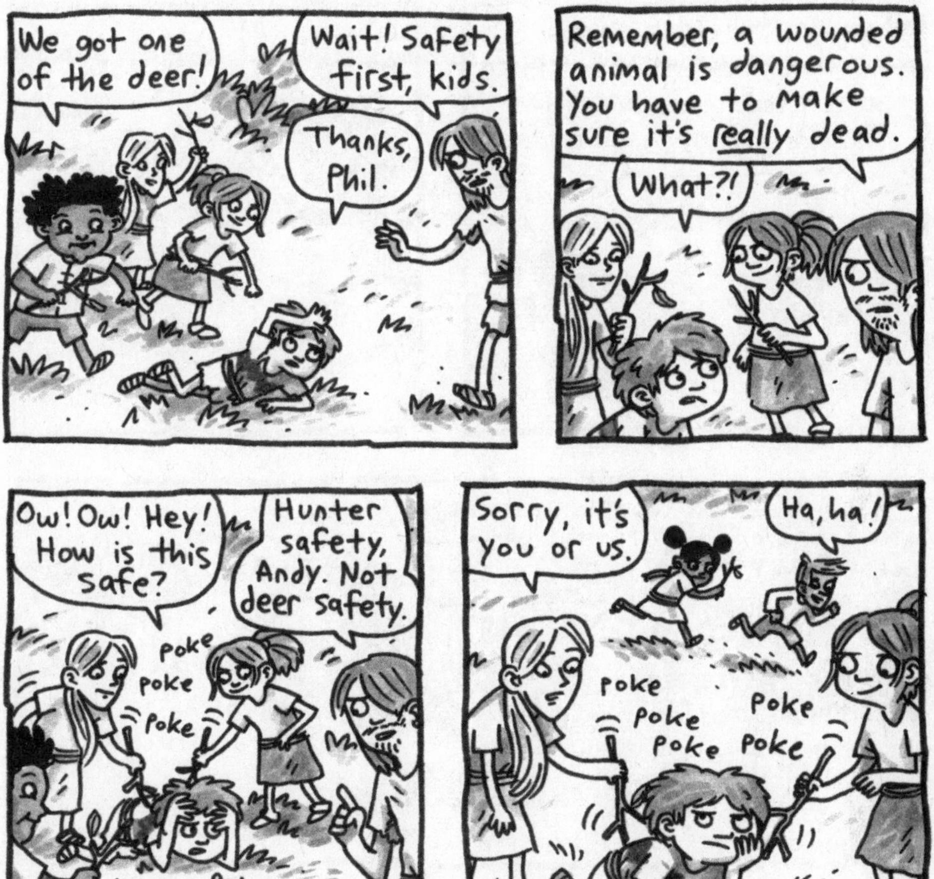
We got one of the deer!
Wait! Safety first, kids.
Thanks, Phil.
Remember, a wounded animal is dangerous. You have to make sure it's really dead.
What?!
Ow! Ow! Hey! How is this safe?
Hunter safety, Andy. Not deer safety.
poke poke poke
poke poke
Sorry, it's you or us.
Ha, ha!
poke poke poke
poke poke

Humans have bodies suited for running. Scientists think early humans may have hunted in open spaces where it's easier to track animals, and chased their prey until it was tired.

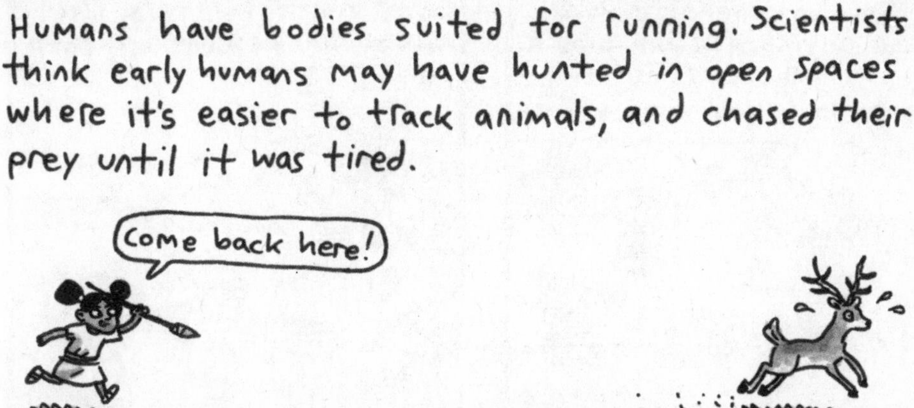
Come back here!

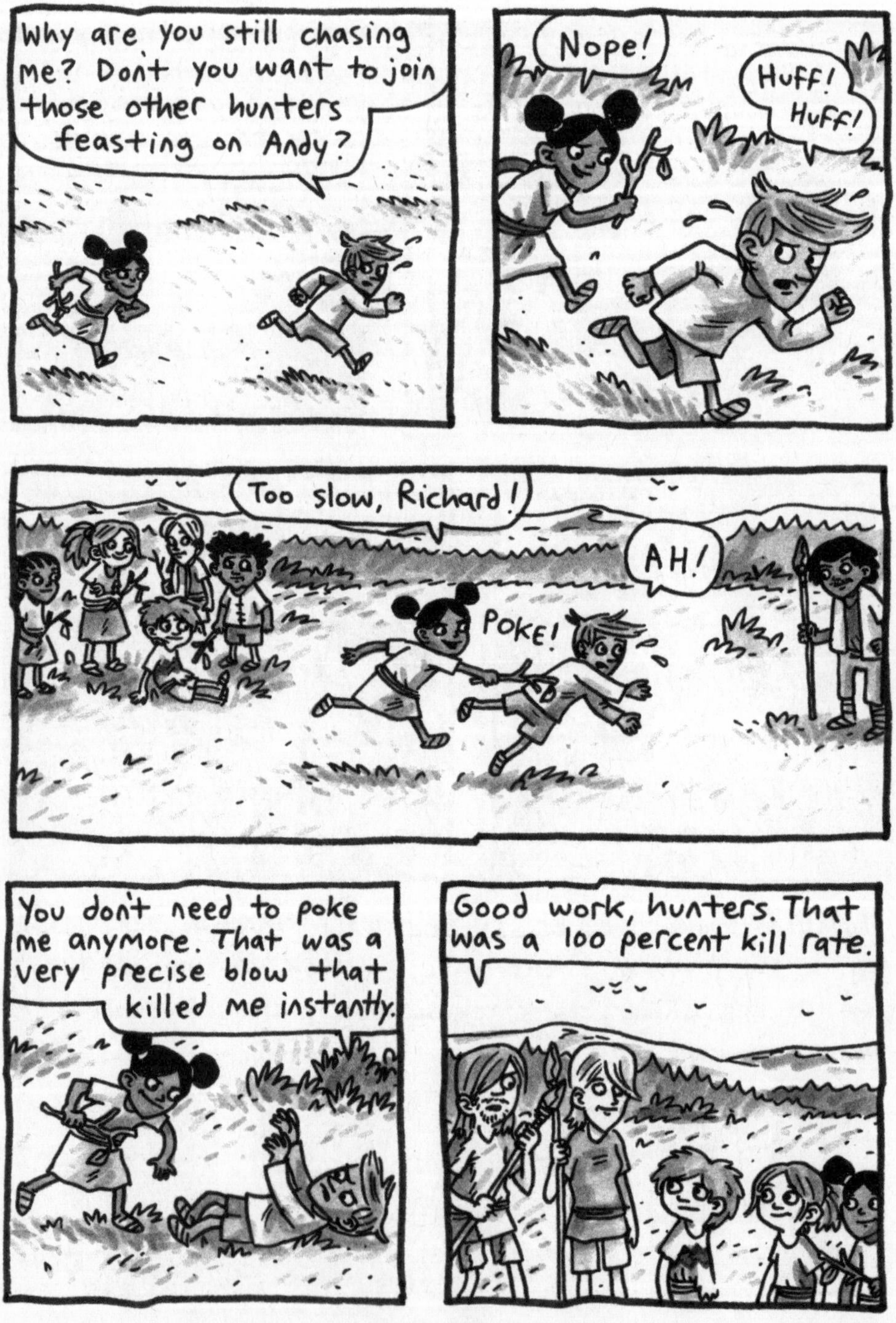
Why are you still chasing me? Don't you want to join those other hunters feasting on Andy?
Nope!
Huff! Huff!
Too slow, Richard!
AH!
POKE!
You don't need to poke me anymore. That was a very precise blow that killed me instantly.
Good work, hunters. That was a 100 percent kill rate.

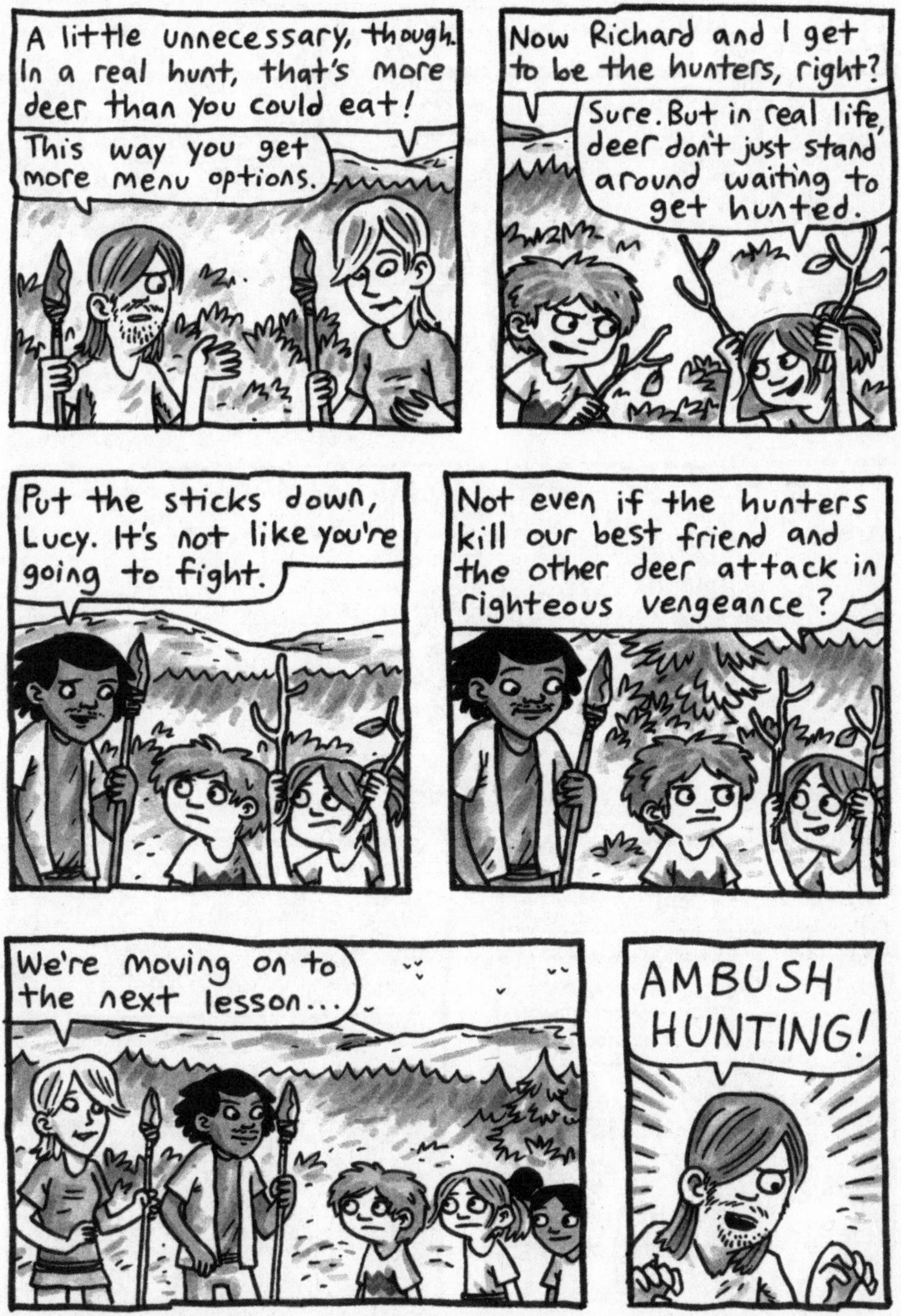
A little unnecessary, though. In a real hunt, that's more deer than you could eat!
This way you get more menu options.
Now Richard and I get to be the hunters, right?
Sure. But in real life, deer don't just stand around waiting to get hunted.
Put the sticks down, Lucy. It's not like you're going to fight.
Not even if the hunters kill our best friend and the other deer attack in righteous vengeance?
We're moving on to the next lesson...
AMBUSH HUNTING!

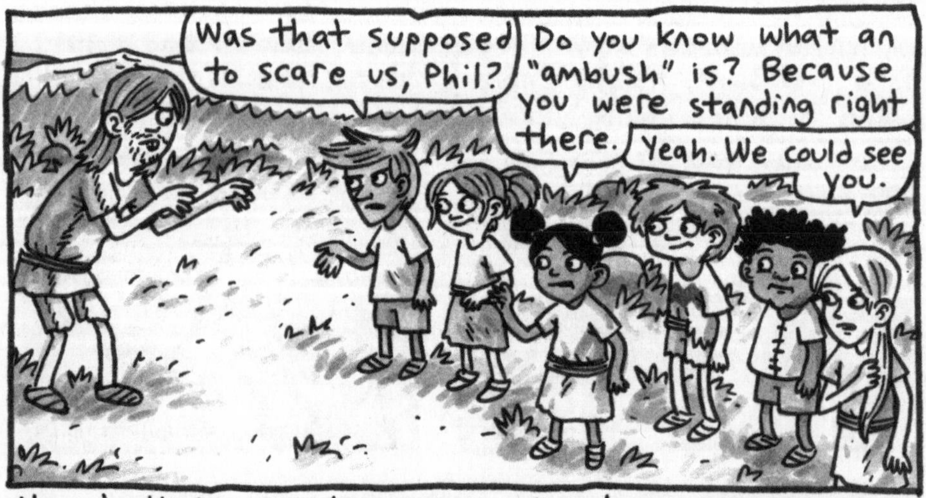

Was that supposed to scare us, Phil?
Do you know what an "ambush" is? Because you were standing right there.
Yeah. We could see you.

Neanderthals may have specialized in ambushing animals and killing them at close quarters.

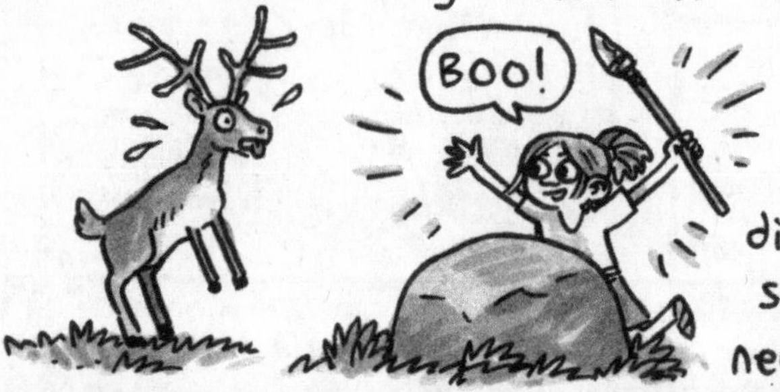

BOO!

Prey most likely didn't drop dead from surprise, and so still needed to be killed.

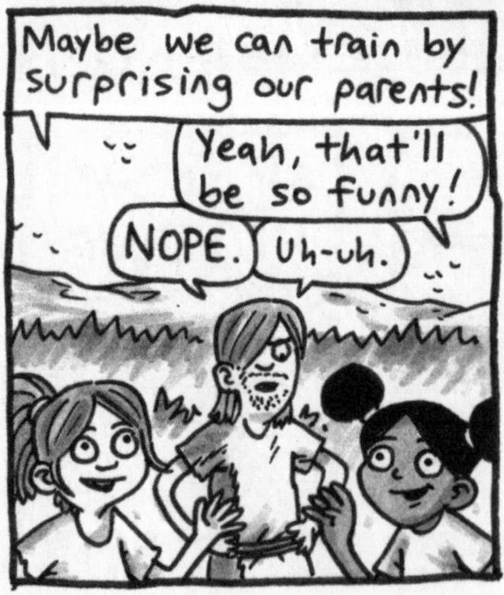

Maybe we can train by surprising our parents!
Yeah, that'll be so funny!
NOPE.
Uh-uh.

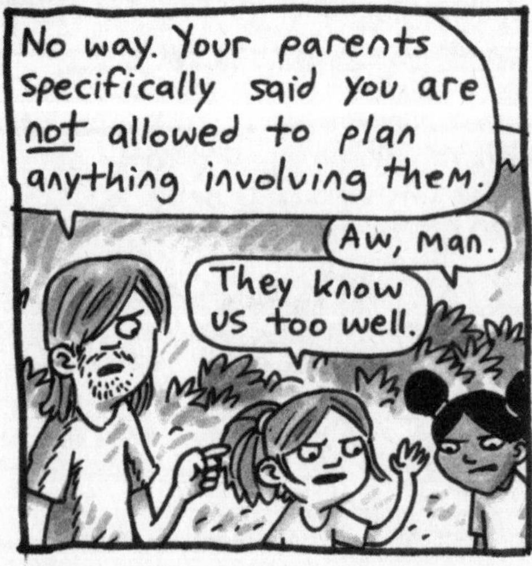

No way. Your parents specifically said you are not allowed to plan anything involving them.
Aw, man.
They know us too well.

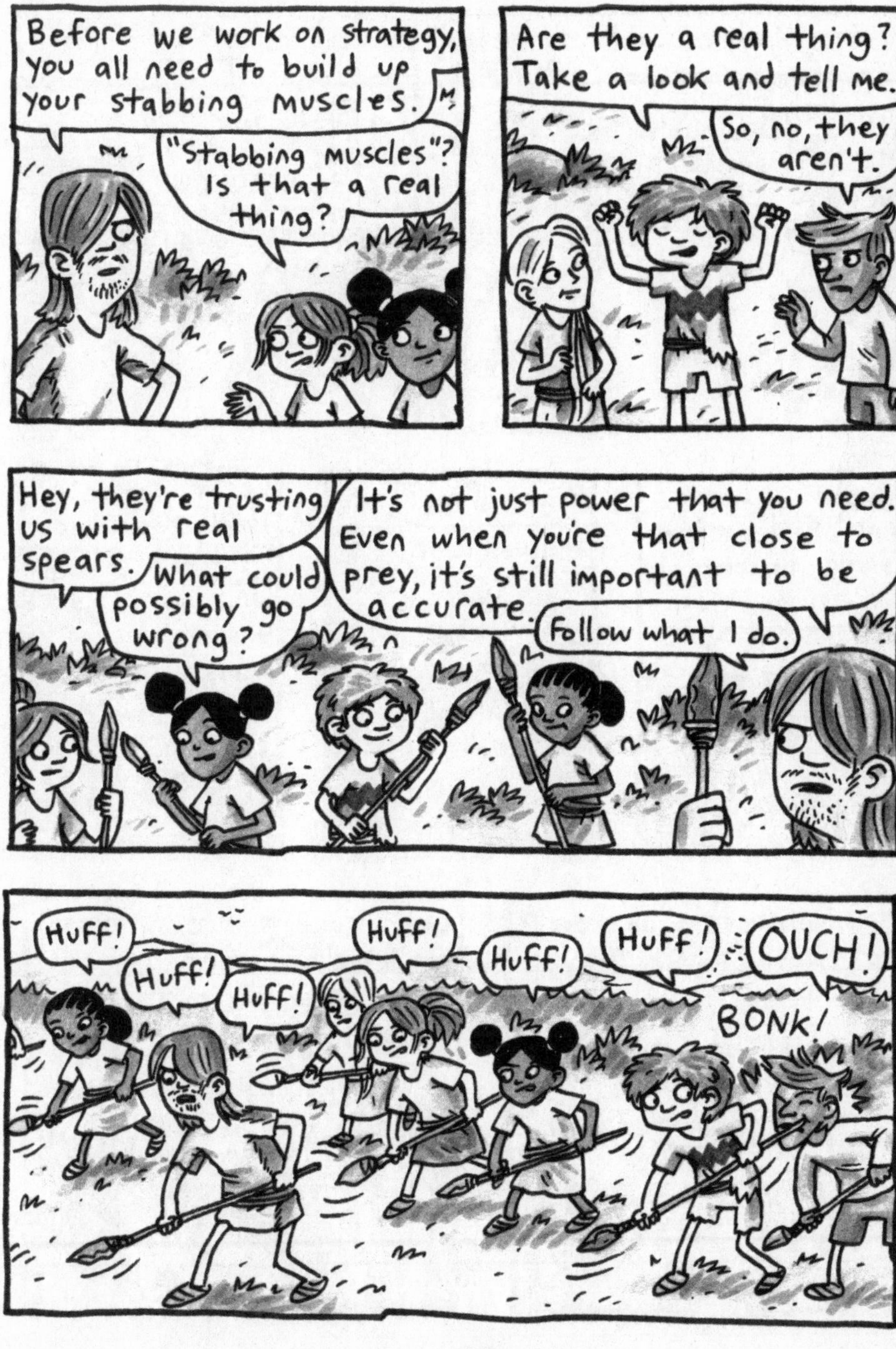
Before we work on strategy, you all need to build up your stabbing muscles.
"Stabbing muscles"? Is that a real thing?
Are they a real thing? Take a look and tell me.
So, no, they aren't.
Hey, they're trusting us with real spears.
What could possibly go wrong?
It's not just power that you need. Even when you're that close to prey, it's still important to be accurate.
Follow what I do.
Huff!
Huff!
Huff!
Huff!
Huff!
Huff!
OUCH!
BONK!

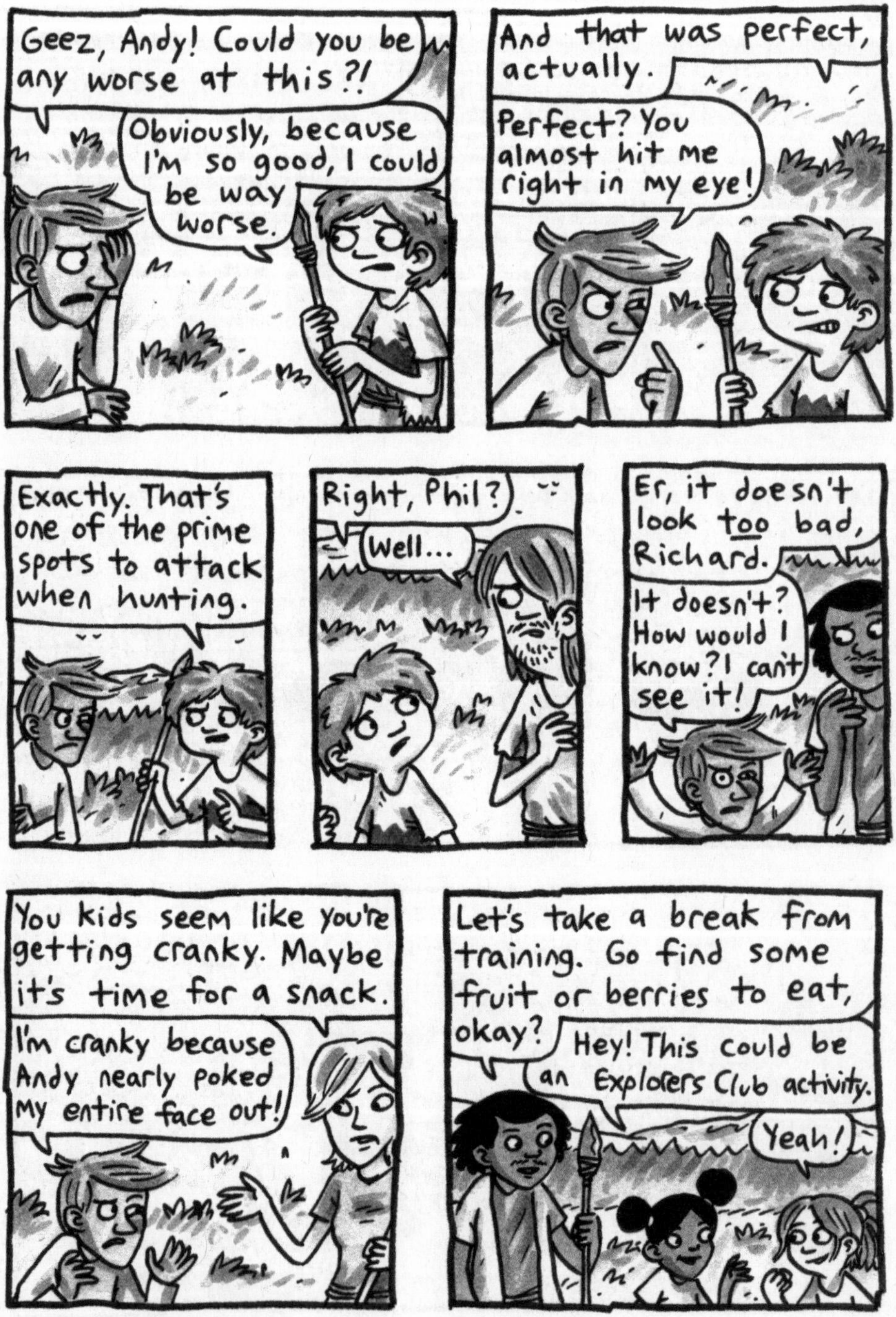
Geez, Andy! Could you be any worse at this?!
Obviously, because I'm so good, I could be way worse.
And that was perfect, actually.
Perfect? You almost hit me right in my eye!
Exactly. That's one of the prime spots to attack when hunting.
Right, Phil?
Well...
Er, it doesn't look too bad, Richard.
It doesn't? How would I know?! I can't see it!
You kids seem like you're getting cranky. Maybe it's time for a snack.
I'm cranky because Andy nearly poked my entire face out!
Let's take a break from training. Go find some fruit or berries to eat, okay?
Hey! This could be an Explorers Club activity.
Yeah!

Just don't wander off too far.

Or do.

Phil!

What? They're explorers!

Could we be in the club now, Lucy?

Fine. Just one condition...

No more drama?

That would be unrealistic. No, you and Richard have to do Sasha's and my chores for a week.

Okay.

Sure.

Hm. They didn't even hesitate. I'm surprised.

Yeah.

Lucy just did her chores, so I won't have anything to do all week.

I can't do anything until my eye is better and Sasha will forget about this by then.

It looks like someone ate all the berries.

I guess we can find some veggies instead.

Maybe those guys are eating everything.

What guys?

35

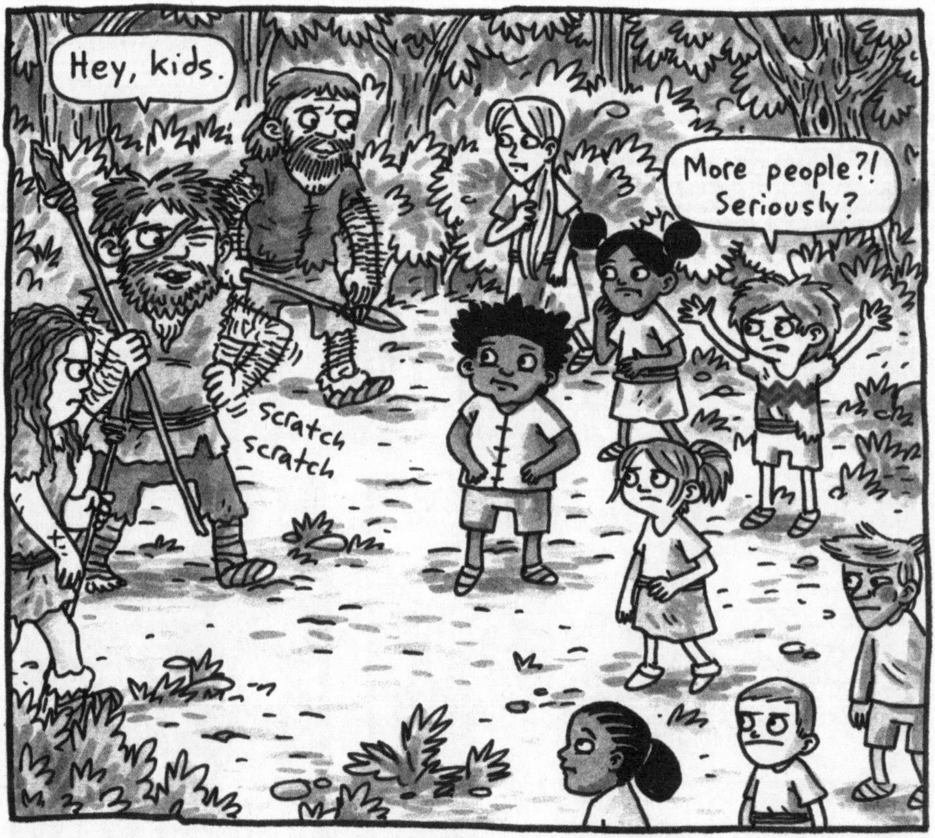
Hey, kids.
More people?! Seriously?
scratch scratch

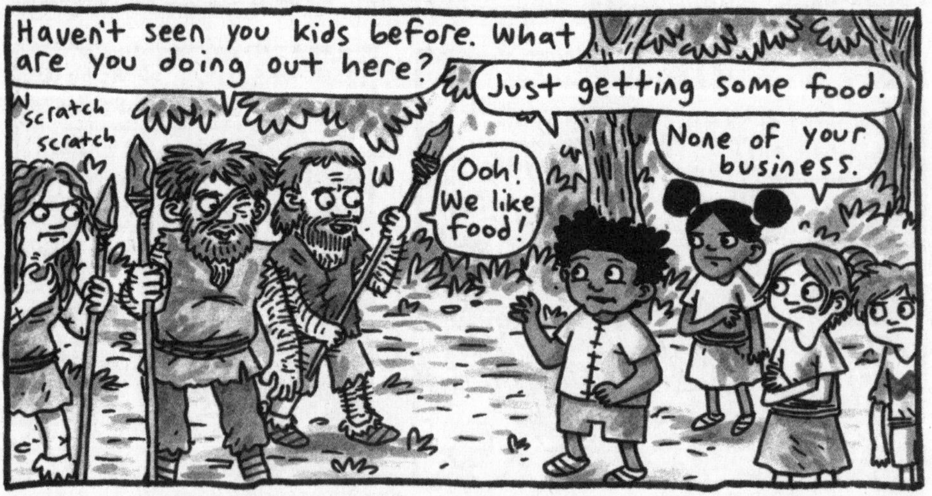
Haven't seen you kids before. What are you doing out here?
scratch scratch
Just getting some food.
None of your business.
Ooh! We like food!

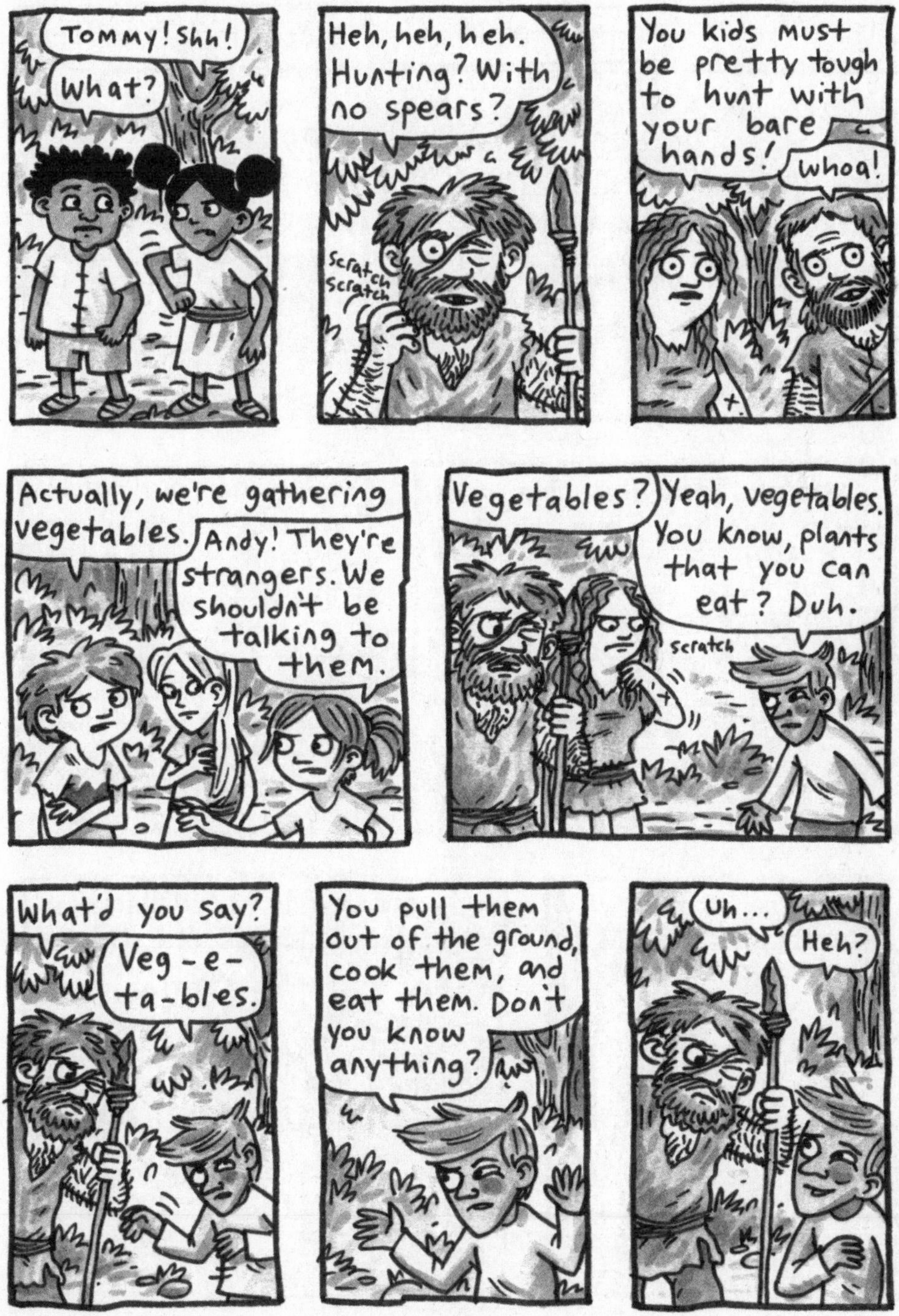
TOMMY! Shh!
What?
Heh, heh, heh. Hunting? With no spears?
Scratch scratch
You kids must be pretty tough to hunt with your bare hands!
Whoa!
Actually, we're gathering vegetables.
Andy! They're strangers. We shouldn't be talking to them.
Vegetables?
Yeah, vegetables. You know, plants that you can eat? Duh.
scratch
What'd you say?
Veg-e-ta-bles.
You pull them out of the ground, cook them, and eat them. Don't you know anything?
Uh...
Heh?

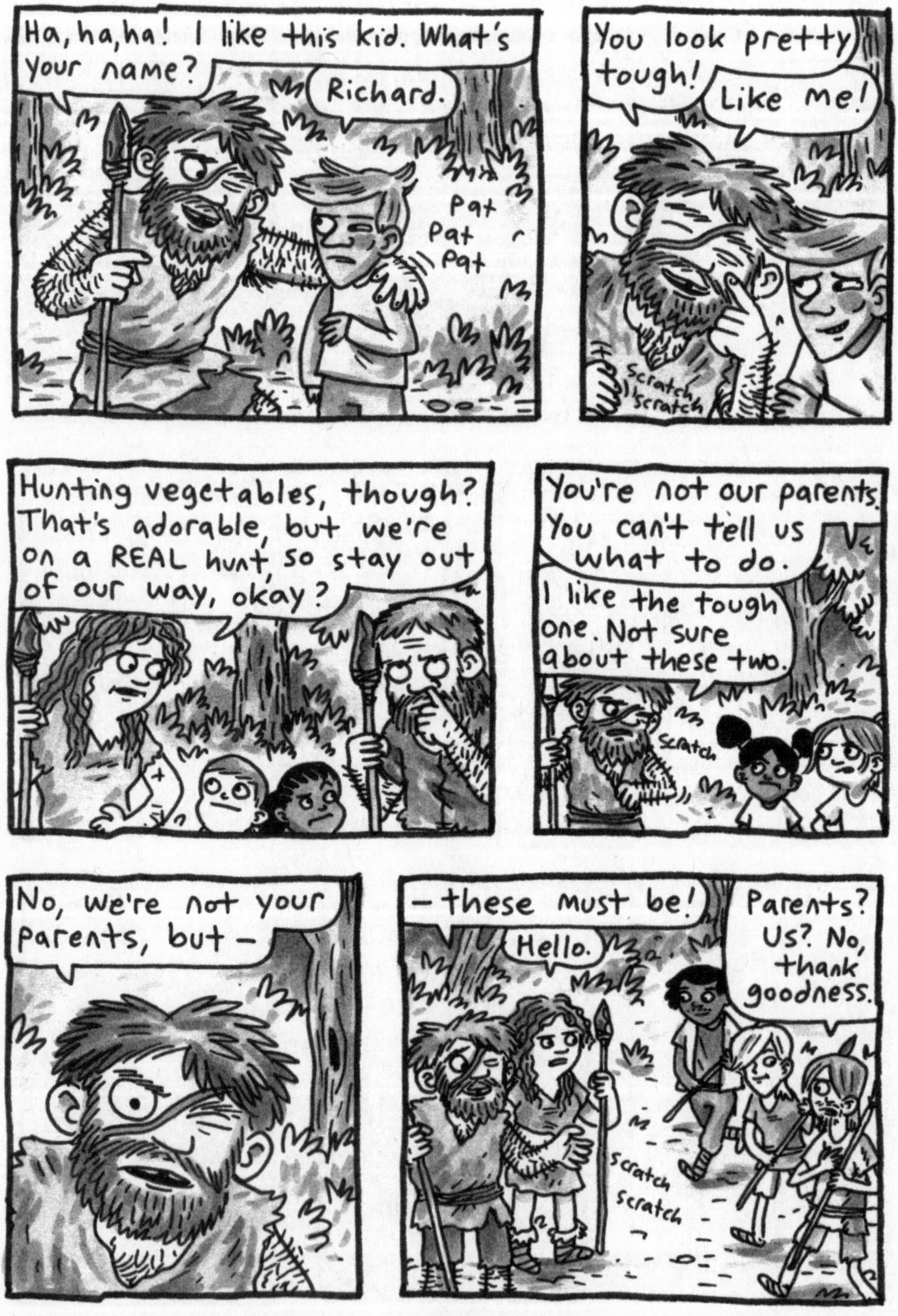

Ha, ha, ha! I like this kid. What's your name?
Richard.
Pat
Pat
Pat
You look pretty tough!
Like me!
Scratch
Scratch
Hunting vegetables, though? That's adorable, but we're on a REAL hunt, so stay out of our way, okay?
You're not our parents. You can't tell us what to do.
I like the tough one. Not sure about these two.
Scratch
No, we're not your parents, but—
—these must be!
Hello.
Parents? Us? No, thank goodness.
Scratch
Scratch

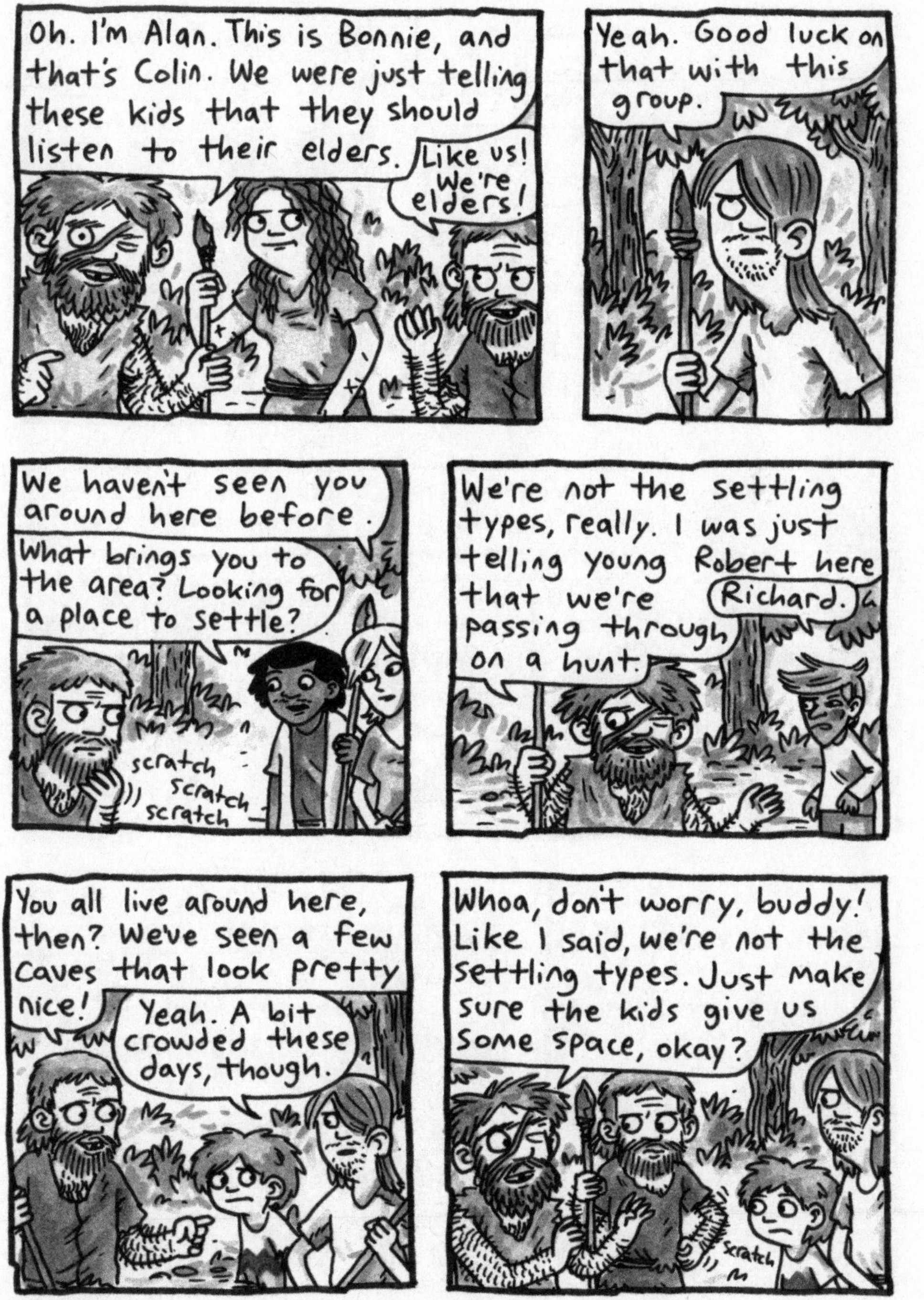
Oh. I'm Alan. This is Bonnie, and that's Colin. We were just telling these kids that they should listen to their elders.
Like us! We're elders!
Yeah. Good luck on that with this group.
We haven't seen you around here before.
What brings you to the area? Looking for a place to settle?
scratch
scratch
scratch
We're not the settling types, really. I was just telling young Robert here that we're passing through on a hunt.
Richard.
You all live around here, then? We've seen a few caves that look pretty nice!
Yeah. A bit crowded these days, though.
Whoa, don't worry, buddy! Like I said, we're not the settling types. Just make sure the kids give us some space, okay?
scratch

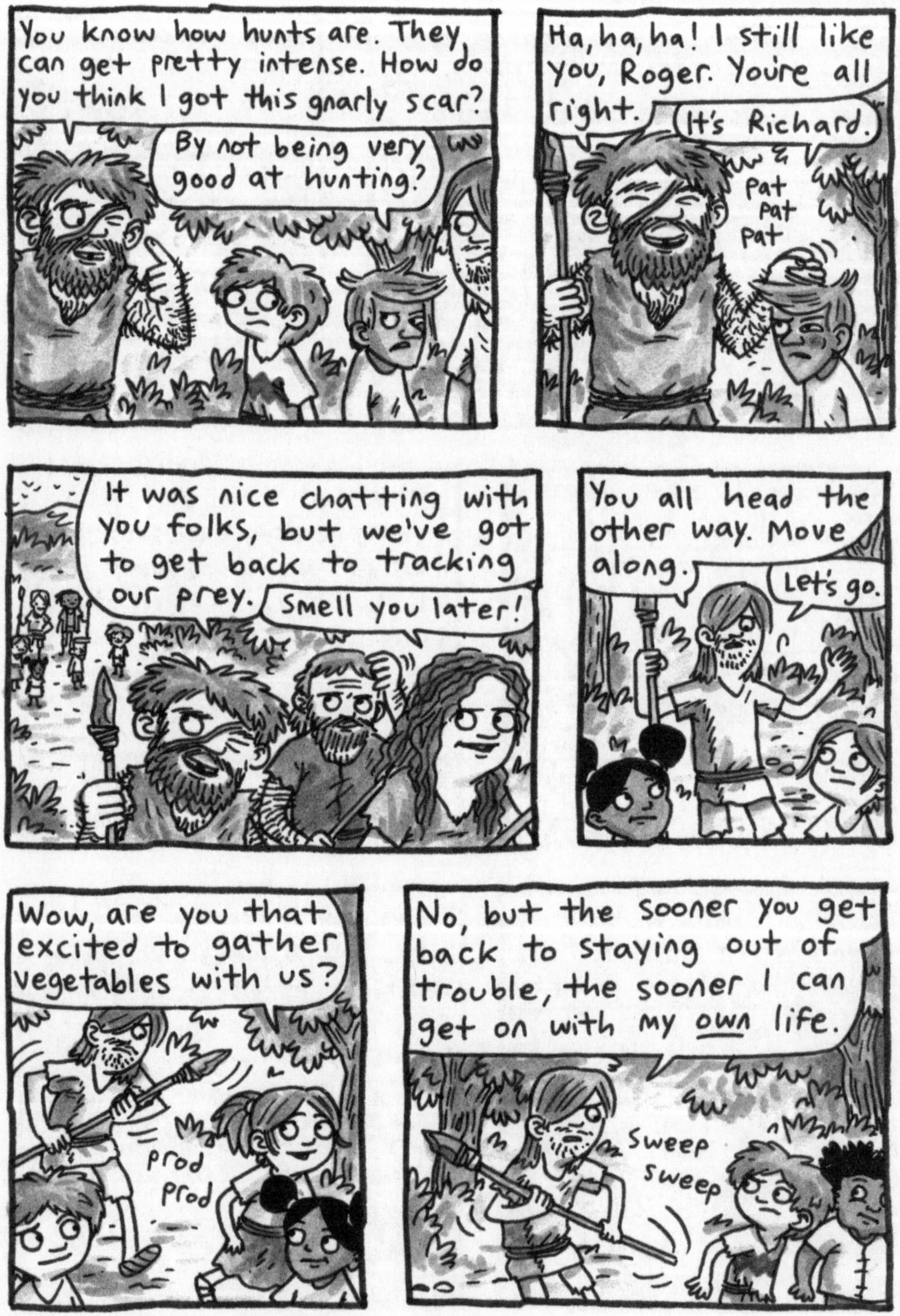
You know how hunts are. They can get pretty intense. How do you think I got this gnarly scar?
By not being very good at hunting?
Ha, ha, ha! I still like you, Roger. You're all right.
It's Richard.
pat pat pat
It was nice chatting with you folks, but we've got to get back to tracking our prey.
Smell you later!
You all head the other way. Move along.
Let's go.
Wow, are you that excited to gather vegetables with us?
prod prod
No, but the sooner you get back to staying out of trouble, the sooner I can get on with my own life.
Sweep sweep

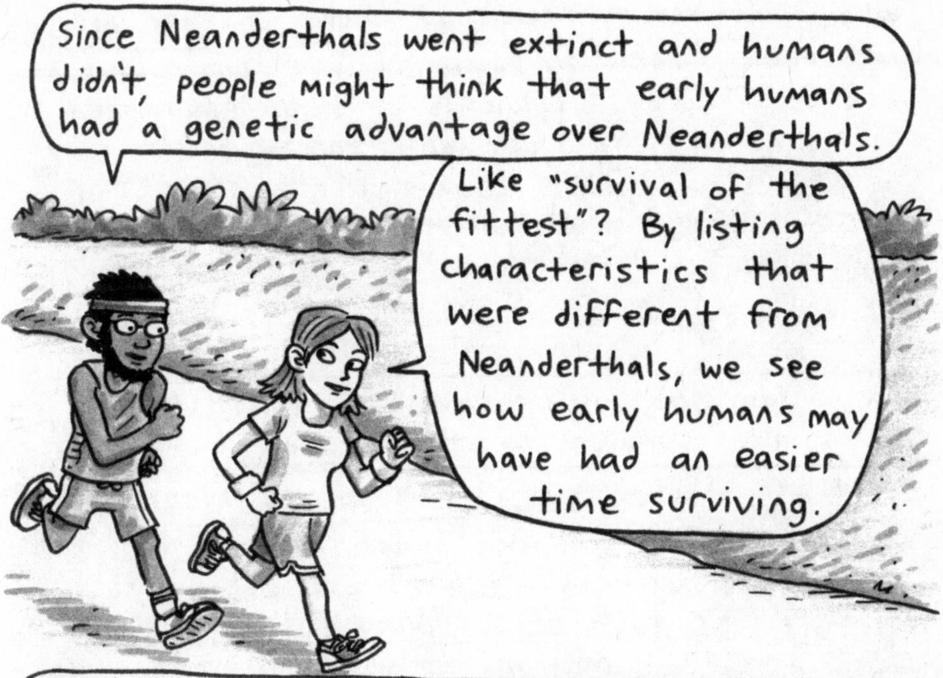
Since Neanderthals went extinct and humans didn't, people might think that early humans had a genetic advantage over Neanderthals.
Like "survival of the fittest"? By listing characteristics that were different from Neanderthals, we see how early humans may have had an easier time surviving.

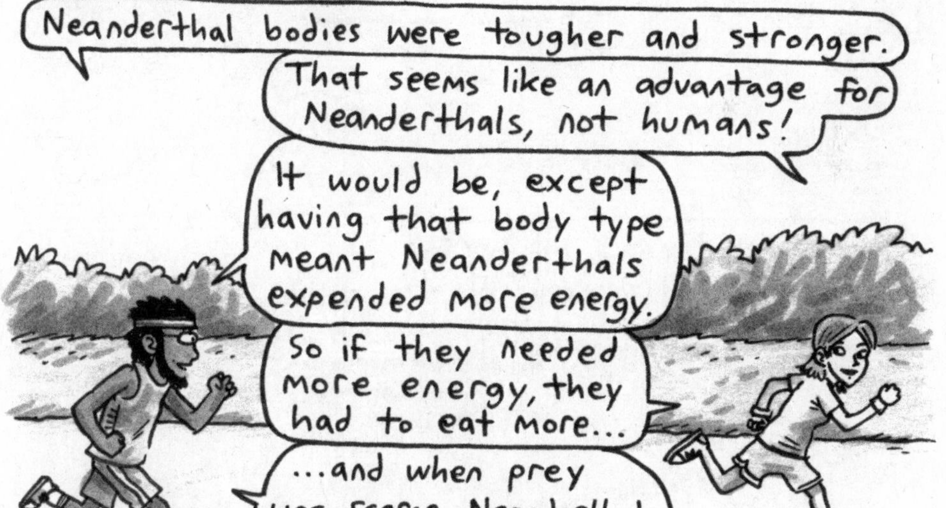
Neanderthal bodies were tougher and stronger.
That seems like an advantage for Neanderthals, not humans!
It would be, except having that body type meant Neanderthals expended more energy.
So if they needed more energy, they had to eat more...
...and when prey was scarce, Neanderthals would have been at a disadvantage!

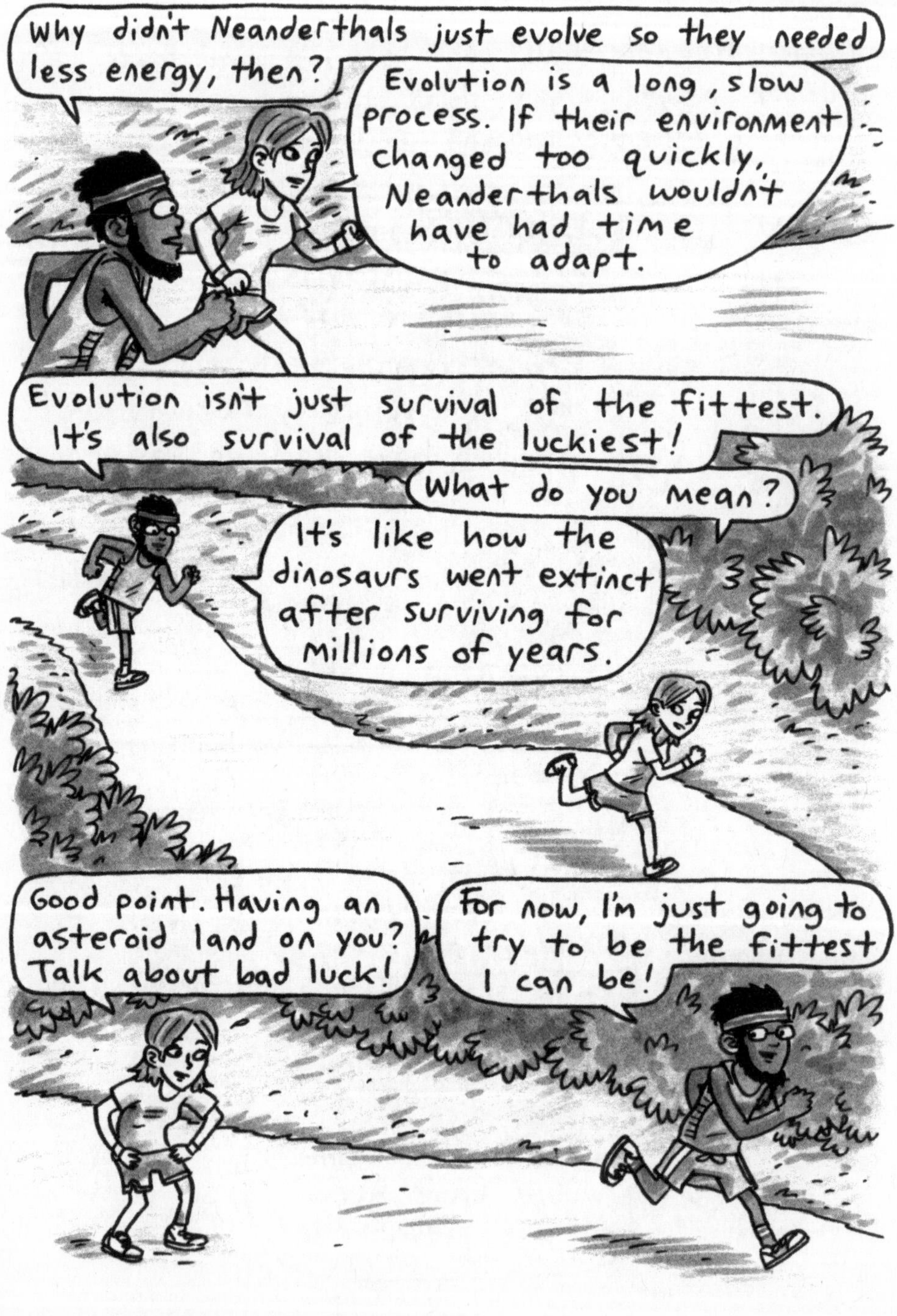
Why didn't Neanderthals just evolve so they needed less energy, then?
Evolution is a long, slow process. If their environment changed too quickly, Neanderthals wouldn't have had time to adapt.
Evolution isn't just survival of the fittest. It's also survival of the luckiest!
What do you mean?
It's like how the dinosaurs went extinct after surviving for millions of years.
Good point. Having an asteroid land on you? Talk about bad luck!
For now, I'm just going to try to be the fittest I can be!

BROKEN FUNNY BONES

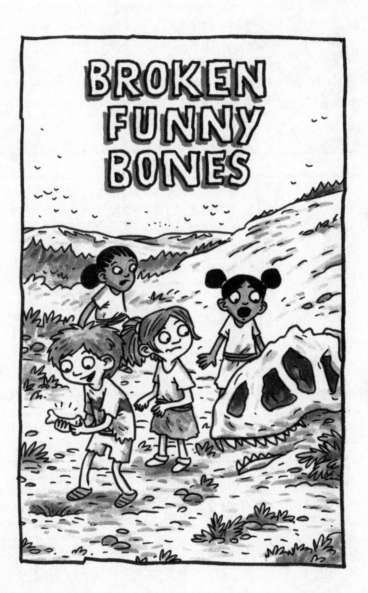

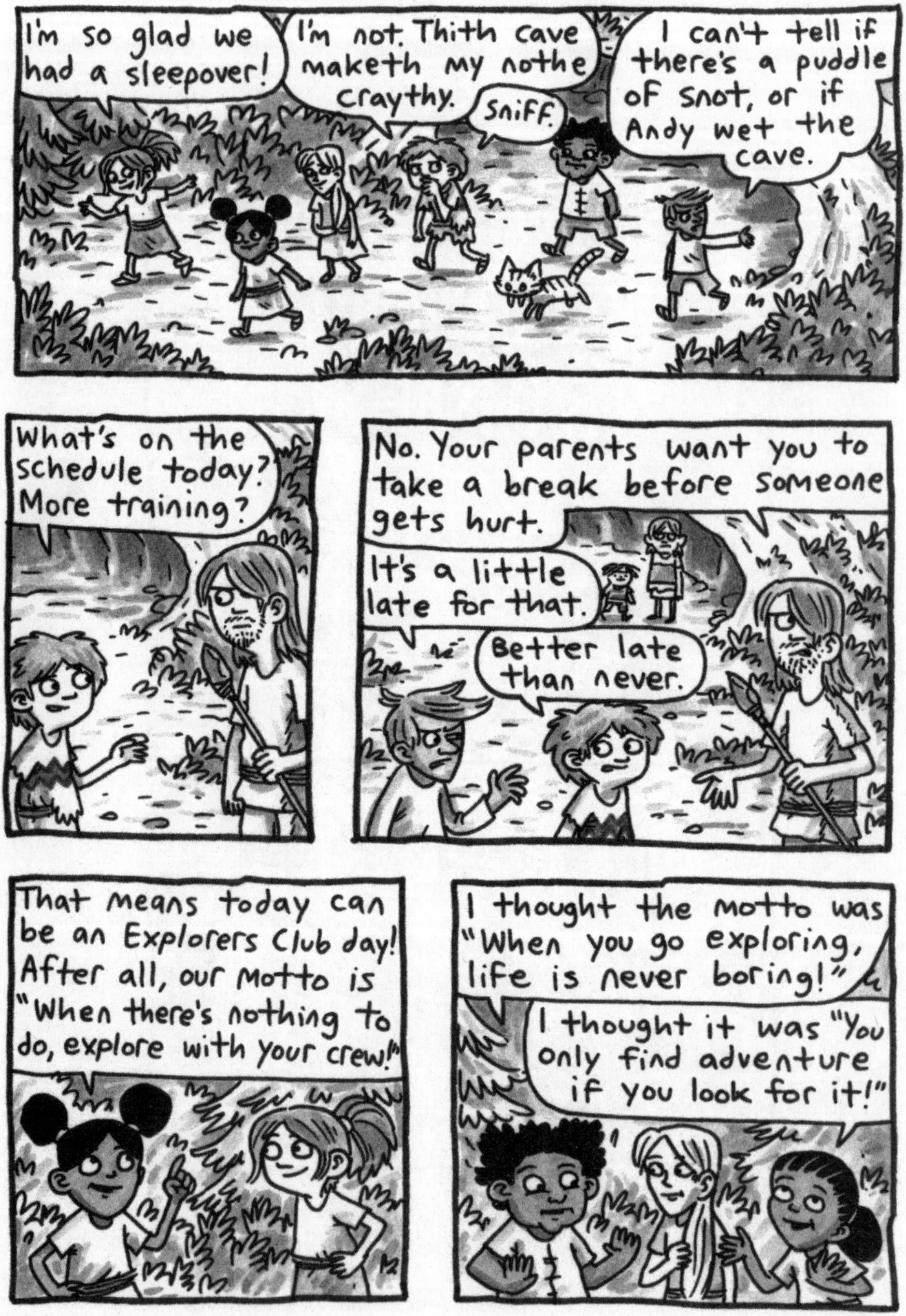
I'm so glad we had a sleepover!
I'm not. Thith cave maketh my nothe craythy.
Sniff.
I can't tell if there's a puddle of snot, or if Andy wet the cave.
What's on the schedule today? More training?
No. Your parents want you to take a break before someone gets hurt.
It's a little late for that.
Better late than never.
That means today can be an Explorers Club day! After all, our motto is "When there's nothing to do, explore with your crew!"
I thought the motto was "When you go exploring, life is never boring!"
I thought it was "You only find adventure if you look for it!"

It seems like you guys are making this up as you go.

Definitely not! But I can see how you'd think that, since our motto is "If you don't have it, make it!"

Everyone, grab your walking sticks and let's head out!

That's not a stick, Richard.

Sure it is. It just has a pointy end.

I have two sticks with pointy ends. Why do you need two?

I don't, but it looks cool.

Where are we going?

Exploring, dummy.

I know. I mean, WHERE?

Let's see what we can find down by the river.

Hurry, before Margaret tries to make us take Danny.

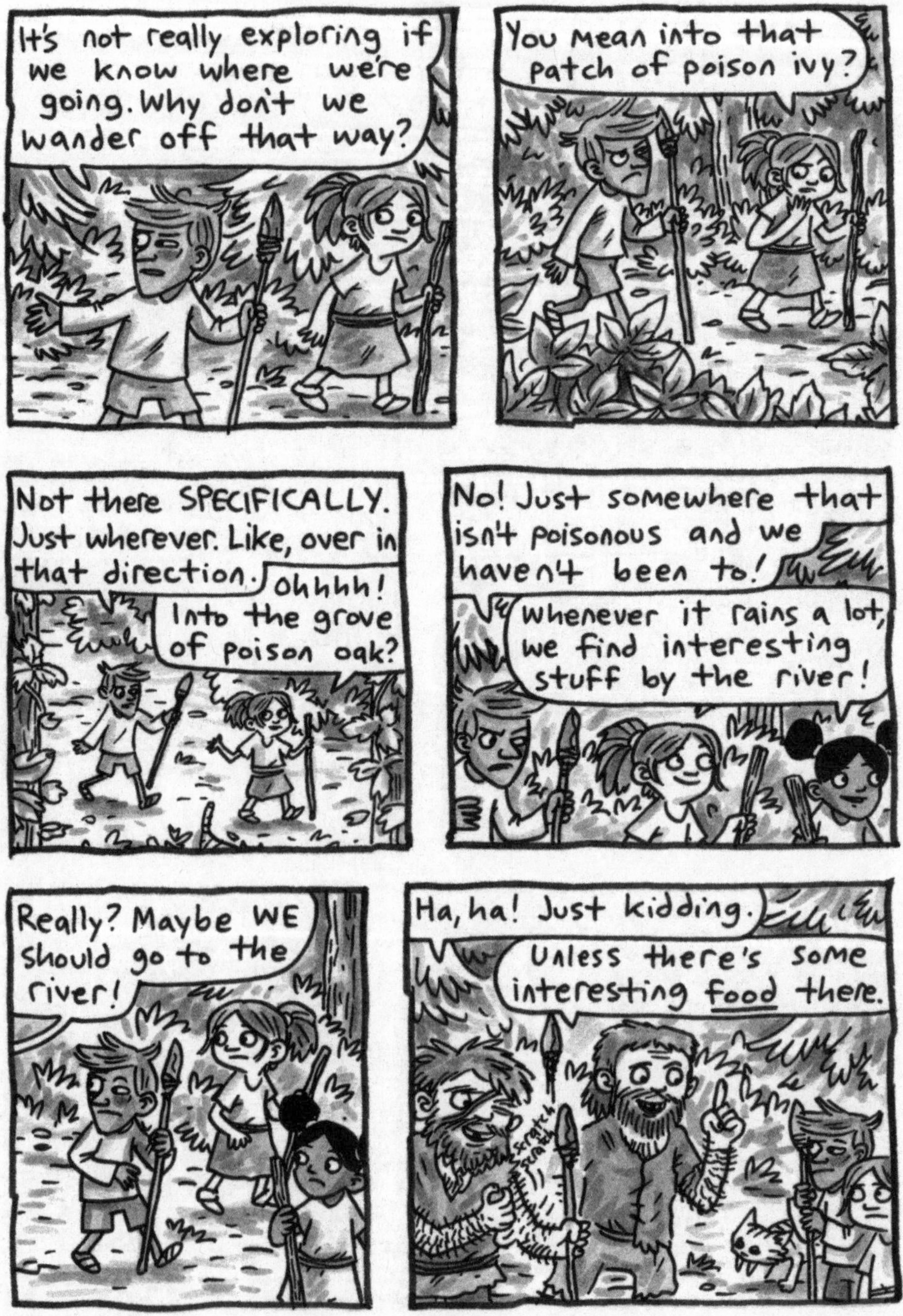
It's not really exploring if we know where we're going. Why don't we wander off that way?
You mean into that patch of poison ivy?
Not there SPECIFICALLY. Just wherever. Like, over in that direction.
Ohhhh! Into the grove of poison oak?
No! Just somewhere that isn't poisonous and we haven't been to!
Whenever it rains a lot, we find interesting stuff by the river!
Really? Maybe WE should go to the river!
Ha, ha! Just kidding.
Unless there's some interesting food there.
scratch scratch

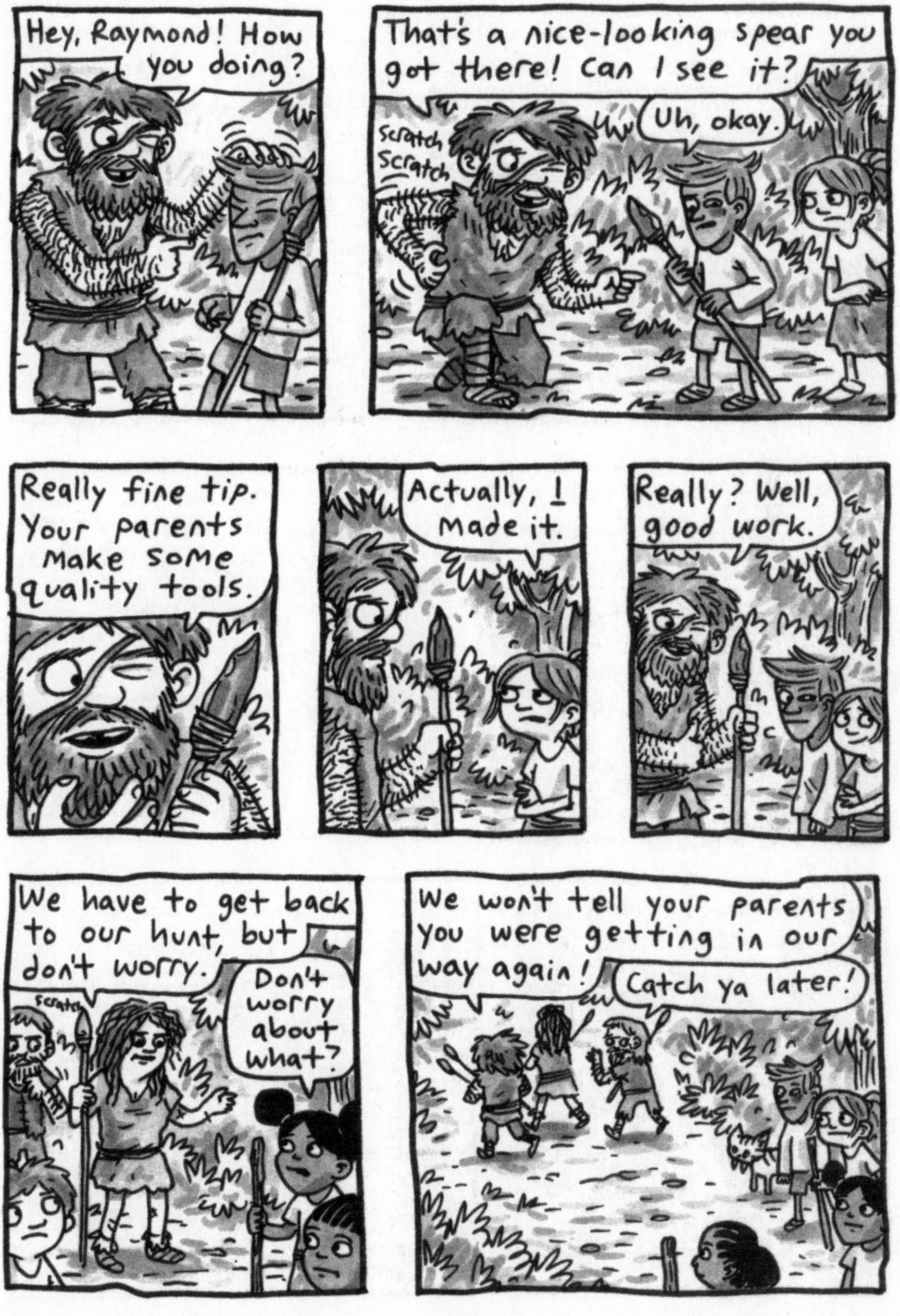
Hey, Raymond! How you doing?
That's a nice-looking spear you got there! Can I see it?
Scratch
Scratch
Uh, okay.
Really fine tip. Your parents make some quality tools.
Actually, I made it.
Really? Well, good work.
We have to get back to our hunt, but don't worry.
Don't worry about what?
We won't tell your parents you were getting in our way again!
Catch ya later!

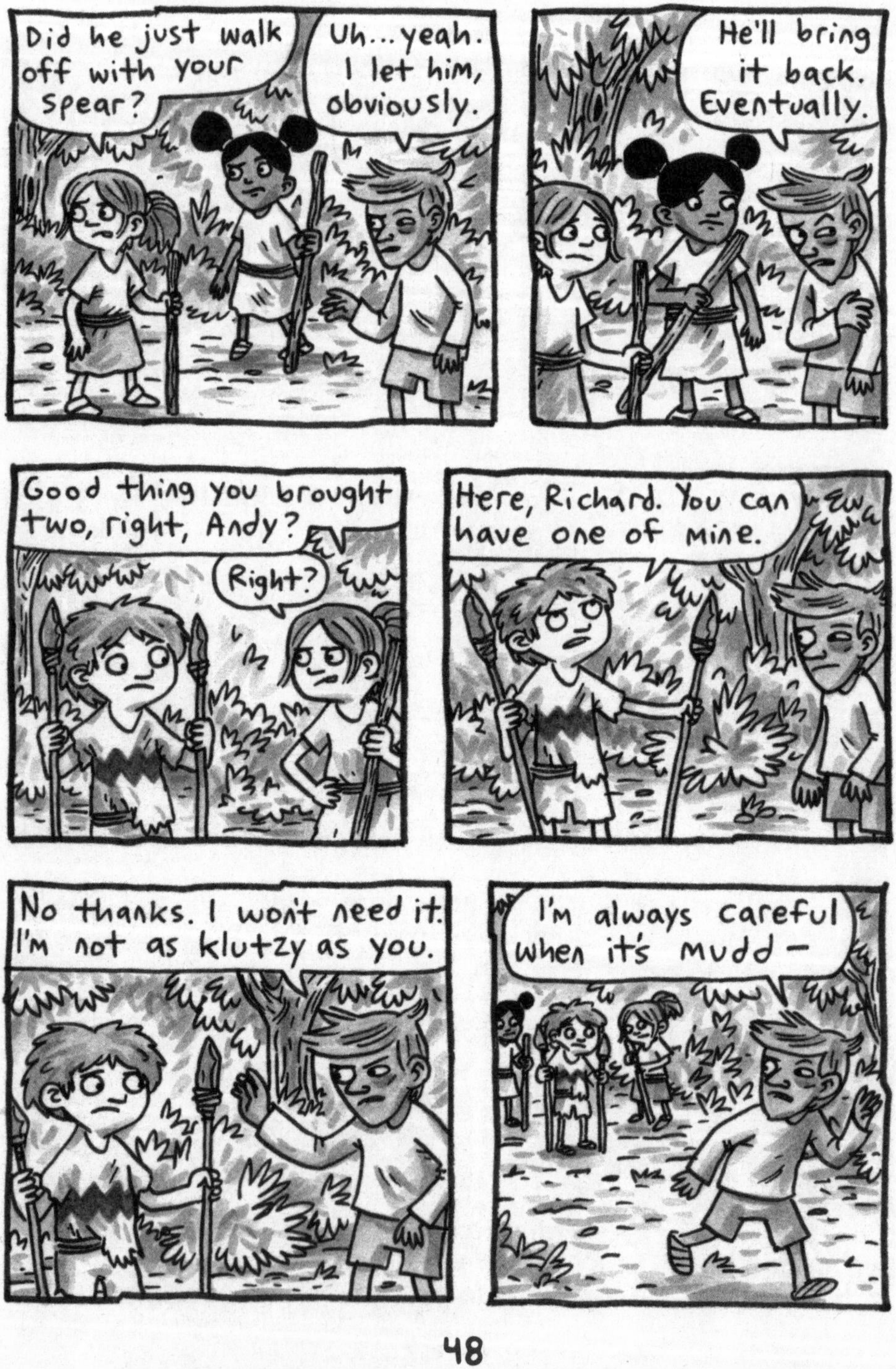
Did he just walk off with your spear?
Uh... yeah. I let him, obviously.
He'll bring it back. Eventually.
Good thing you brought two, right, Andy?
Right?
Here, Richard. You can have one of mine.
No thanks. I won't need it. I'm not as klutzy as you.
I'm always careful when it's mudd–

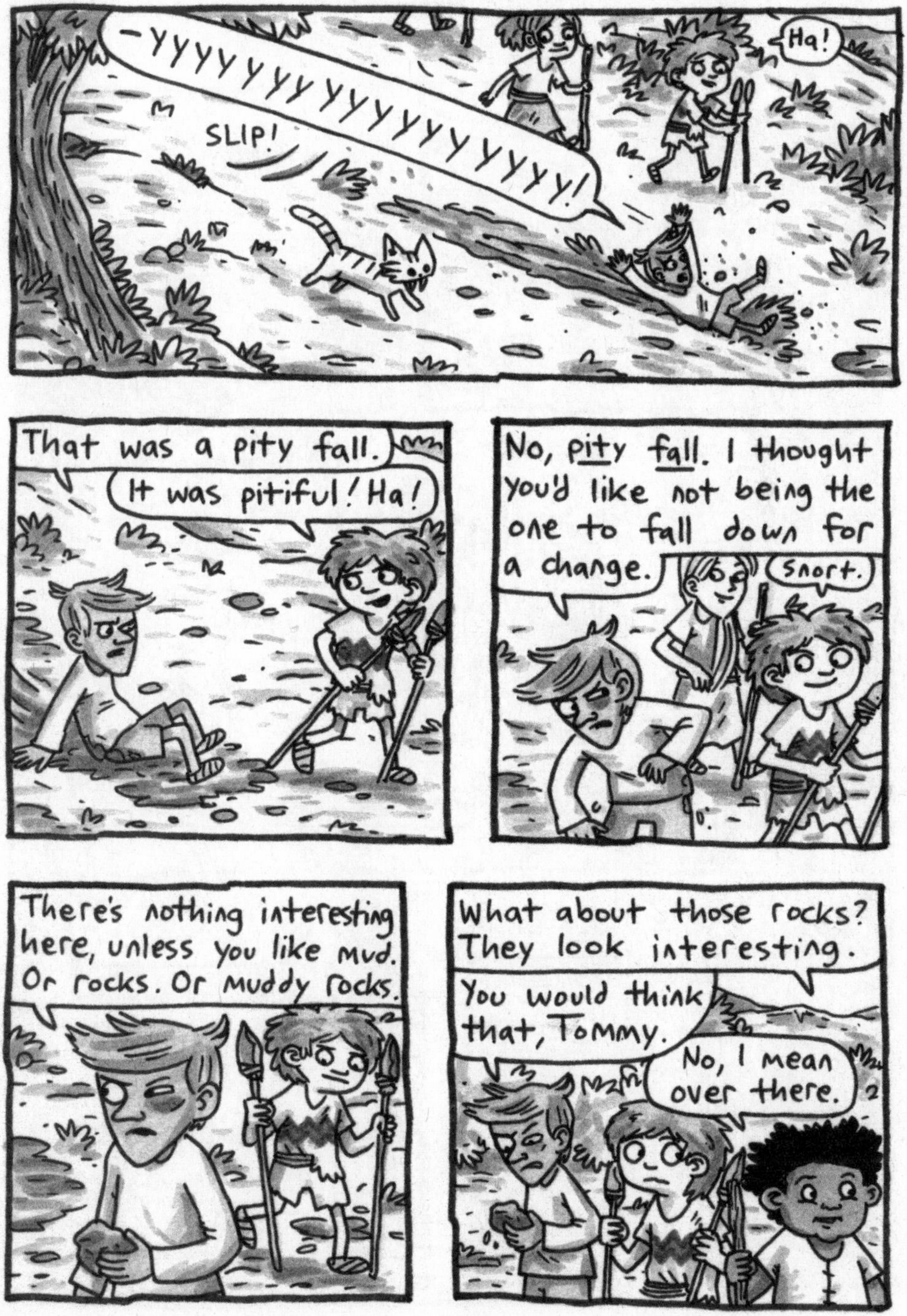
-YYYYYYYYYYYYYYYYYYYYYY!
SLIP!
Ha!
That was a pity fall.
It was pitiful! Ha!
No, pity fall. I thought you'd like not being the one to fall down for a change.
Snort.
There's nothing interesting here, unless you like mud. Or rocks. Or muddy rocks.
What about those rocks? They look interesting.
You would think that, Tommy.
No, I mean over there.

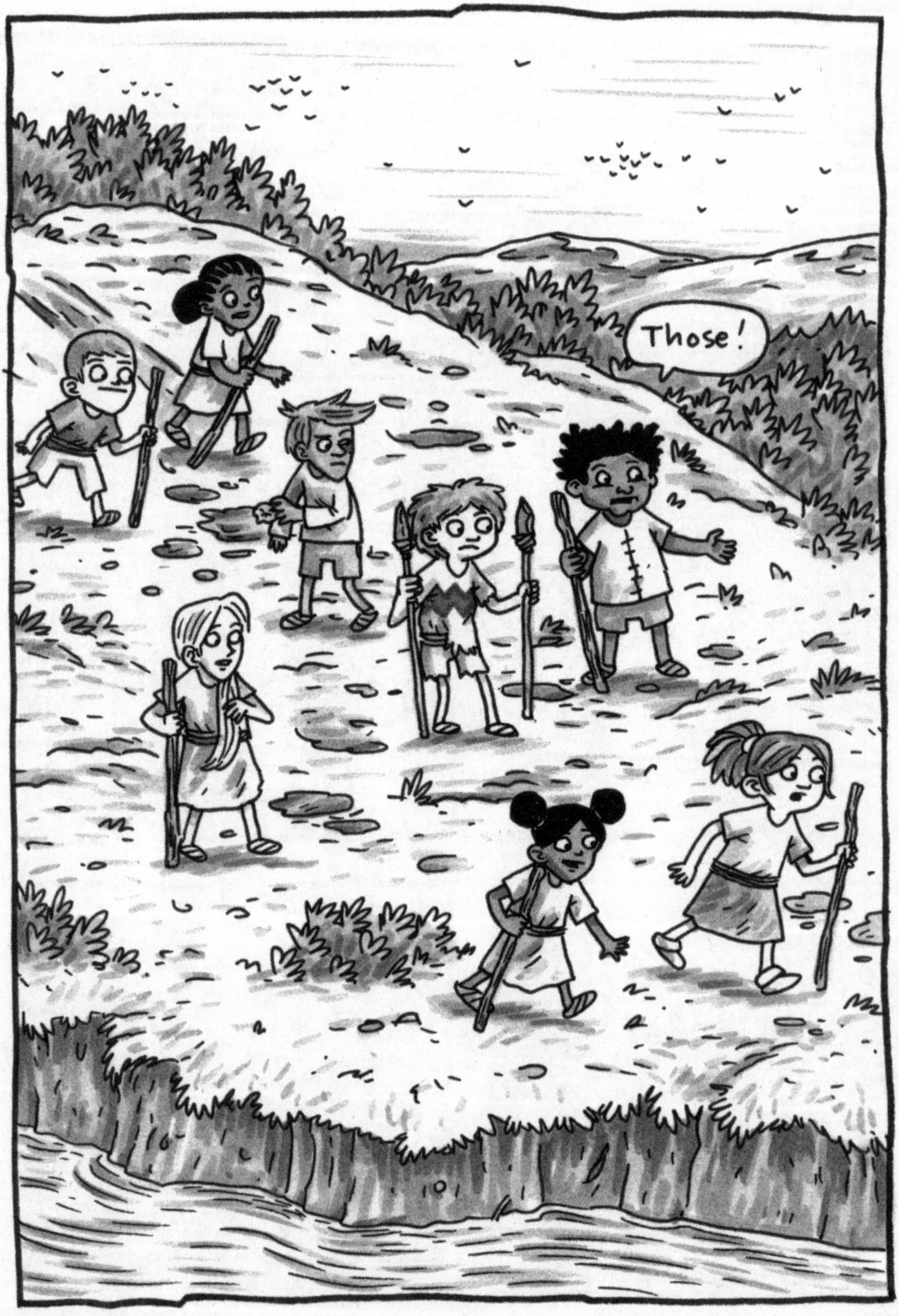
Those!

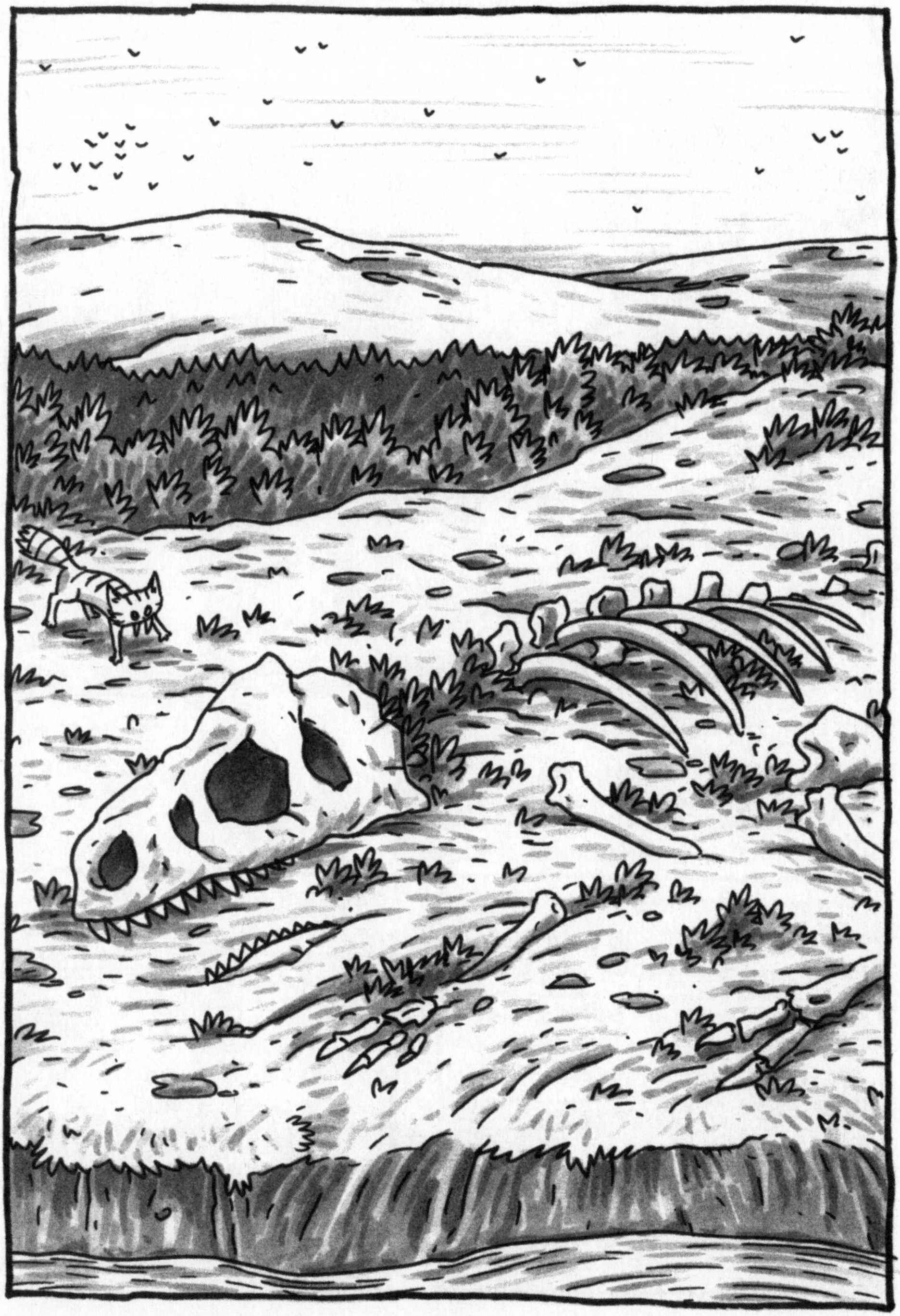

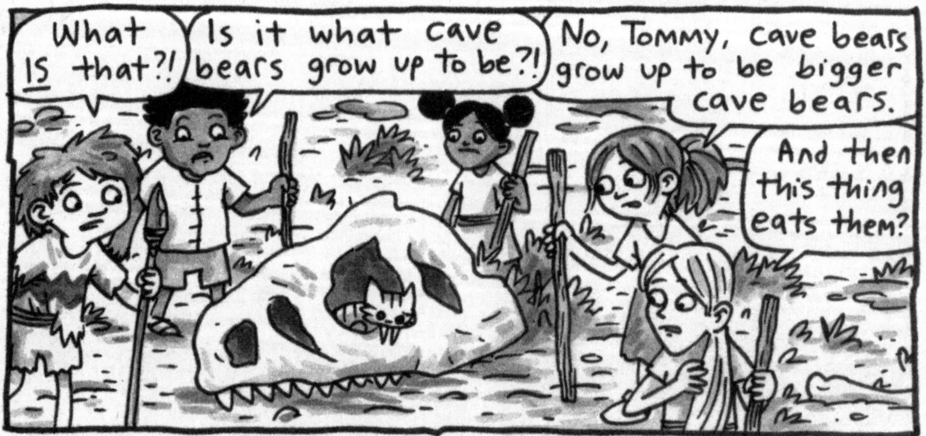
What IS that?!
Is it what cave bears grow up to be?!
No, Tommy, cave bears grow up to be bigger cave bears.
And then this thing eats them?

Dinosaurs last roamed the earth about 65 million years ago — long before humans and Neanderthals appeared!

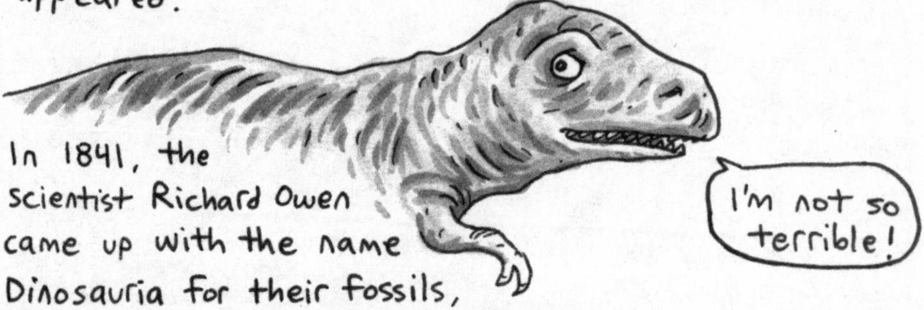
I'm not so terrible!

In 1841, the scientist Richard Owen came up with the name Dinosauria for their fossils, which means "terrible lizards."

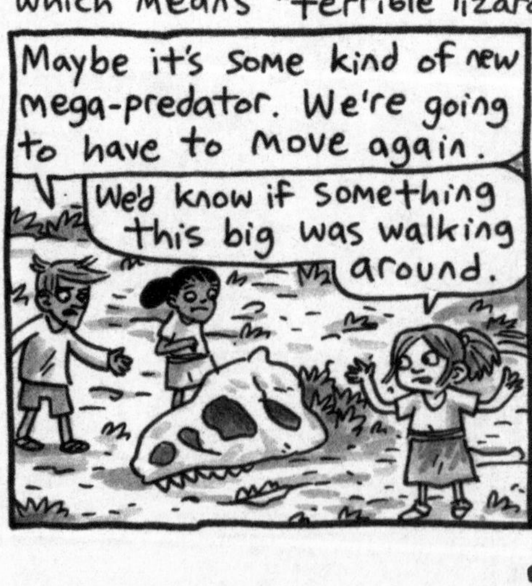
Maybe it's some kind of new mega-predator. We're going to have to move again.
We'd know if something this big was walking around.

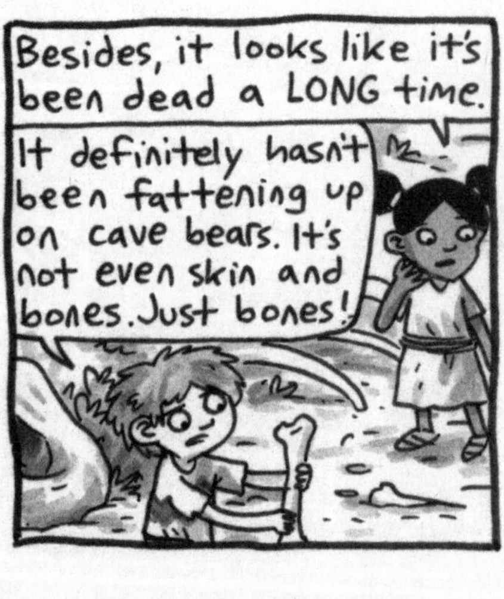
Besides, it looks like it's been dead a LONG time.
It definitely hasn't been fattening up on cave bears. It's not even skin and bones. Just bones!

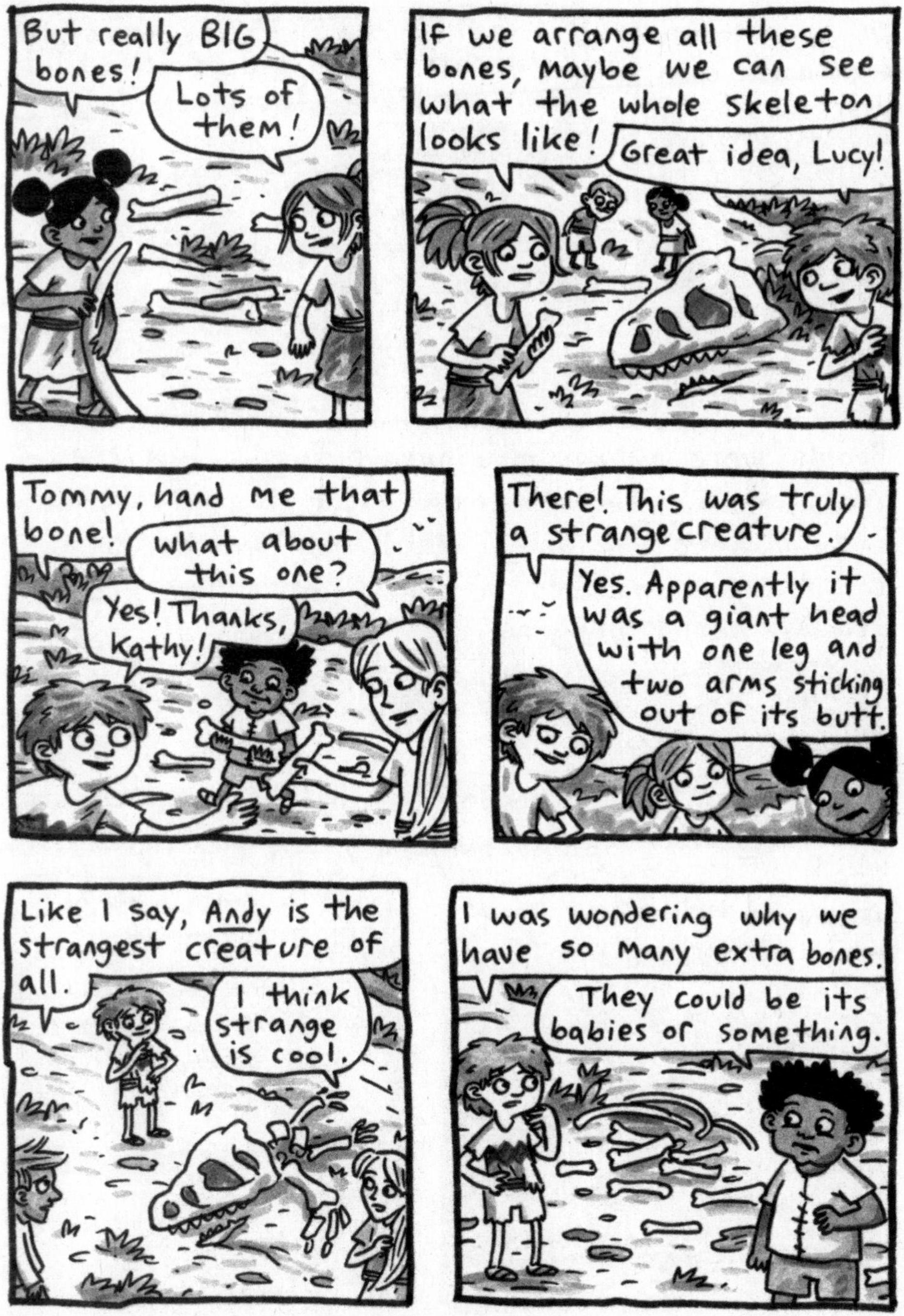
But really BIG bones!
Lots of them!
If we arrange all these bones, maybe we can see what the whole skeleton looks like!
Great idea, Lucy!
Tommy, hand me that bone!
What about this one?
Yes! Thanks, Kathy!
There! This was truly a strange creature.
Yes. Apparently it was a giant head with one leg and two arms sticking out of its butt.
Like I say, Andy is the strangest creature of all.
I think strange is cool.
I was wondering why we have so many extra bones.
They could be its babies or something.

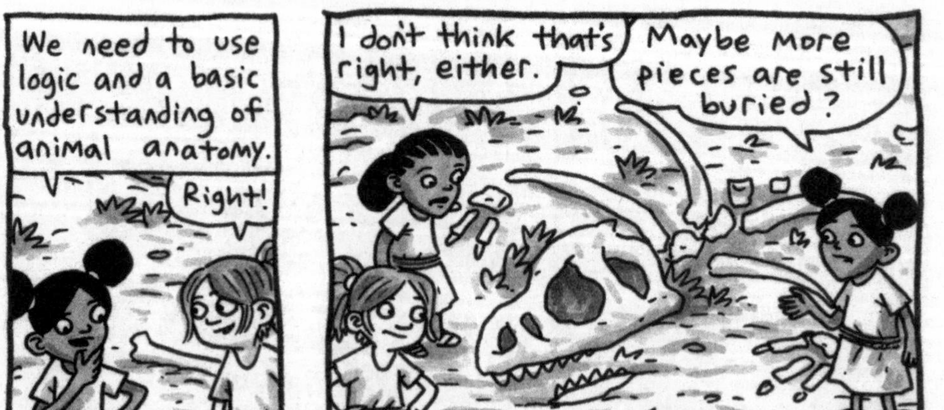
We need to use logic and a basic understanding of animal anatomy.
Right!
I don't think that's right, either.
Maybe more pieces are still buried?

People were aware of dinosaur fossils hundreds of years ago but had no idea what they really were. They thought the bones might be from mythical creatures—dinosaurs may have been the origin of stories about dragons!

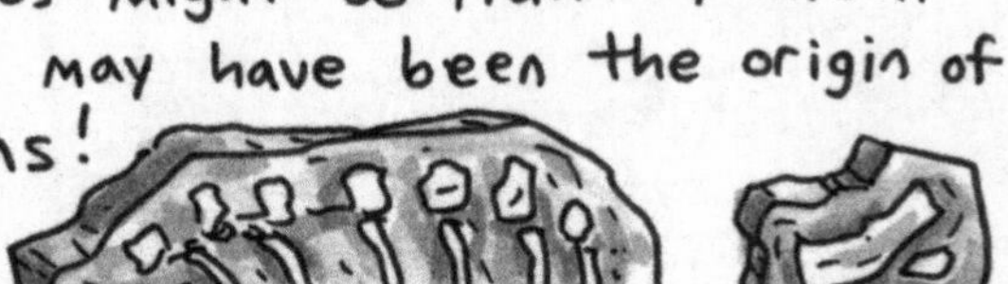

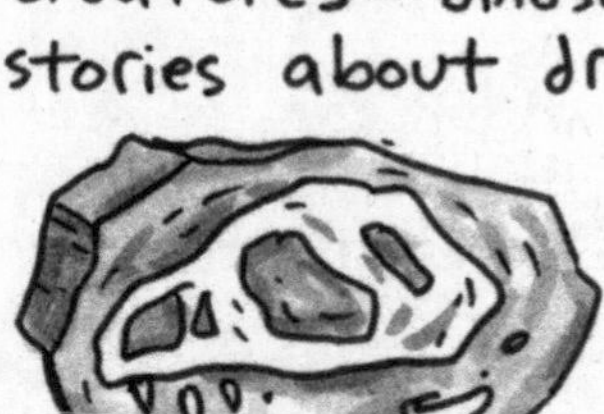

Maybe Neanderthals found dinosaur skulls! Unfortunately, they didn't make any cave paintings of them.

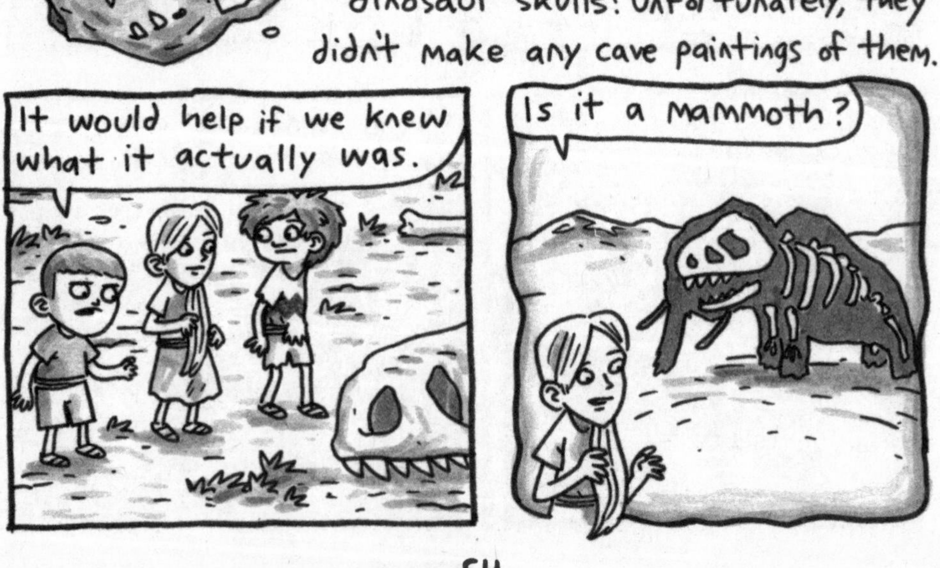
It would help if we knew what it actually was.
Is it a mammoth?

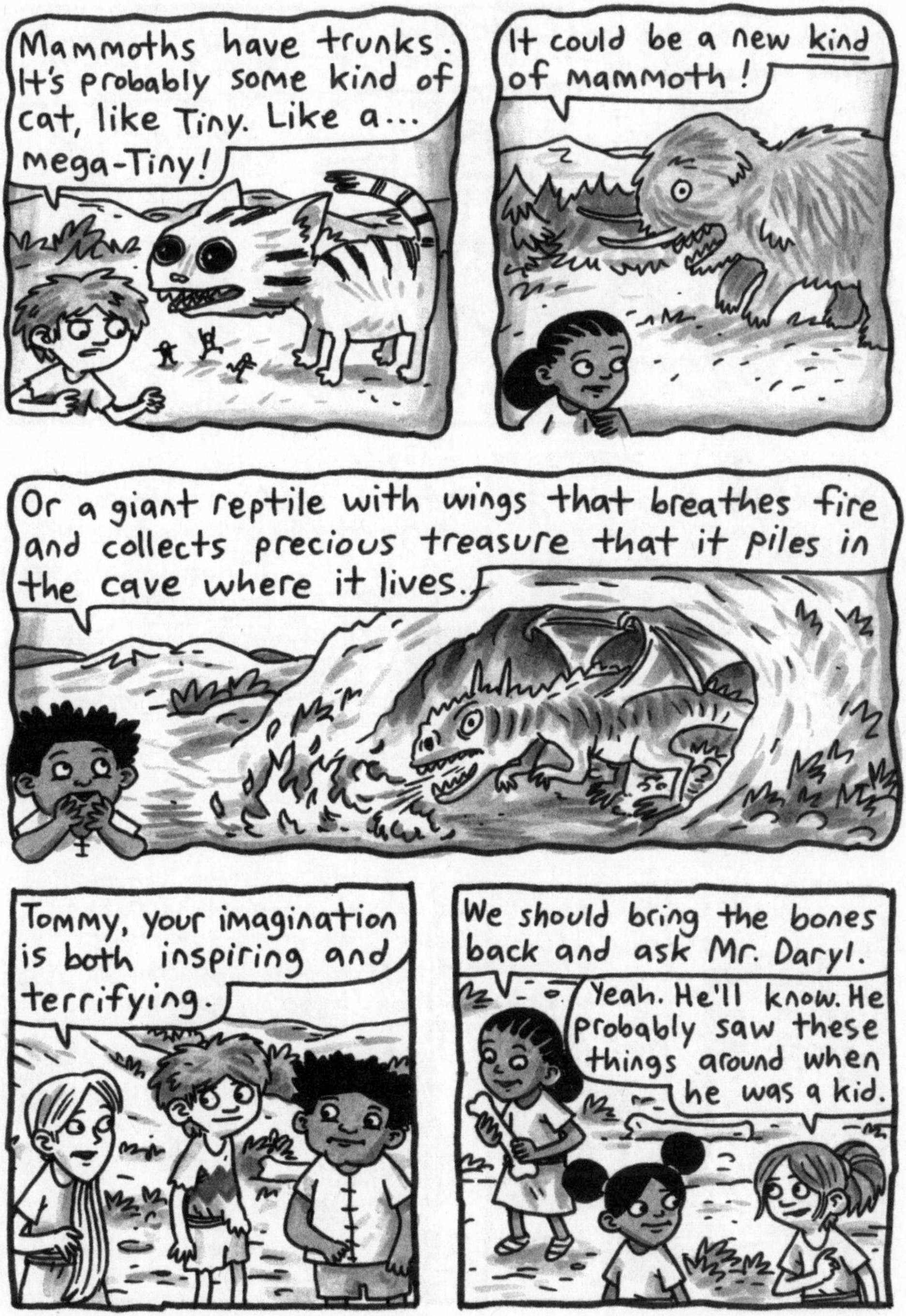
Mammoths have trunks. It's probably some kind of cat, like Tiny. Like a... mega-Tiny!
It could be a new kind of mammoth!
Or a giant reptile with wings that breathes fire and collects precious treasure that it piles in the cave where it lives.
Tommy, your imagination is both inspiring and terrifying.
We should bring the bones back and ask Mr. Daryl.
Yeah. He'll know. He probably saw these things around when he was a kid.

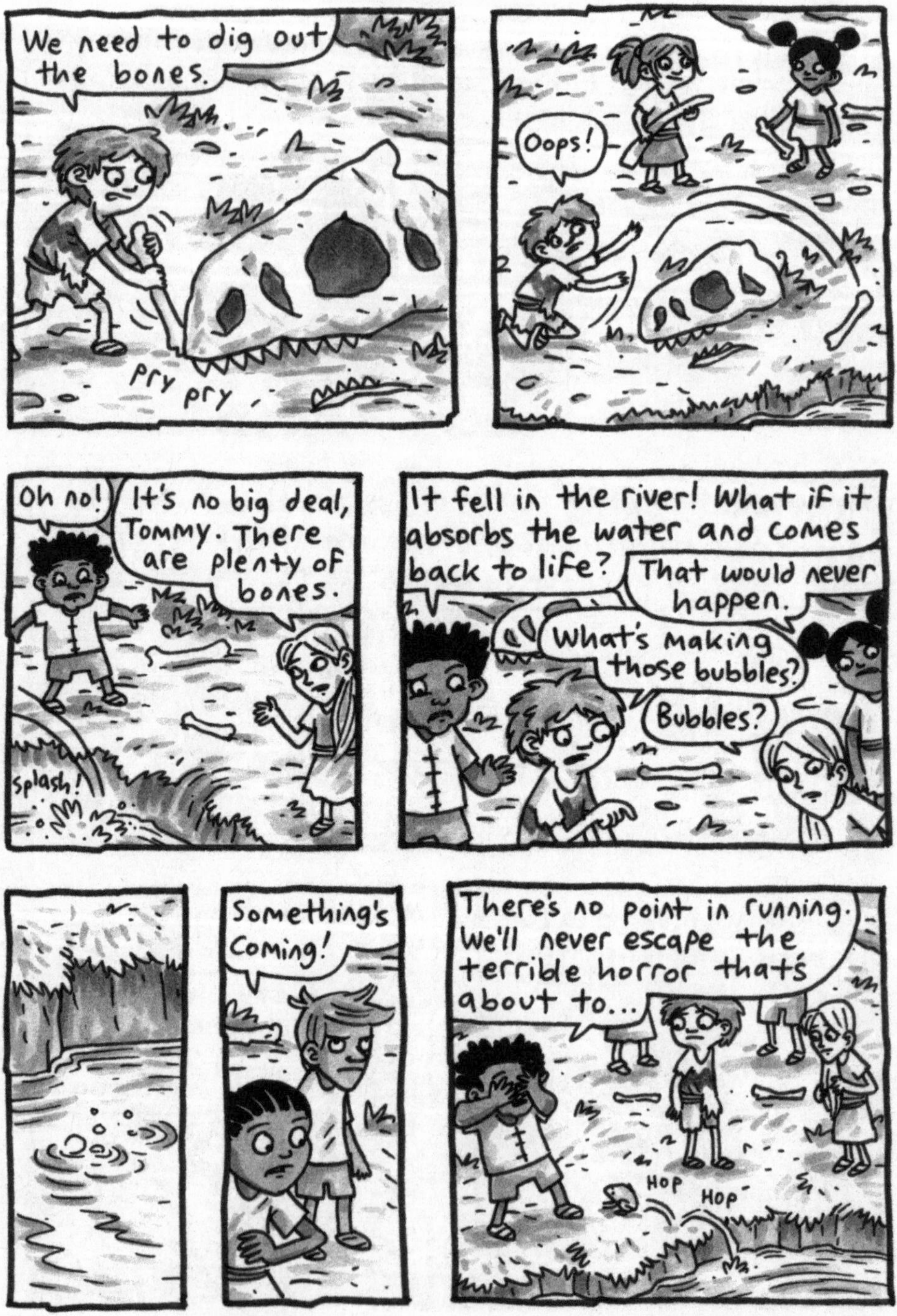
We need to dig out the bones.
pry pry
Oops!
Oh no!
It's no big deal, Tommy. There are plenty of bones.
splash!
It fell in the river! What if it absorbs the water and comes back to life?
That would never happen.
What's making those bubbles?
Bubbles?
Something's coming!
There's no point in running. We'll never escape the terrible horror that's about to...
HOP
HOP

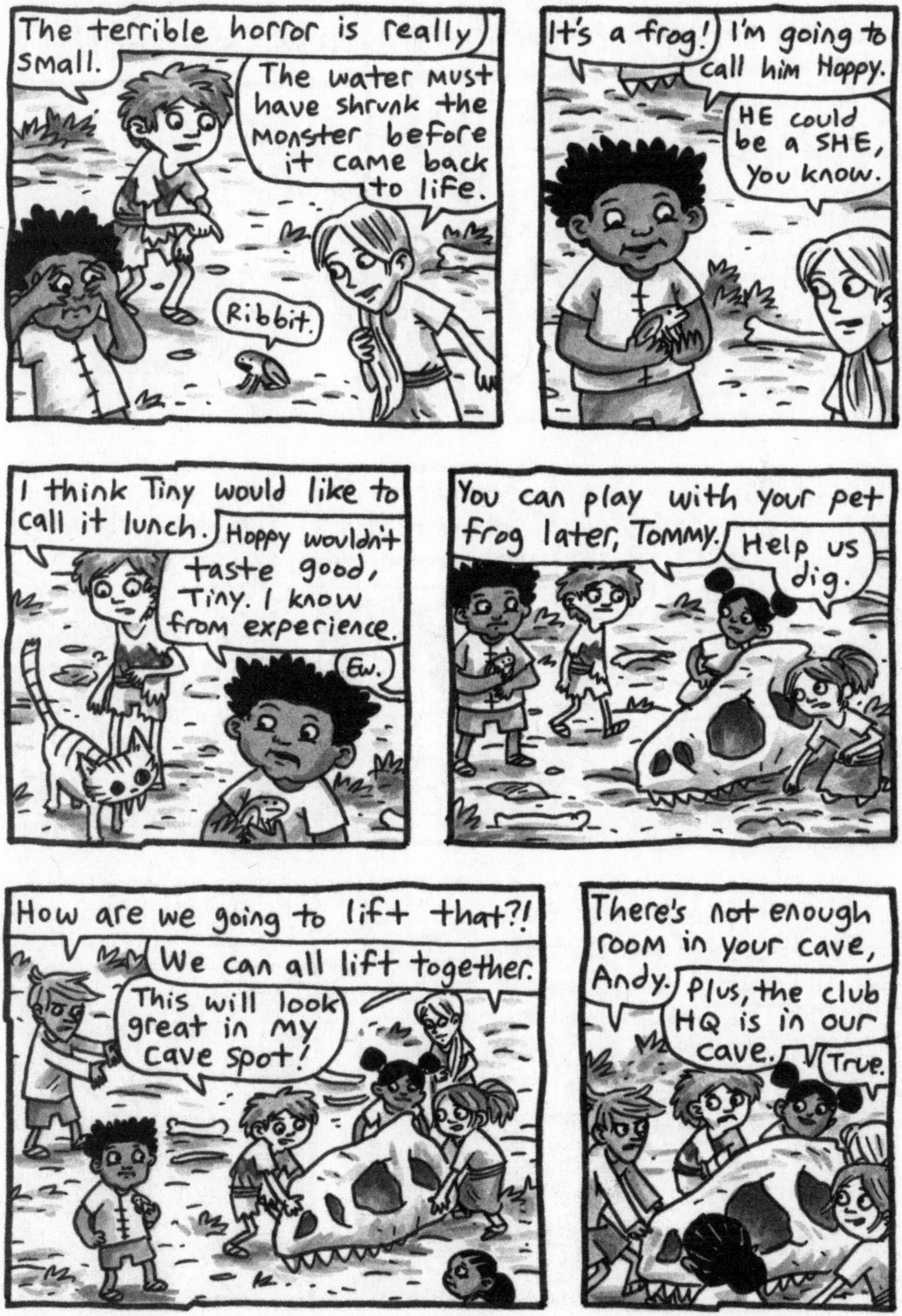
The terrible horror is really small.
The water must have shrunk the monster before it came back to life.
Ribbit.
It's a frog! I'm going to call him Hoppy.
HE could be a SHE, you know.
I think Tiny would like to call it lunch.
Hoppy wouldn't taste good, Tiny. I know from experience.
Ew.
You can play with your pet frog later, Tommy.
Help us dig.
How are we going to lift that?!
We can all lift together.
This will look great in my cave spot!
There's not enough room in your cave, Andy.
Plus, the club HQ is in our cave.
True.

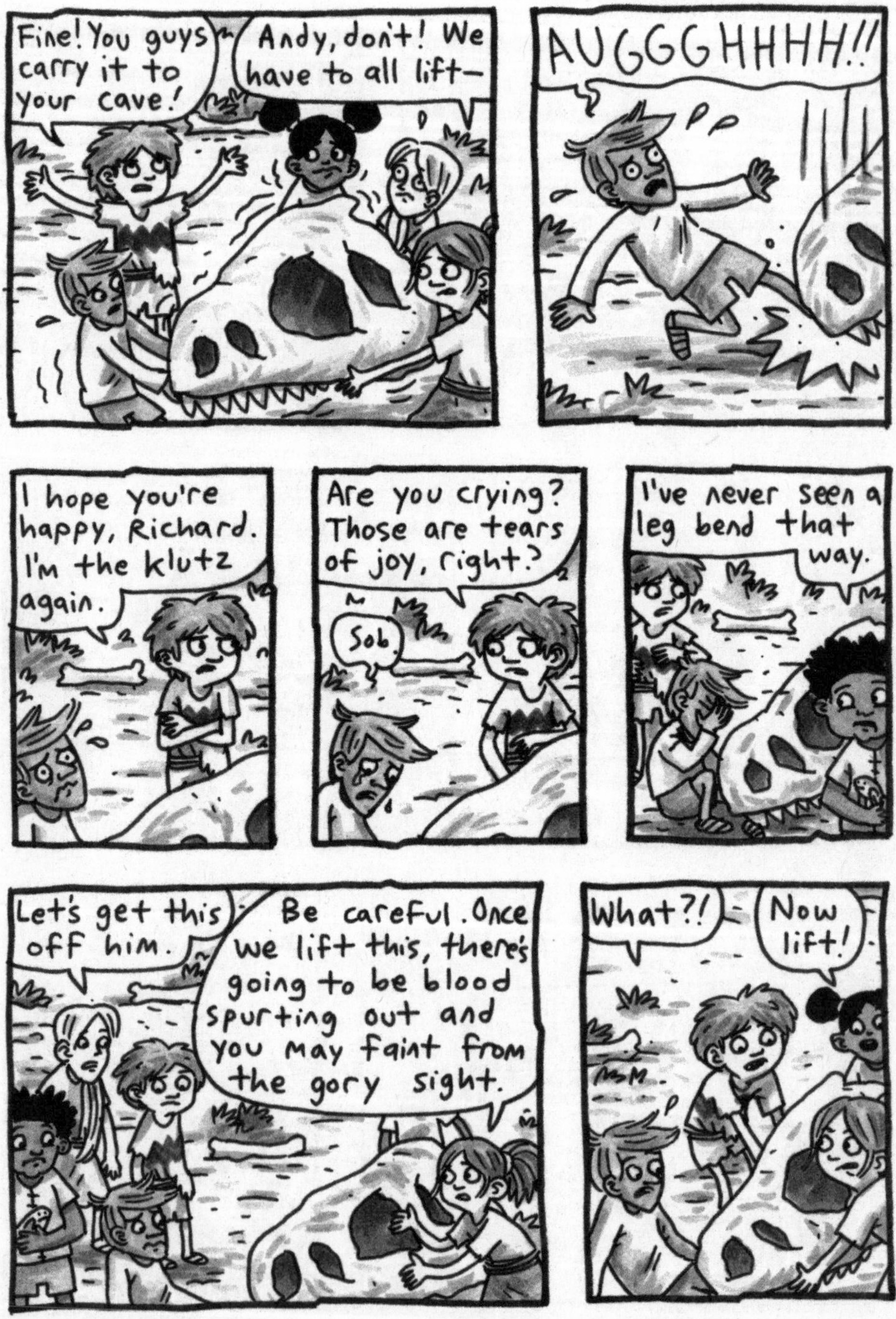
Fine! You guys carry it to your cave!
Andy, don't! We have to all lift—
AUGGGHHHH!!
I hope you're happy, Richard. I'm the klutz again.
Are you crying? Those are tears of joy, right?
Sob.
I've never seen a leg bend that way.
Let's get this off him.
Be careful. Once we lift this, there's going to be blood spurting out and you may faint from the gory sight.
What?!
Now lift!

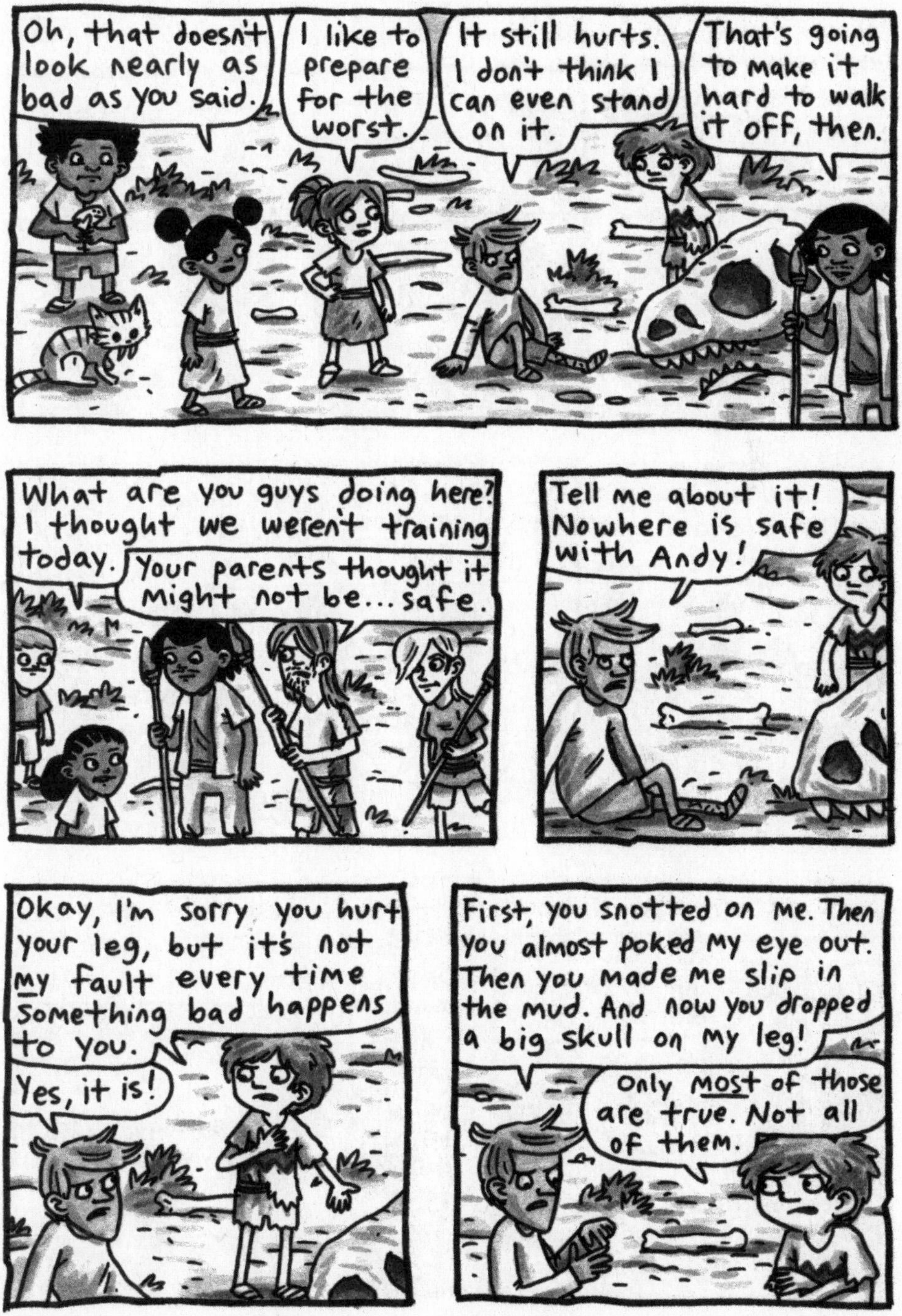

Oh, that doesn't look nearly as bad as you said.
I like to prepare for the worst.
It still hurts. I don't think I can even stand on it.
That's going to make it hard to walk it off, then.
What are you guys doing here? I thought we weren't training today.
Your parents thought it might not be... safe.
Tell me about it! Nowhere is safe with Andy!
Okay, I'm sorry you hurt your leg, but it's not my fault every time something bad happens to you.
Yes, it is!
First, you snotted on me. Then you almost poked my eye out. Then you made me slip in the mud. And now you dropped a big skull on my leg!
Only MOST of those are true. Not all of them.

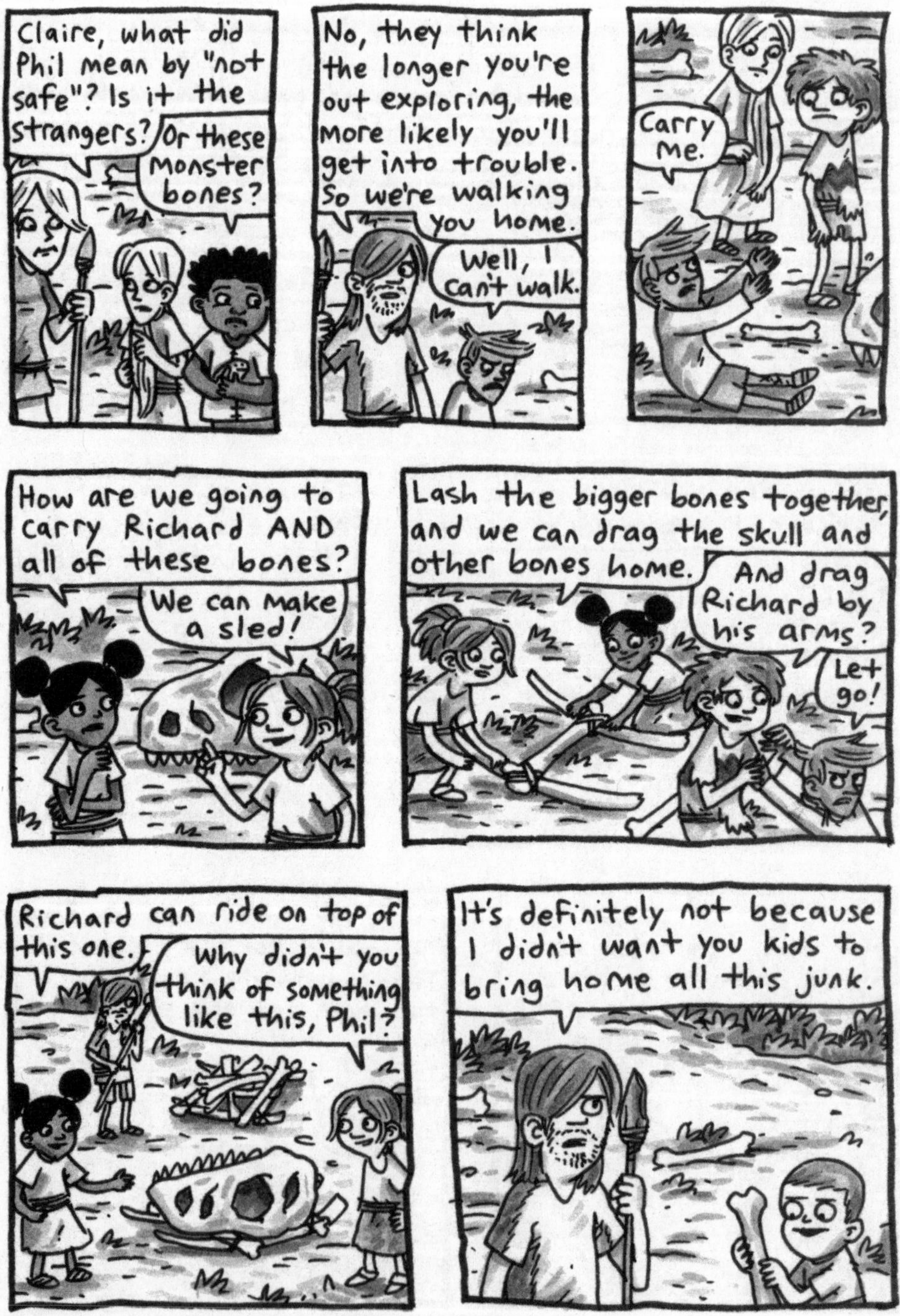
Claire, what did Phil mean by "not safe"? Is it the strangers?
Or these monster bones?
No, they think the longer you're out exploring, the more likely you'll get into trouble. So we're walking you home.
Well, I can't walk.
Carry me.
How are we going to carry Richard AND all of these bones?
We can make a sled!
Lash the bigger bones together, and we can drag the skull and other bones home.
And drag Richard by his arms?
Let go!
Richard can ride on top of this one.
Why didn't you think of something like this, Phil?
It's definitely not because I didn't want you kids to bring home all this junk.

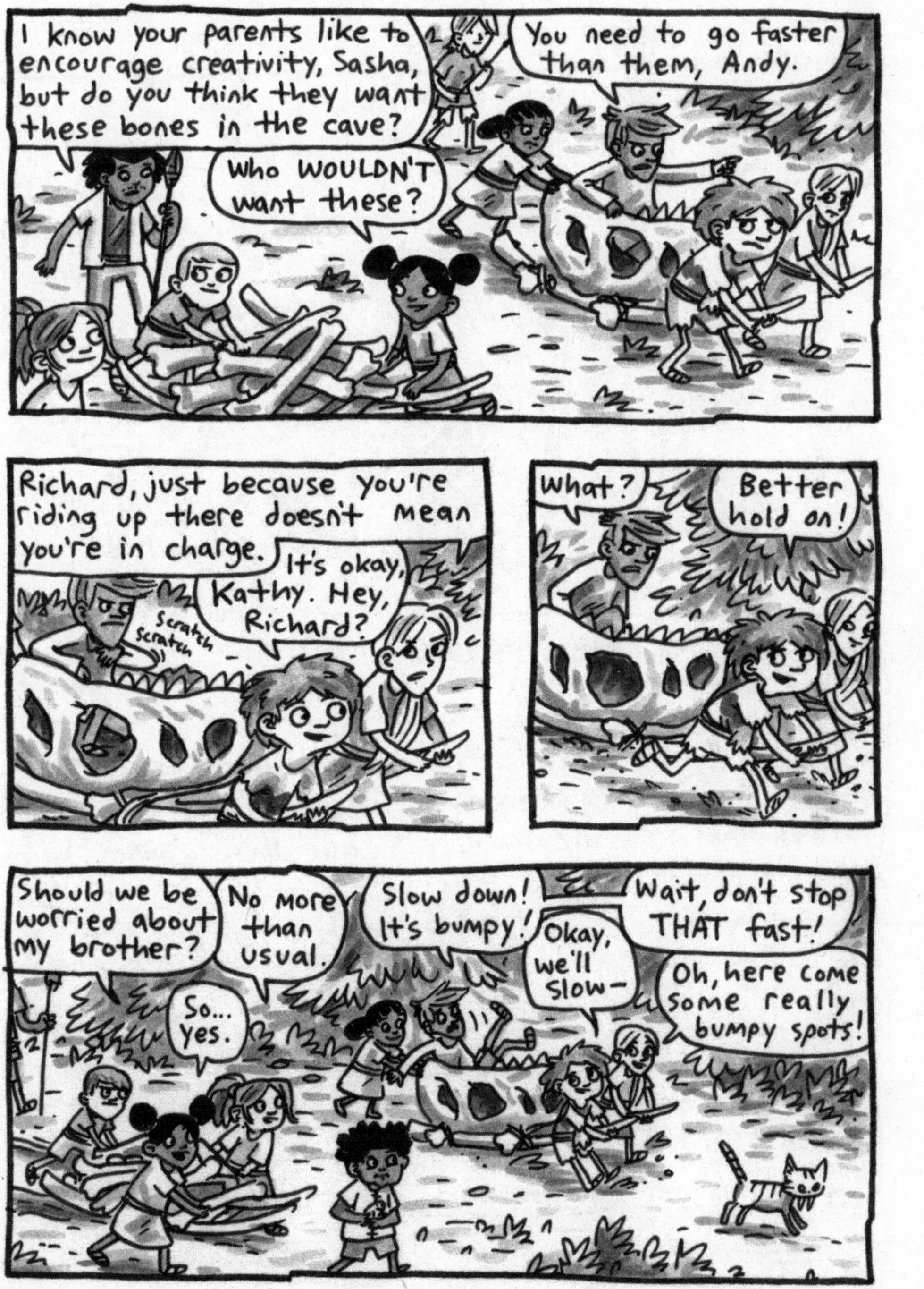
I know your parents like to encourage creativity, Sasha, but do you think they want these bones in the cave?
Who WOULDN'T want these?
You need to go faster than them, Andy.
Richard, just because you're riding up there doesn't mean you're in charge.
It's okay, Kathy. Hey, Richard?
Scratch Scratch
What?
Better hold on!
Should we be worried about my brother?
No more than usual.
So... yes.
Slow down! It's bumpy!
Okay, we'll slow—
Wait, don't stop THAT fast!
Oh, here come some really bumpy spots!

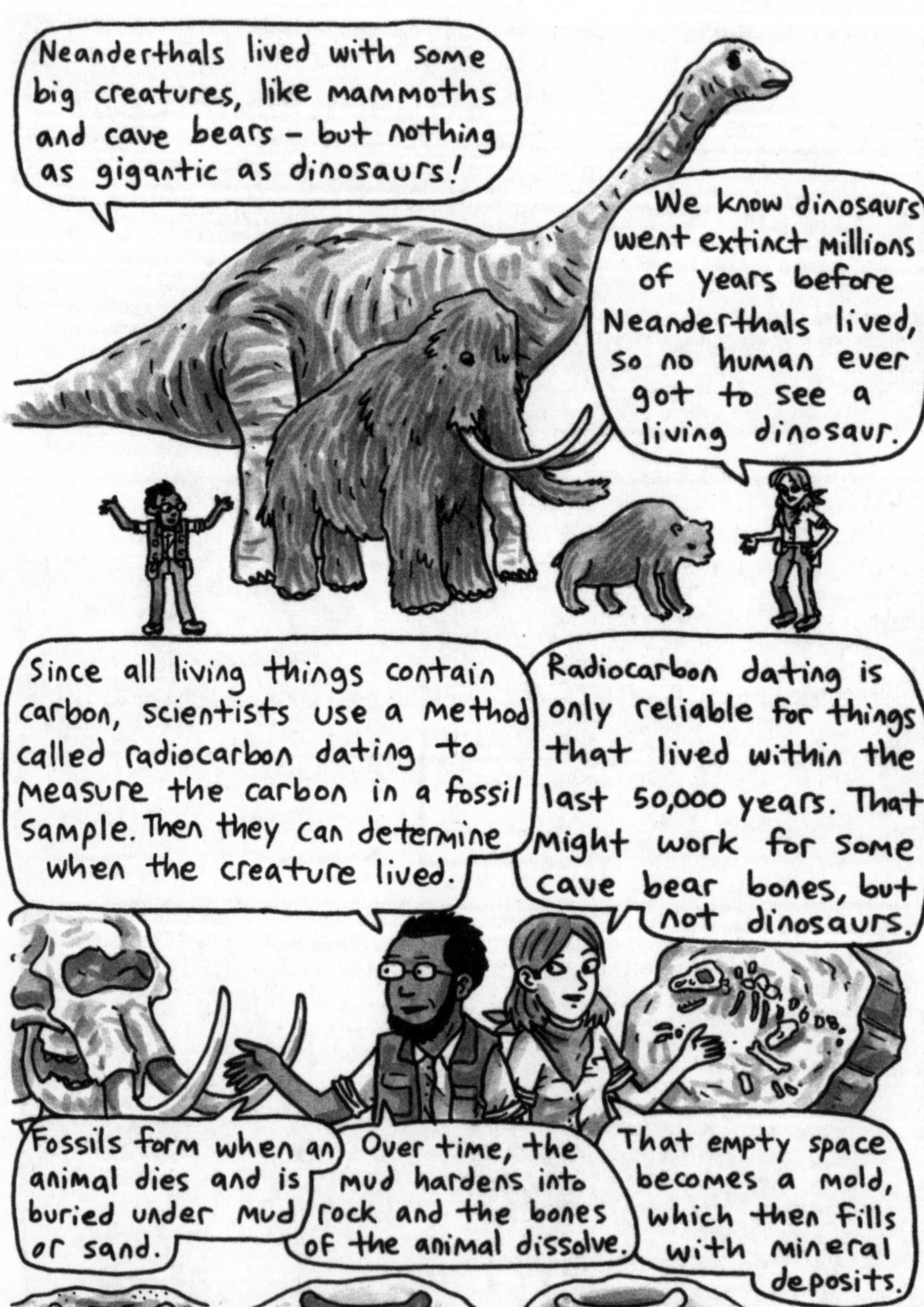
Neanderthals lived with some big creatures, like mammoths and cave bears – but nothing as gigantic as dinosaurs!
We know dinosaurs went extinct millions of years before Neanderthals lived, so no human ever got to see a living dinosaur.
Since all living things contain carbon, scientists use a method called radiocarbon dating to measure the carbon in a fossil sample. Then they can determine when the creature lived.
Radiocarbon dating is only reliable for things that lived within the last 50,000 years. That might work for some cave bear bones, but not dinosaurs.
Fossils form when an animal dies and is buried under mud or sand.
Over time, the mud hardens into rock and the bones of the animal dissolve.
That empty space becomes a mold, which then fills with mineral deposits.

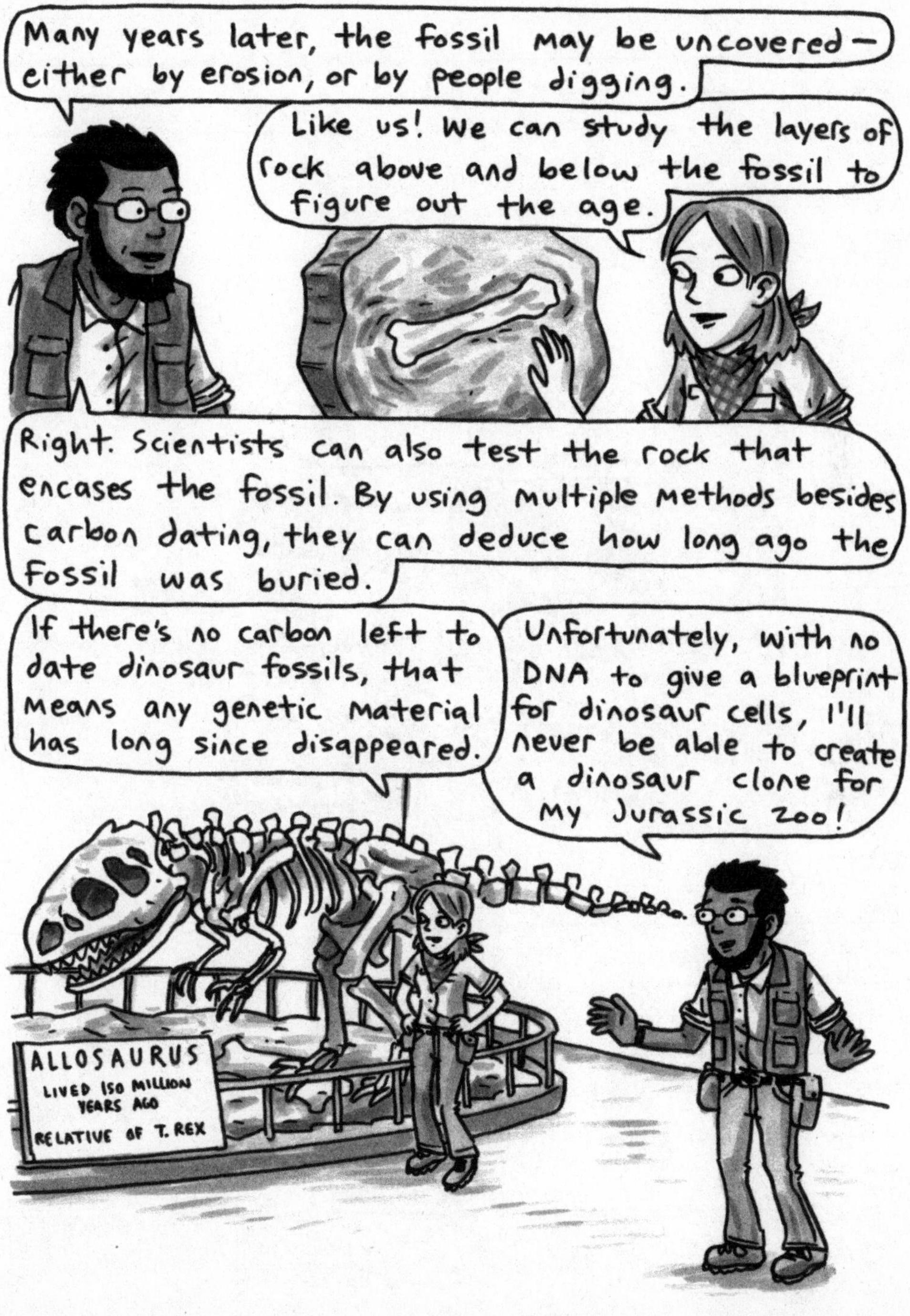
Many years later, the fossil may be uncovered— either by erosion, or by people digging.
Like us! We can study the layers of rock above and below the fossil to figure out the age.
Right. Scientists can also test the rock that encases the fossil. By using multiple methods besides carbon dating, they can deduce how long ago the fossil was buried.
If there's no carbon left to date dinosaur fossils, that means any genetic material has long since disappeared.
Unfortunately, with no DNA to give a blueprint for dinosaur cells, I'll never be able to create a dinosaur clone for my Jurassic zoo!
ALLOSAURUS
LIVED 150 MILLION YEARS AGO
RELATIVE OF T. REX

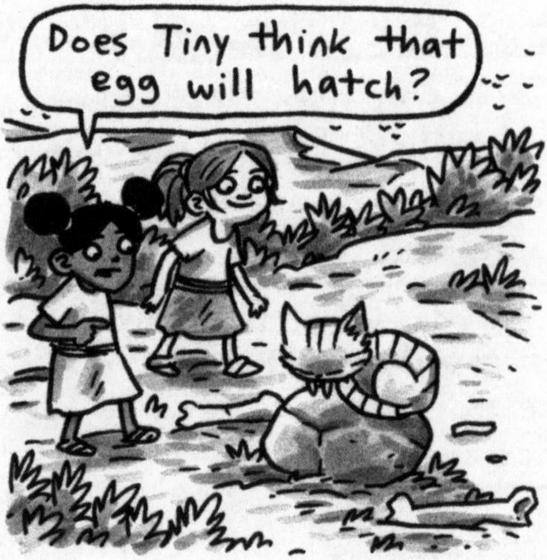
Does Tiny think that egg will hatch?

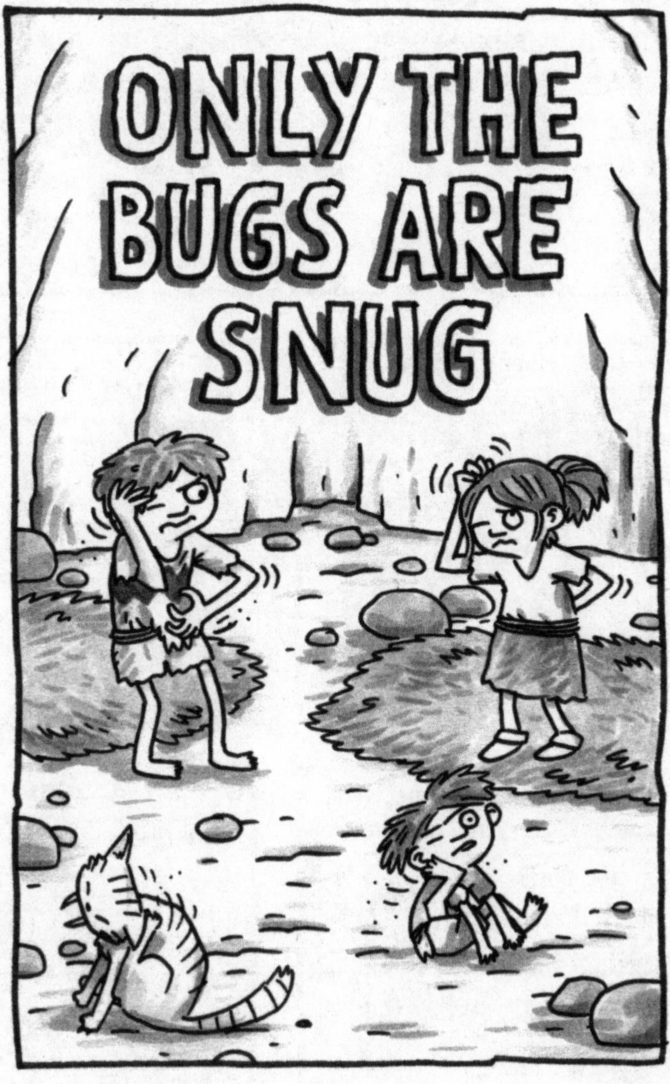
ONLY THE BUGS ARE SNUG

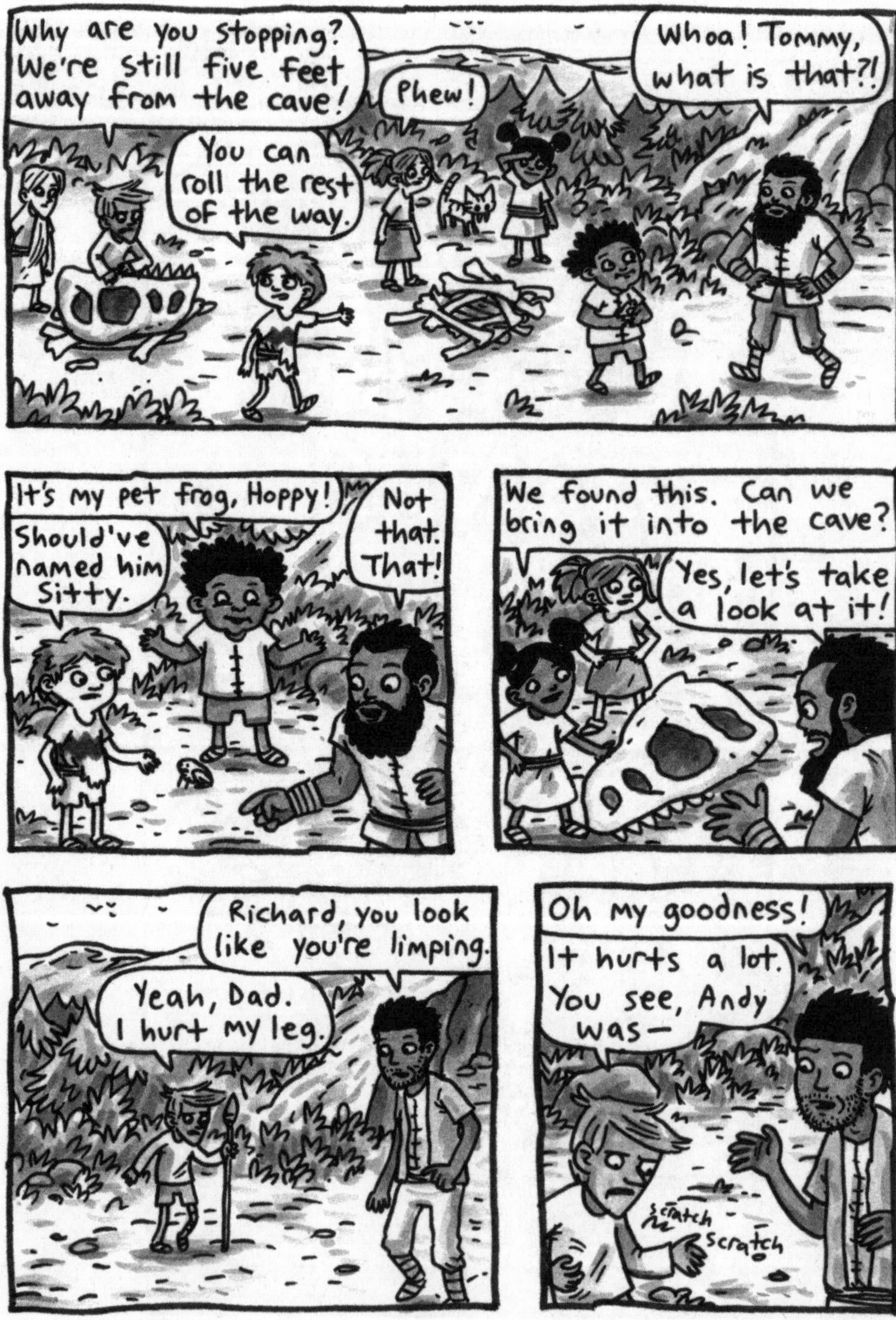
Why are you stopping? We're still five feet away from the cave!
You can roll the rest of the way.
Phew!
Whoa! Tommy, what is that?!
It's my pet frog, Hoppy!
Should've named him Sitty.
Not that. That!
We found this. Can we bring it into the cave?
Yes, let's take a look at it!
Richard, you look like you're limping.
Yeah, Dad. I hurt my leg.
Oh my goodness!
It hurts a lot. You see, Andy was—
scratch
scratch

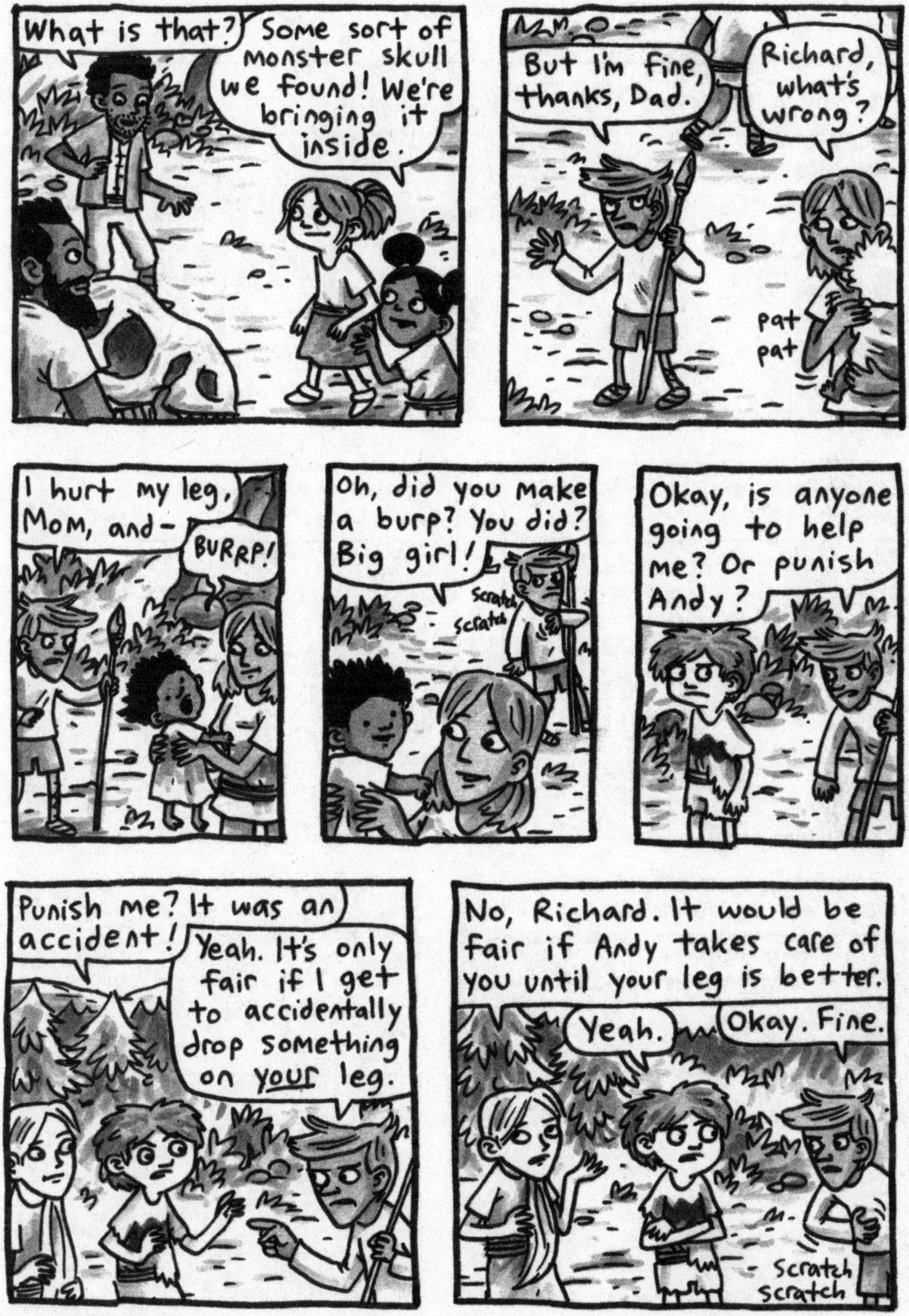
What is that?
Some sort of monster skull we found! We're bringing it inside.
But I'm fine, thanks, Dad.
Richard, what's wrong?
pat pat
I hurt my leg, Mom, and–
BURRP!
Oh, did you make a burp? You did? Big girl!
Scratch scratch
Okay, is anyone going to help me? Or punish Andy?
Punish me? It was an accident!
Yeah. It's only fair if I get to accidentally drop something on your leg.
No, Richard. It would be fair if Andy takes care of you until your leg is better.
Yeah.
Okay. Fine.
Scratch scratch

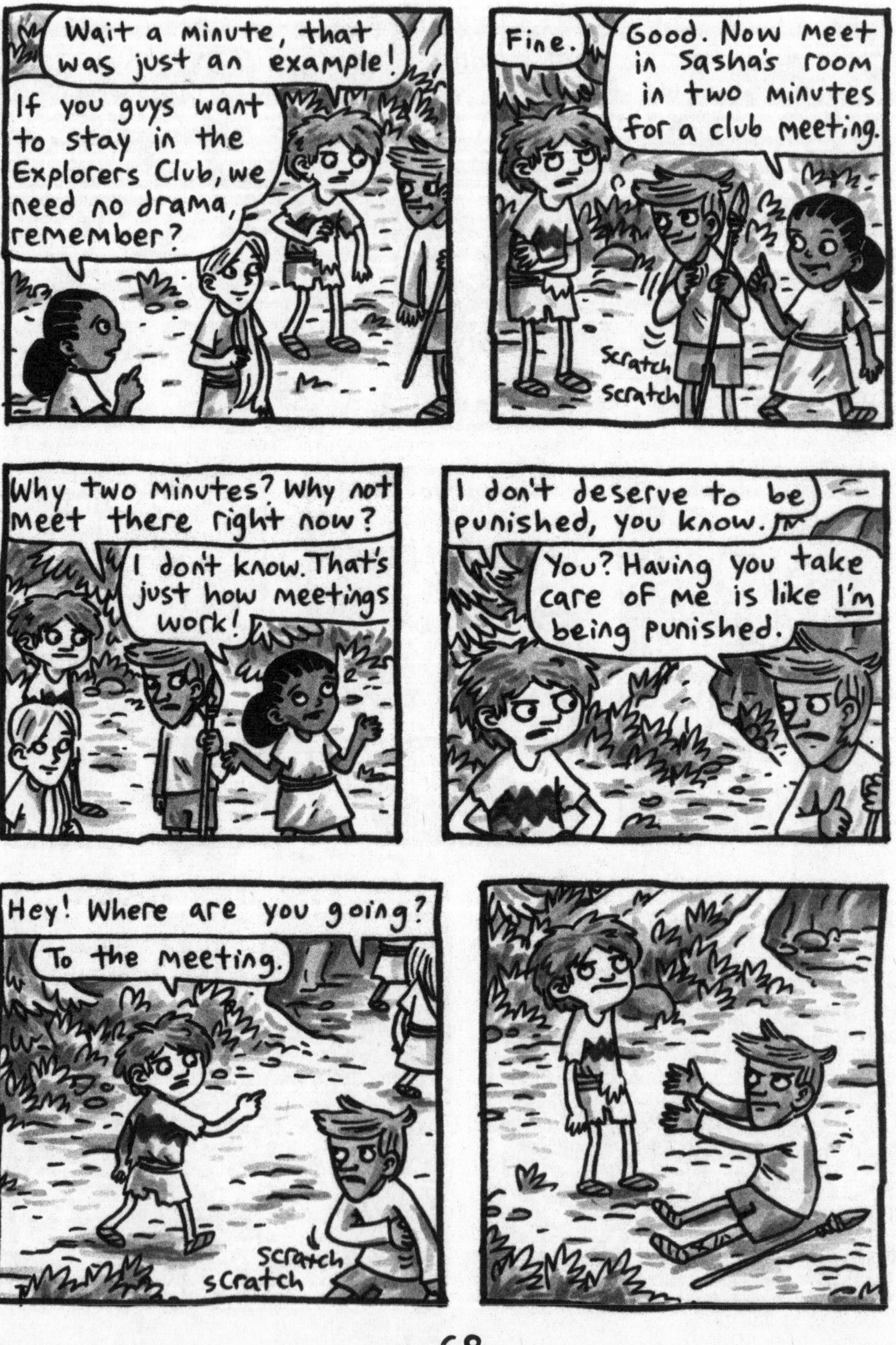
Wait a minute, that was just an example!
If you guys want to stay in the Explorers Club, we need no drama, remember?
Fine.
Good. Now meet in Sasha's room in two minutes for a club meeting.
Scratch
scratch
Why two minutes? Why not meet there right now?
I don't know. That's just how meetings work!
I don't deserve to be punished, you know.
You? Having you take care of me is like I'm being punished.
Hey! Where are you going?
To the meeting.
scratch
scratch

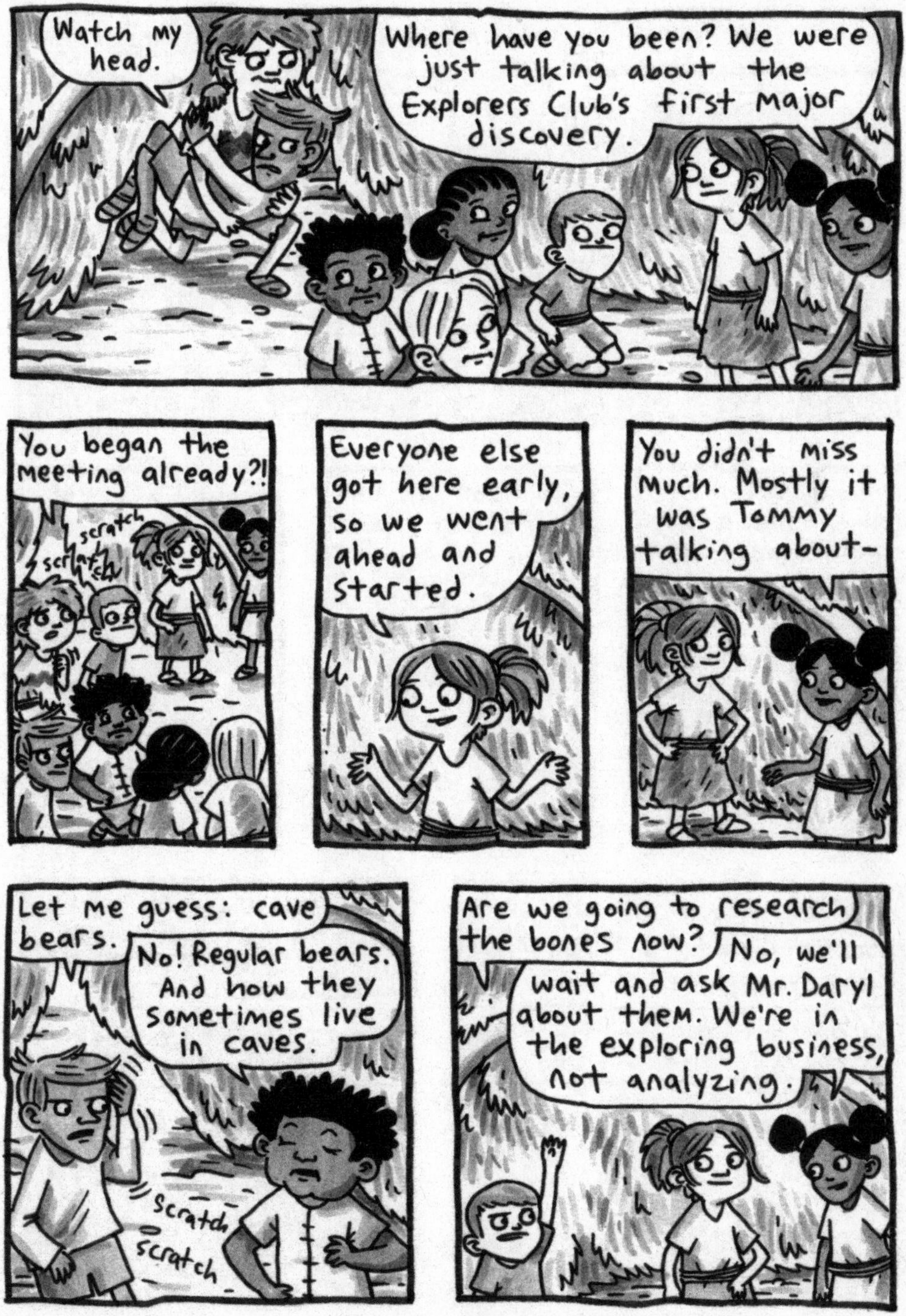
Watch my head.
Where have you been? We were just talking about the Explorers Club's first major discovery.
You began the meeting already?!
scratch
scratch
Everyone else got here early, so we went ahead and started.
You didn't miss much. Mostly it was Tommy talking about-
Let me guess: cave bears.
No! Regular bears. And how they sometimes live in caves.
scratch
scratch
Are we going to research the bones now?
No, we'll wait and ask Mr. Daryl about them. We're in the exploring business, not analyzing.

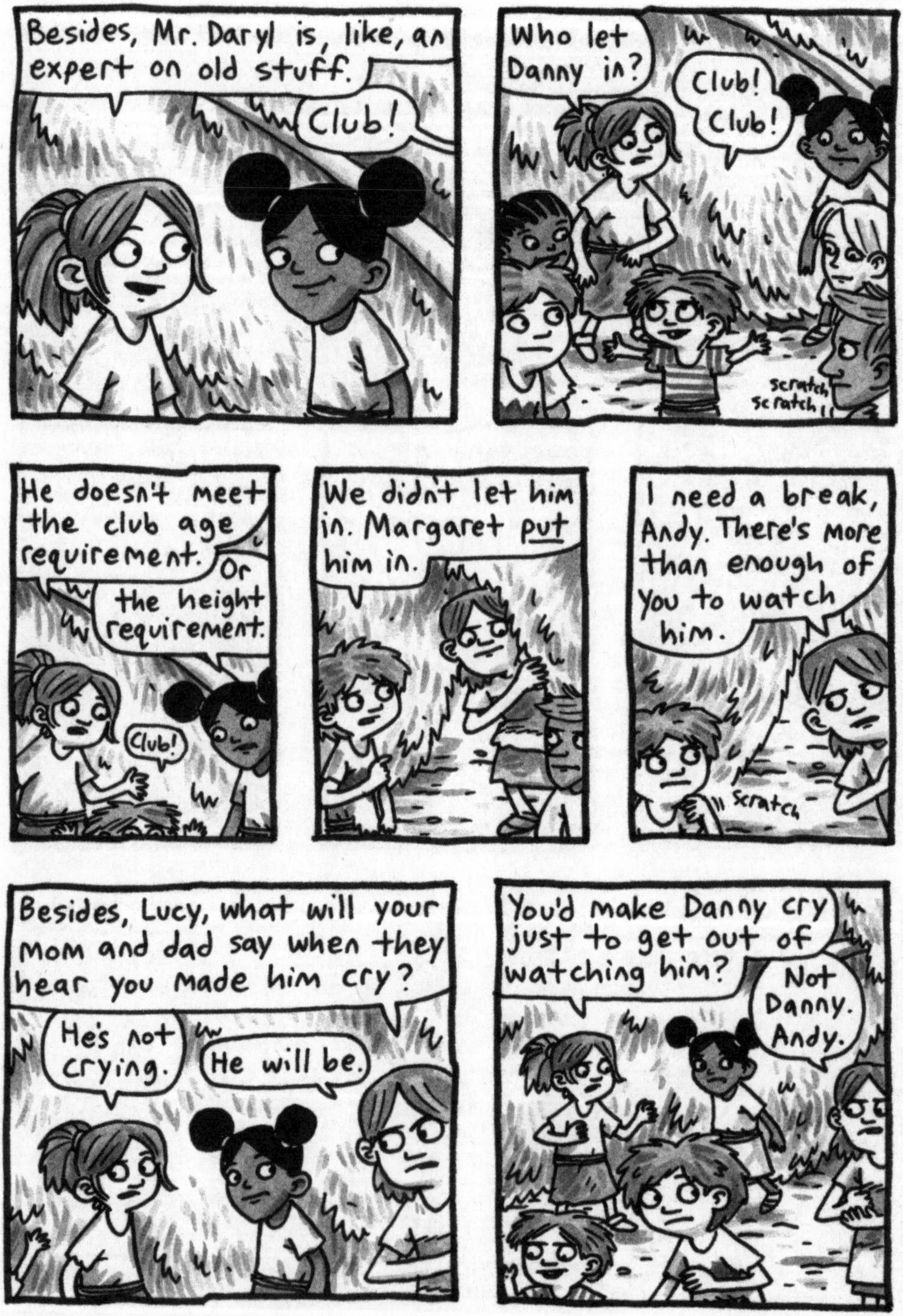
Besides, Mr. Daryl is, like, an expert on old stuff.
Club!
Who let Danny in?
Club! Club!
scratch scratch
He doesn't meet the club age requirement.
Or the height requirement.
Club!
We didn't let him in. Margaret put him in.
I need a break, Andy. There's more than enough of you to watch him.
scratch
Besides, Lucy, what will your mom and dad say when they hear you made him cry?
He's not crying.
He will be.
You'd make Danny cry just to get out of watching him?
Not Danny. Andy.

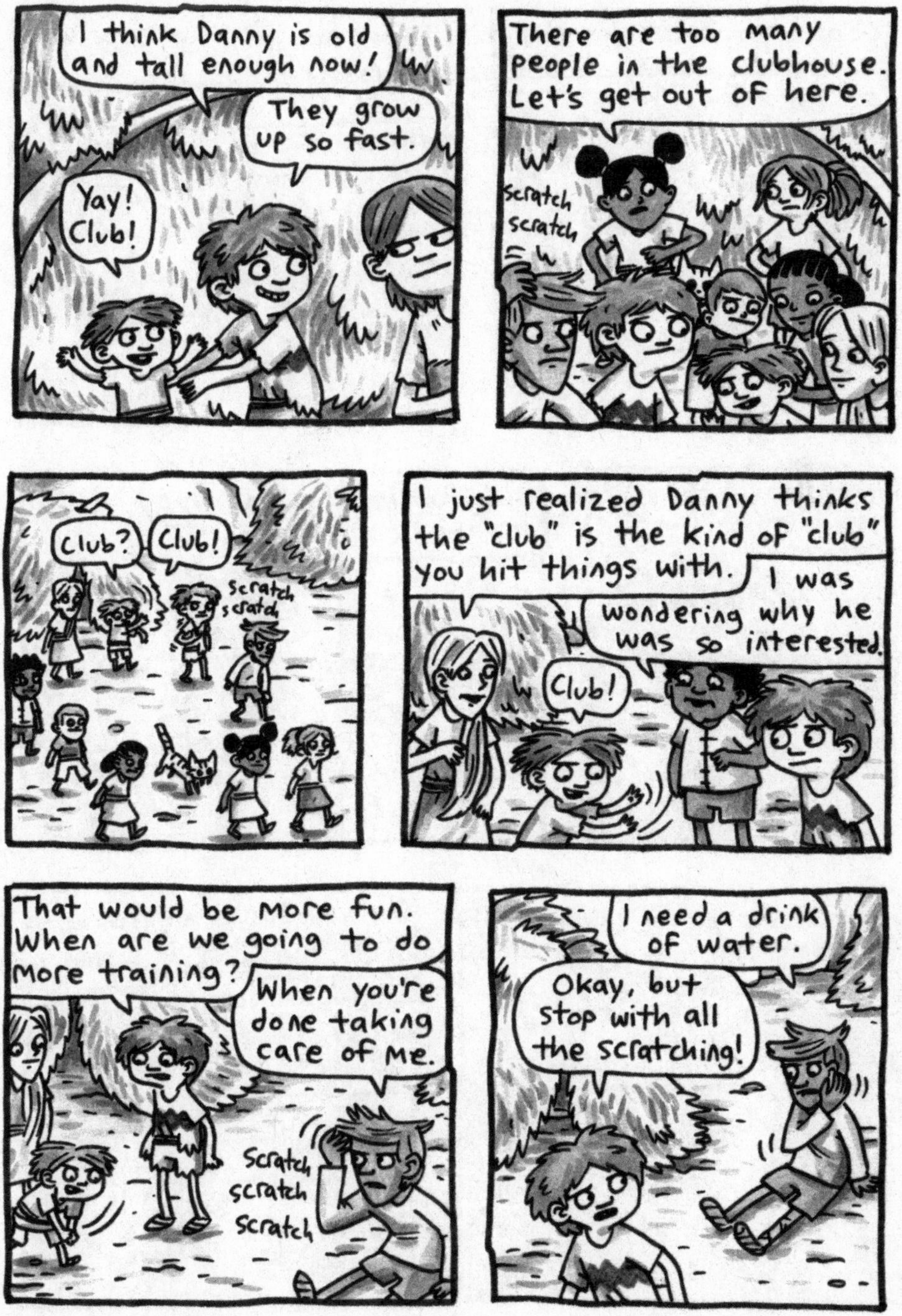
I think Danny is old and tall enough now!
They grow up so fast.
Yay! Club!
There are too many people in the clubhouse. Let's get out of here.
scratch scratch
Club?
Club!
scratch scratch
I just realized Danny thinks the "club" is the kind of "club" you hit things with.
I was wondering why he was so interested.
Club!
That would be more fun. When are we going to do more training?
When you're done taking care of me.
scratch scratch scratch
I need a drink of water.
Okay, but stop with all the scratching!

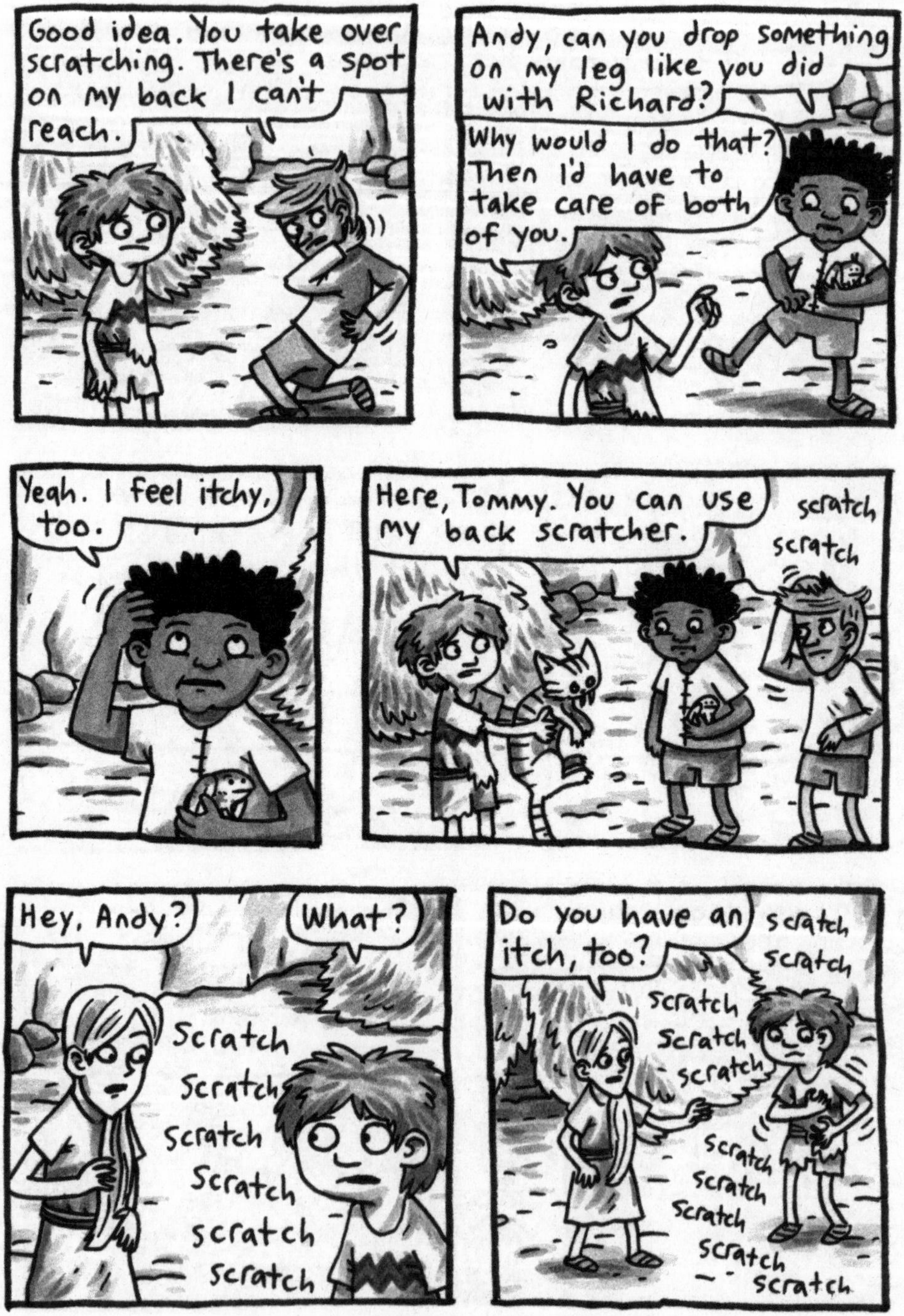
Good idea. You take over scratching. There's a spot on my back I can't reach.
Andy, can you drop something on my leg like you did with Richard?
Why would I do that? Then I'd have to take care of both of you.
Yeah. I feel itchy, too.
Here, Tommy. You can use my back scratcher.
scratch
scratch
Hey, Andy?
What?
Scratch
Scratch
Scratch
Scratch
scratch
scratch
Do you have an itch, too?
scratch
scratch
Scratch
Scratch
scratch
Scratch
Scratch
Scratch
Scratch
scratch

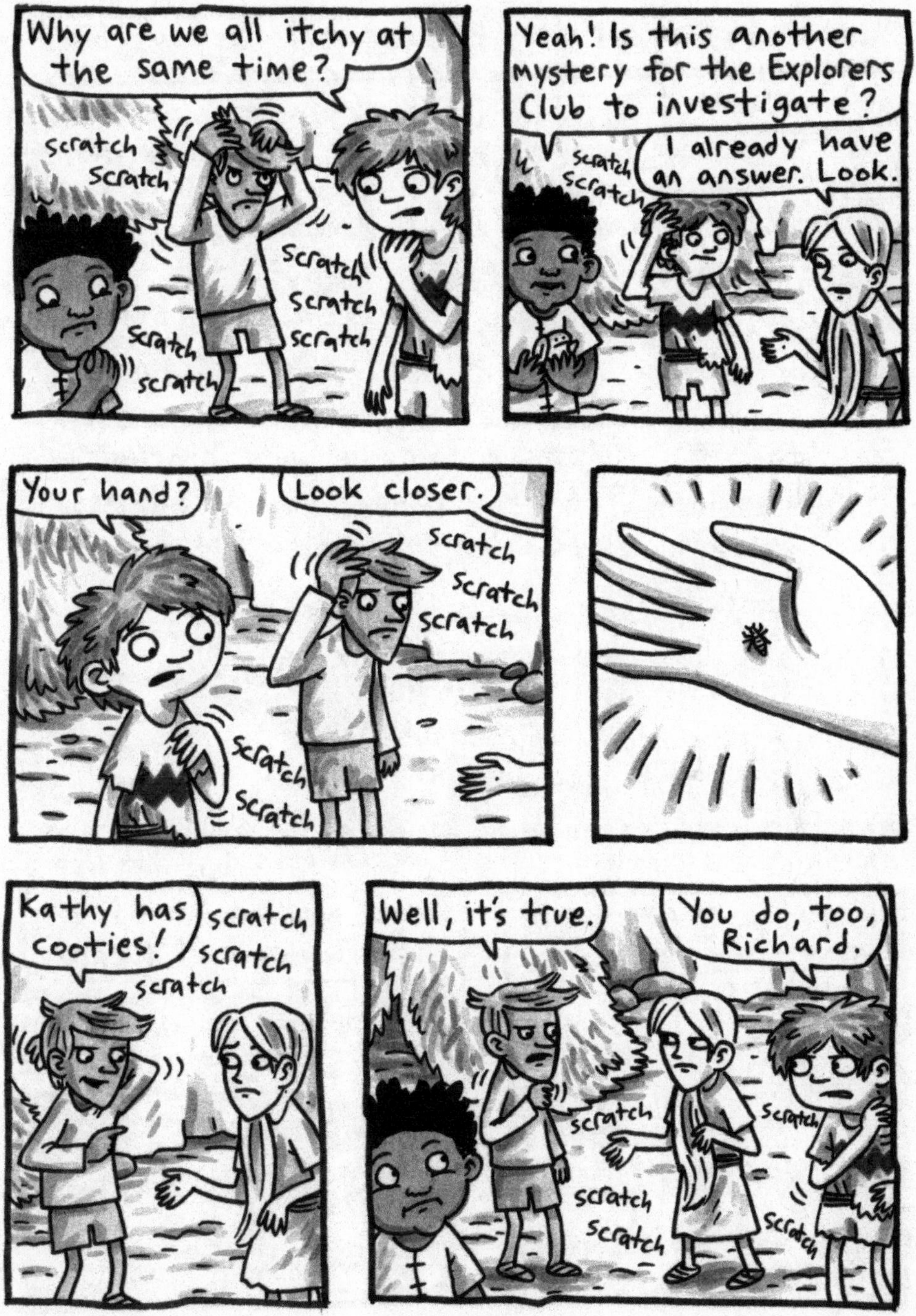
Why are we all itchy at the same time?
scratch
scratch
scratch
scratch
scratch
scratch
scratch
Yeah! Is this another mystery for the Explorers Club to investigate?
scratch
scratch
I already have an answer. Look.
Your hand?
Look closer.
scratch
scratch
scratch
scratch
scratch
Kathy has cooties!
scratch
scratch
scratch
Well, it's true.
You do, too, Richard.
scratch
scratch
scratch
scratch
scratch

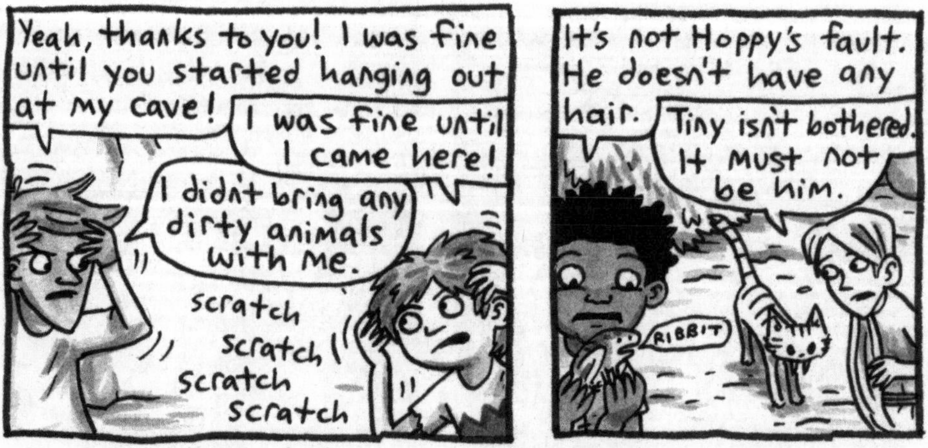
Yeah, thanks to you! I was fine until you started hanging out at my cave!
I was fine until I came here!
I didn't bring any dirty animals with me.
scratch
scratch
scratch
scratch
It's not Hoppy's fault. He doesn't have any hair.
Tiny isn't bothered. It must not be him.
RIBBIT

Since the 1950s, kids have used the word "cooties" for imaginary illness. The term comes from a real pest that has been around since before Neanderthals—lice!

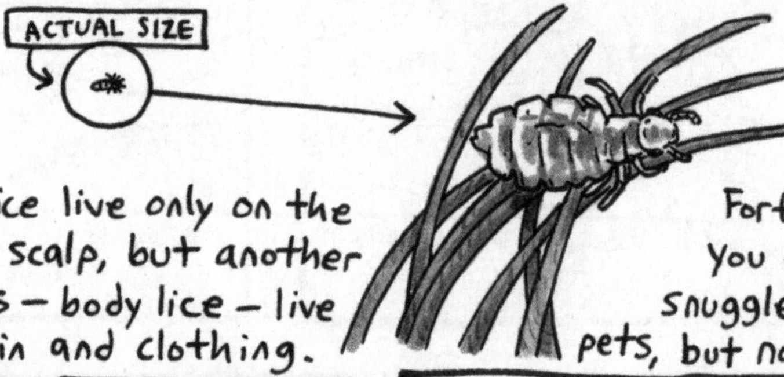
ACTUAL SIZE

Head lice live only on the human scalp, but another species—body lice—live on skin and clothing.

Fortunately, you can get snuggles from pets, but not lice!

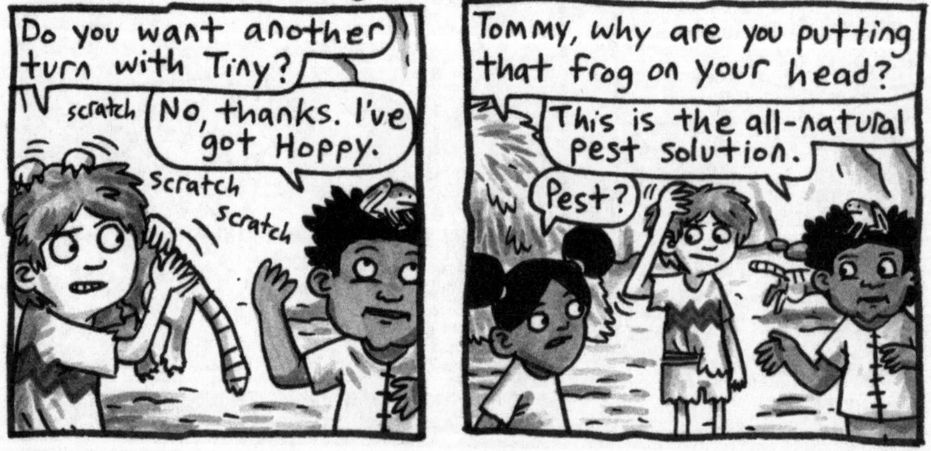
Do you want another turn with Tiny?
scratch
No, thanks. I've got Hoppy.
scratch
scratch
Tommy, why are you putting that frog on your head?
This is the all-natural pest solution.
Pest?

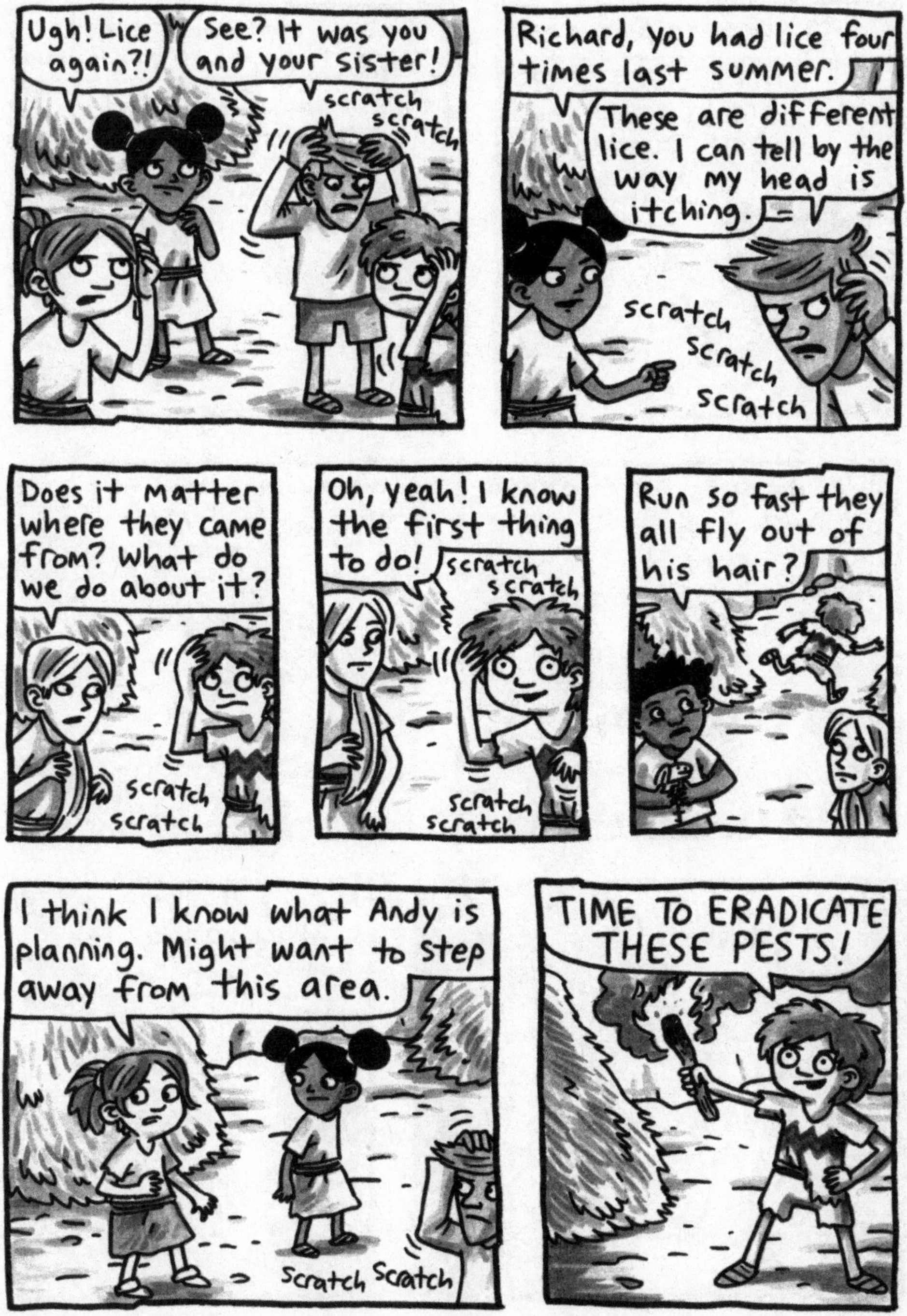

Ugh! Lice again?!
See? It was you and your sister!
scratch scratch
Richard, you had lice four times last summer.
These are different lice. I can tell by the way my head is itching.
scratch scratch scratch
Does it matter where they came from? What do we do about it?
scratch scratch
Oh, yeah! I know the first thing to do!
scratch scratch
scratch scratch
Run so fast they all fly out of his hair?
I think I know what Andy is planning. Might want to step away from this area.
Scratch Scratch
TIME TO ERADICATE THESE PESTS!

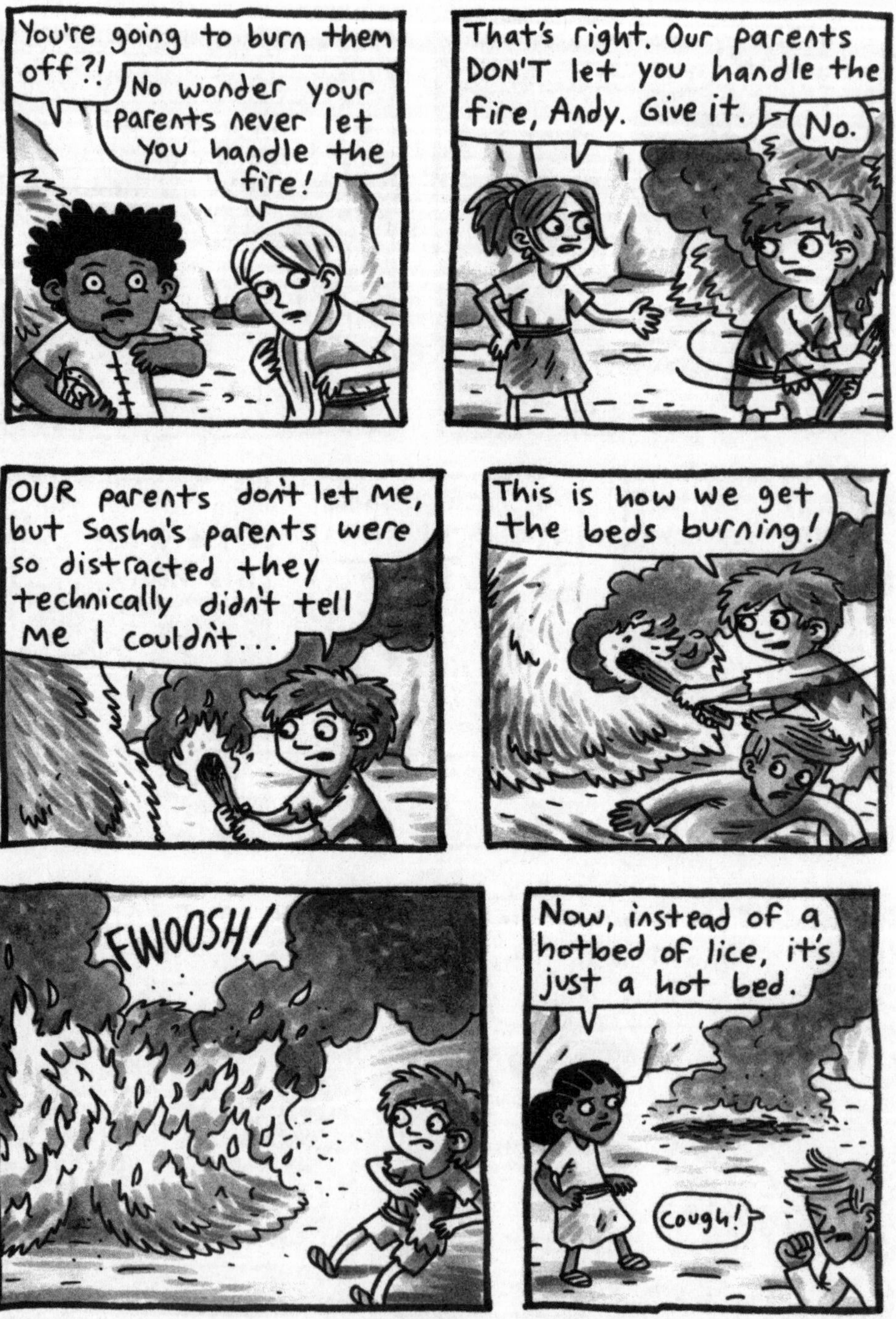
You're going to burn them off?!
No wonder your parents never let you handle the fire!
That's right. Our parents DON'T let you handle the fire, Andy. Give it.
No.
OUR parents don't let me, but Sasha's parents were so distracted they technically didn't tell me I couldn't...
This is how we get the beds burning!
FWOOSH!
Now, instead of a hotbed of lice, it's just a hot bed.
Cough!

Neanderthal beds were made of grass and other plants, then covered with animal fur.

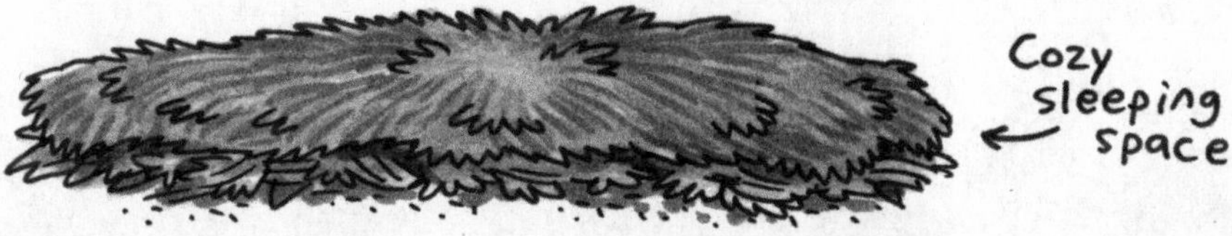
Cozy sleeping space

Because there were no washing machines, Neanderthals burned their beds instead! The new layer of ash helped keep bugs away and was softer than the hard ground.

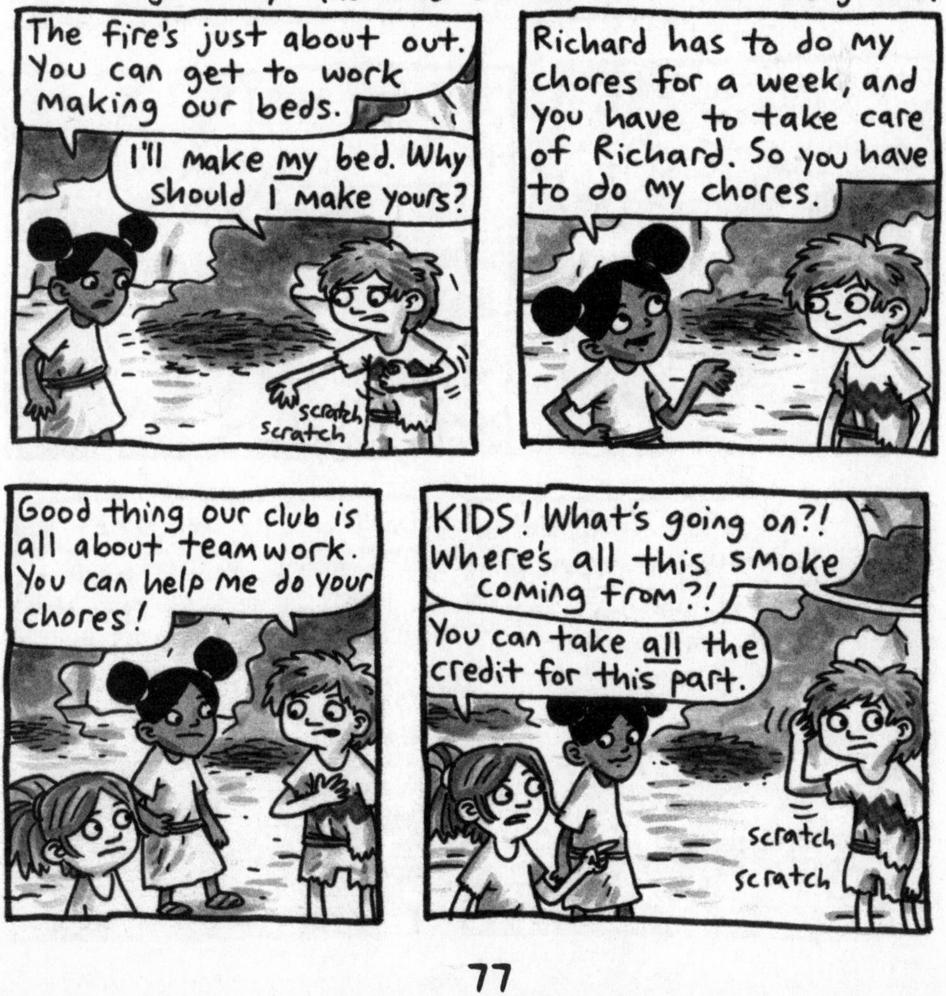
The fire's just about out. You can get to work making our beds.
I'll make my bed. Why should I make yours?
scratch scratch
Richard has to do my chores for a week, and you have to take care of Richard. So you have to do my chores.
Good thing our club is all about teamwork. You can help me do your chores!
KIDS! What's going on?! Where's all this smoke coming from?!
You can take all the credit for this part.
scratch scratch

What happened?!
Andy just set everything on fire and made a huge mess.
You're welcome.
scratch scratch
scratch scratch
All our stuff is ruined, too.
Not everything. Richard's spear is okay.
You pulled it out of the fire?!
No, Richard gave his spear to the strangers.
You kids were supposed to stay away from them.
I LOANED it to them.
scratch scratch scratch
This is all pretty disappointing, but I can't say I'm surprised.
Please don't tell my parents!
Don't worry, we won't.
Oh, good! Thank - oh. They're standing right behind me, aren't they?

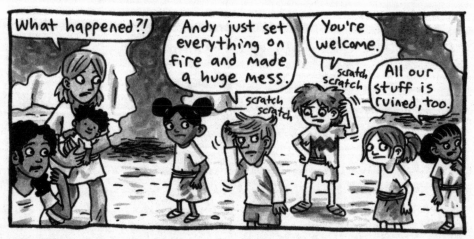

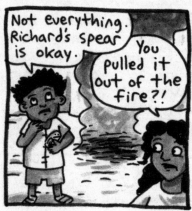

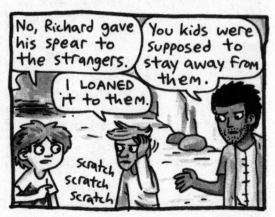

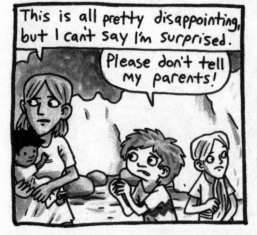

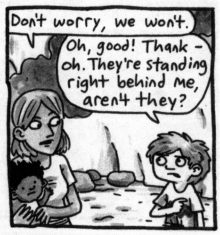

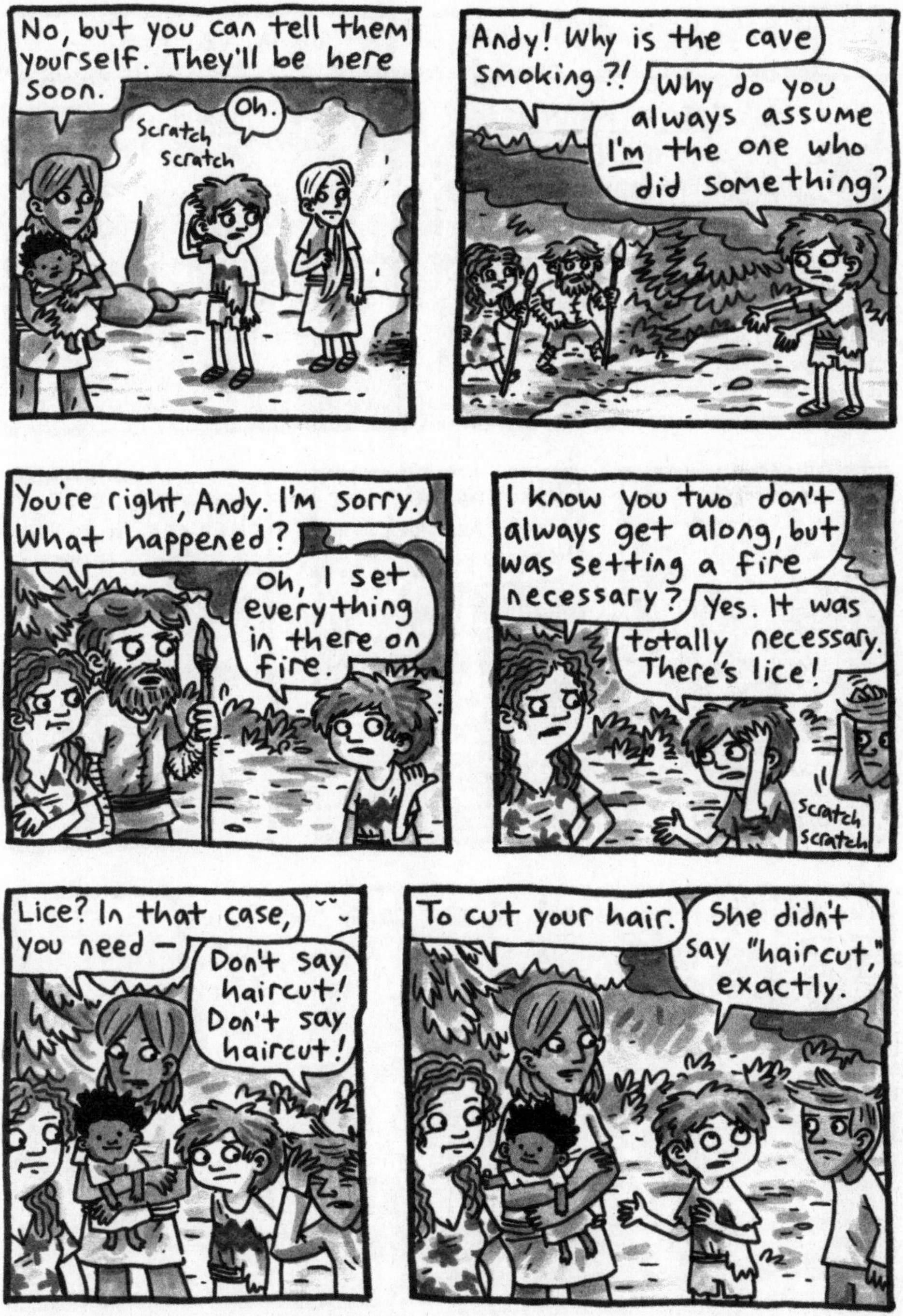
No, but you can tell them yourself. They'll be here soon.
Oh.
Scratch scratch
Andy! Why is the cave smoking?!
Why do you always assume I'm the one who did something?
You're right, Andy. I'm sorry. What happened?
Oh, I set everything in there on fire.
I know you two don't always get along, but was setting a fire necessary?
Yes. It was totally necessary. There's lice!
Scratch scratch
Lice? In that case, you need—
Don't say haircut! Don't say haircut!
To cut your hair.
She didn't say "haircut," exactly.

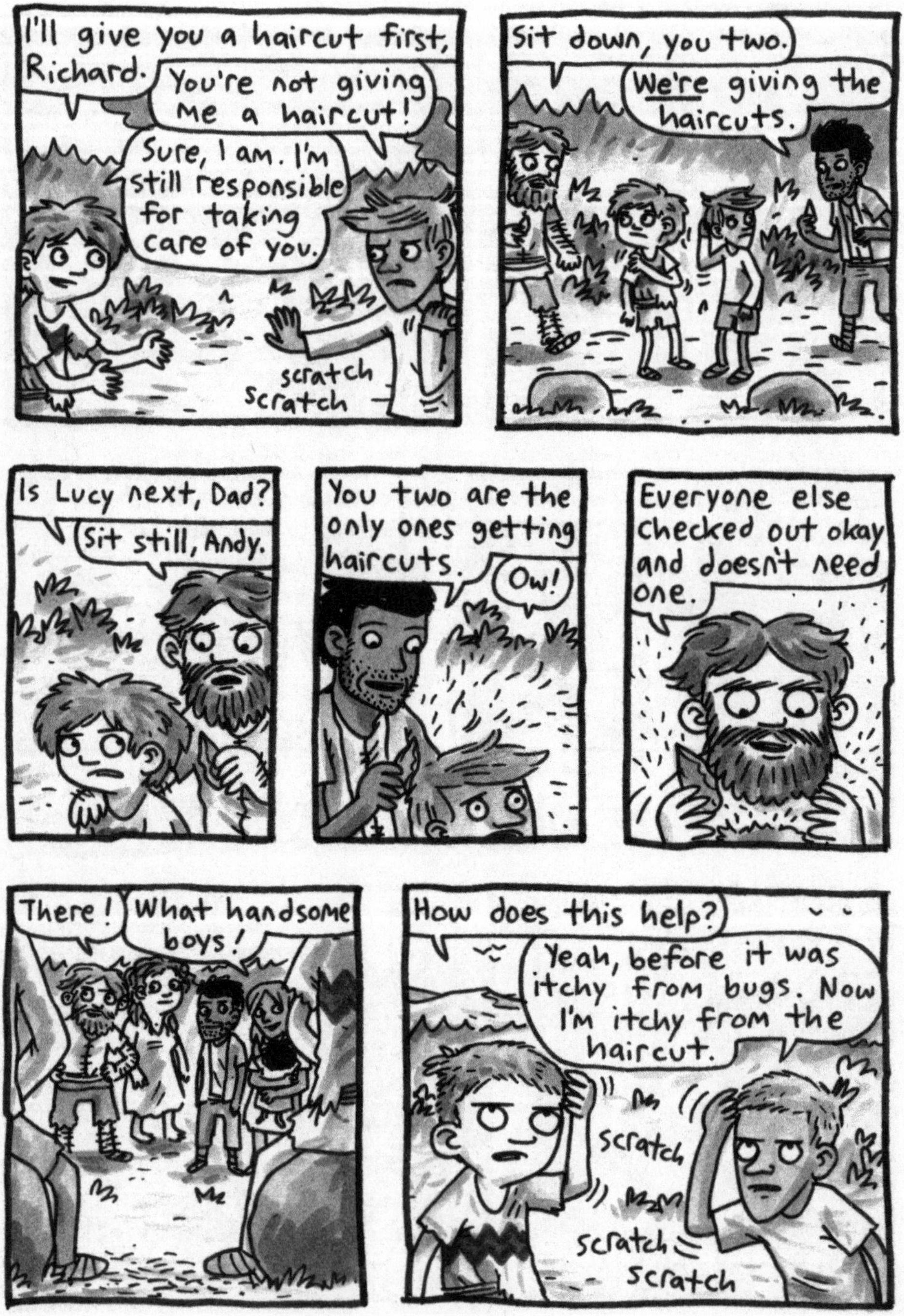
I'll give you a haircut first, Richard.
You're not giving me a haircut!
Sure, I am. I'm still responsible for taking care of you.
scratch
scratch
Sit down, you two.
We're giving the haircuts.
Is Lucy next, Dad?
Sit still, Andy.
You two are the only ones getting haircuts.
Ow!
Everyone else checked out okay and doesn't need one.
There!
What handsome boys!
How does this help?
Yeah, before it was itchy from bugs. Now I'm itchy from the haircut.
scratch
scratch
scratch

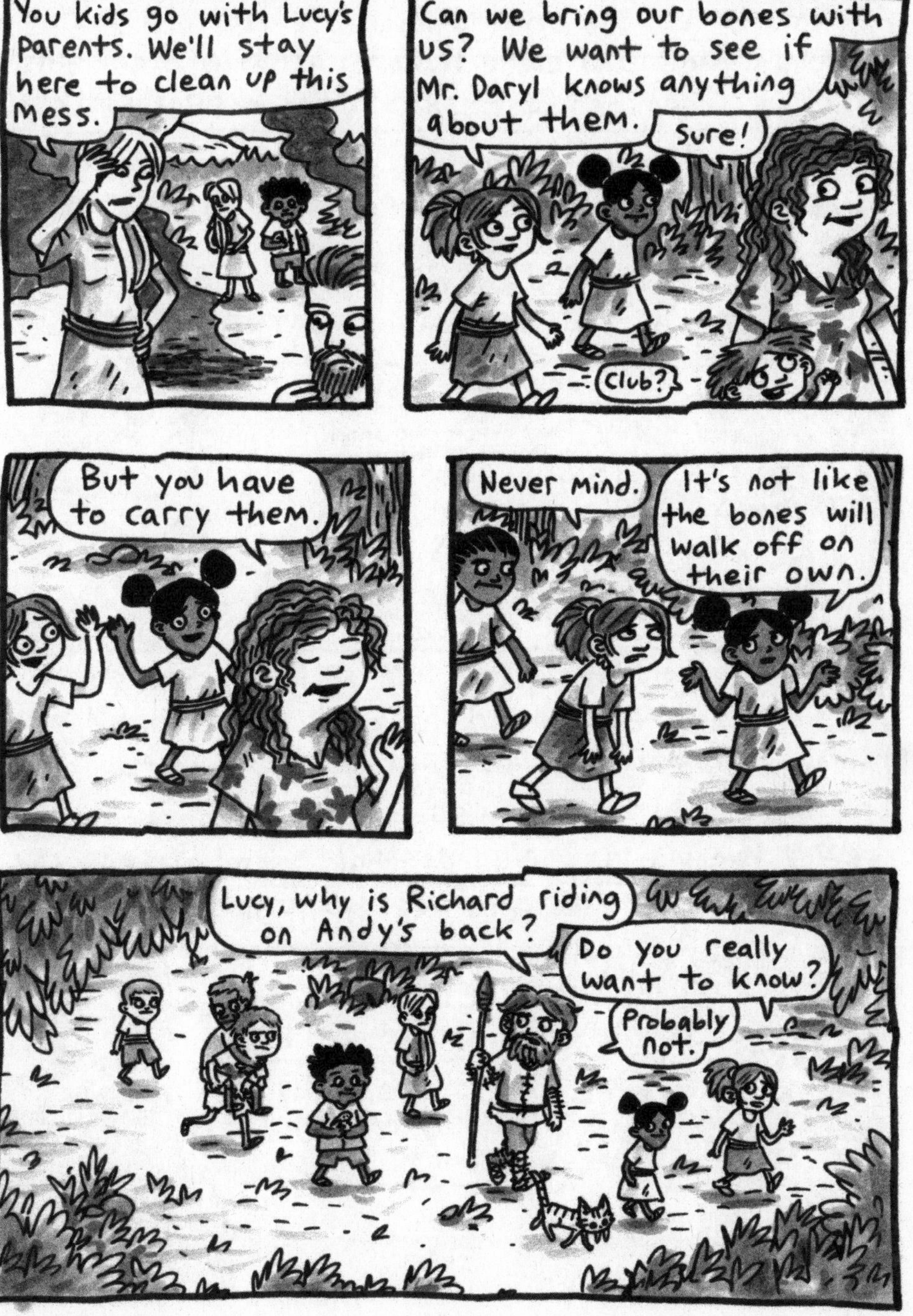
You kids go with Lucy's parents. We'll stay here to clean up this mess.
Can we bring our bones with us? We want to see if Mr. Daryl knows anything about them.
Sure!
Club?
But you have to carry them.
Never mind.
It's not like the bones will walk off on their own.
Lucy, why is Richard riding on Andy's back?
Do you really want to know?
Probably not.

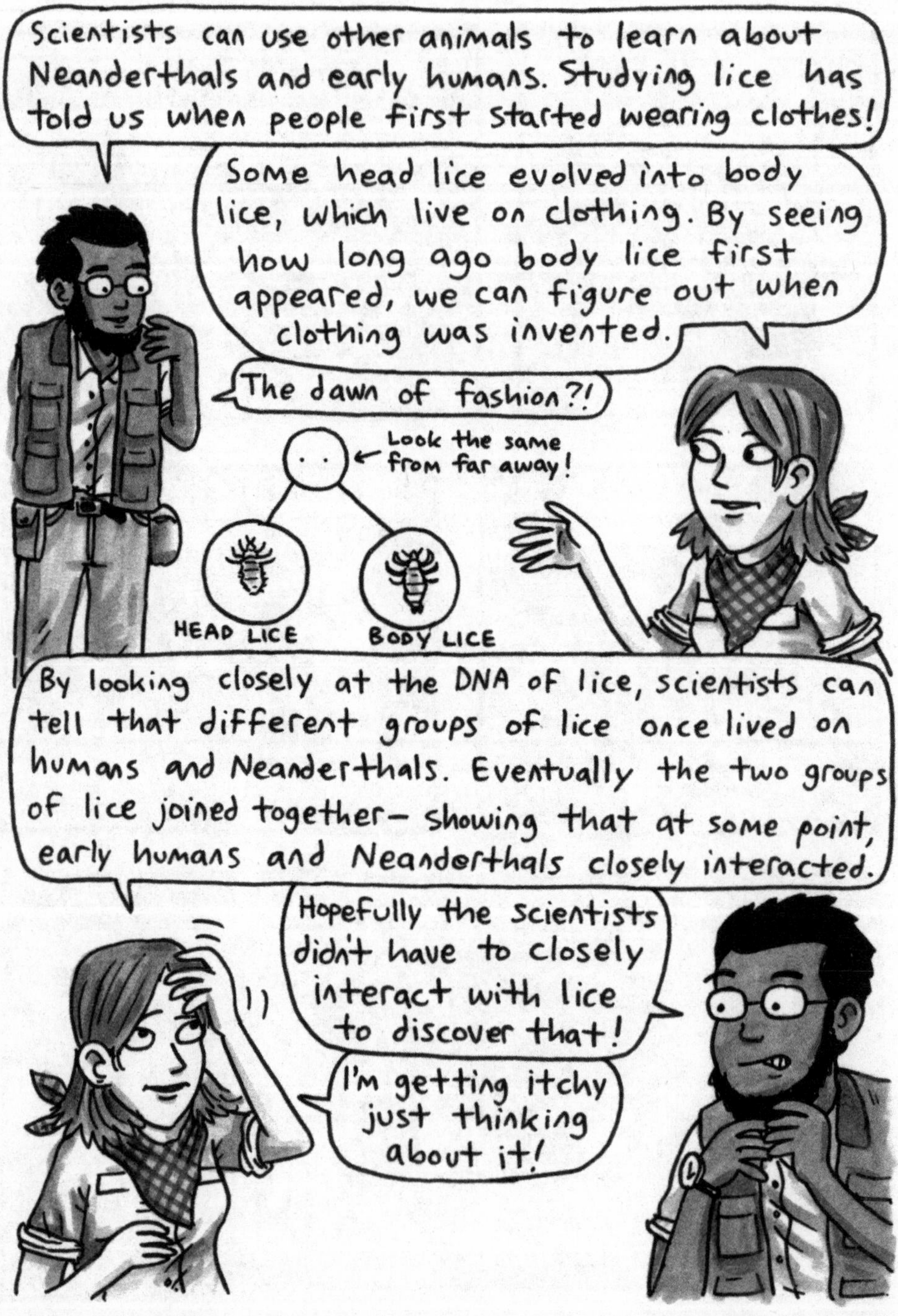
Scientists can use other animals to learn about Neanderthals and early humans. Studying lice has told us when people first started wearing clothes!
Some head lice evolved into body lice, which live on clothing. By seeing how long ago body lice first appeared, we can figure out when clothing was invented.
The dawn of fashion?!
Look the same from far away!
HEAD LICE
BODY LICE
By looking closely at the DNA of lice, scientists can tell that different groups of lice once lived on humans and Neanderthals. Eventually the two groups of lice joined together— showing that at some point, early humans and Neanderthals closely interacted.
Hopefully the scientists didn't have to closely interact with lice to discover that!
I'm getting itchy just thinking about it!

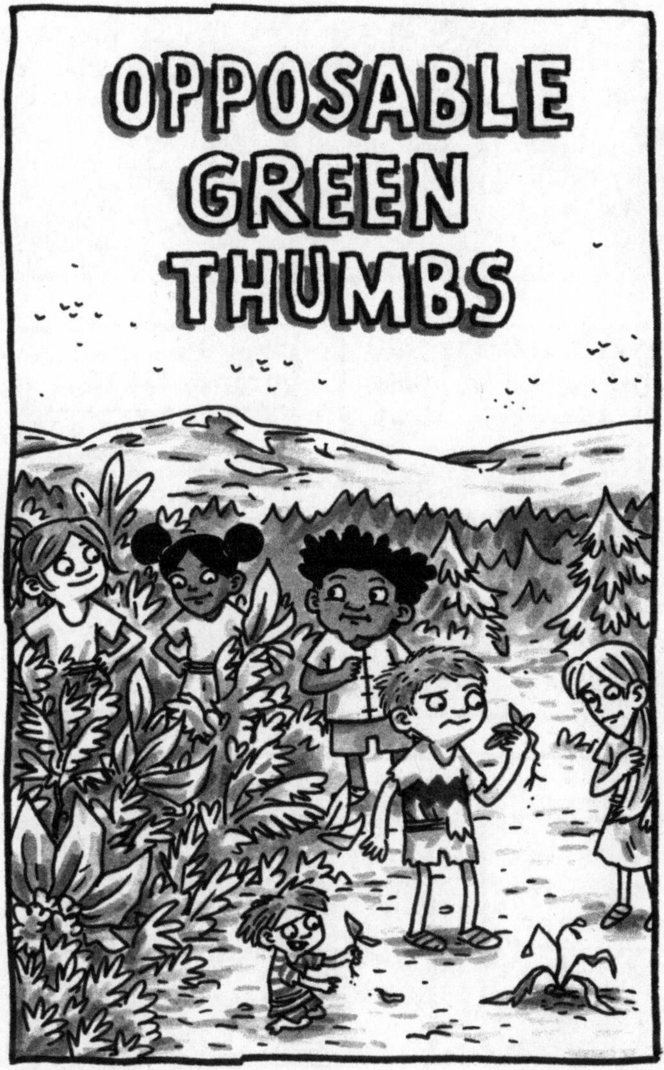
OPPOSABLE GREEN THUMBS

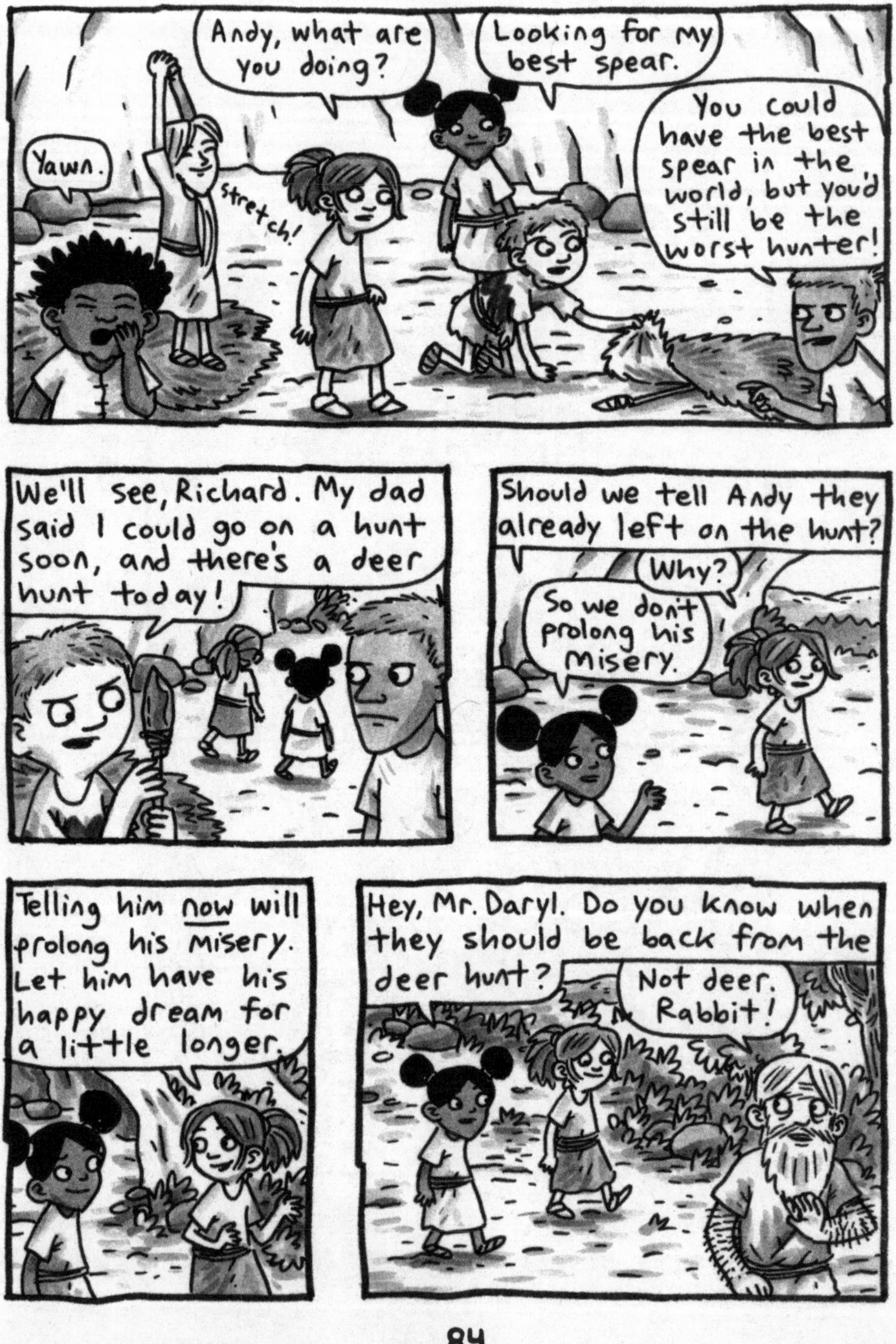
Yawn.
Stretch!
Andy, what are you doing?
Looking for my best spear.
You could have the best spear in the world, but you'd still be the worst hunter!
We'll see, Richard. My dad said I could go on a hunt soon, and there's a deer hunt today!
Should we tell Andy they already left on the hunt?
Why?
So we don't prolong his misery.
Telling him now will prolong his misery. Let him have his happy dream for a little longer.
Hey, Mr. Daryl. Do you know when they should be back from the deer hunt?
Not deer. Rabbit!

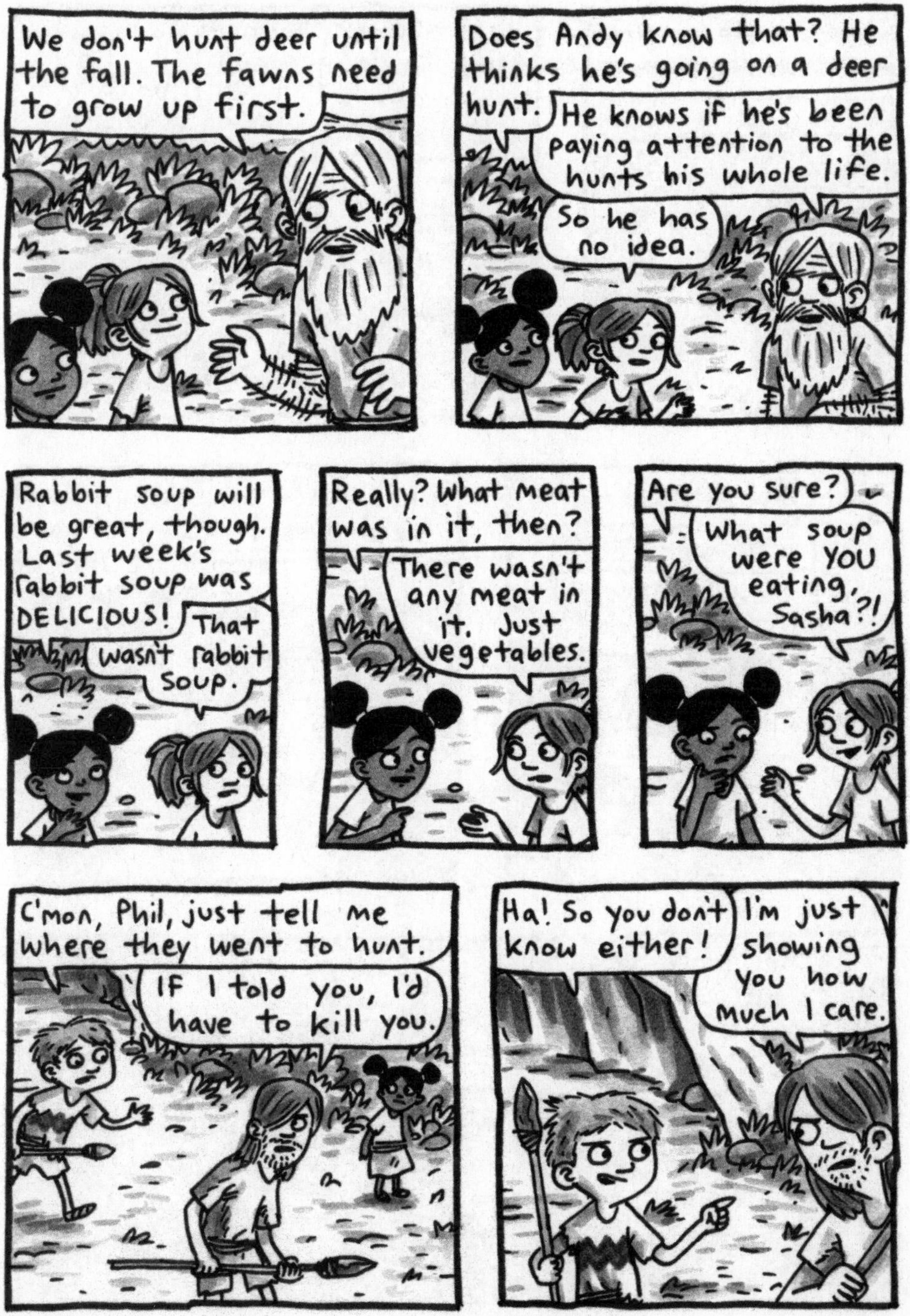
We don't hunt deer until the fall. The fawns need to grow up first.
Does Andy know that? He thinks he's going on a deer hunt.
He knows if he's been paying attention to the hunts his whole life.
So he has no idea.
Rabbit soup will be great, though. Last week's rabbit soup was DELICIOUS!
That wasn't rabbit soup.
Really? What meat was in it, then?
There wasn't any meat in it. Just vegetables.
Are you sure?
What soup were YOU eating, Sasha?!
C'mon, Phil, just tell me where they went to hunt.
If I told you, I'd have to kill you.
Ha! So you don't know either!
I'm just showing you how much I care.

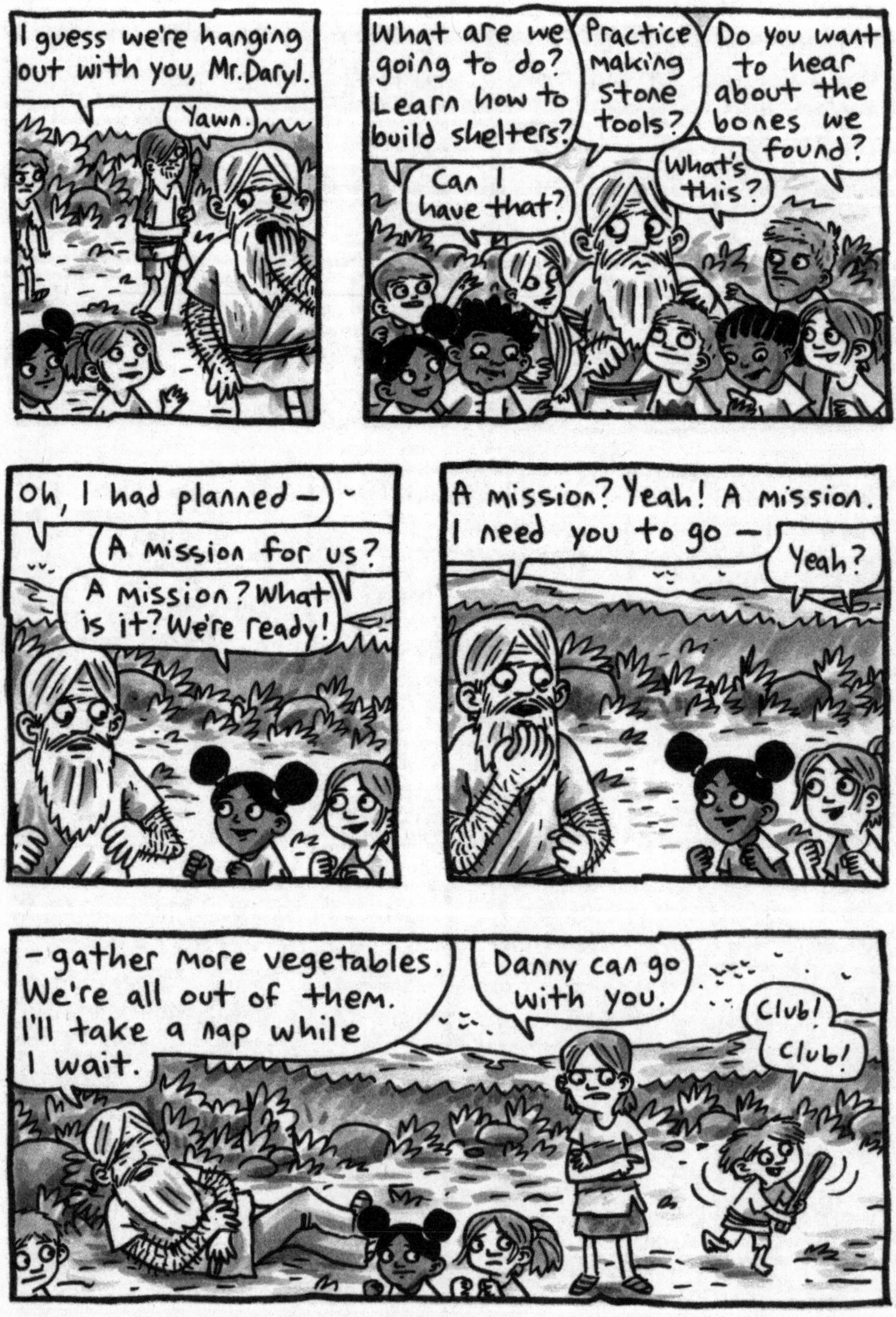
I guess we're hanging out with you, Mr. Daryl.
Yawn.
What are we going to do? Learn how to build shelters?
Practice making stone tools?
Do you want to hear about the bones we found?
Can I have that?
What's this?
Oh, I had planned —
A mission for us?
A mission? What is it? We're ready!
A mission? Yeah! A mission. I need you to go —
Yeah?
— gather more vegetables. We're all out of them. I'll take a nap while I wait.
Danny can go with you.
Club!
Club!

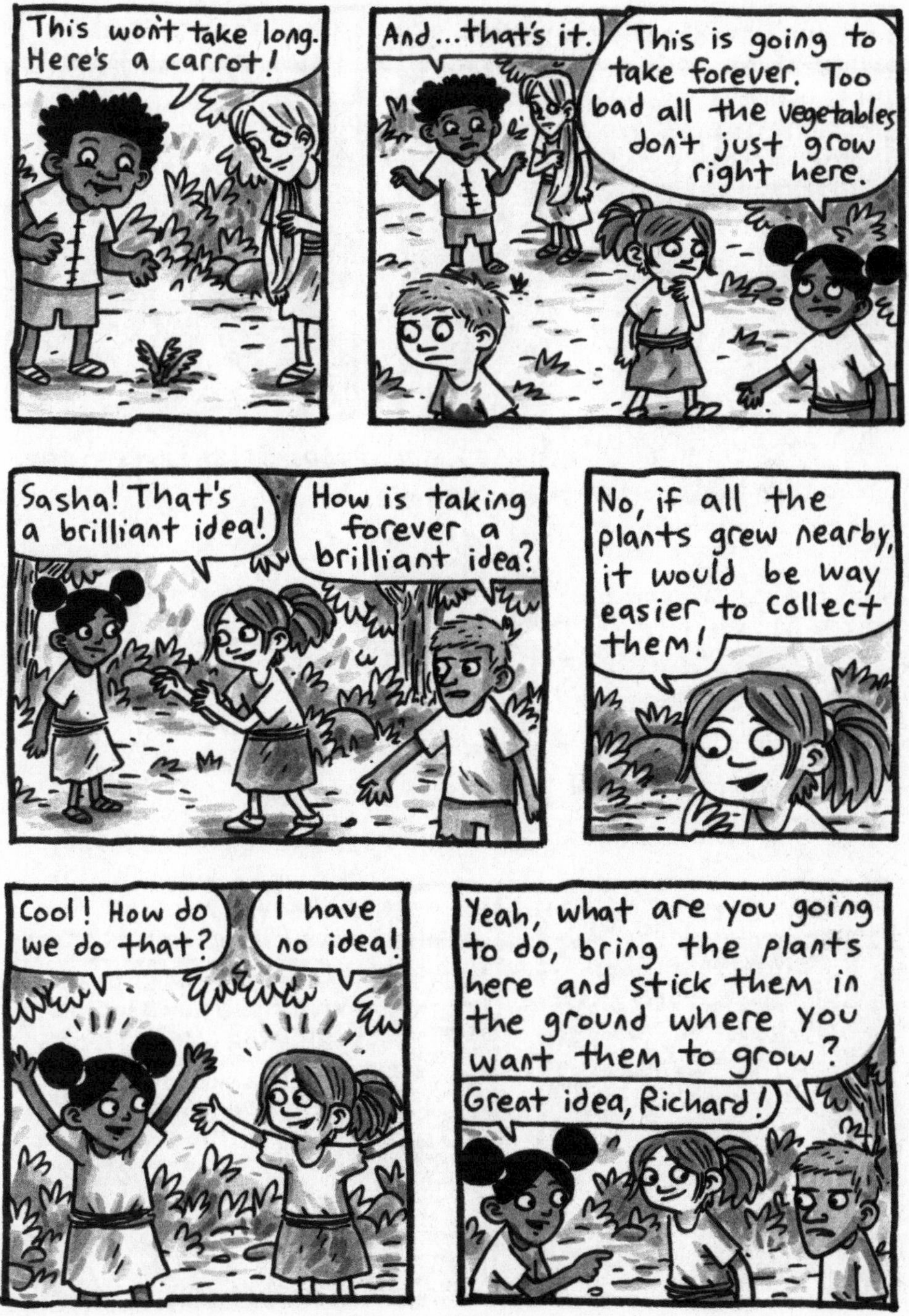
This won't take long. Here's a carrot!
And...that's it.
This is going to take forever. Too bad all the vegetables don't just grow right here.
Sasha! That's a brilliant idea!
How is taking forever a brilliant idea?
No, if all the plants grew nearby, it would be way easier to collect them!
Cool! How do we do that?
I have no idea!
Yeah, what are you going to do, bring the plants here and stick them in the ground where you want them to grow?
Great idea, Richard!

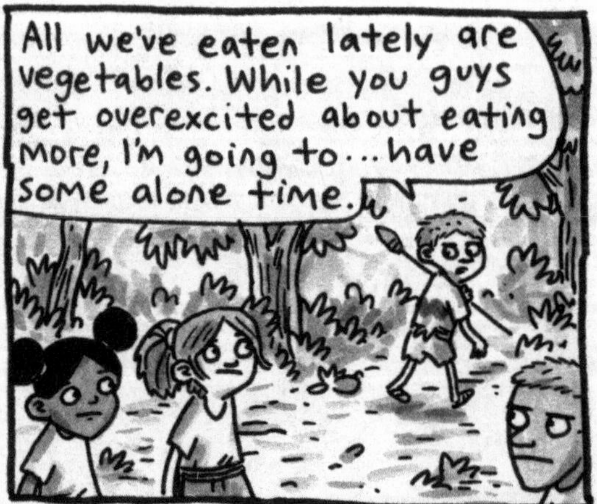
All we've eaten lately are vegetables. While you guys get overexcited about eating more, I'm going to... have some alone time.

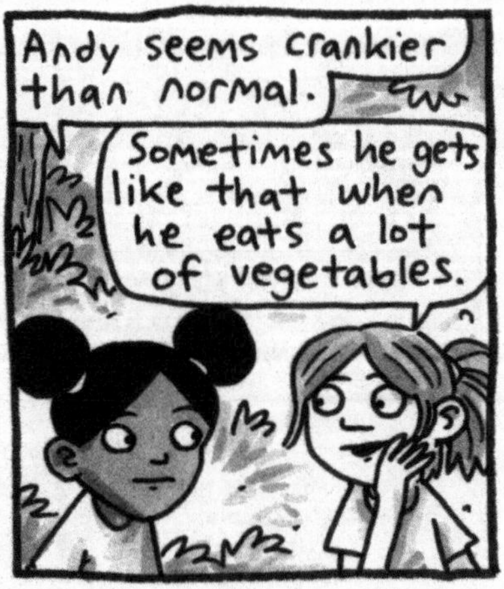
Andy seems crankier than normal.
Sometimes he gets like that when he eats a lot of vegetables.

By studying teeth, bones, and poop, scientists know Neanderthals ate their veggies!

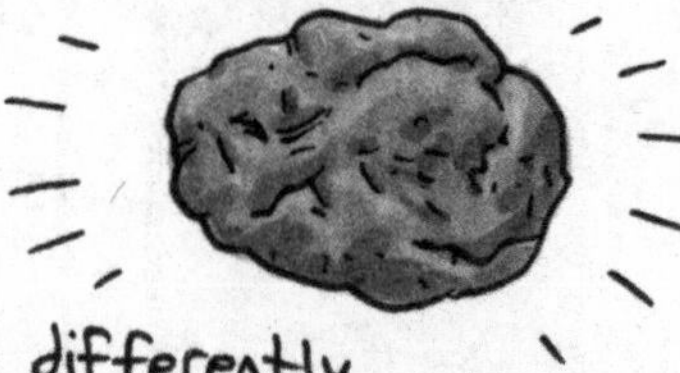

Fortunately, fossilized poop doesn't stink!

People digest food differently from other animals. By analyzing the composition of fossil poop, scientists can identify who created it, and determine what they ate.

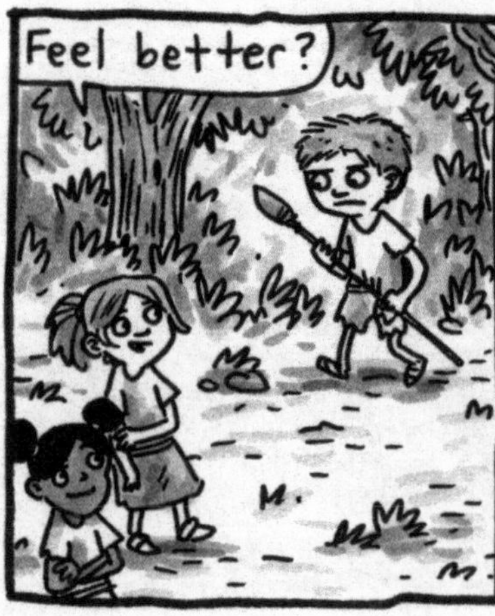
Feel better?

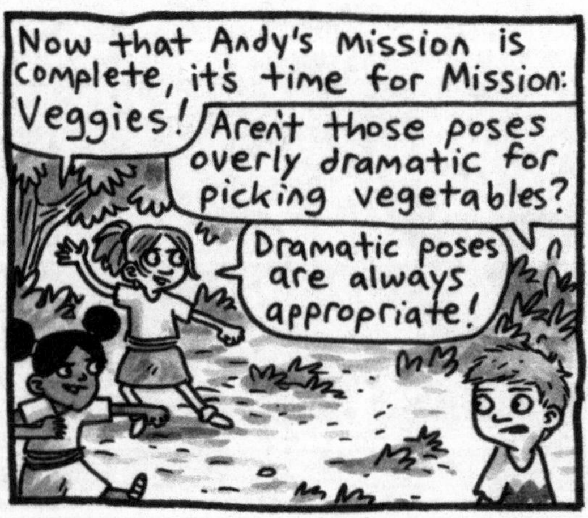
Now that Andy's mission is complete, it's time for Mission: Veggies!
Aren't those poses overly dramatic for picking vegetables?
Dramatic poses are always appropriate!

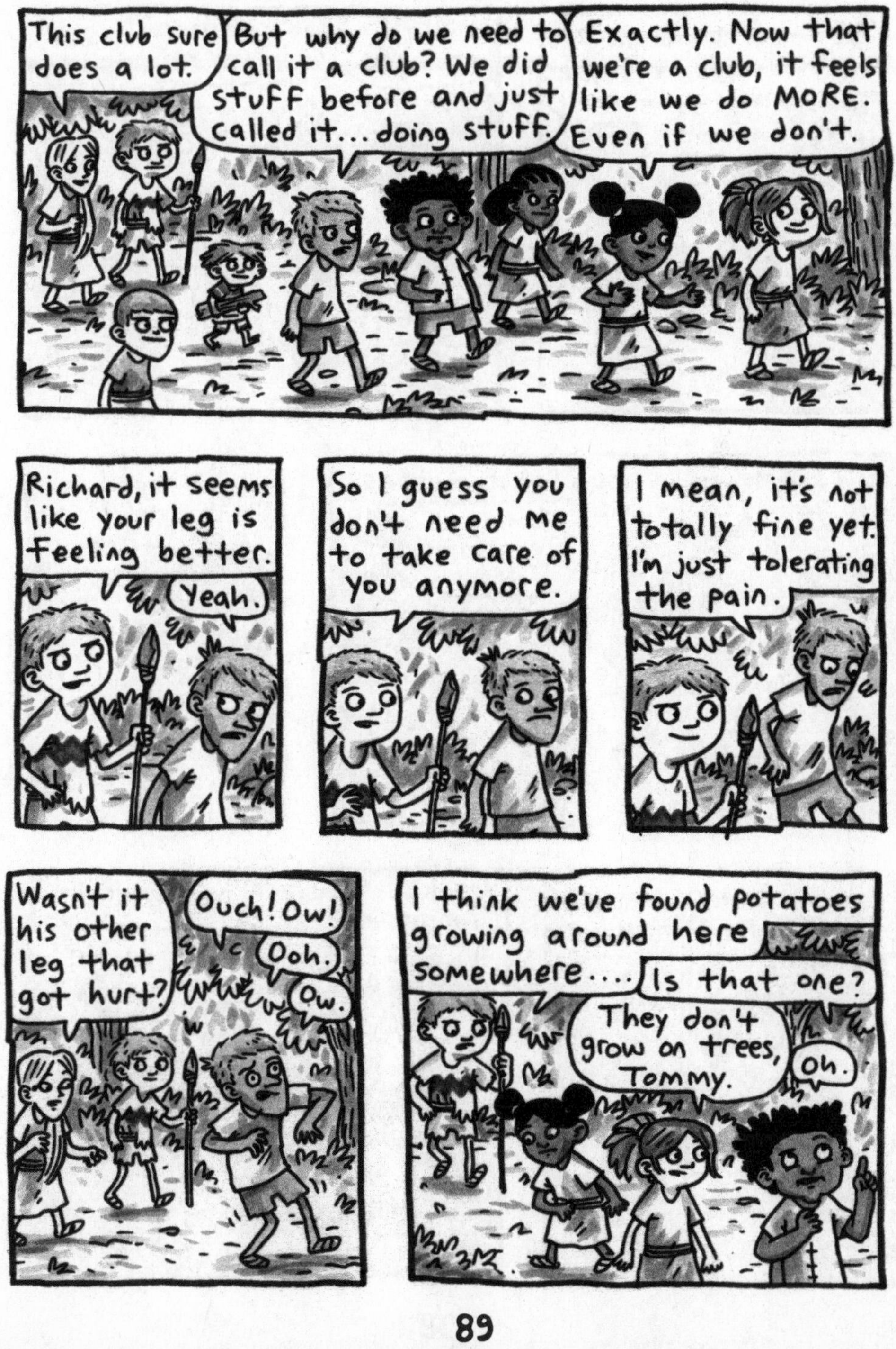

This club sure does a lot.
But why do we need to call it a club? We did stuff before and just called it... doing stuff.
Exactly. Now that we're a club, it feels like we do MORE. Even if we don't.
Richard, it seems like your leg is feeling better.
Yeah.
So I guess you don't need me to take care of you anymore.
I mean, it's not totally fine yet. I'm just tolerating the pain.
Wasn't it his other leg that got hurt?
Ouch! Ow!
Ooh.
Ow.
I think we've found potatoes growing around here somewhere....
Is that one?
They don't grow on trees, Tommy.
Oh.

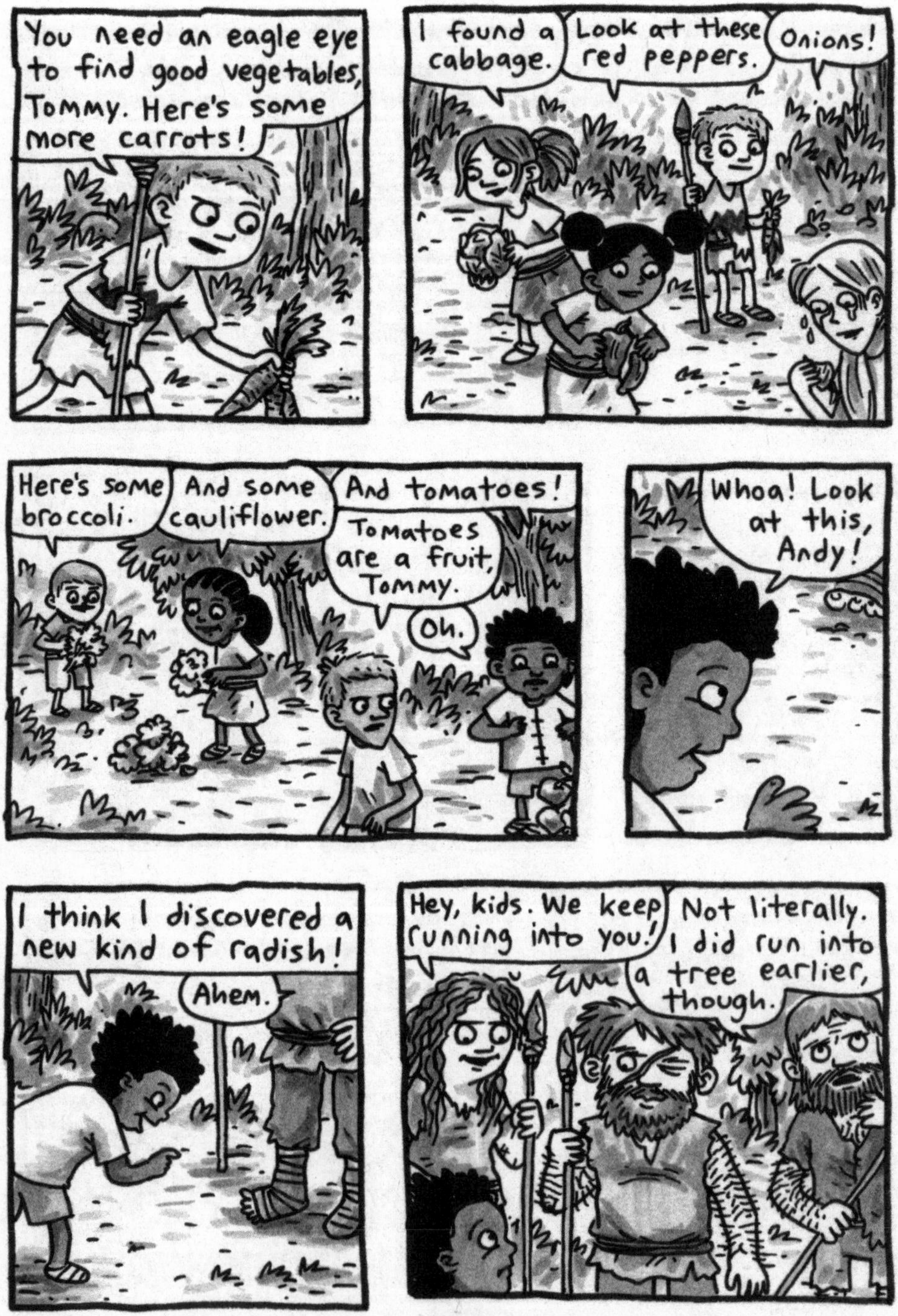
You need an eagle eye to find good vegetables, Tommy. Here's some more carrots!
I found a cabbage.
Look at these red peppers.
Onions!
Here's some broccoli.
And some cauliflower.
And tomatoes!
Tomatoes are a fruit, Tommy.
Oh.
Whoa! Look at this, Andy!
I think I discovered a new kind of radish!
Ahem.
Hey, kids. We keep running into you!
Not literally. I did run into a tree earlier, though.

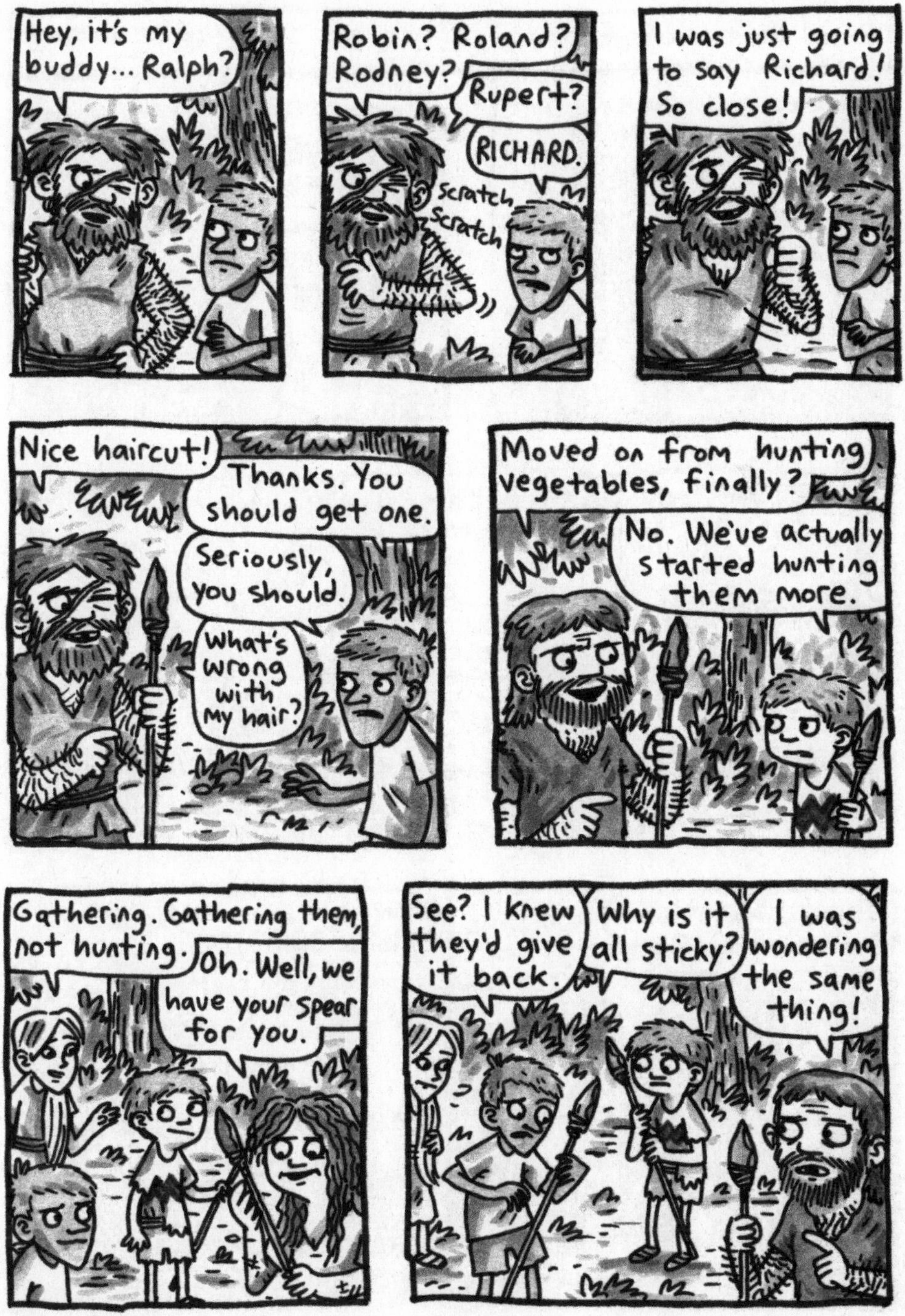
Hey, it's my buddy... Ralph?
Robin? Roland? Rodney?
Rupert?
RICHARD.
scratch scratch
I was just going to say Richard! So close!
Nice haircut!
Thanks. You should get one.
Seriously, you should.
What's wrong with my hair?
Moved on from hunting vegetables, finally?
No. We've actually started hunting them more.
Gathering. Gathering them, not hunting.
Oh. Well, we have your spear for you.
See? I knew they'd give it back.
Why is it all sticky?
I was wondering the same thing!

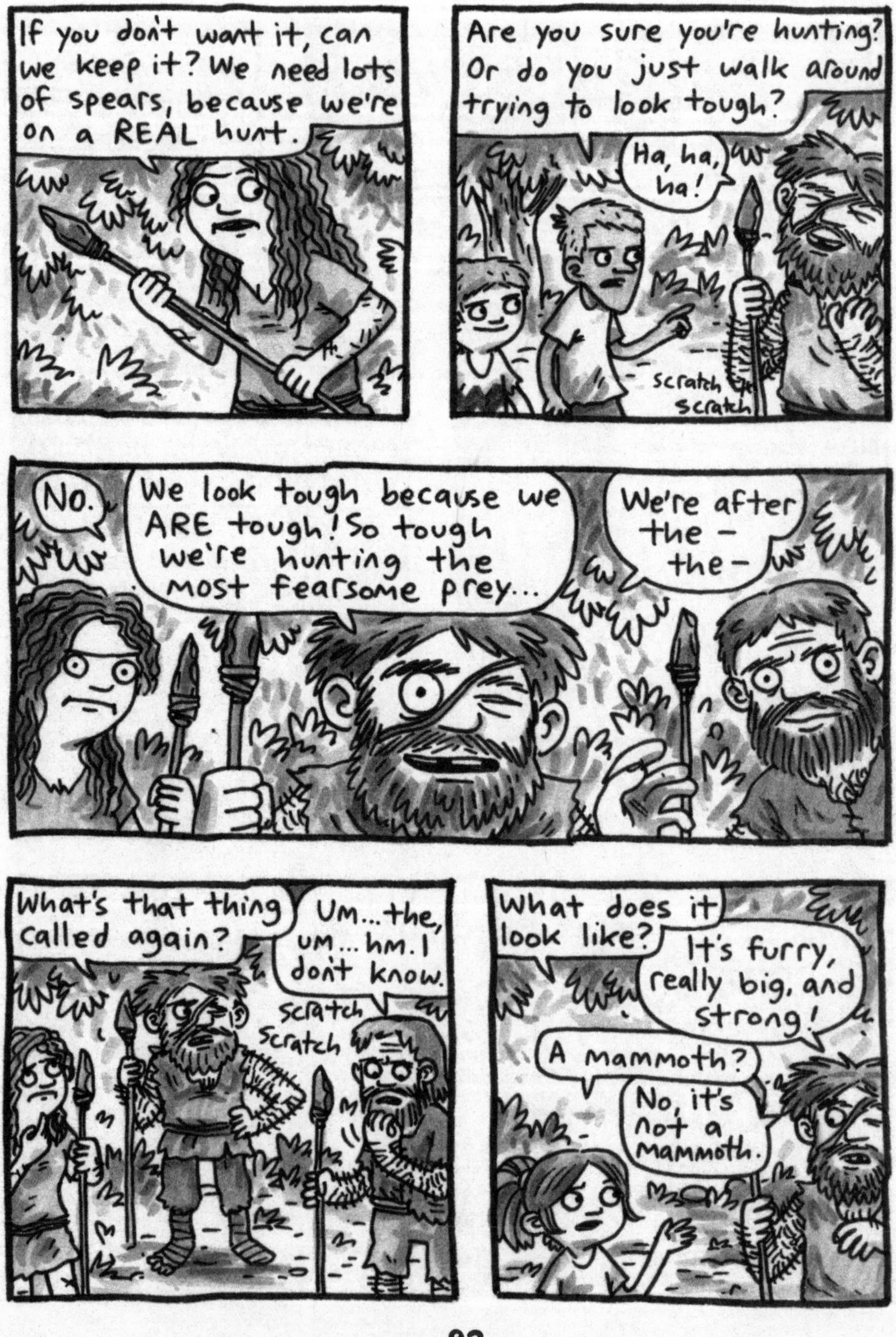
If you don't want it, can we keep it? We need lots of spears, because we're on a REAL hunt.
Are you sure you're hunting? Or do you just walk around trying to look tough?
Ha, ha, ha!
scratch scratch
No.
We look tough because we ARE tough! So tough we're hunting the most fearsome prey...
We're after the – the –
What's that thing called again?
Um...the, um...hm. I don't know.
scratch scratch
What does it look like?
It's furry, really big, and strong!
A mammoth?
No, it's not a mammoth.

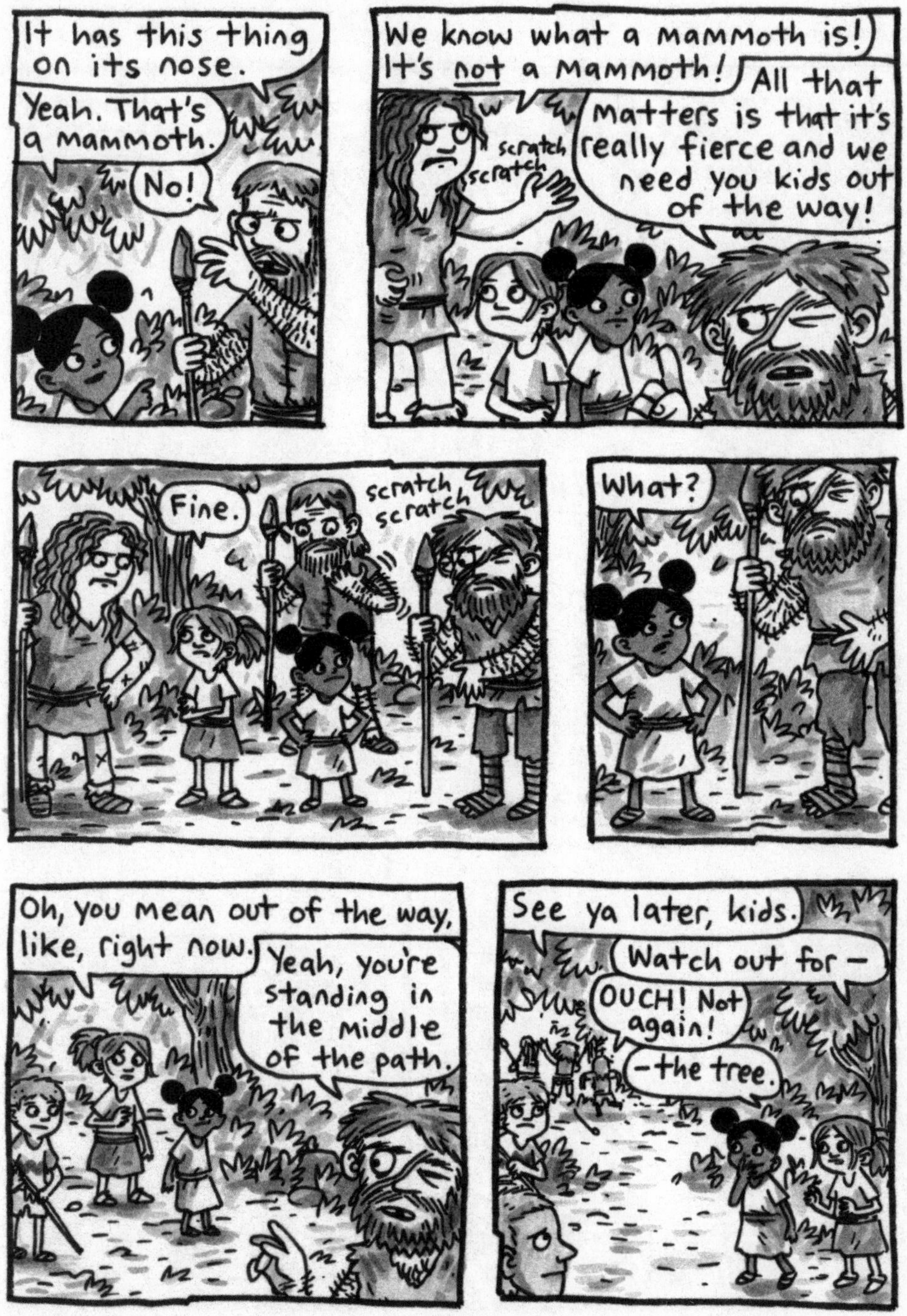
It has this thing on its nose.
Yeah. That's a mammoth.
No!
We know what a mammoth is! It's not a mammoth!
All that matters is that it's really fierce and we need you kids out of the way!
scratch scratch
Fine.
scratch scratch
What?
Oh, you mean out of the way, like, right now.
Yeah, you're standing in the middle of the path.
See ya later, kids.
Watch out for—
OUCH! Not again!
—the tree.

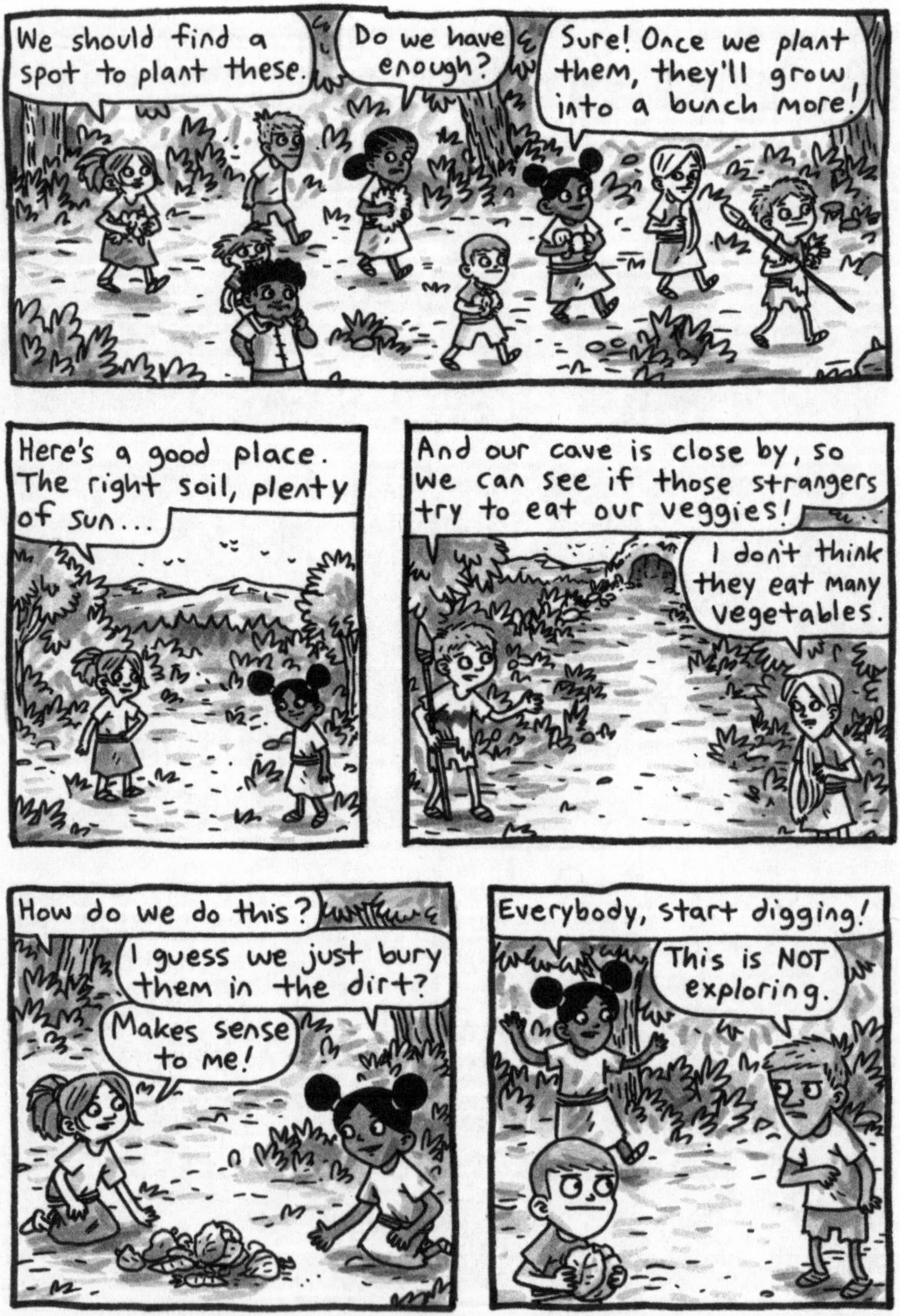
We should find a spot to plant these.
Do we have enough?
Sure! Once we plant them, they'll grow into a bunch more!
Here's a good place. The right soil, plenty of sun...
And our cave is close by, so we can see if those strangers try to eat our veggies!
I don't think they eat many vegetables.
How do we do this?
I guess we just bury them in the dirt?
Makes sense to me!
Everybody, start digging!
This is NOT exploring.

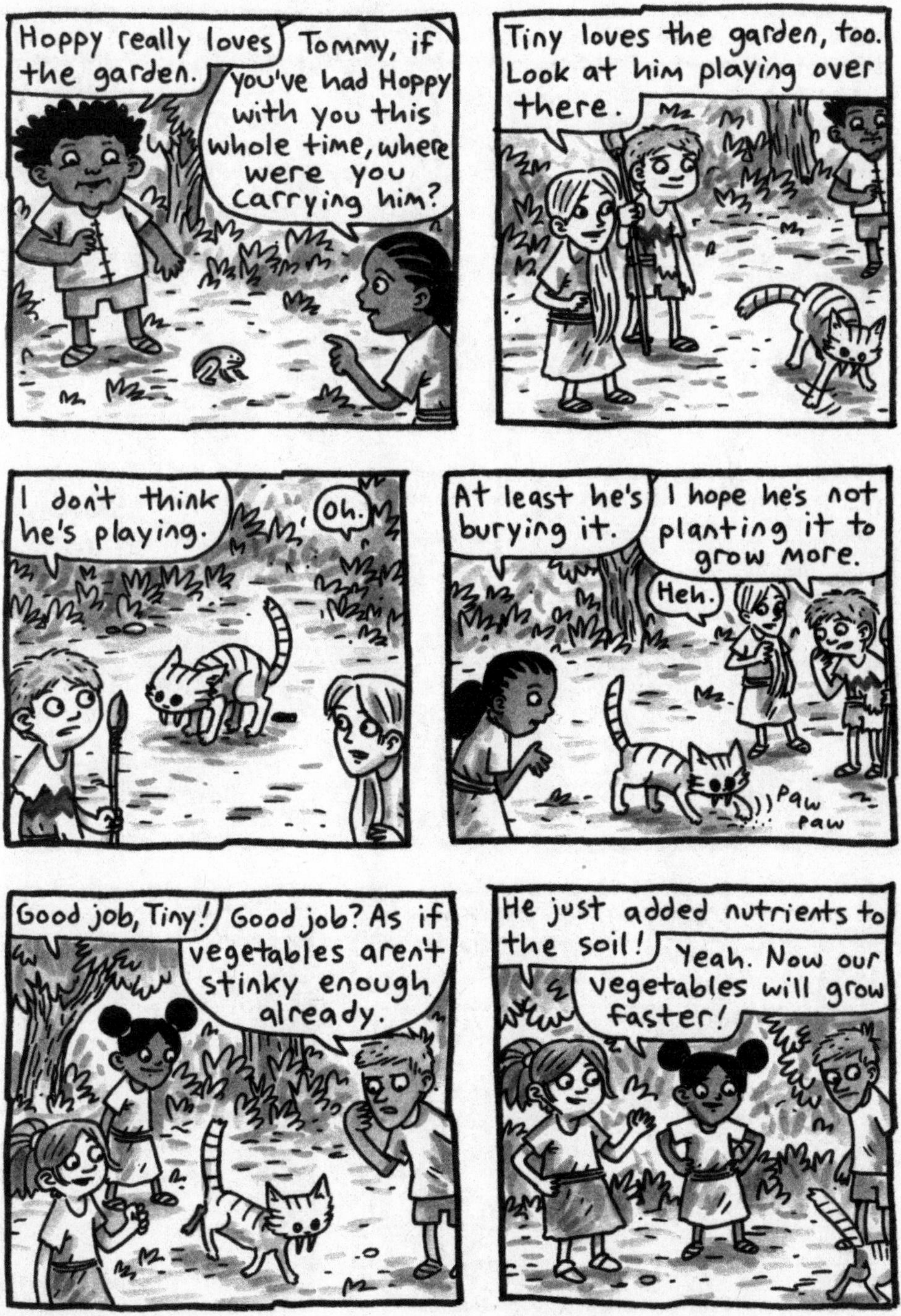
Hoppy really loves the garden.
Tommy, if you've had Hoppy with you this whole time, where were you carrying him?
Tiny loves the garden, too. Look at him playing over there.
I don't think he's playing.
Oh.
At least he's burying it.
I hope he's not planting it to grow more.
Heh.
Paw paw
Good job, Tiny!
Good job? As if vegetables aren't stinky enough already.
He just added nutrients to the soil!
Yeah. Now our vegetables will grow faster!

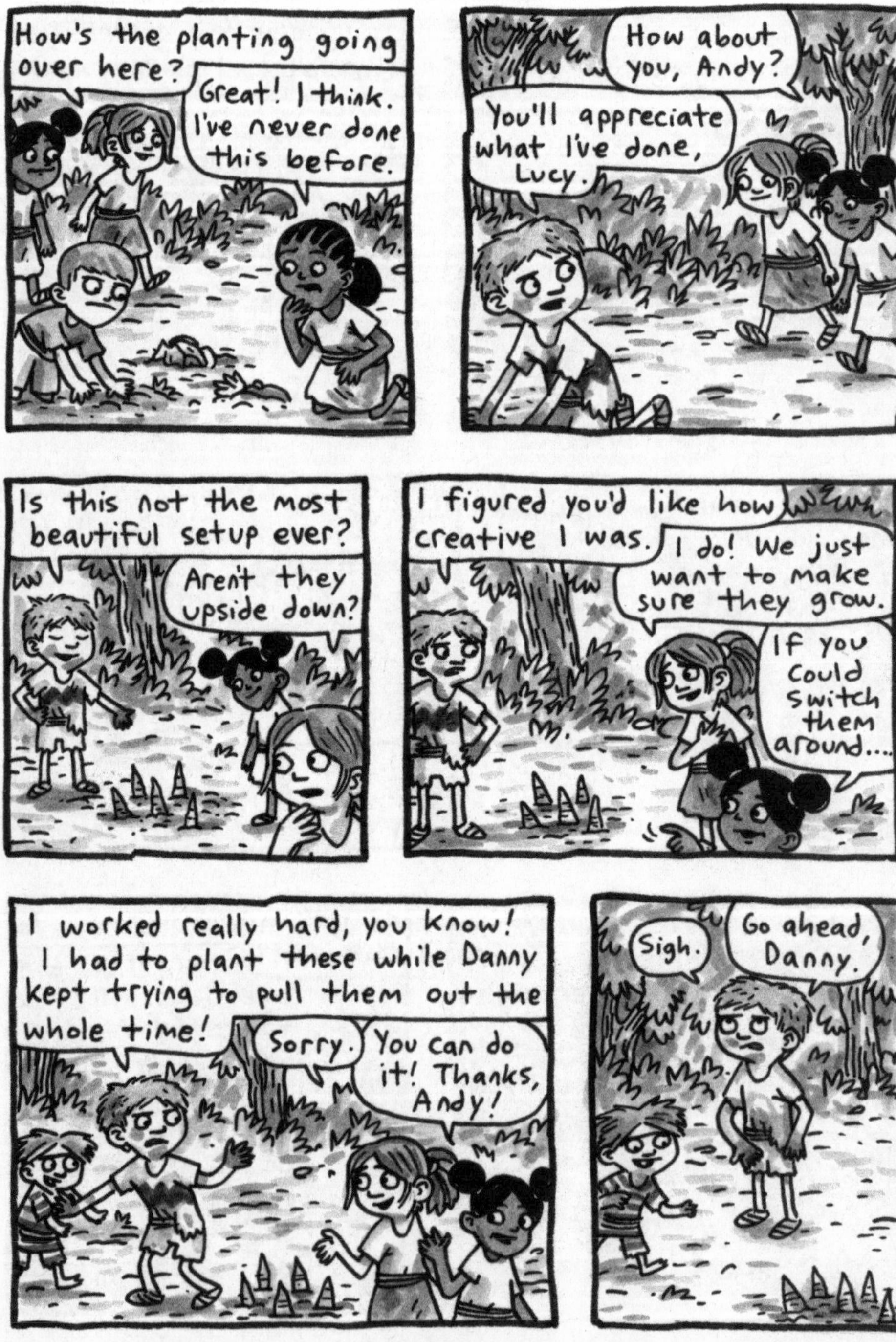
How's the planting going over here?
Great! I think. I've never done this before.
How about you, Andy?
You'll appreciate what I've done, Lucy.
Is this not the most beautiful setup ever?
Aren't they upside down?
I figured you'd like how creative I was.
I do! We just want to make sure they grow.
If you could switch them around....
I worked really hard, you know! I had to plant these while Danny kept trying to pull them out the whole time!
Sorry.
You can do it! Thanks, Andy!
Sigh.
Go ahead, Danny.

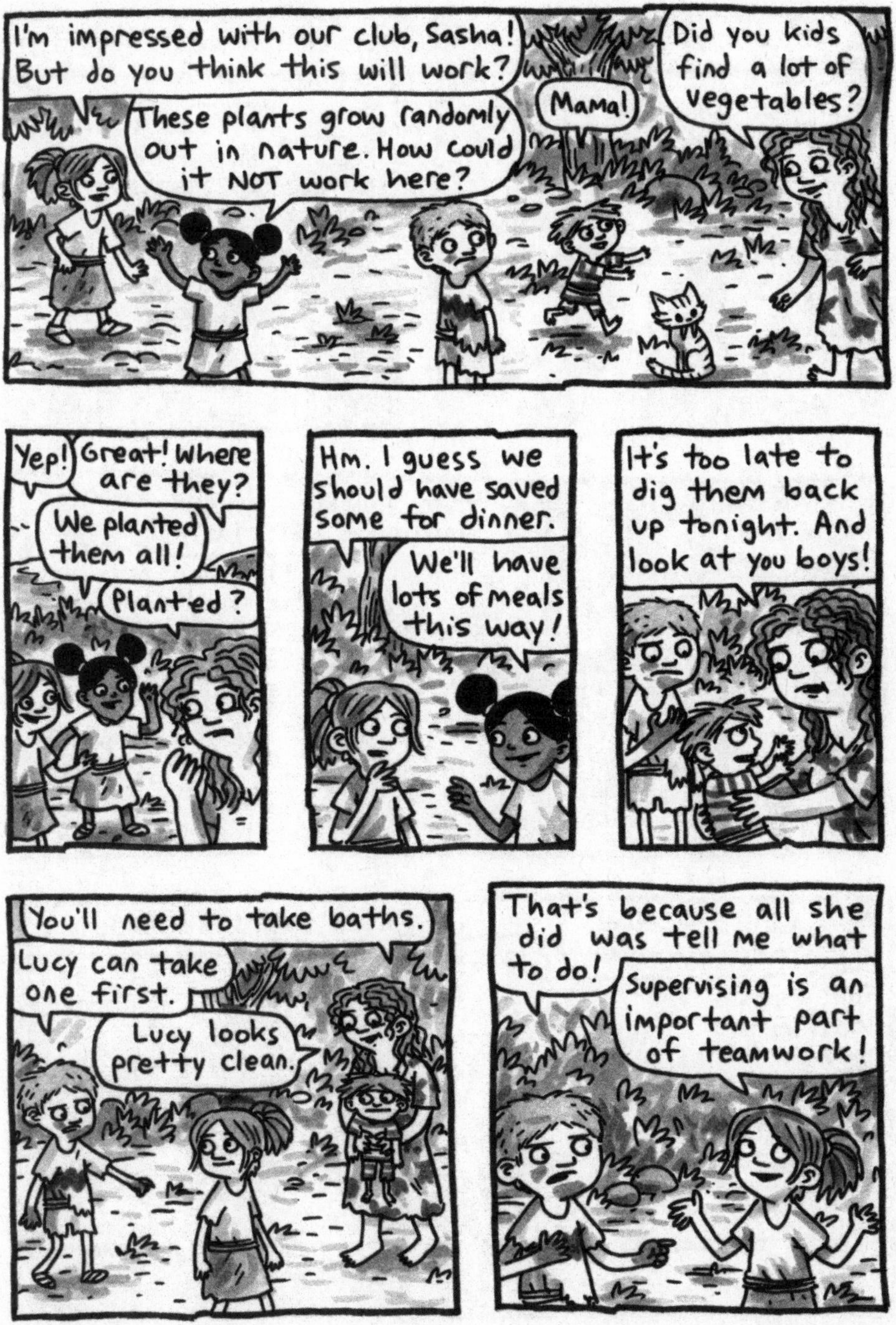

I'm impressed with our club, Sasha! But do you think this will work?
These plants grow randomly out in nature. How could it NOT work here?
Mama!
Did you kids find a lot of vegetables?
Yep!
Great! Where are they?
We planted them all!
Planted?
Hm. I guess we should have saved some for dinner.
We'll have lots of meals this way!
It's too late to dig them back up tonight. And look at you boys!
You'll need to take baths.
Lucy can take one first.
Lucy looks pretty clean.
That's because all she did was tell me what to do!
Supervising is an important part of teamwork!

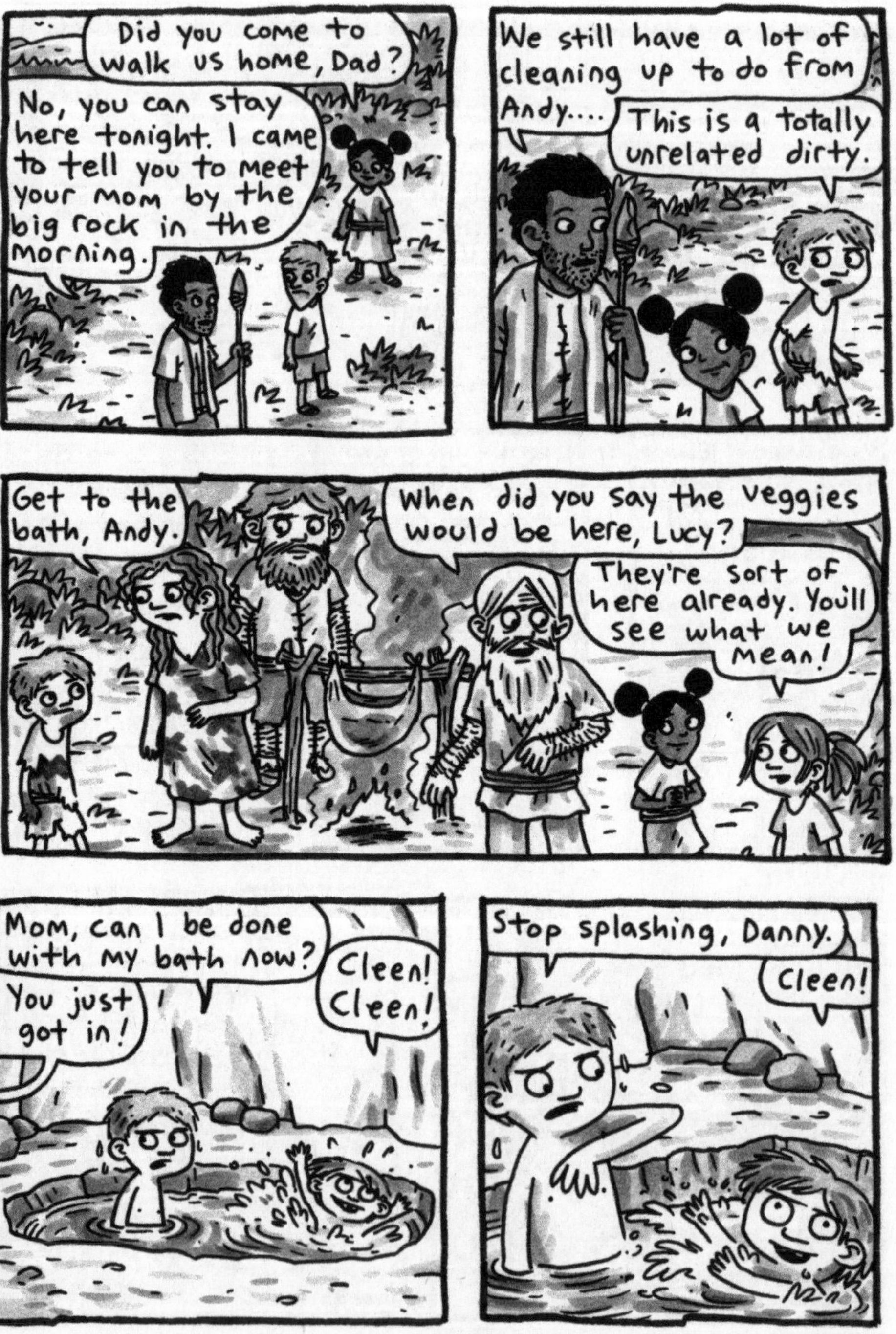
Did you come to walk us home, Dad?
No, you can stay here tonight. I came to tell you to meet your mom by the big rock in the morning.
We still have a lot of cleaning up to do from Andy....
This is a totally unrelated dirty.
Get to the bath, Andy.
When did you say the veggies would be here, Lucy?
They're sort of here already. You'll see what we mean!
Mom, can I be done with my bath now?
You just got in!
Cleen! Cleen!
Stop splashing, Danny.
Cleen!

Neanderthals may have taken hot baths!

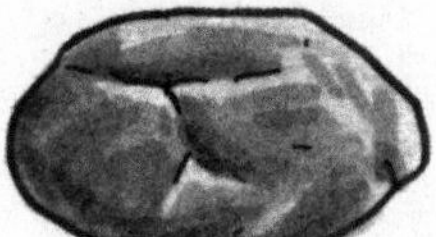

Shallow pits in Neanderthal caves may have held water. Some of these pits contain rocks that had cracks from being heated.

Scientists don't know if Neanderthal kids complained about bathtime, though.

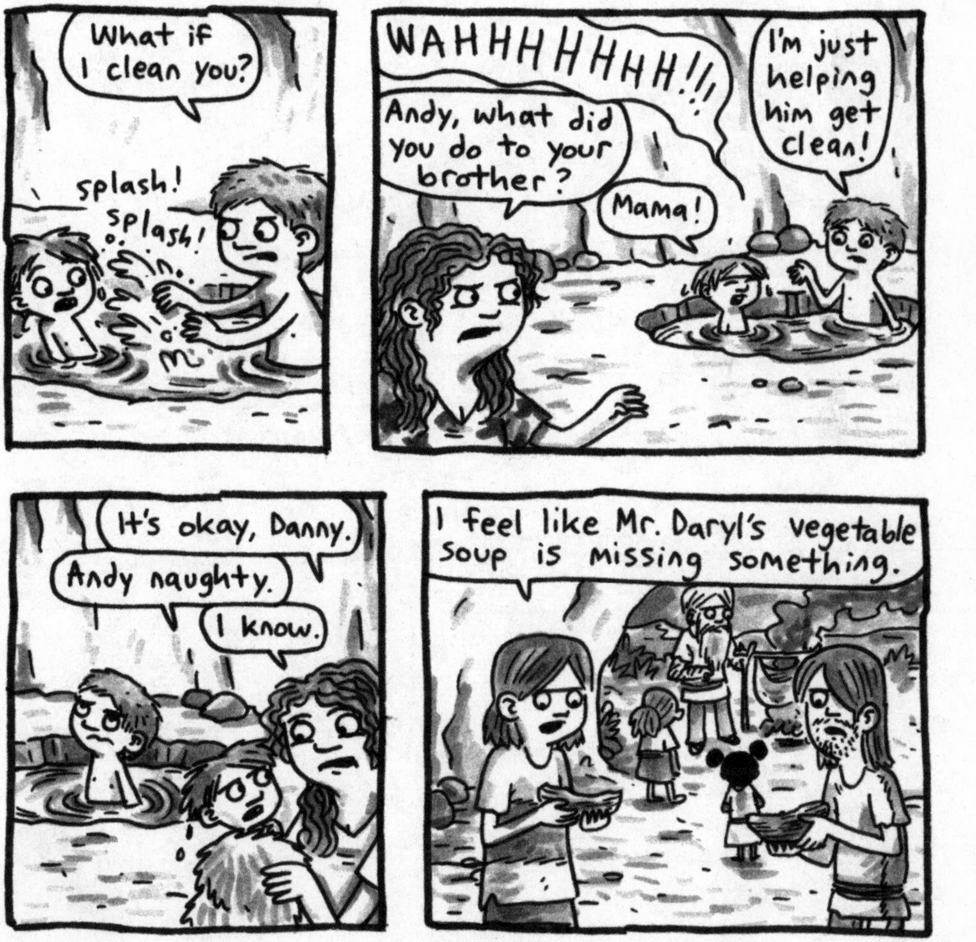
What if I clean you?
splash!
splash!
WAHHHHHHHH!!!
Andy, what did you do to your brother?
Mama!
I'm just helping him get clean!
It's okay, Danny.
Andy naughty.
I know.
I feel like Mr. Daryl's vegetable soup is missing something.

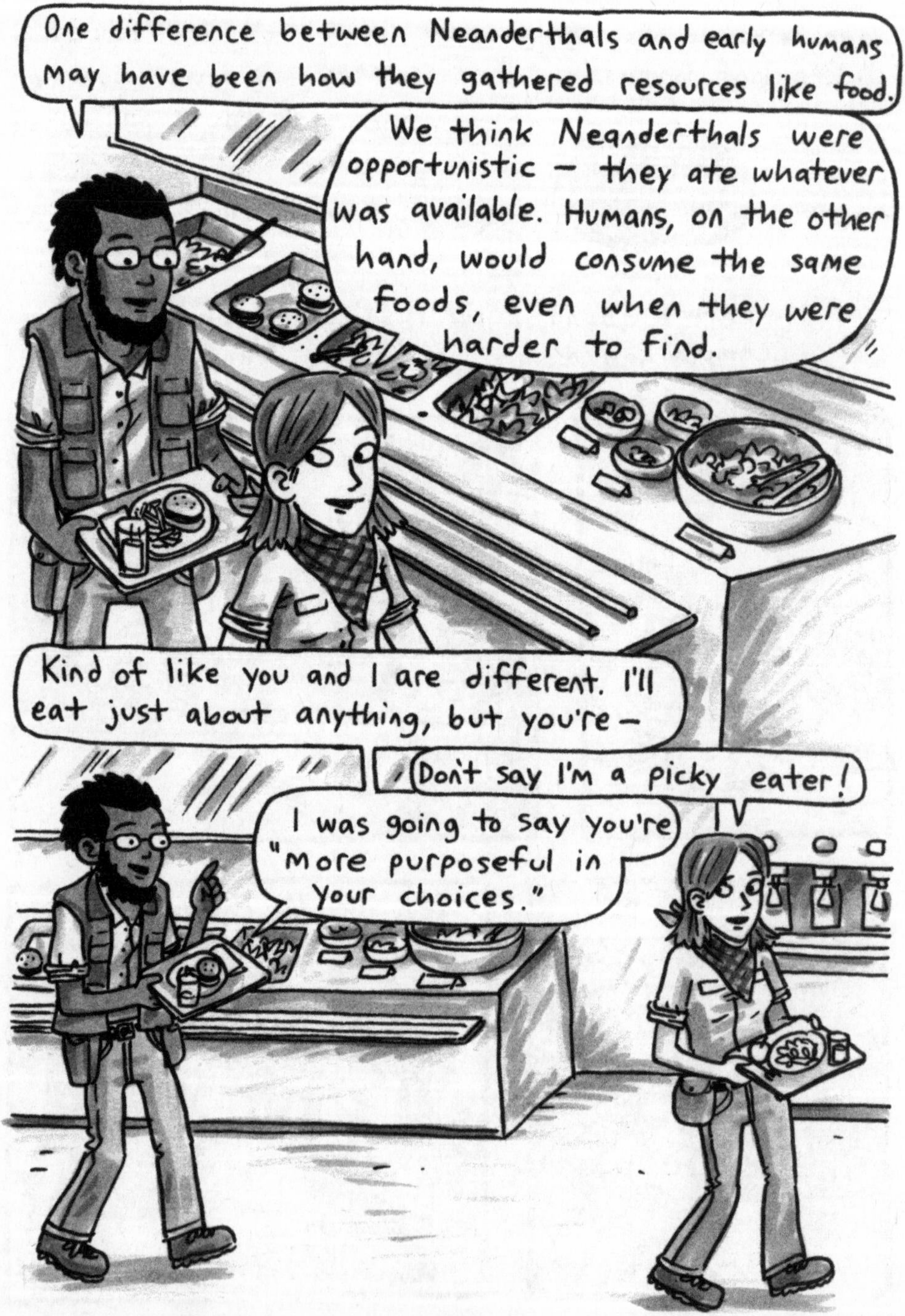
One difference between Neanderthals and early humans may have been how they gathered resources like food.
We think Neanderthals were opportunistic – they ate whatever was available. Humans, on the other hand, would consume the same foods, even when they were harder to find.
Kind of like you and I are different. I'll eat just about anything, but you're–
Don't say I'm a picky eater!
I was going to say you're "more purposeful in your choices."

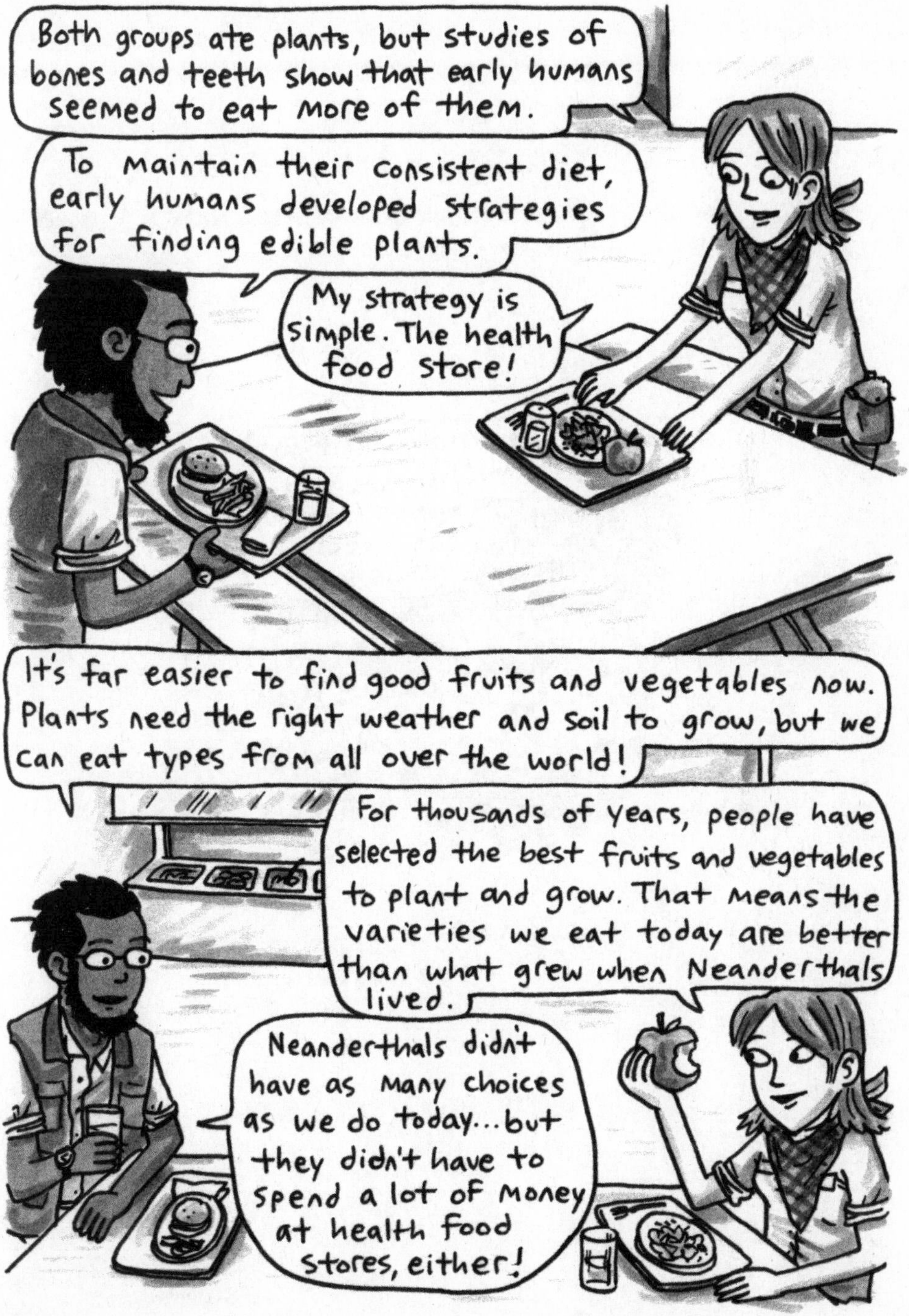
Both groups ate plants, but studies of bones and teeth show that early humans seemed to eat more of them.
To maintain their consistent diet, early humans developed strategies for finding edible plants.
My strategy is simple. The health food store!
It's far easier to find good fruits and vegetables now. Plants need the right weather and soil to grow, but we can eat types from all over the world!
For thousands of years, people have selected the best fruits and vegetables to plant and grow. That means the varieties we eat today are better than what grew when Neanderthals lived.
Neanderthals didn't have as many choices as we do today...but they didn't have to spend a lot of money at health food stores, either!

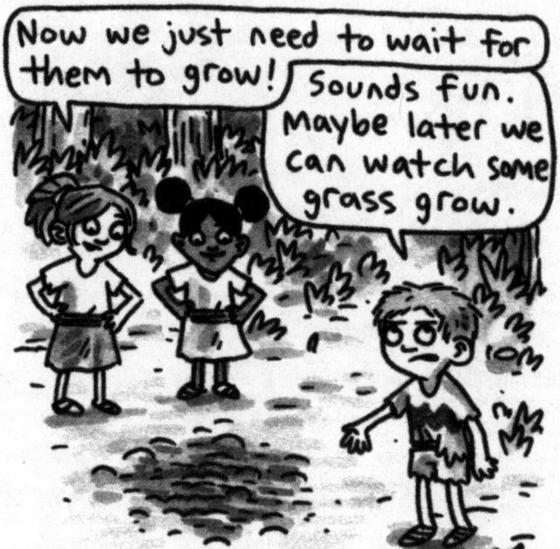
Now we just need to wait for them to grow!
Sounds fun. Maybe later we can watch some grass grow.

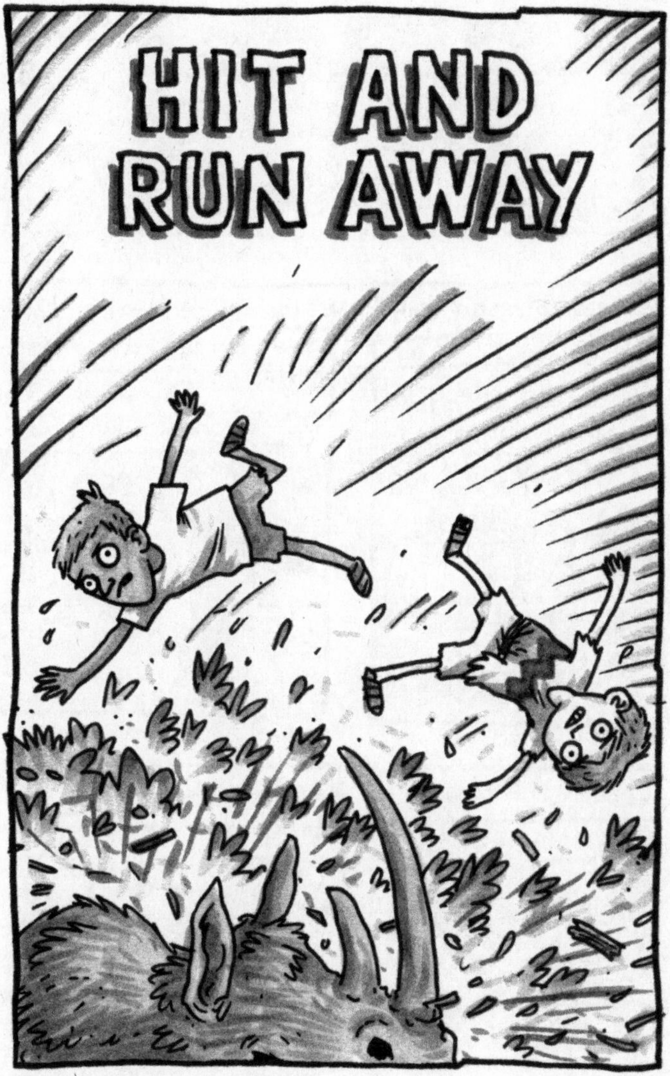
HIT AND RUN AWAY

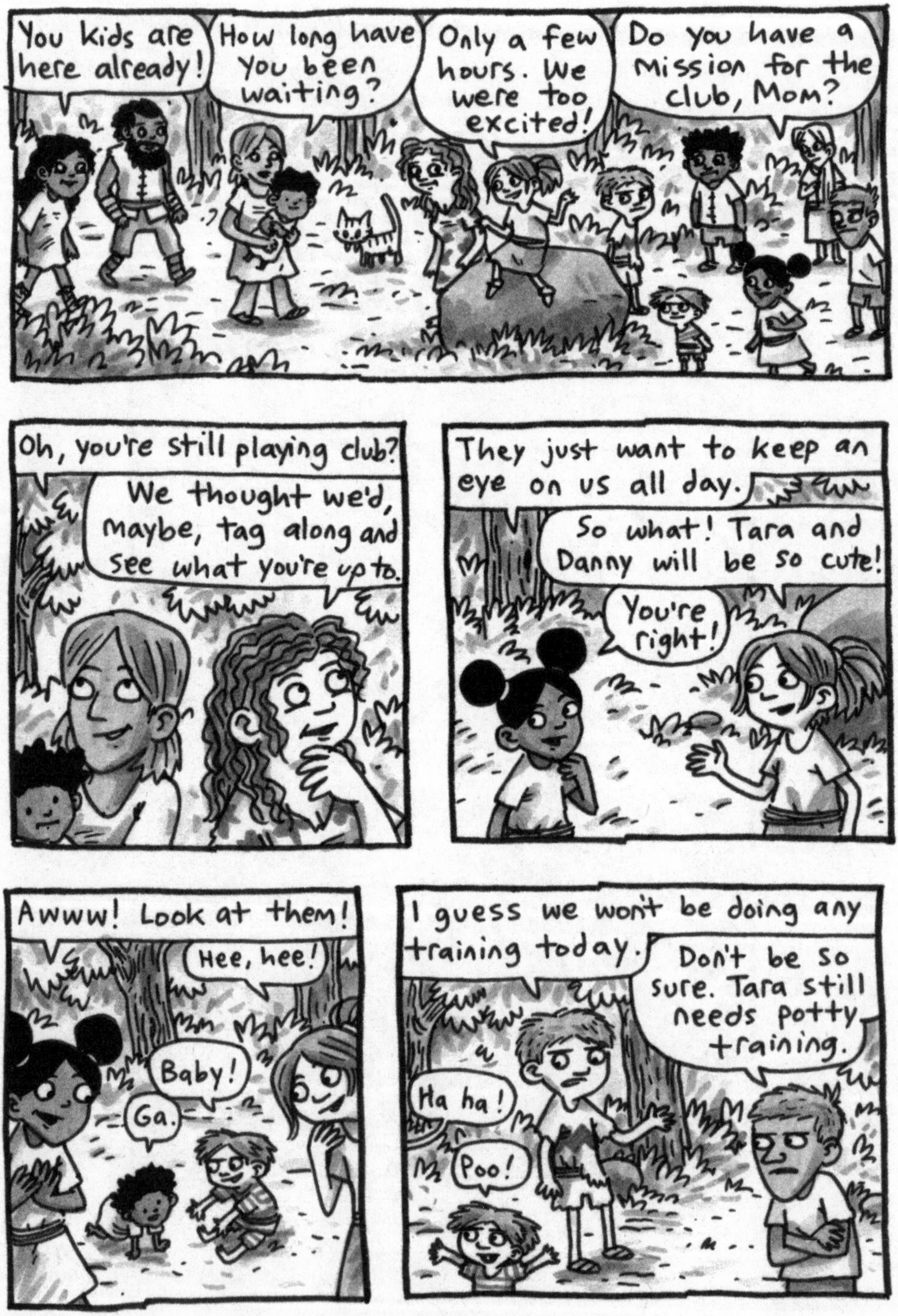
You kids are here already!
How long have you been waiting?
Only a few hours. We were too excited!
Do you have a mission for the club, Mom?
Oh, you're still playing club?
We thought we'd, maybe, tag along and see what you're up to.
They just want to keep an eye on us all day.
So what! Tara and Danny will be so cute!
You're right!
Awww! Look at them!
Hee, hee!
Baby!
Ga.
I guess we won't be doing any training today.
Don't be so sure. Tara still needs potty training.
Ha ha!
Poo!

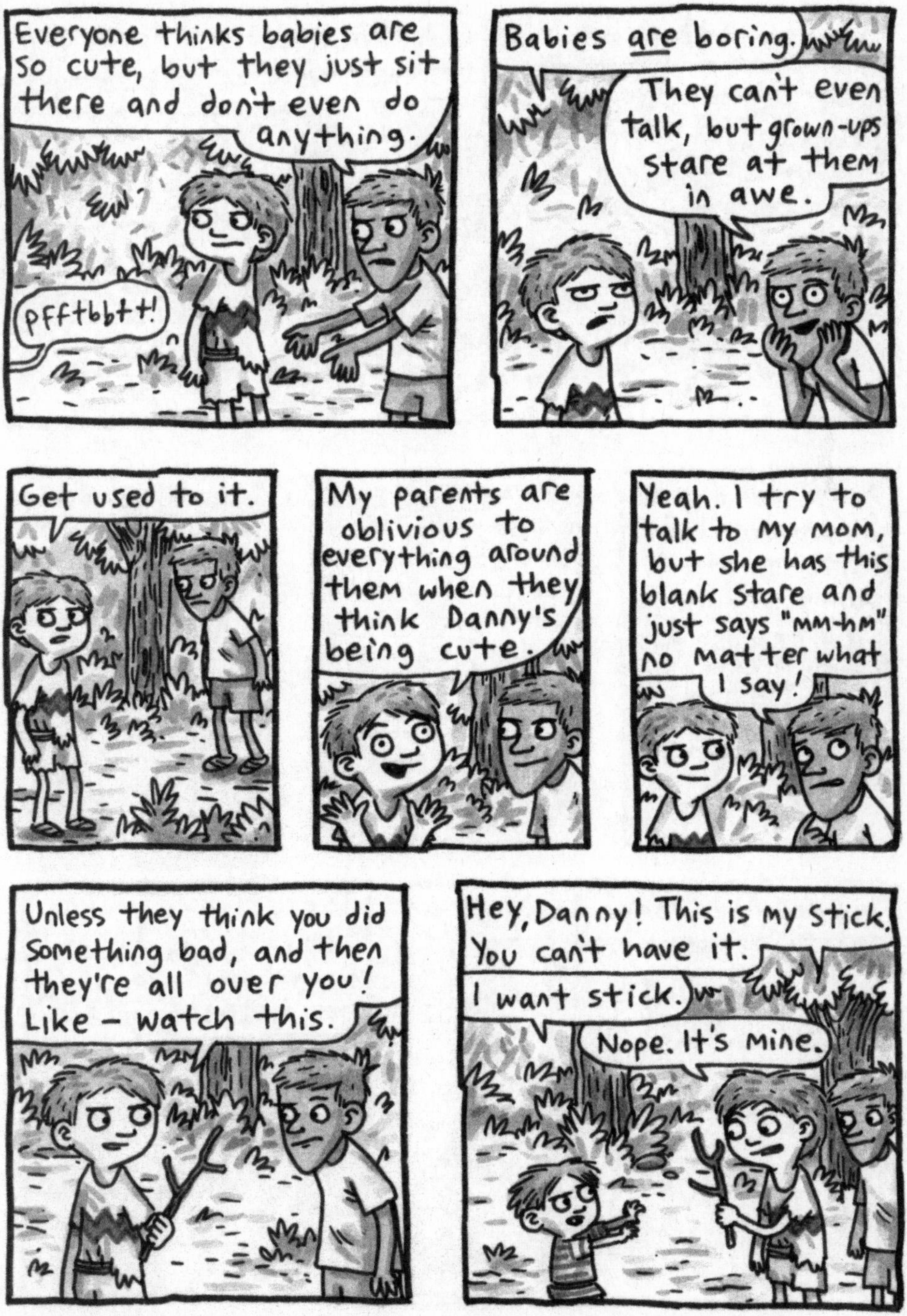
Everyone thinks babies are so cute, but they just sit there and don't even do anything.
pfftbbtt!
Babies are boring.
They can't even talk, but grown-ups stare at them in awe.
Get used to it.
My parents are oblivious to everything around them when they think Danny's being cute.
Yeah. I try to talk to my mom, but she has this blank stare and just says "mm-hm" no matter what I say!
Unless they think you did something bad, and then they're all over you! Like - watch this.
Hey, Danny! This is my stick. You can't have it.
I want stick.
Nope. It's mine.

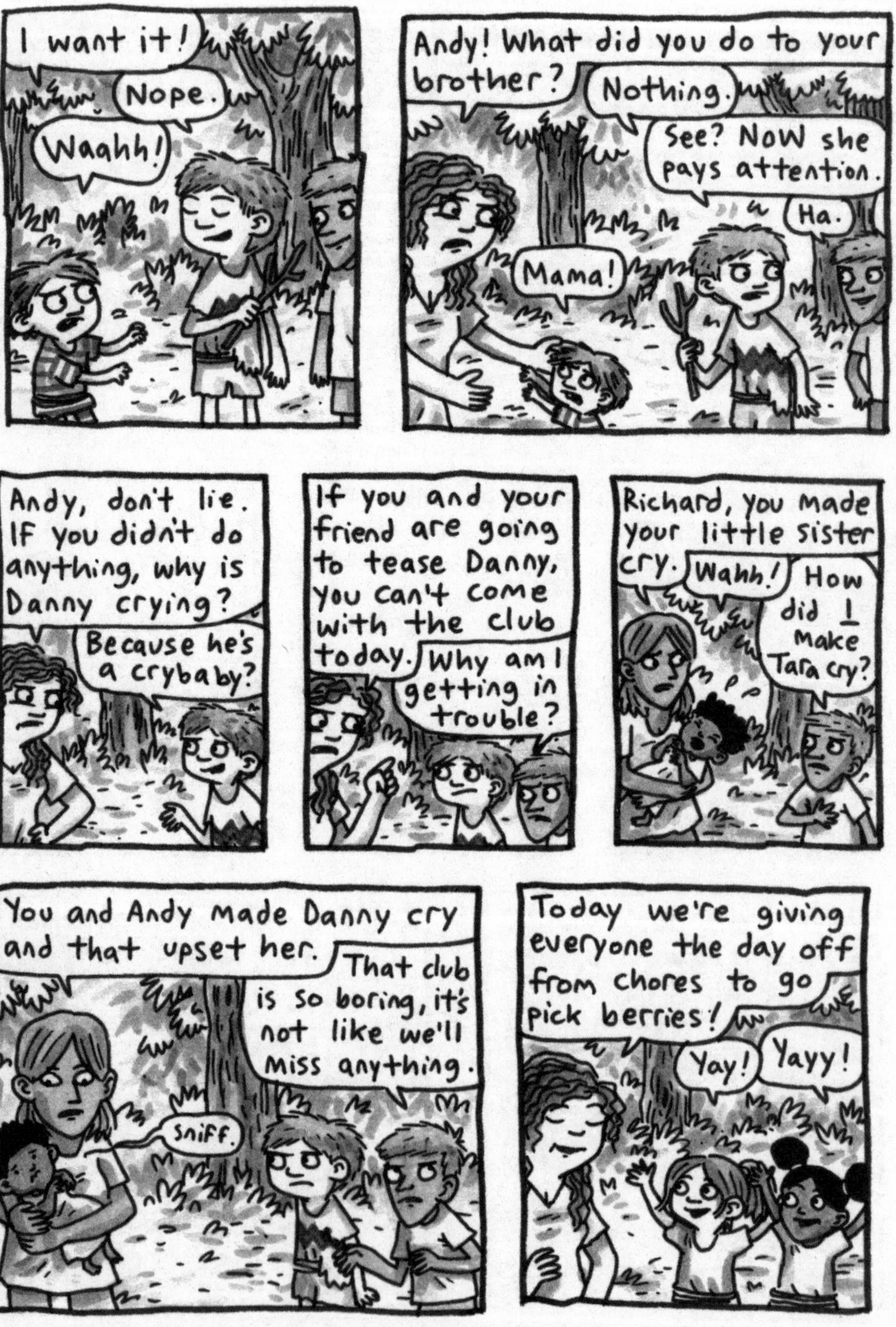
I want it!
Nope.
Waahh!
Andy! What did you do to your brother?
Nothing.
See? NOW she pays attention.
Ha.
Mama!
Andy, don't lie. If you didn't do anything, why is Danny crying?
Because he's a crybaby?
If you and your friend are going to tease Danny, you can't come with the club today.
Why am I getting in trouble?
Richard, you made your little sister cry.
Wahh!
How did I make Tara cry?
You and Andy made Danny cry and that upset her.
That club is so boring, it's not like we'll miss anything.
Sniff.
Today we're giving everyone the day off from chores to go pick berries!
Yay!
Yayy!

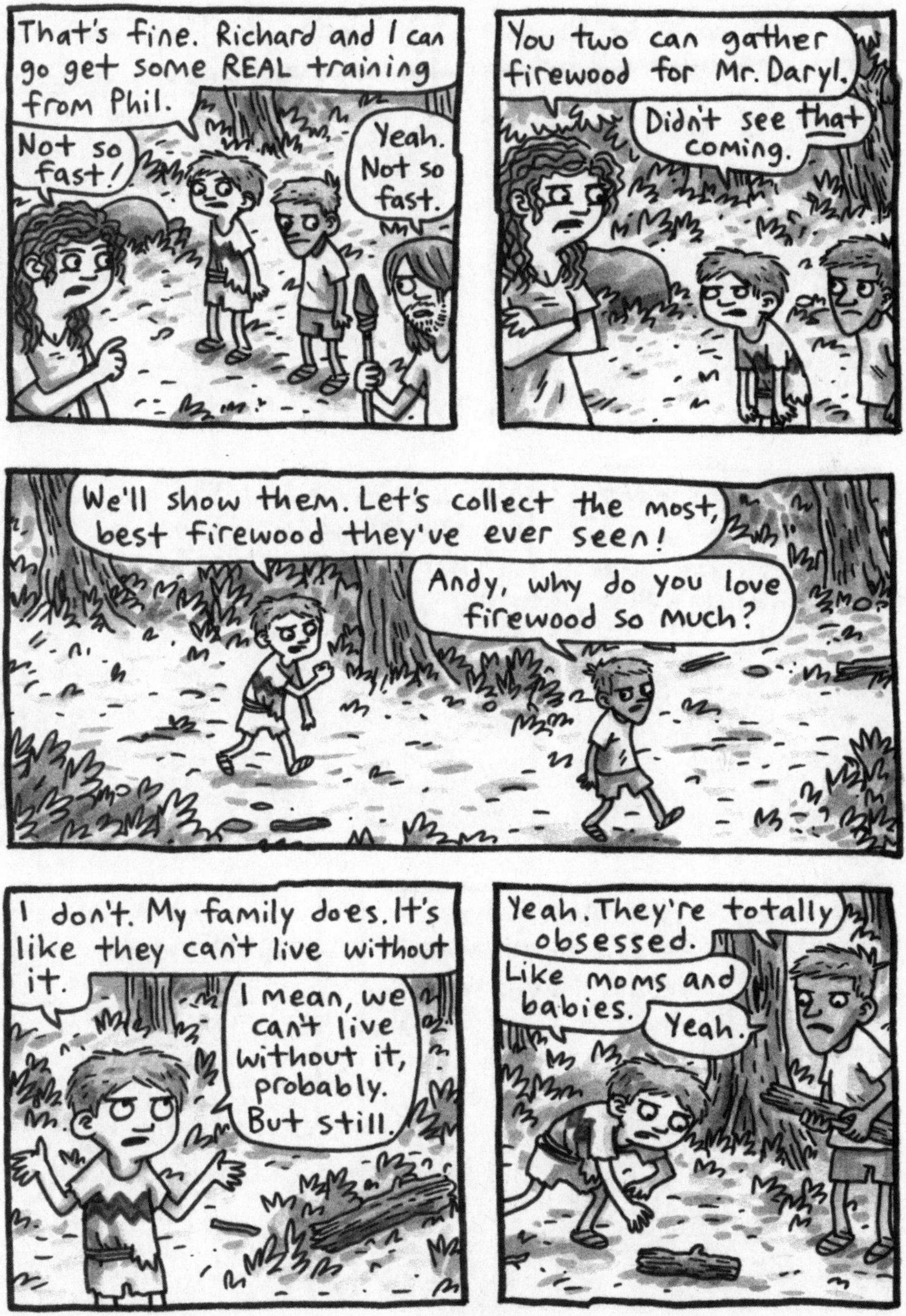

That's fine. Richard and I can go get some REAL training from Phil.
Not so fast!
Yeah. Not so fast.
You two can gather firewood for Mr. Daryl.
Didn't see that coming.
We'll show them. Let's collect the most, best firewood they've ever seen!
Andy, why do you love firewood so much?
I don't. My family does. It's like they can't live without it.
I mean, we can't live without it, probably. But still.
Yeah. They're totally obsessed.
Like moms and babies.
Yeah.

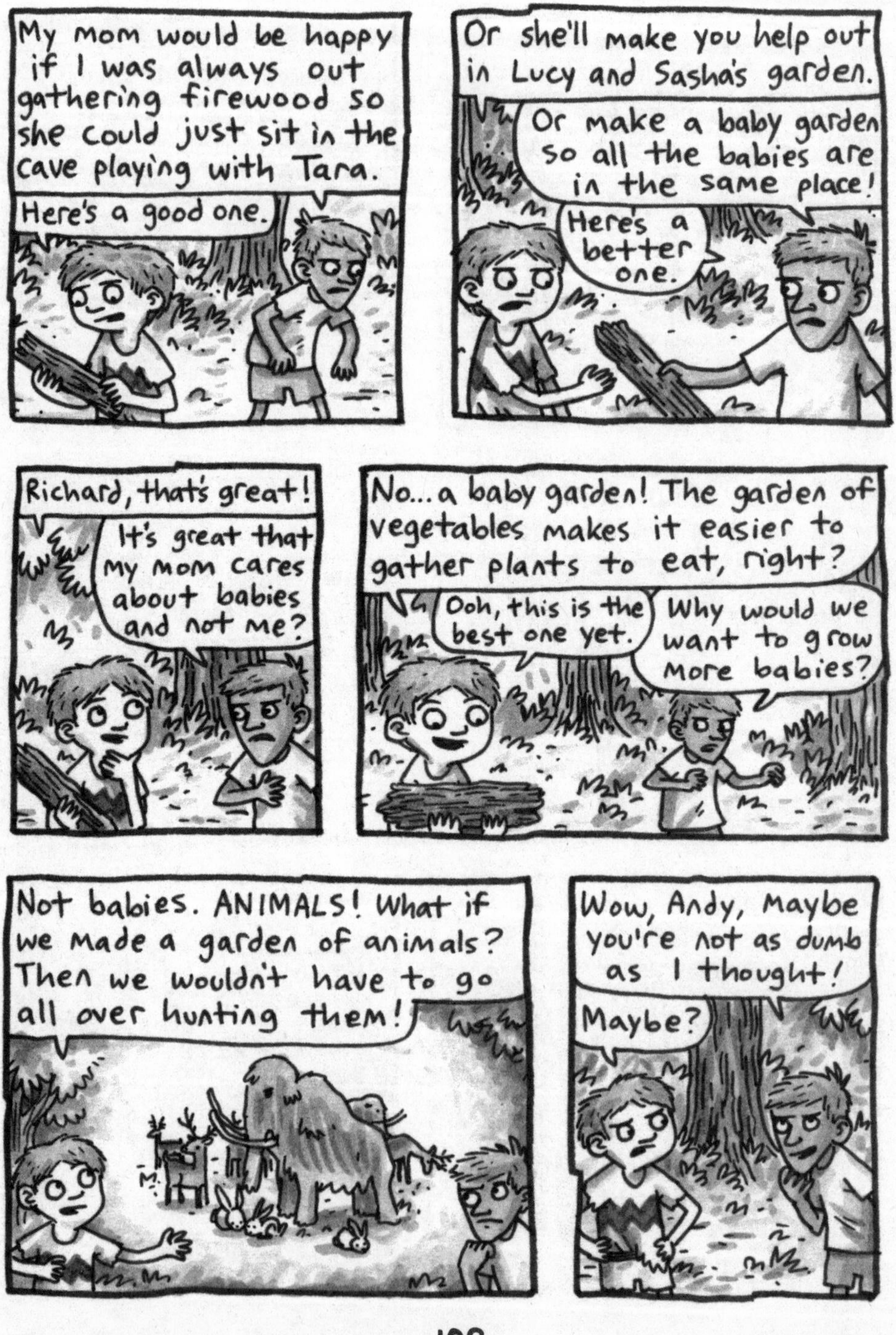
My mom would be happy if I was always out gathering firewood so she could just sit in the cave playing with Tara.
Here's a good one.
Or she'll make you help out in Lucy and Sasha's garden.
Or make a baby garden so all the babies are in the same place!
Here's a better one.
Richard, that's great!
It's great that my mom cares about babies and not me?
No...a baby garden! The garden of vegetables makes it easier to gather plants to eat, right?
Ooh, this is the best one yet.
Why would we want to grow more babies?
Not babies. ANIMALS! What if we made a garden of animals? Then we wouldn't have to go all over hunting them!
Wow, Andy, maybe you're not as dumb as I thought!
Maybe?

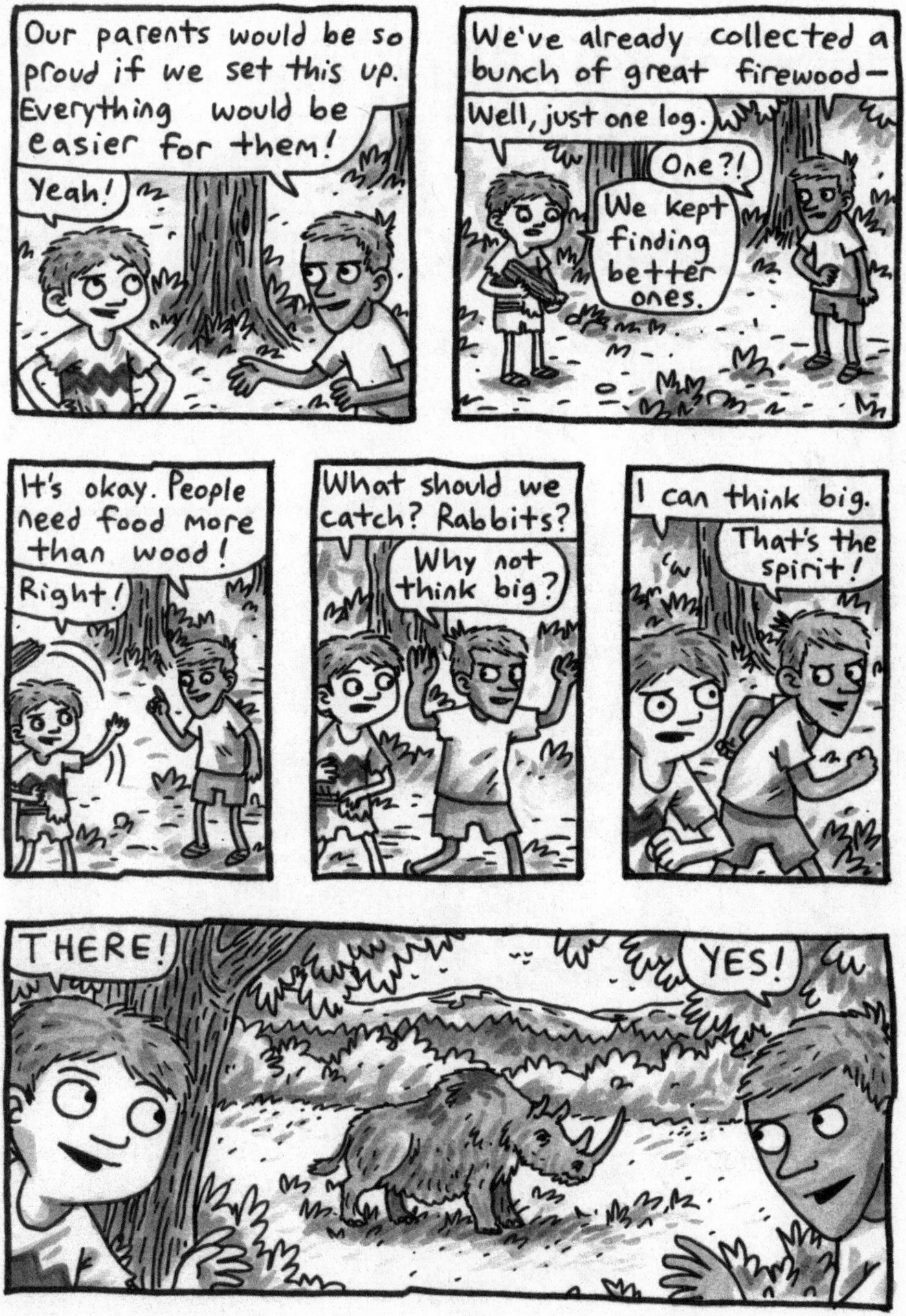
Our parents would be so proud if we set this up. Everything would be easier for them!
Yeah!
We've already collected a bunch of great firewood—
Well, just one log.
One?!
We kept finding better ones.
It's okay. People need food more than wood!
Right!
What should we catch? Rabbits?
Why not think big?
I can think big.
That's the spirit!
THERE!
YES!

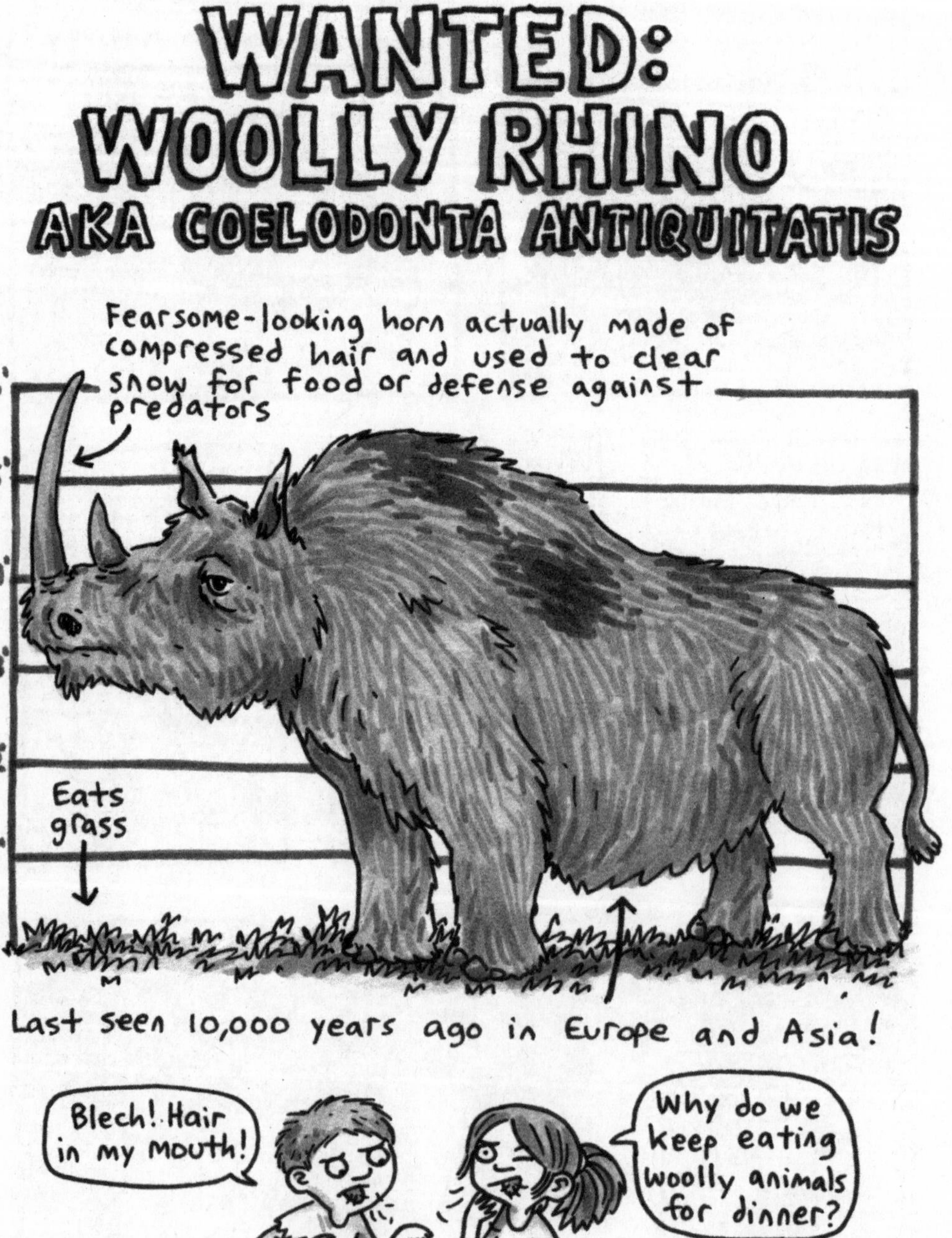
WANTED:
WOOLLY RHINO
AKA COELODONTA ANTIQUITATIS
Fearsome-looking horn actually made of compressed hair and used to clear snow for food or defense against predators
6'
5'
4'
3'
2'
1'
Eats grass
Last seen 10,000 years ago in Europe and Asia!
Blech! Hair in my mouth!
Why do we keep eating woolly animals for dinner?

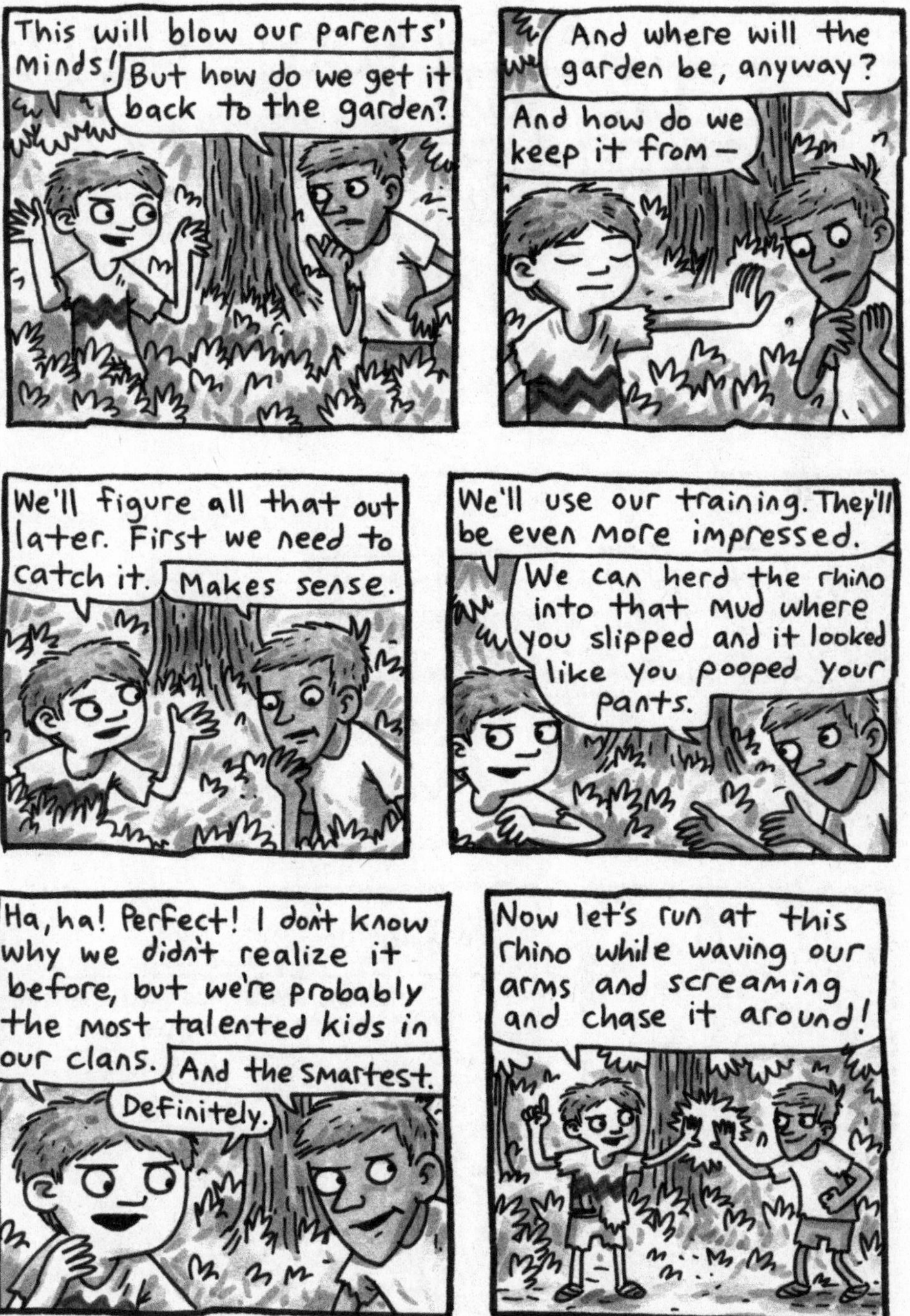
This will blow our parents' minds!
But how do we get it back to the garden?
And where will the garden be, anyway?
And how do we keep it from—
We'll figure all that out later. First we need to catch it.
Makes sense.
We'll use our training. They'll be even more impressed.
We can herd the rhino into that mud where you slipped and it looked like you pooped your pants.
Ha, ha! Perfect! I don't know why we didn't realize it before, but we're probably the most talented kids in our clans.
And the smartest.
Definitely.
Now let's run at this rhino while waving our arms and screaming and chase it around!

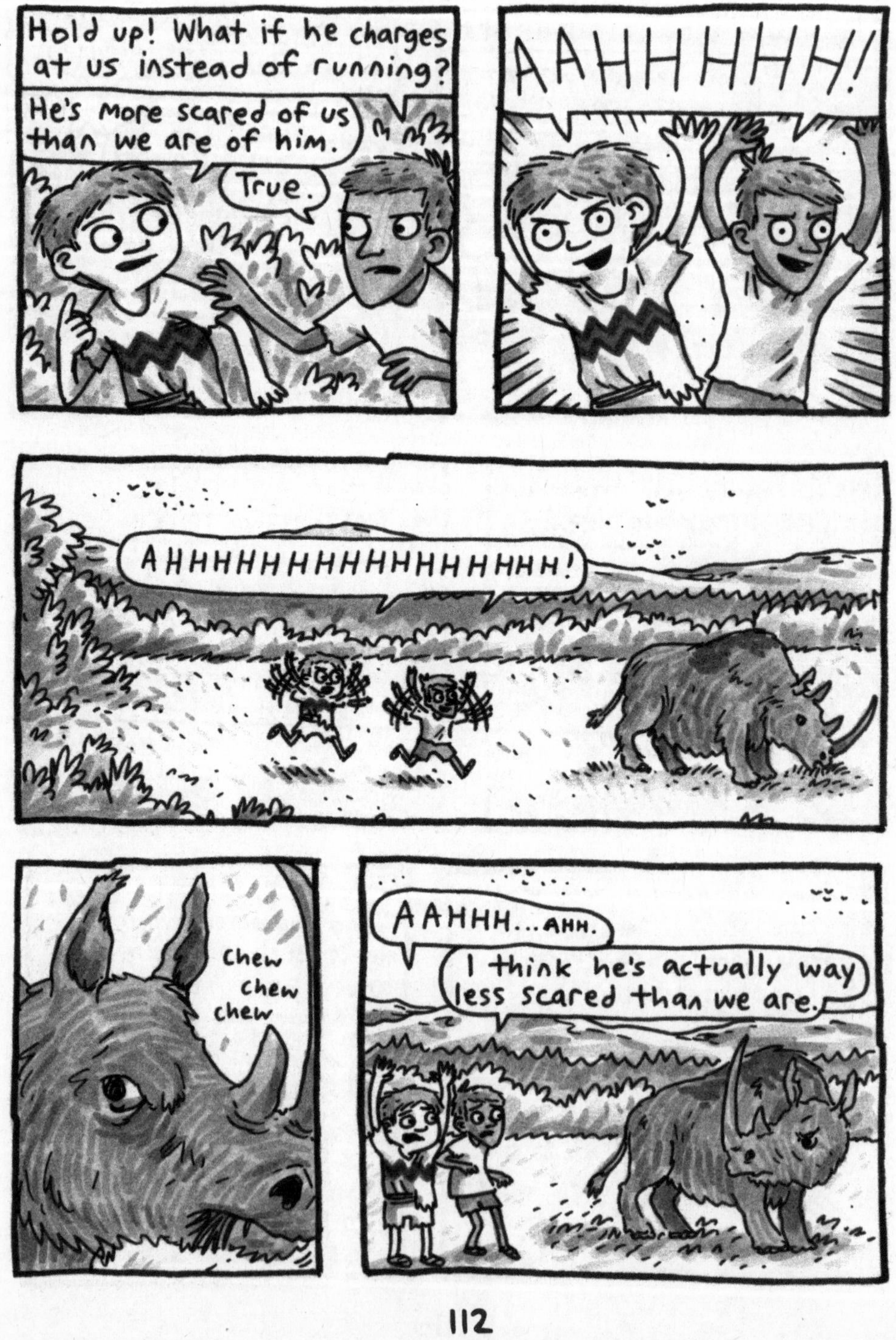
Hold up! What if he charges at us instead of running?
He's more scared of us than we are of him.
True.
AAHHHHHH!
AHHHHHHHHHHHHHHHHHH!
chew chew chew
AAHHH...AHH.
I think he's actually way less scared than we are.

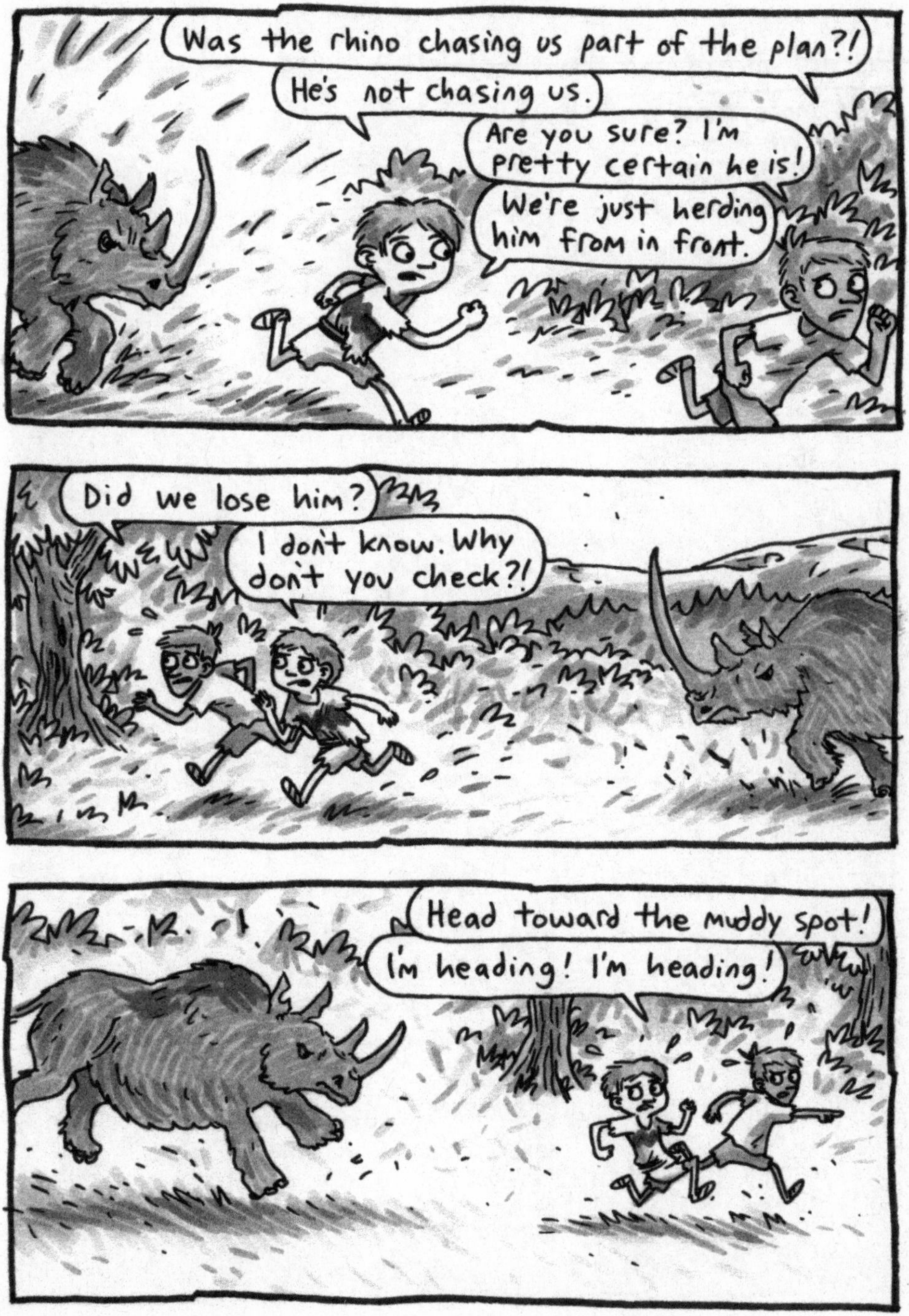
Was the rhino chasing us part of the plan?!
He's not chasing us.
Are you sure? I'm pretty certain he is!
We're just herding him from in front.
Did we lose him?
I don't know. Why don't you check?!
Head toward the muddy spot!
I'm heading! I'm heading!

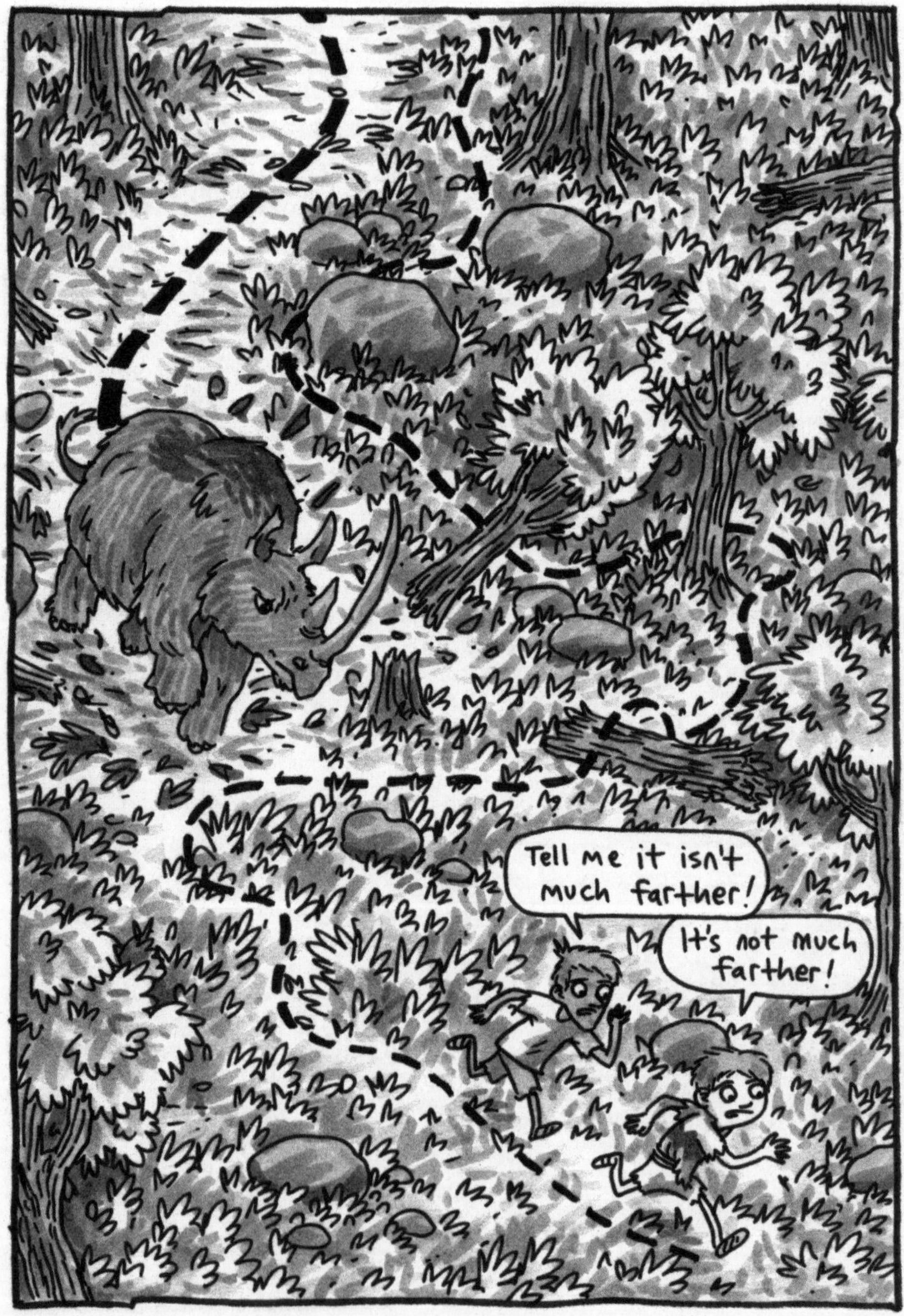
Tell me it isn't much farther!
It's not much farther!

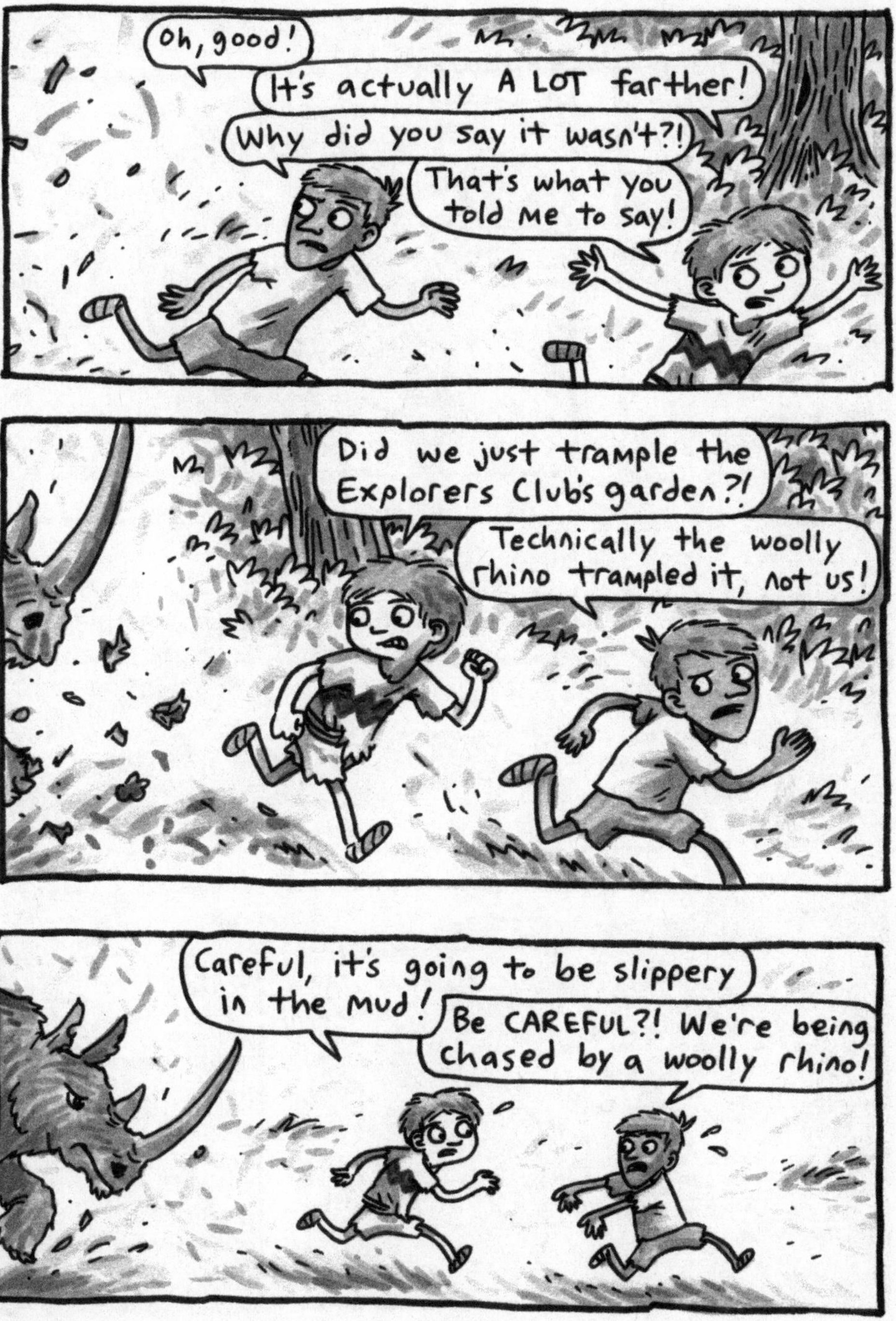
Oh, good!
It's actually A LOT farther!
Why did you say it wasn't?!
That's what you told me to say!
Did we just trample the Explorers Club's garden?!
Technically the woolly rhino trampled it, not us!
Careful, it's going to be slippery in the mud!
Be CAREFUL?! We're being chased by a woolly rhino!

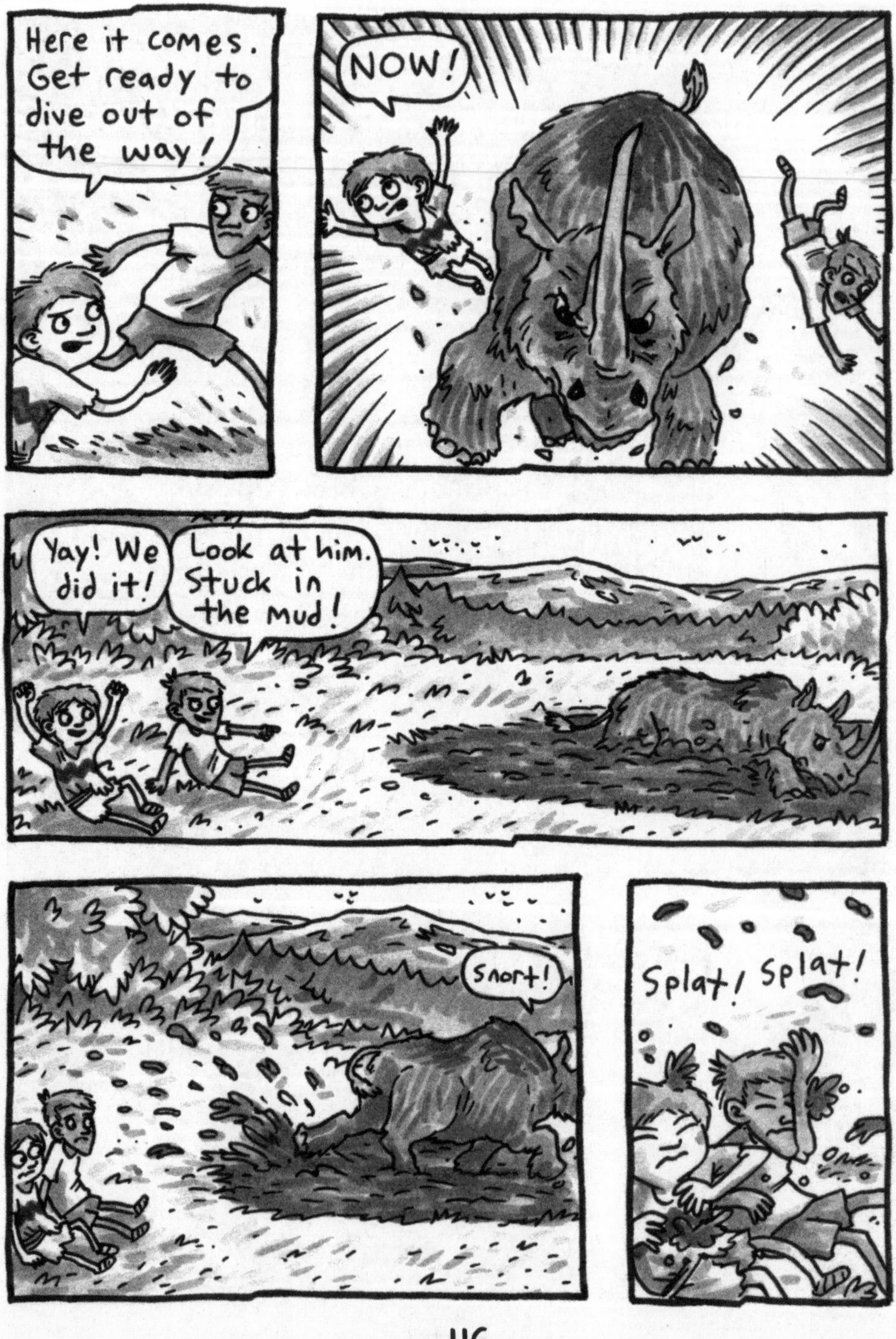
Here it comes. Get ready to dive out of the way!
NOW!
Yay! We did it!
Look at him. Stuck in the mud!
Snort!
Splat! Splat!

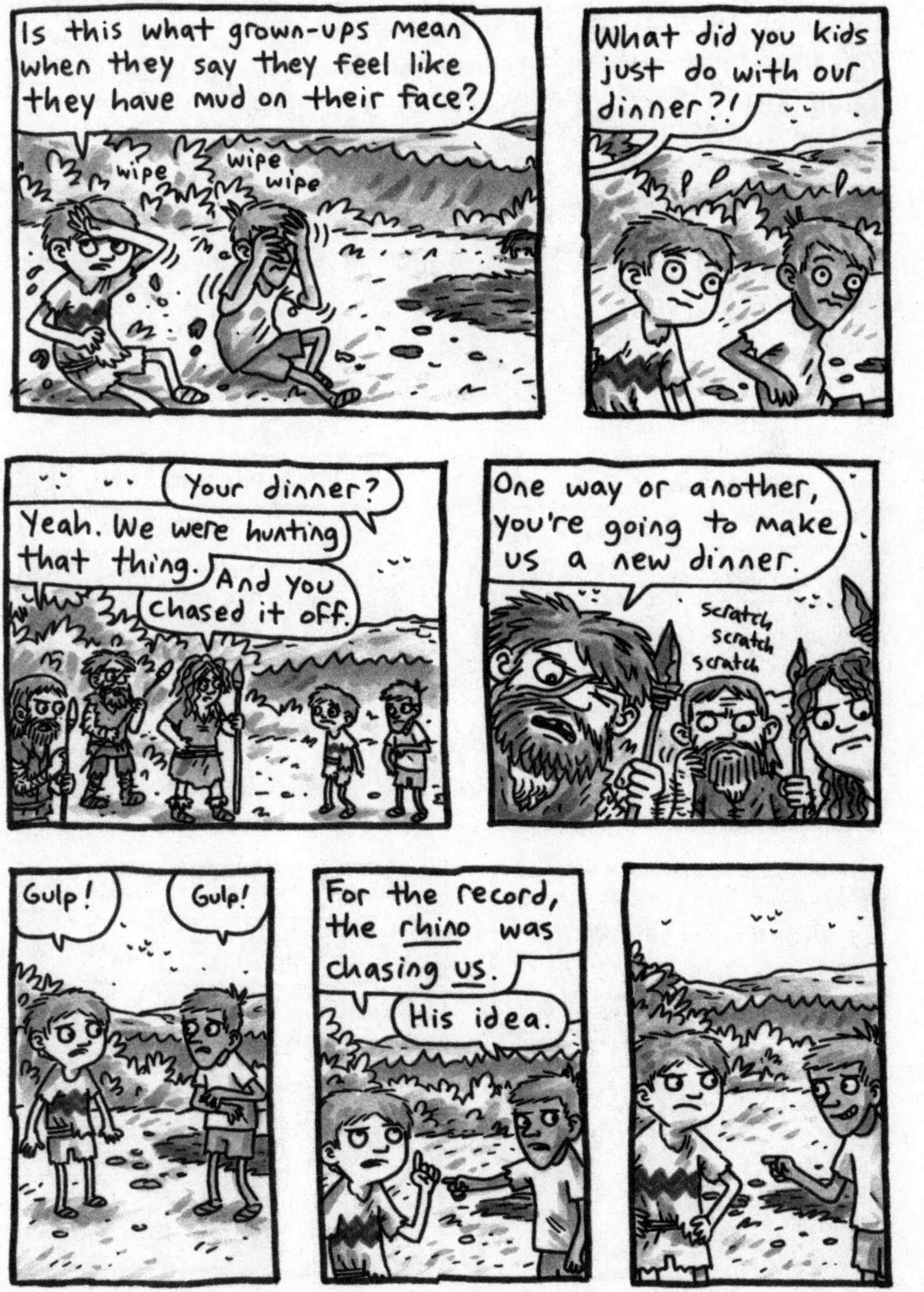
Is this what grown-ups mean when they say they feel like they have mud on their face?
wipe
wipe
wipe
What did you kids just do with our dinner?!
Your dinner?
Yeah. We were hunting that thing.
And you chased it off.
One way or another, you're going to make us a new dinner.
scratch
scratch
scratch
Gulp!
Gulp!
For the record, the rhino was chasing us.
His idea.

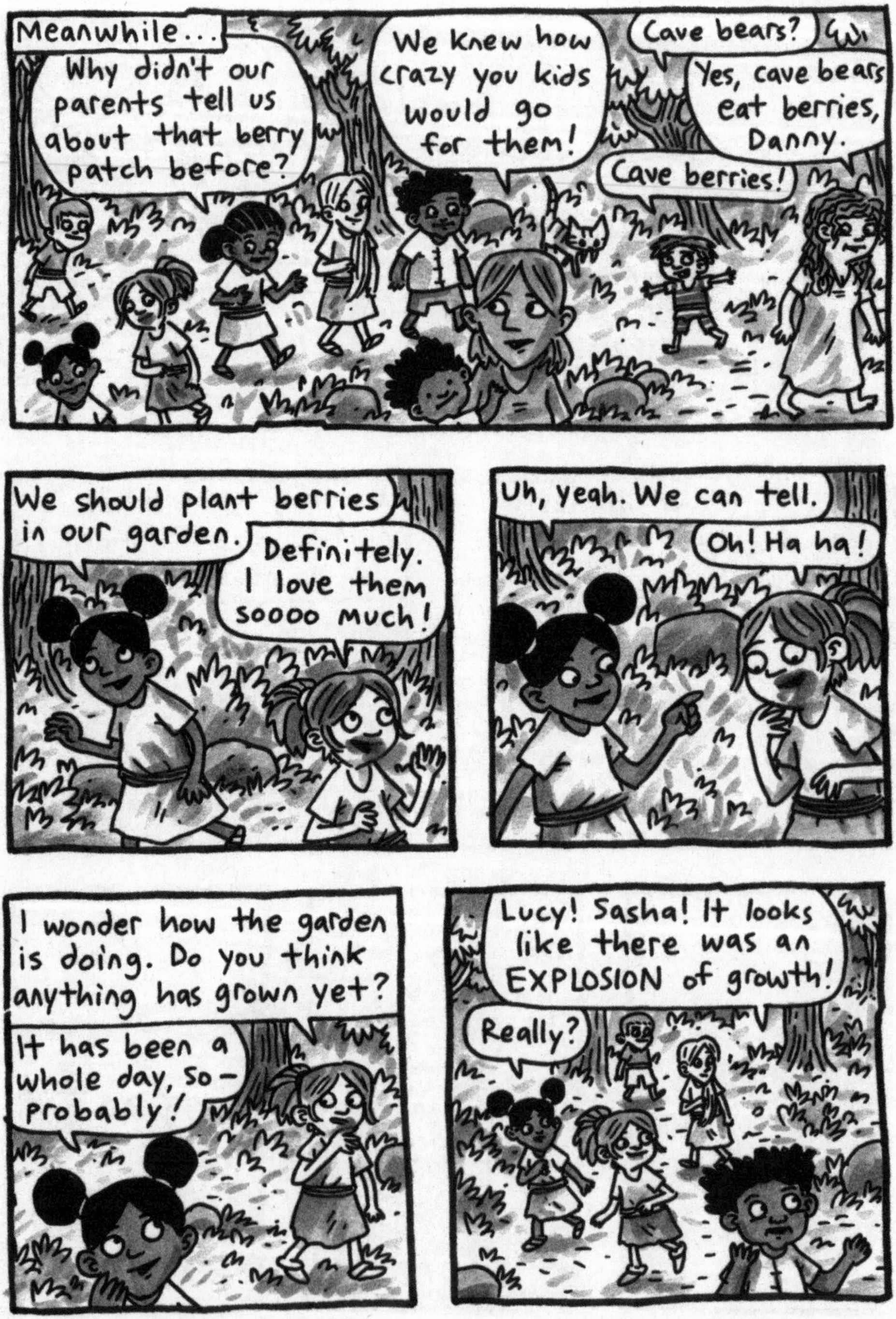
Meanwhile...
Why didn't our parents tell us about that berry patch before?
We knew how crazy you kids would go for them!
Cave bears?
Yes, cave bears eat berries, Danny.
Cave berries!
We should plant berries in our garden.
Definitely. I love them soooo much!
Uh, yeah. We can tell.
Oh! Ha ha!
I wonder how the garden is doing. Do you think anything has grown yet?
It has been a whole day, so—probably!
Lucy! Sasha! It looks like there was an EXPLOSION of growth!
Really?

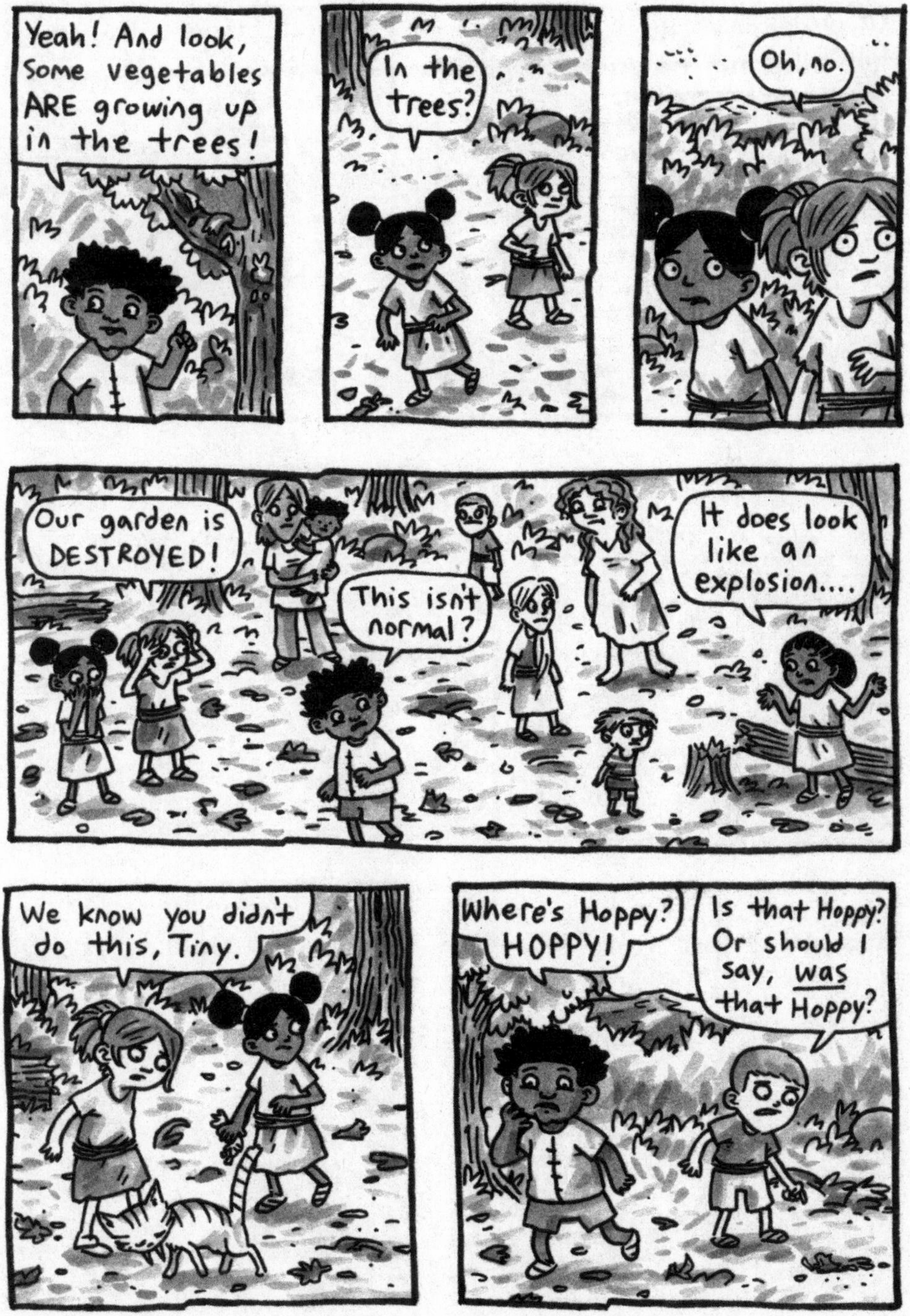
Yeah! And look, some vegetables ARE growing up in the trees!
In the trees?
Oh, no.
Our garden is DESTROYED!
This isn't normal?
It does look like an explosion....
We know you didn't do this, Tiny.
Where's Hoppy? HOPPY!
Is that Hoppy? Or should I say, was that Hoppy?

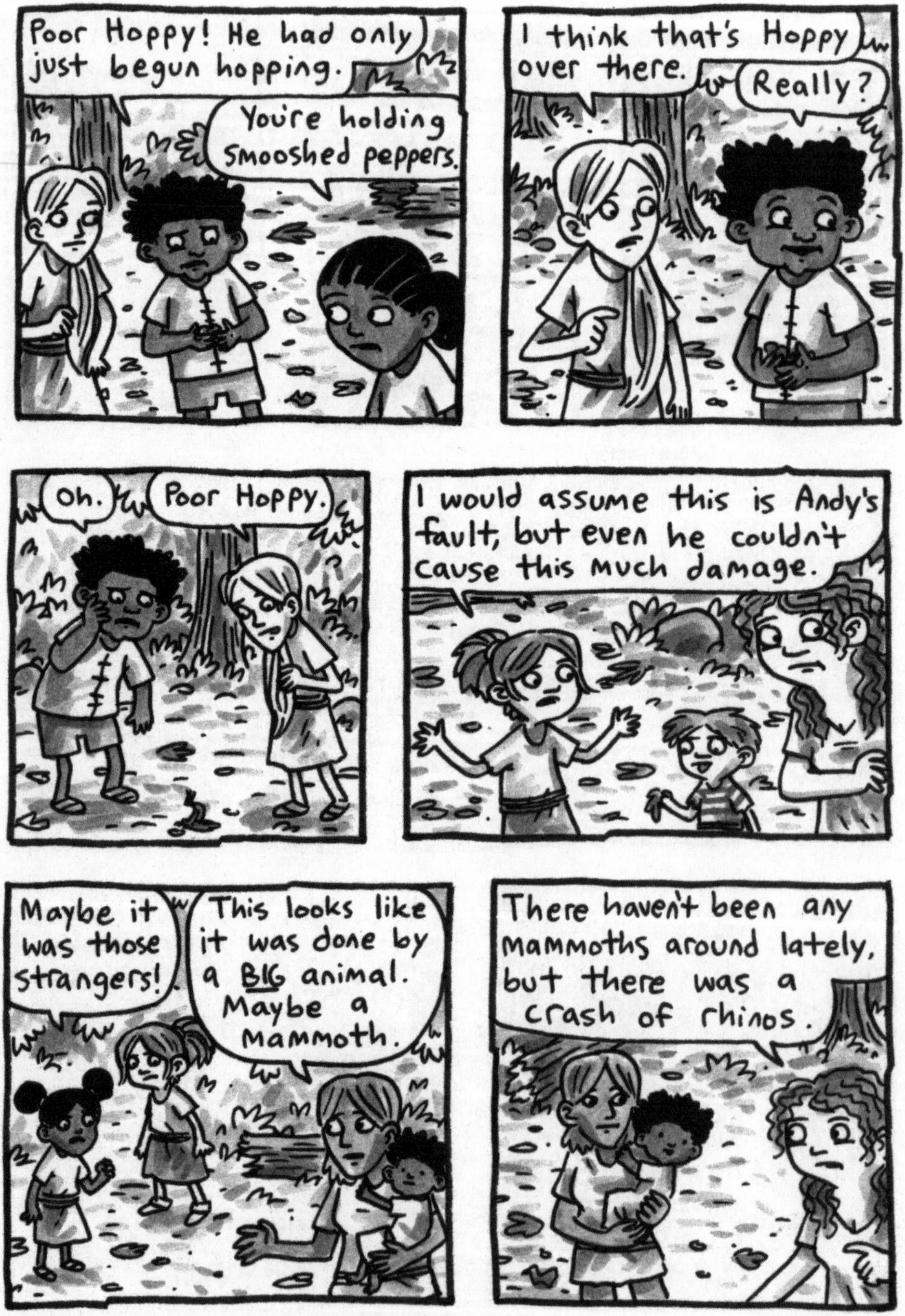
Poor Hoppy! He had only just begun hopping.
You're holding smooshed peppers.
I think that's Hoppy over there.
Really?
Oh.
Poor Hoppy.
I would assume this is Andy's fault, but even he couldn't cause this much damage.
Maybe it was those strangers!
This looks like it was done by a BIG animal. Maybe a mammoth.
There haven't been any mammoths around lately, but there was a crash of rhinos.

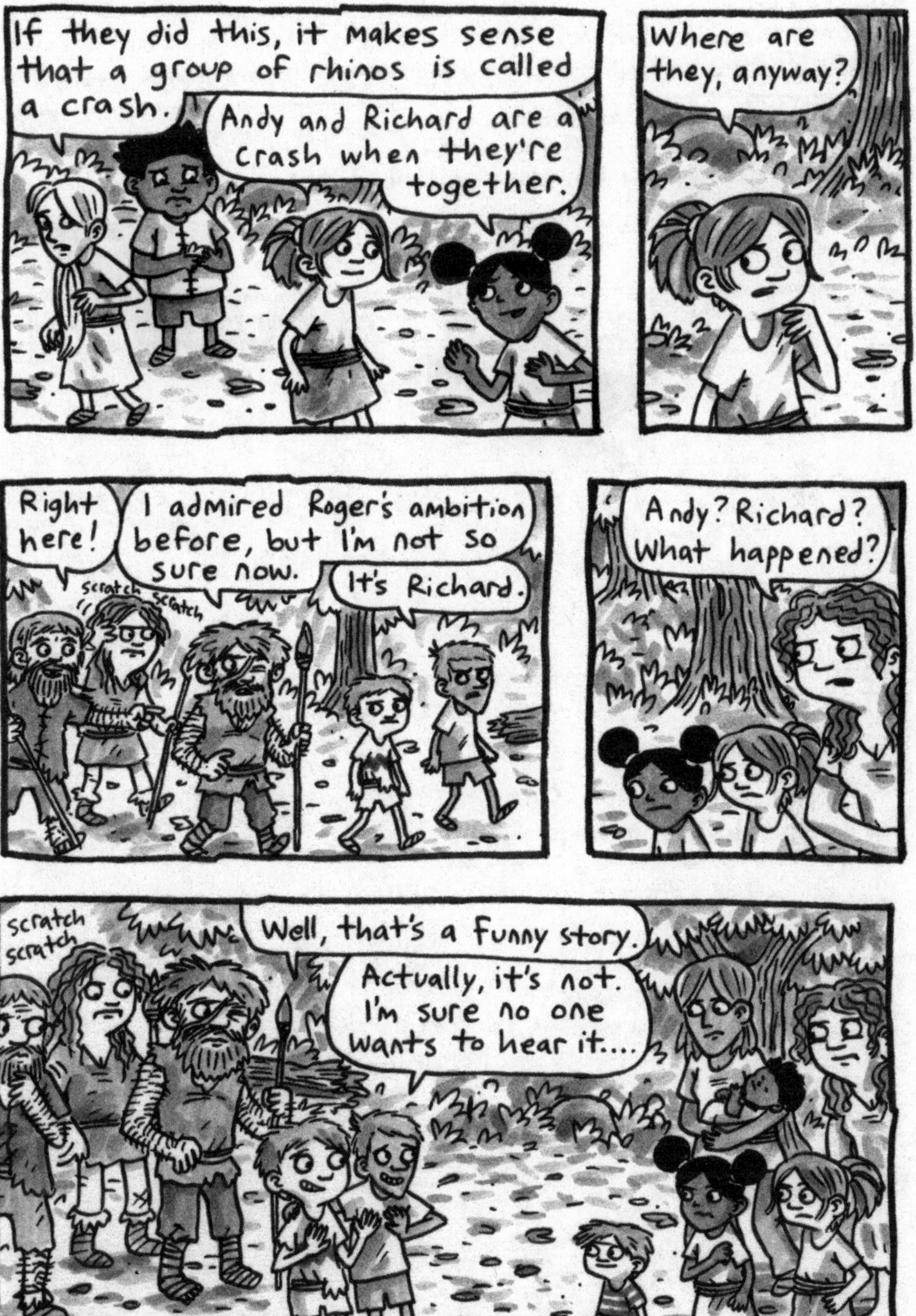
If they did this, it makes sense that a group of rhinos is called a crash.
Andy and Richard are a crash when they're together.
Where are they, anyway?
Right here!
I admired Roger's ambition before, but I'm not so sure now.
scratch scratch
It's Richard.
Andy? Richard? What happened?
scratch scratch
Well, that's a funny story.
Actually, it's not. I'm sure no one wants to hear it....

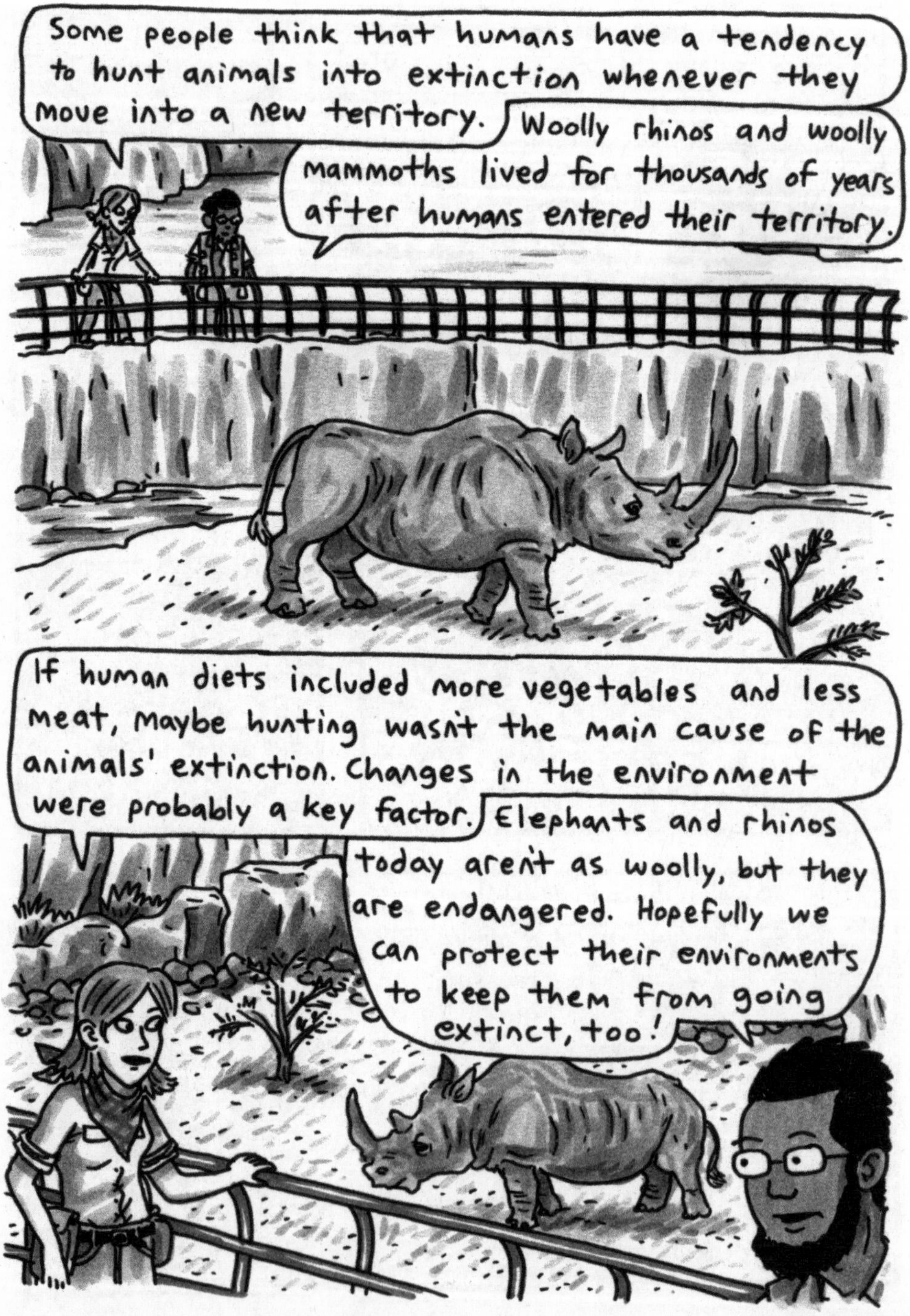
Some people think that humans have a tendency to hunt animals into extinction whenever they move into a new territory.
Woolly rhinos and woolly mammoths lived for thousands of years after humans entered their territory.
If human diets included more vegetables and less meat, maybe hunting wasn't the main cause of the animals' extinction. Changes in the environment were probably a key factor.
Elephants and rhinos today aren't as woolly, but they are endangered. Hopefully we can protect their environments to keep them from going extinct, too!

TALK OF THE CAVE

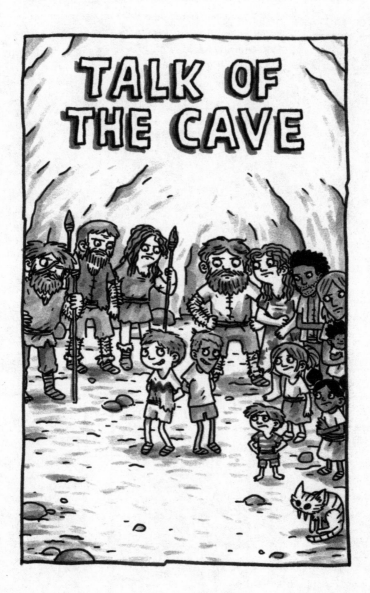

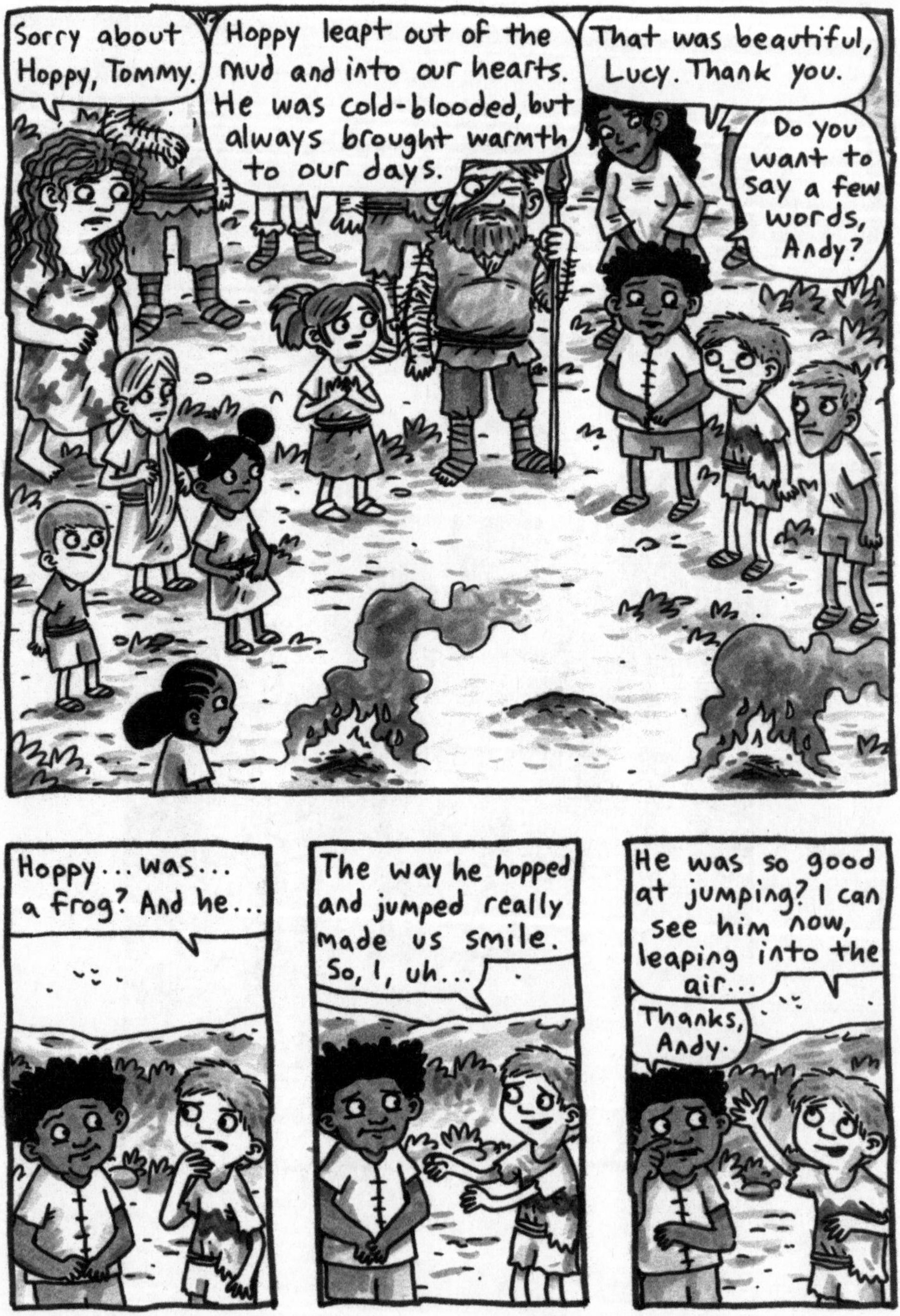
Sorry about Hoppy, Tommy.
Hoppy leapt out of the mud and into our hearts. He was cold-blooded, but always brought warmth to our days.
That was beautiful, Lucy. Thank you.
Do you want to say a few words, Andy?
Hoppy... was... a frog? And he...
The way he hopped and jumped really made us smile.
So, I, uh...
He was so good at jumping? I can see him now, leaping into the air...
Thanks, Andy.

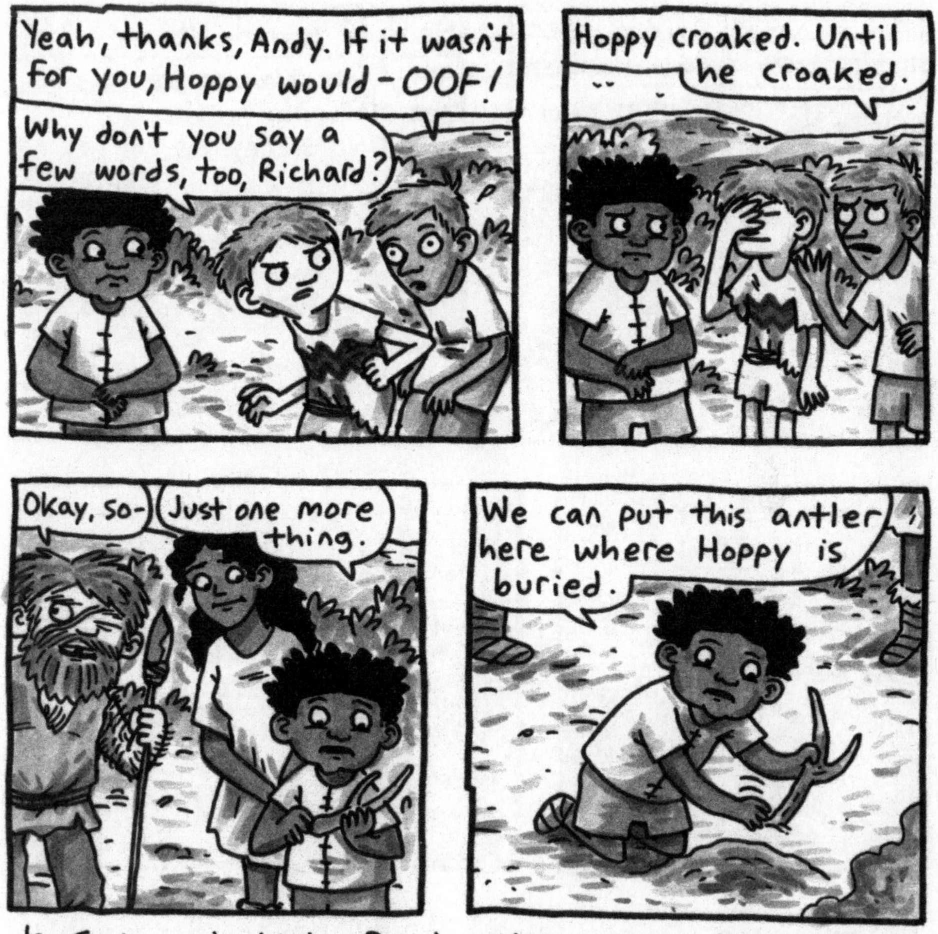
Yeah, thanks, Andy. If it wasn't for you, Hoppy would-OOF!
Why don't you say a few words, too, Richard?
Hoppy croaked. Until he croaked.
Okay, so-
Just one more thing.
We can put this antler here where Hoppy is buried.

In Spain, scientists found evidence that Neanderthals may have used fires in funeral rituals. The fires had been lit for a burial.

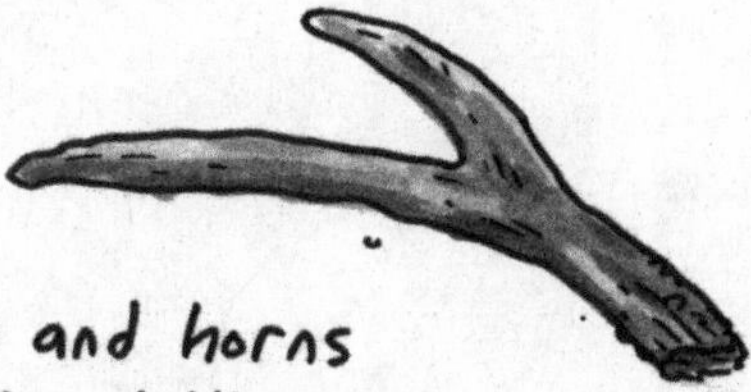

Antlers and horns were also deliberately placed in the fires.

But there's no indication that Neanderthals had funerals for pets. And they didn't have toilets for flushing pet goldfish!

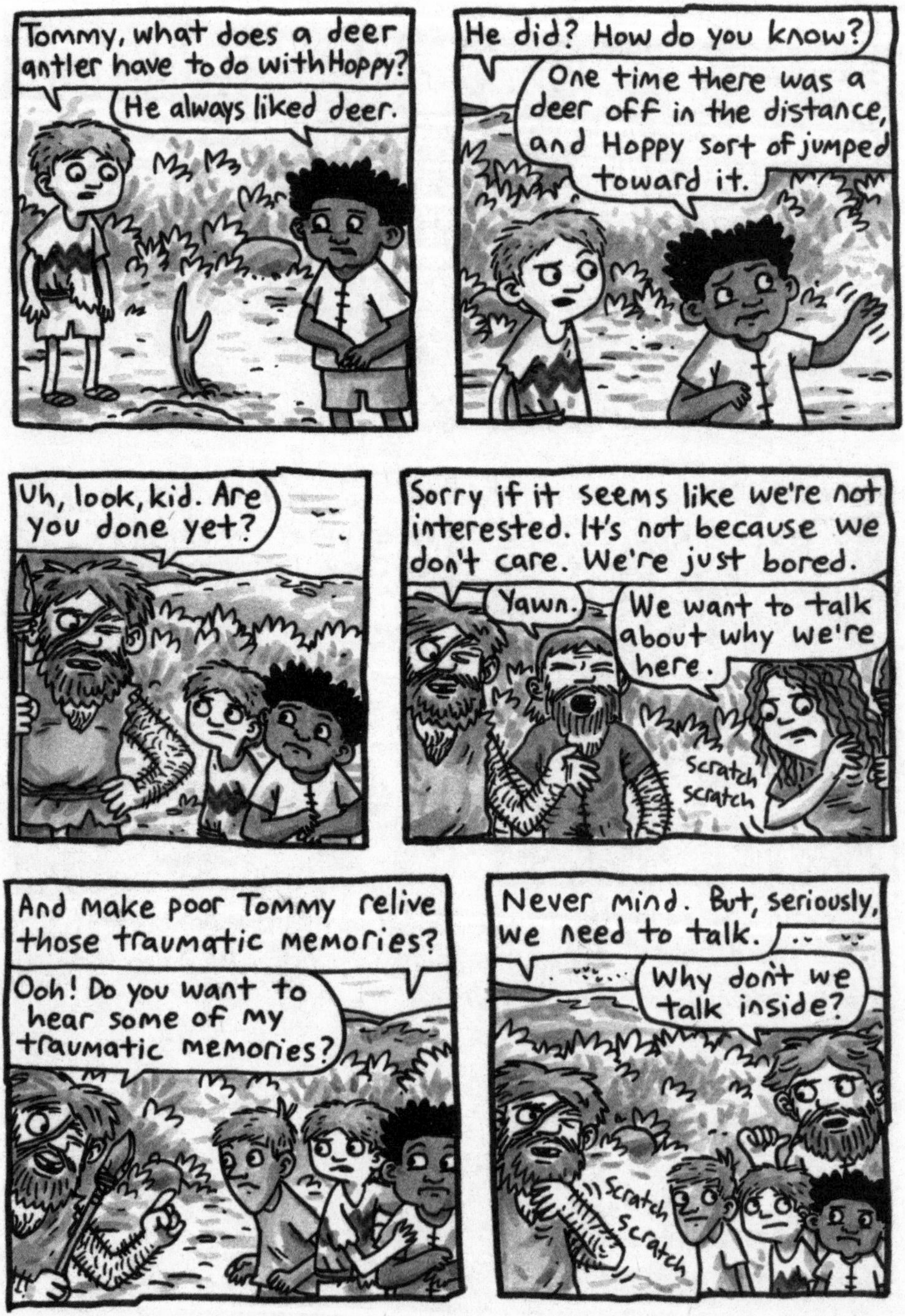
Tommy, what does a deer antler have to do with Hoppy?
He always liked deer.
He did? How do you know?
One time there was a deer off in the distance, and Hoppy sort of jumped toward it.
Uh, look, kid. Are you done yet?
Sorry if it seems like we're not interested. It's not because we don't care. We're just bored.
Yawn.
We want to talk about why we're here.
Scratch scratch
And make poor Tommy relive those traumatic memories?
Ooh! Do you want to hear some of my traumatic memories?
Never mind. But, seriously, we need to talk.
Why don't we talk inside?
Scratch scratch

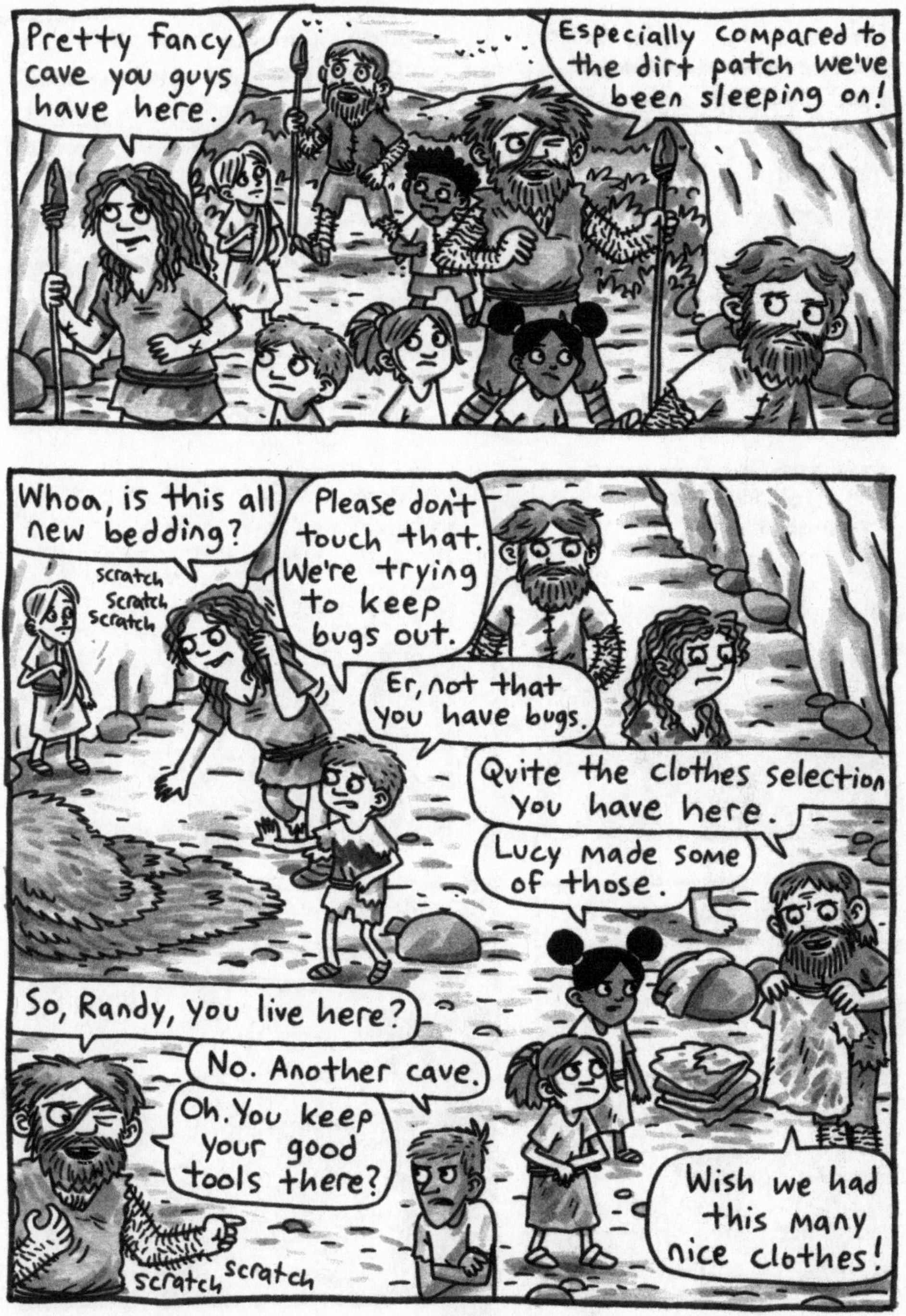
Pretty fancy cave you guys have here.
Especially compared to the dirt patch we've been sleeping on!
Whoa, is this all new bedding?
scratch scratch scratch
Please don't touch that. We're trying to keep bugs out.
Er, not that you have bugs.
Quite the clothes selection you have here.
Lucy made some of those.
So, Randy, you live here?
No. Another cave.
Oh. You keep your good tools there?
scratch scratch
Wish we had this many nice clothes!

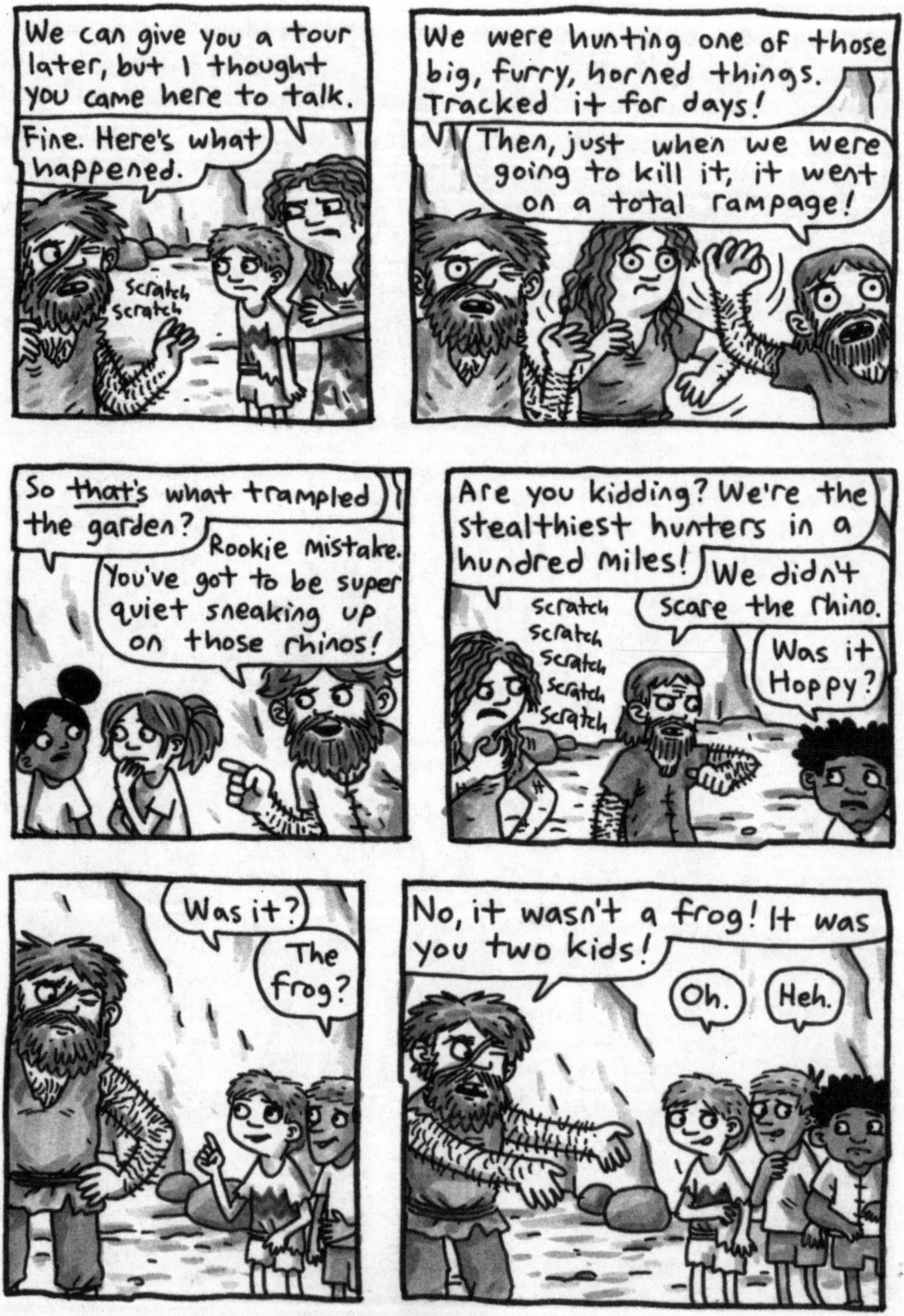
We can give you a tour later, but I thought you came here to talk.
Fine. Here's what happened.
Scratch scratch
We were hunting one of those big, furry, horned things. Tracked it for days!
Then, just when we were going to kill it, it went on a total rampage!
So that's what trampled the garden?
Rookie mistake. You've got to be super quiet sneaking up on those rhinos!
Are you kidding? We're the stealthiest hunters in a hundred miles!
We didn't scare the rhino.
Scratch scratch scratch scratch scratch
Was it Hoppy?
Was it?
The frog?
No, it wasn't a frog! It was you two kids!
Oh.
Heh.

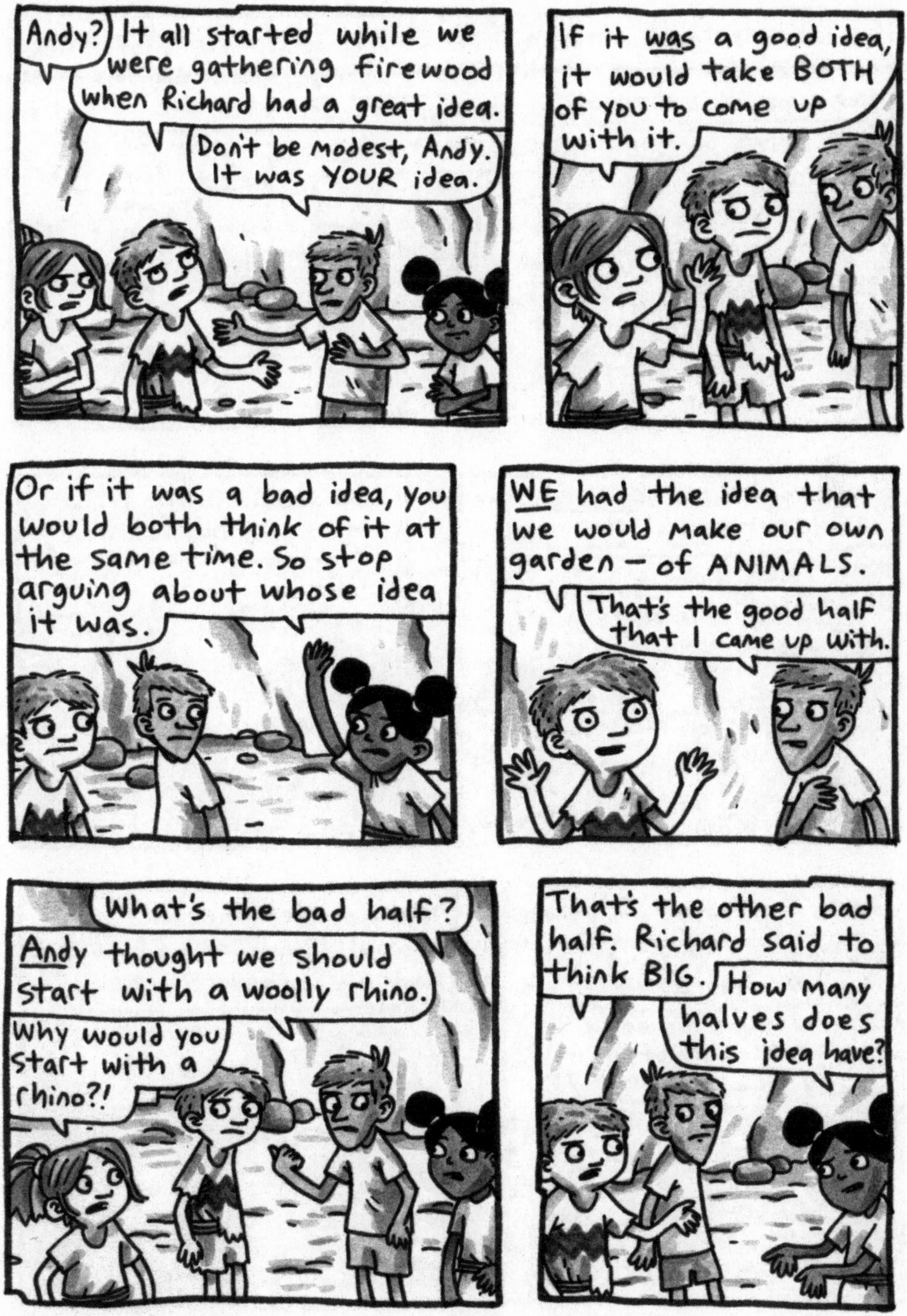
Andy?
It all started while we were gathering firewood when Richard had a great idea.
Don't be modest, Andy. It was YOUR idea.
If it was a good idea, it would take BOTH of you to come up with it.
Or if it was a bad idea, you would both think of it at the same time. So stop arguing about whose idea it was.
WE had the idea that we would make our own garden—of ANIMALS.
That's the good half that I came up with.
What's the bad half?
Andy thought we should start with a woolly rhino.
Why would you start with a rhino?!
That's the other bad half. Richard said to think BIG.
How many halves does this idea have?

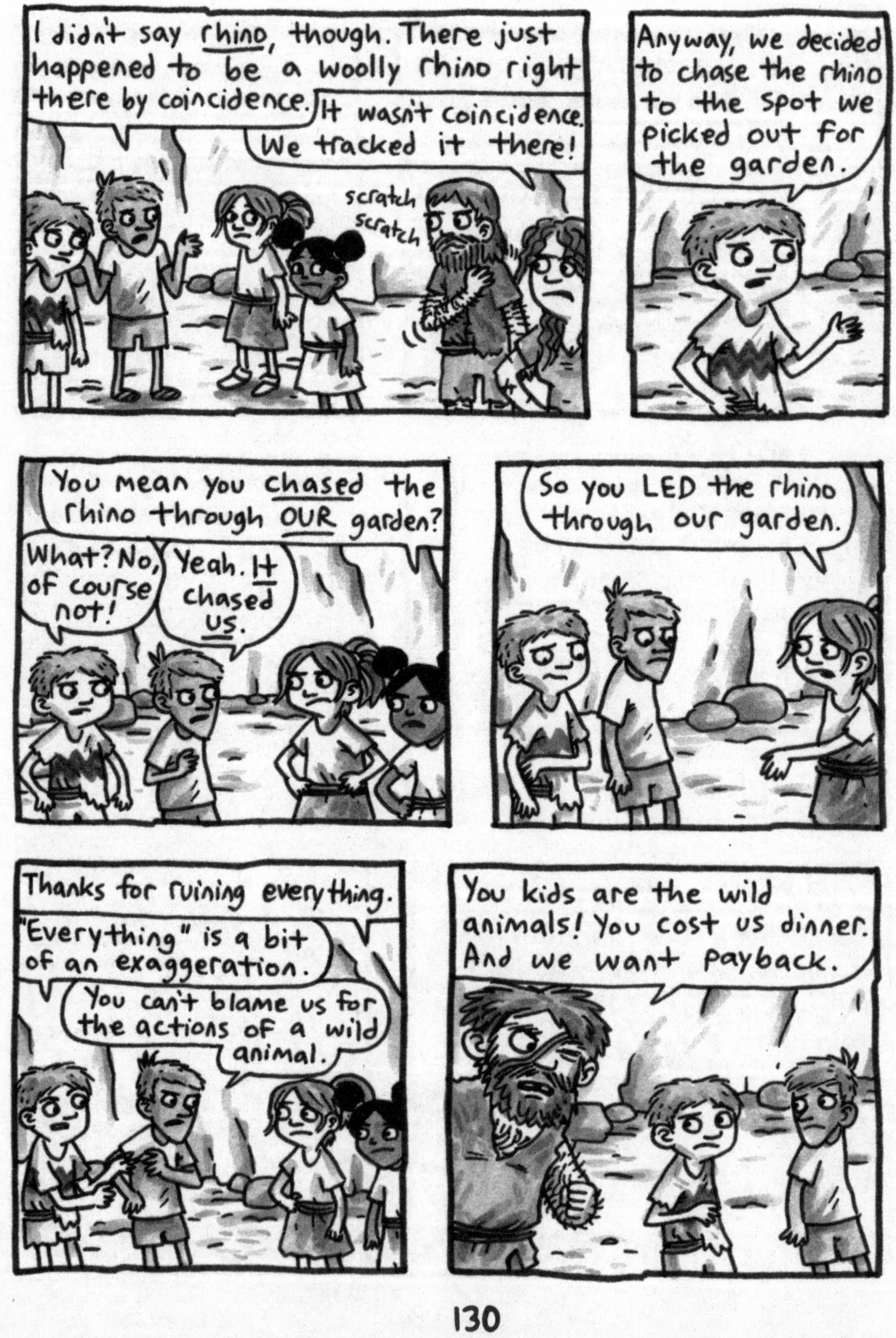
I didn't say rhino, though. There just happened to be a woolly rhino right there by coincidence.
It wasn't coincidence. We tracked it there!
scratch scratch
Anyway, we decided to chase the rhino to the spot we picked out for the garden.
You mean you chased the rhino through OUR garden?
What? No, of course not!
Yeah. It chased us.
So you LED the rhino through our garden.
Thanks for ruining everything.
"Everything" is a bit of an exaggeration.
You can't blame us for the actions of a wild animal.
You kids are the wild animals! You cost us dinner. And we want payback.

You can join us for dinner. We're about to cook up some tortoise soup.
Kids, we need some more tortoises for our guests.
Does this mean we have time for a tour?
I'm tired of catching tortoises. There are too many people.
At least it's easy.
I'll help.
Aren't you mad that we, you know, caused Hoppy's... accident?
It's okay. He was just a frog.

Tortoise shells with marks indicating they were roasted have been found in caves dating back almost 400,000 years ago.

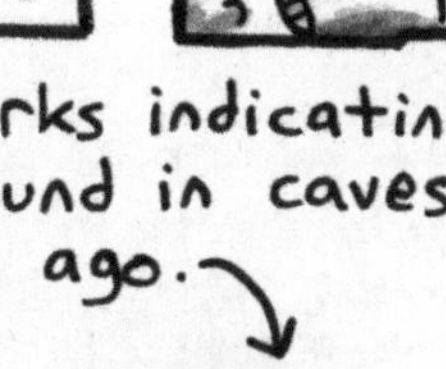

Neanderthals may have mostly eaten large prey, but turtles and tortoises provided additional sources of meat.

Hunting tortoises wasn't as dangerous as hunting rhinos, but it would still hurt to drop one on your foot!

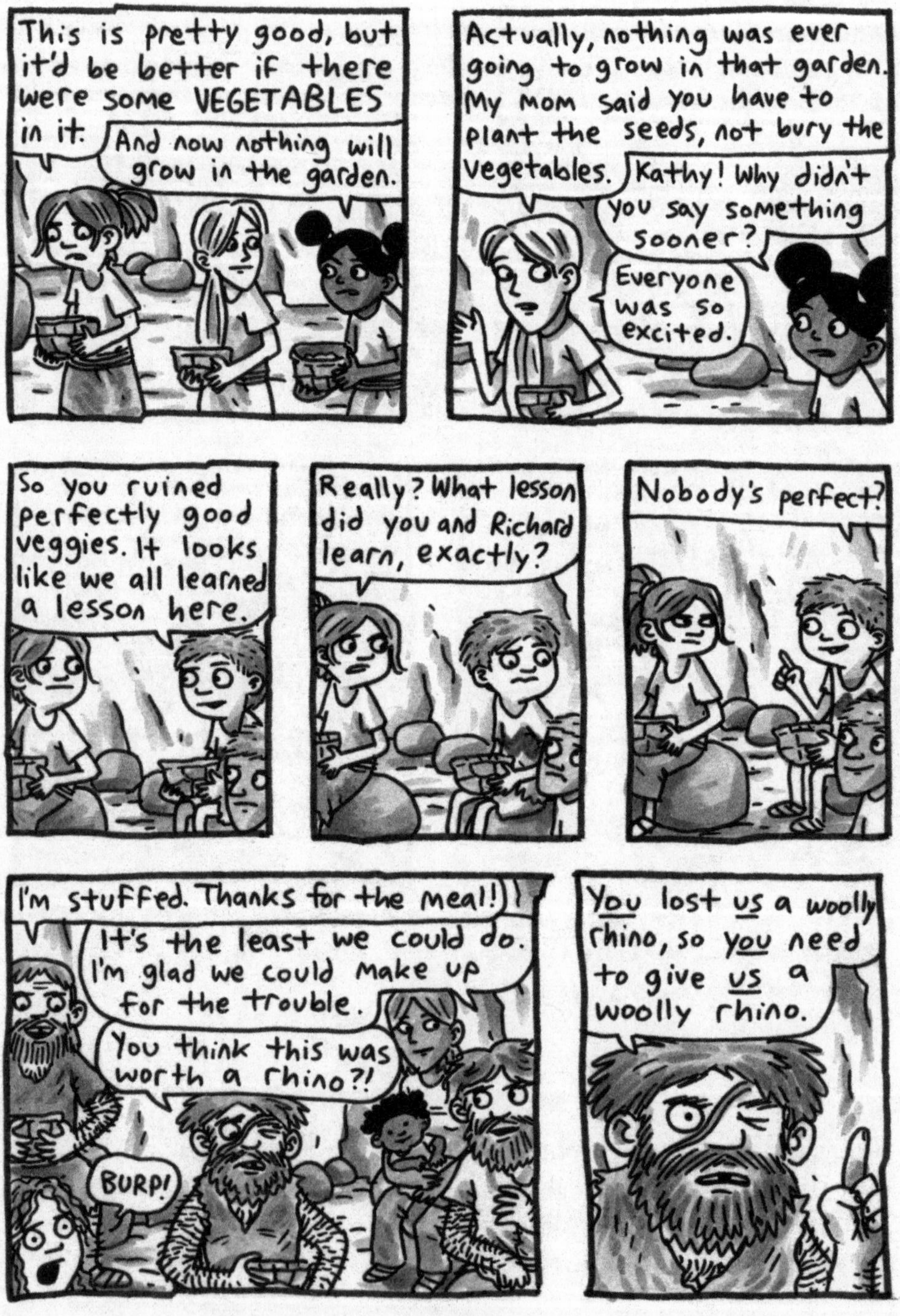
This is pretty good, but it'd be better if there were some VEGETABLES in it.
And now nothing will grow in the garden.
Actually, nothing was ever going to grow in that garden. My mom said you have to plant the seeds, not bury the vegetables.
Kathy! Why didn't you say something sooner?
Everyone was so excited.
So you ruined perfectly good veggies. It looks like we all learned a lesson here.
Really? What lesson did you and Richard learn, exactly?
Nobody's perfect?
I'm stuffed. Thanks for the meal!
It's the least we could do. I'm glad we could make up for the trouble.
You think this was worth a rhino?!
BURP!
You lost us a woolly rhino, so you need to give us a woolly rhino.

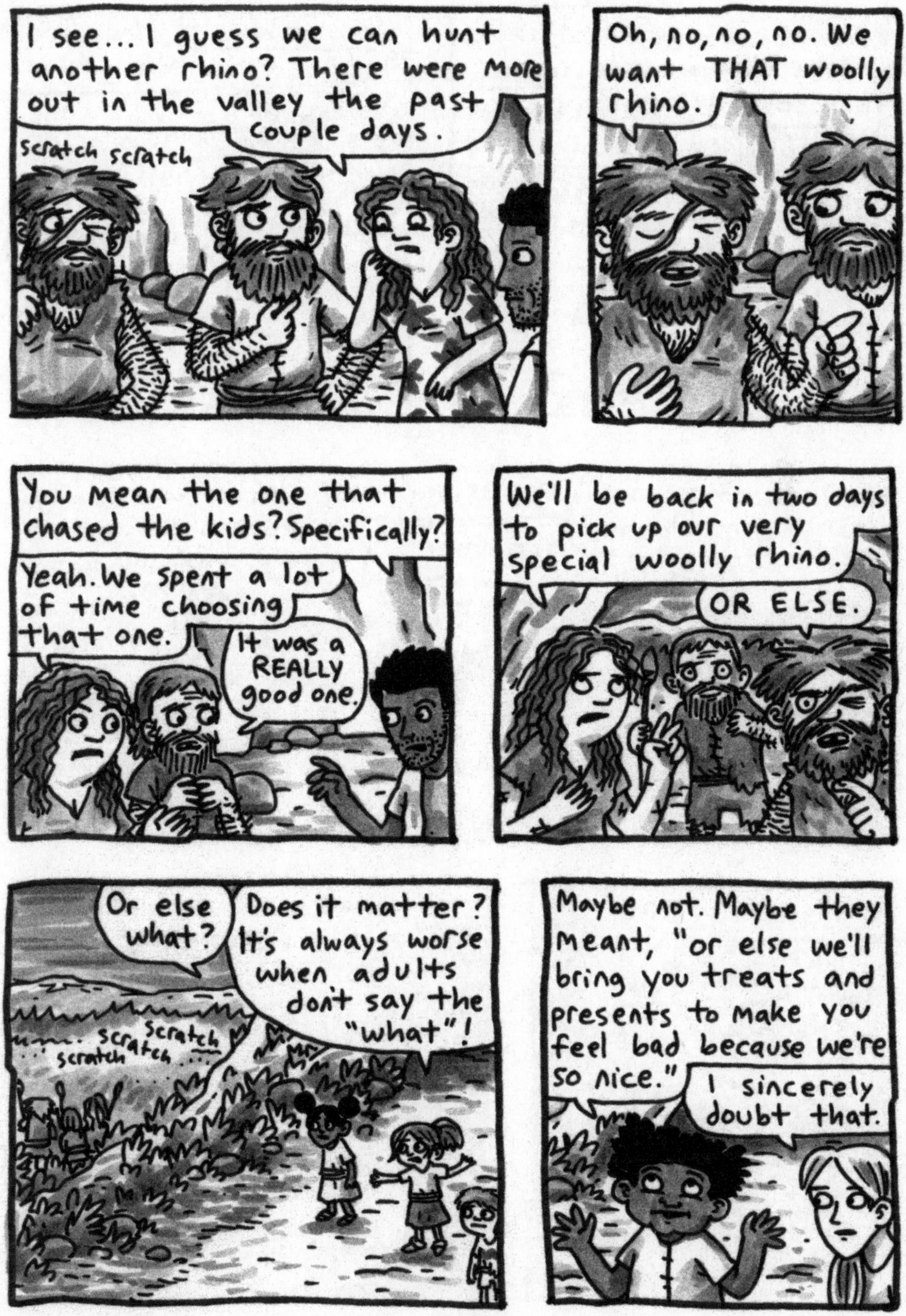
I see... I guess we can hunt another rhino? There were more out in the valley the past couple days.
scratch scratch
Oh, no, no, no. We want THAT woolly rhino.
You mean the one that chased the kids? Specifically?
Yeah. We spent a lot of time choosing that one.
It was a REALLY good one.
We'll be back in two days to pick up our very special woolly rhino.
OR ELSE.
Or else what?
Does it matter? It's always worse when adults don't say the "what"!
scratch scratch scratch
Maybe not. Maybe they meant, "or else we'll bring you treats and presents to make you feel bad because we're so nice."
I sincerely doubt that.

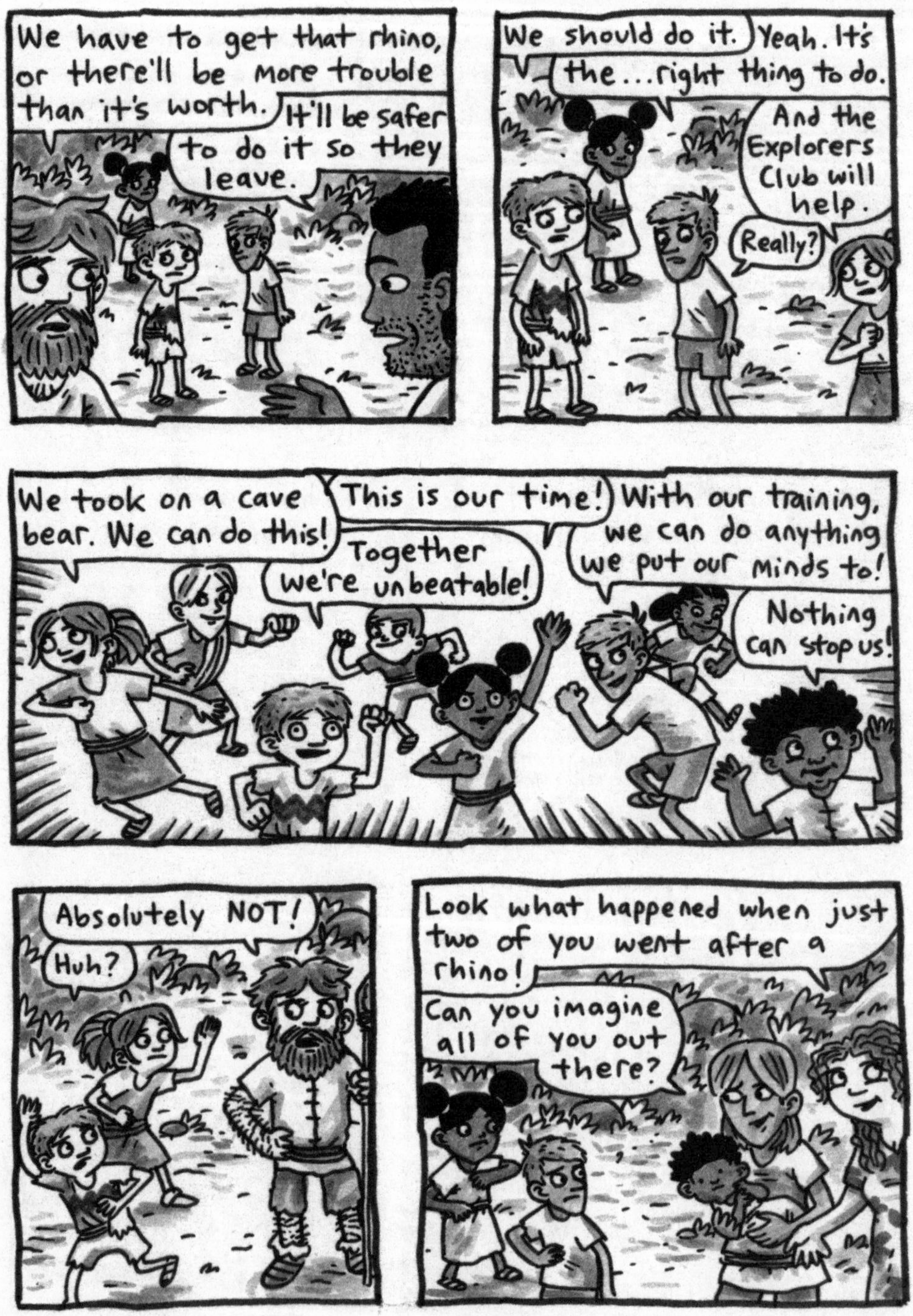
We have to get that rhino, or there'll be more trouble than it's worth.
It'll be safer to do it so they leave.
We should do it.
Yeah. It's the...right thing to do.
And the Explorers Club will help.
Really?
We took on a cave bear. We can do this!
This is our time!
With our training, we can do anything we put our minds to!
Together we're unbeatable!
Nothing can stop us!
Absolutely NOT!
Huh?
Look what happened when just two of you went after a rhino!
Can you imagine all of you out there?

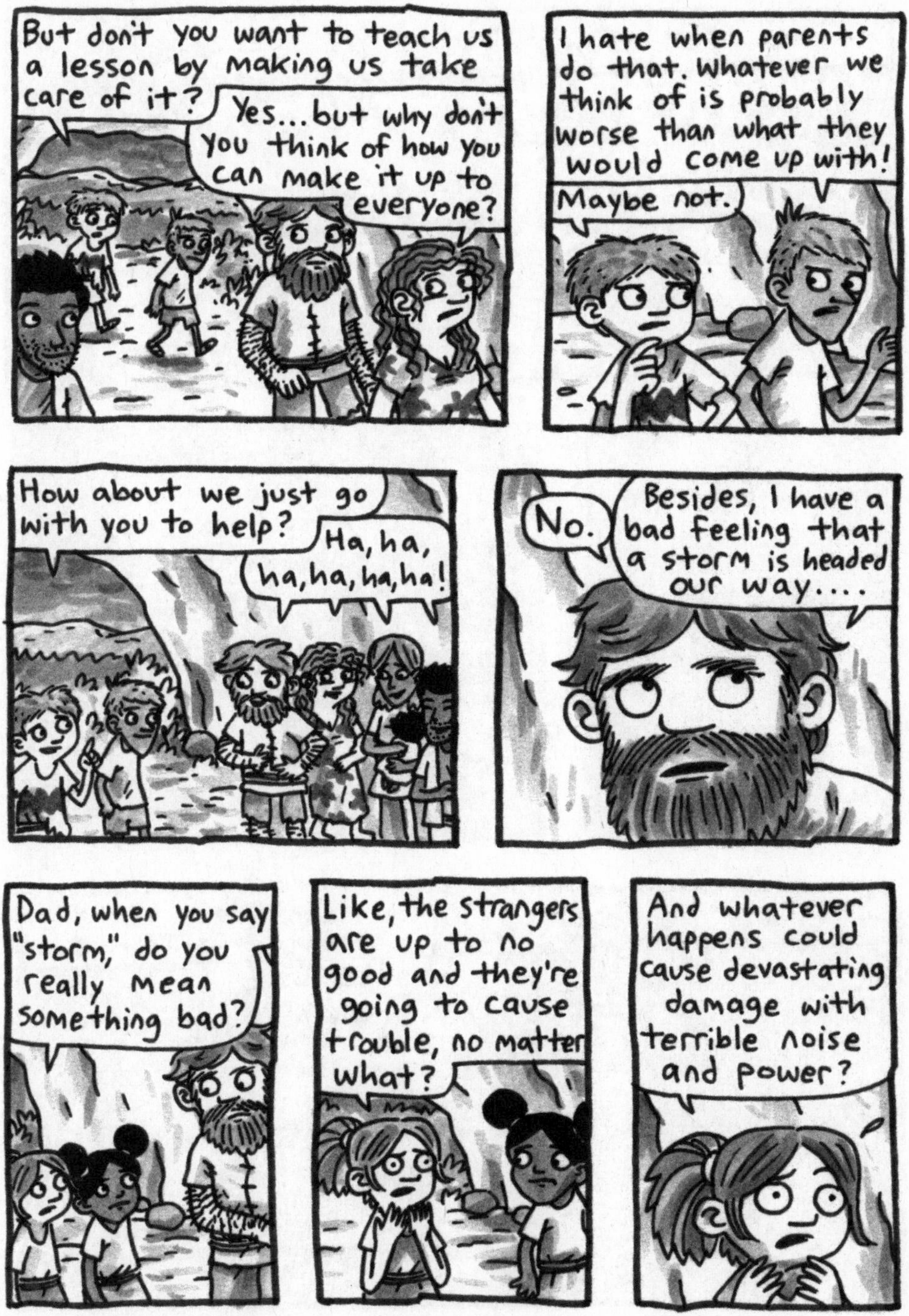
But don't you want to teach us a lesson by making us take care of it?
Yes...but why don't you think of how you can make it up to everyone?
I hate when parents do that. Whatever we think of is probably worse than what they would come up with!
Maybe not.
How about we just go with you to help?
Ha, ha, ha, ha, ha, ha!
No.
Besides, I have a bad feeling that a storm is headed our way....
Dad, when you say "storm," do you really mean something bad?
Like, the strangers are up to no good and they're going to cause trouble, no matter what?
And whatever happens could cause devastating damage with terrible noise and power?

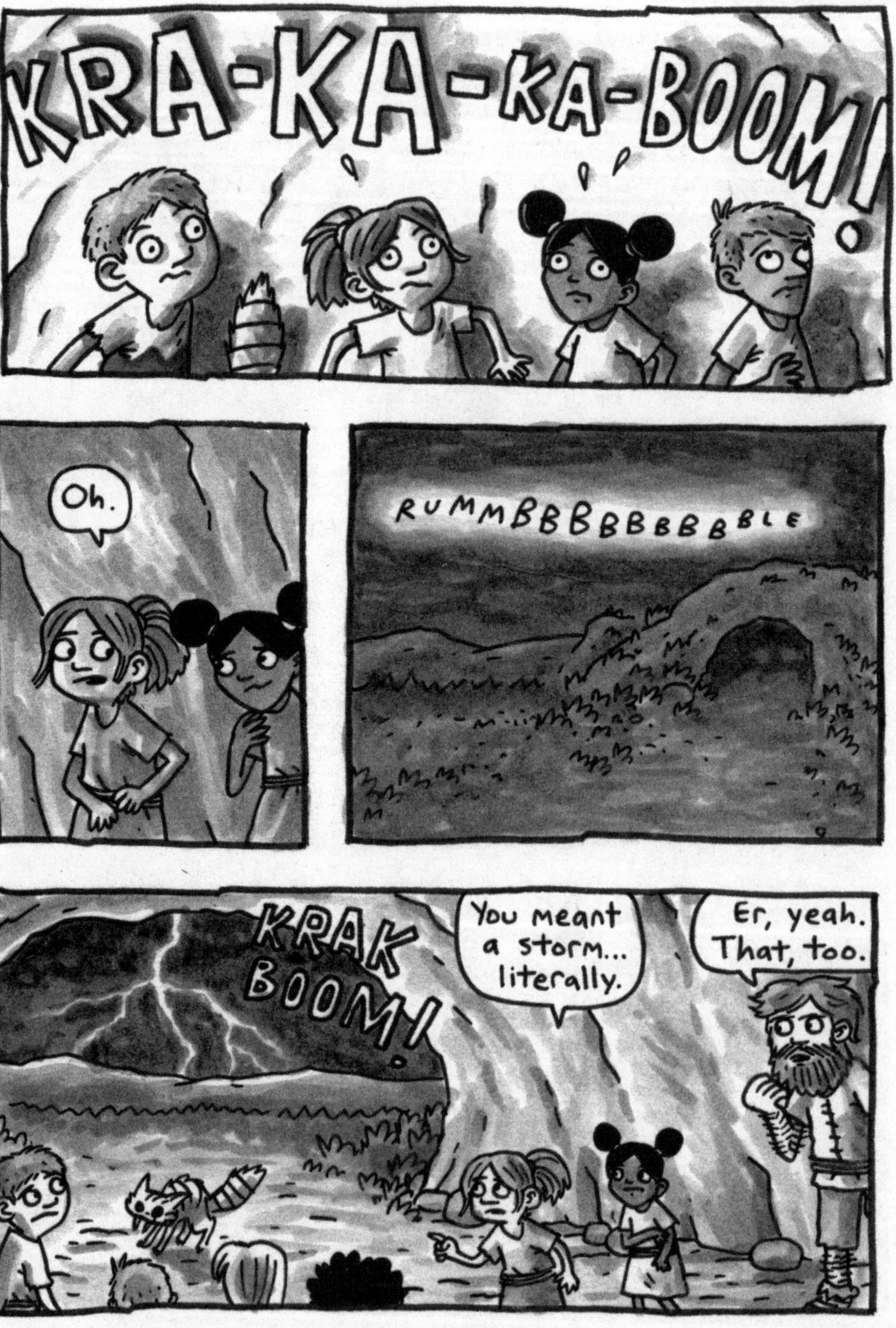
KRA-KA-KA-BOOM!
Oh.
RUMMBBBBBBBBBLE
KRAK BOOM!
You meant a storm... literally.
Er, yeah. That, too.

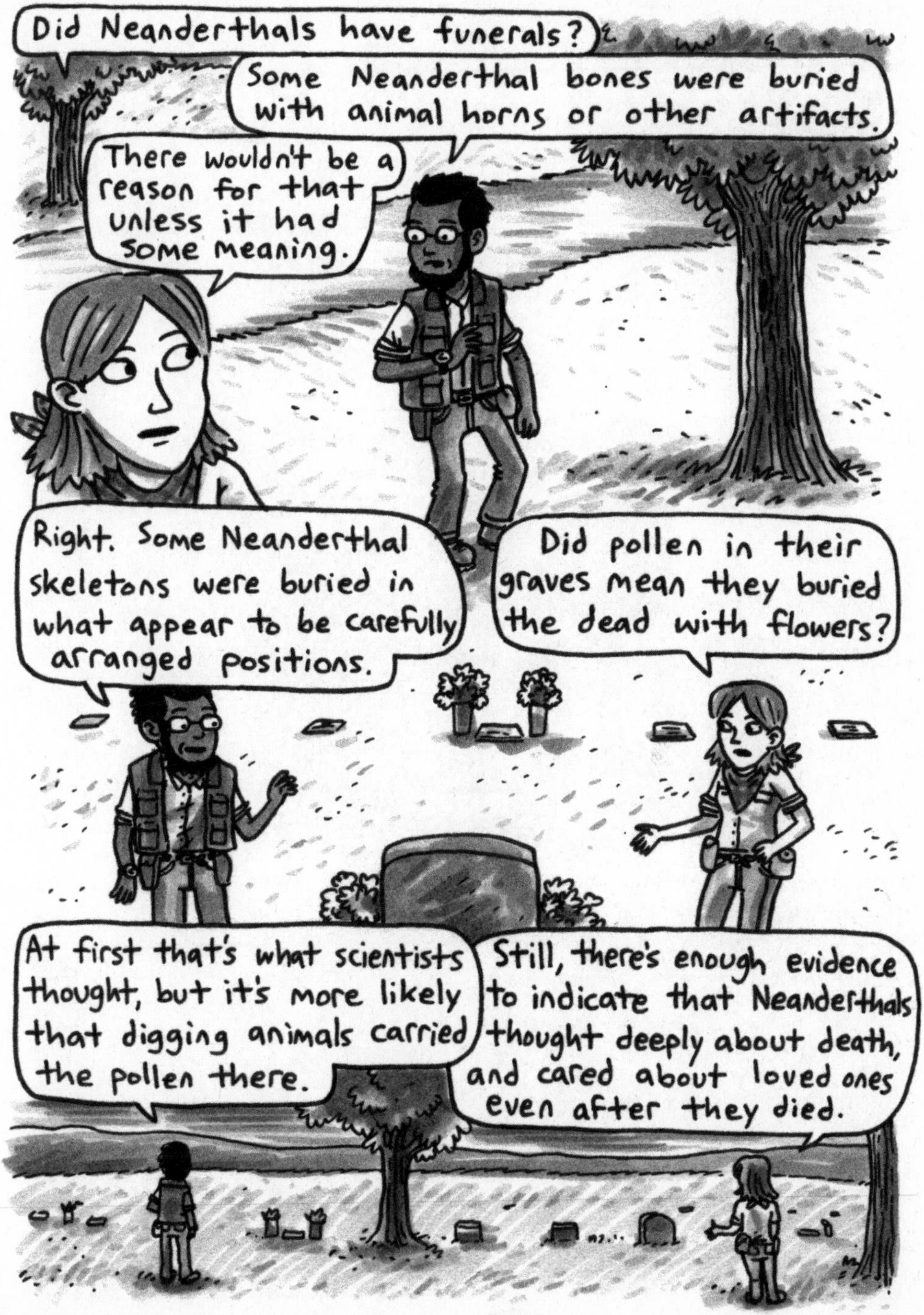
Did Neanderthals have funerals?
Some Neanderthal bones were buried with animal horns or other artifacts.
There wouldn't be a reason for that unless it had some meaning.
Right. Some Neanderthal skeletons were buried in what appear to be carefully arranged positions.
Did pollen in their graves mean they buried the dead with flowers?
At first that's what scientists thought, but it's more likely that digging animals carried the pollen there.
Still, there's enough evidence to indicate that Neanderthals thought deeply about death, and cared about loved ones even after they died.

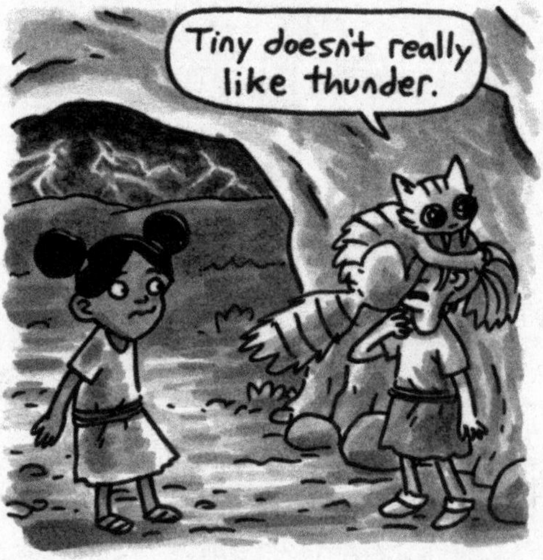
Tiny doesn't really like thunder.

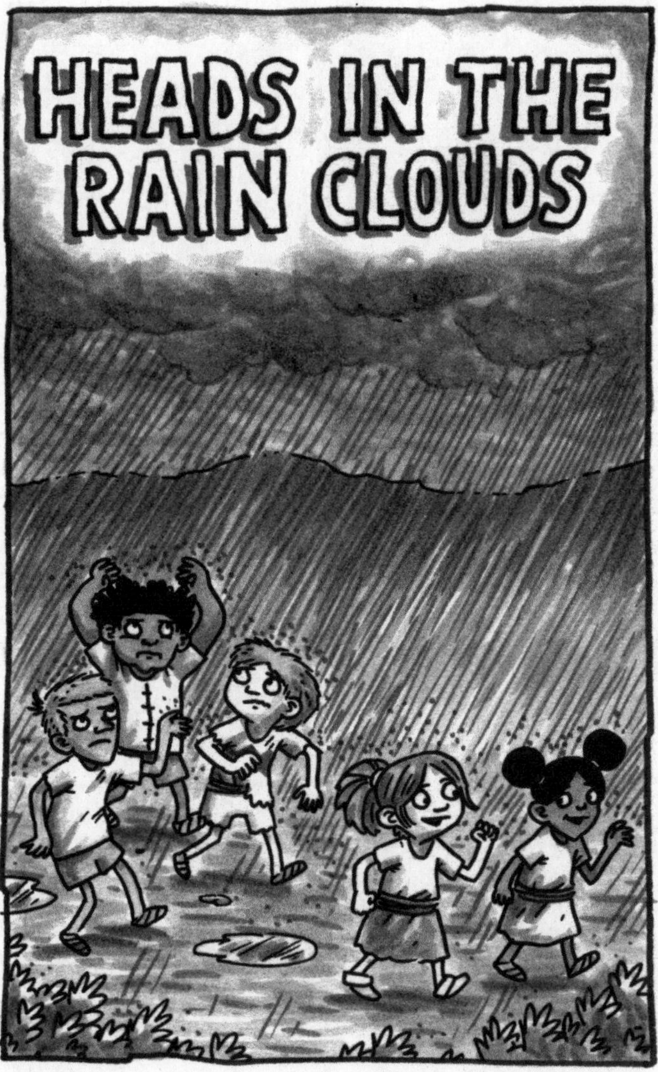
HEADS IN THE
RAIN CLOUDS

Good thing last night's storm has passed. It should be easier to track the rhino.
How would the strangers know which rhino it is, anyway?
Yeah! Dad, why can't you just hunt a different one?
Did the rhino have anything special that could identify it, Richard?
No. Other than the unique pattern of fur on its back.
And one ear was bitten off.
And its horn was bent to the side a little...
And...
I know what the answer's going to be, but... Dad, can I come with you?
Sure!
Sure?
What's the catch?
Catch? There's no catch.
So I can really come on the rhino hunt?
Rhino hunt? No way! I'm not going on the rhino hunt.
Huh?

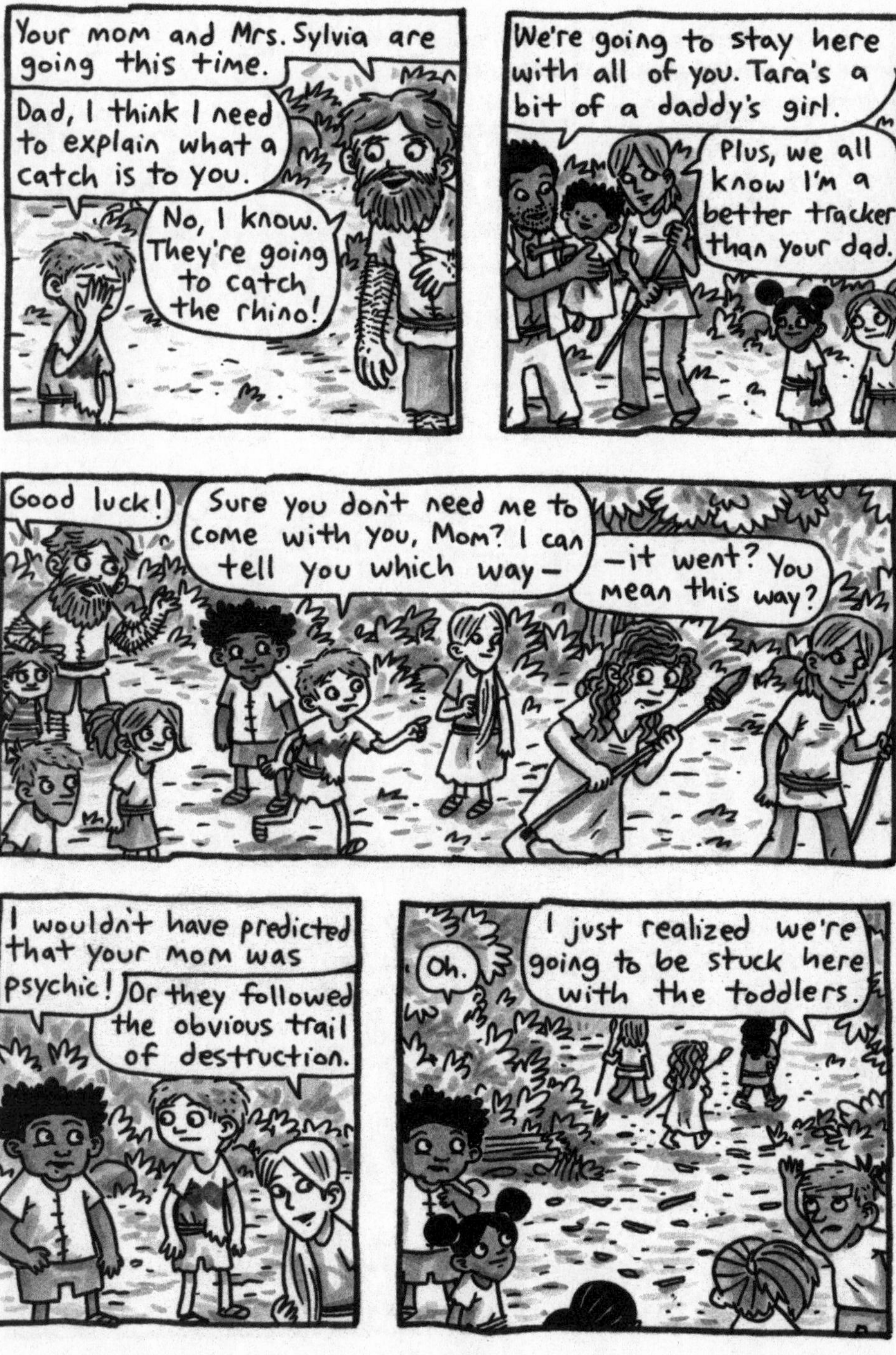
Your mom and Mrs. Sylvia are going this time.
Dad, I think I need to explain what a catch is to you.
No, I know. They're going to catch the rhino!
We're going to stay here with all of you. Tara's a bit of a daddy's girl.
Plus, we all know I'm a better tracker than your dad.
Good luck!
Sure you don't need me to come with you, Mom? I can tell you which way—
—it went? You mean this way?
I wouldn't have predicted that your mom was psychic!
Or they followed the obvious trail of destruction.
Oh.
I just realized we're going to be stuck here with the toddlers.

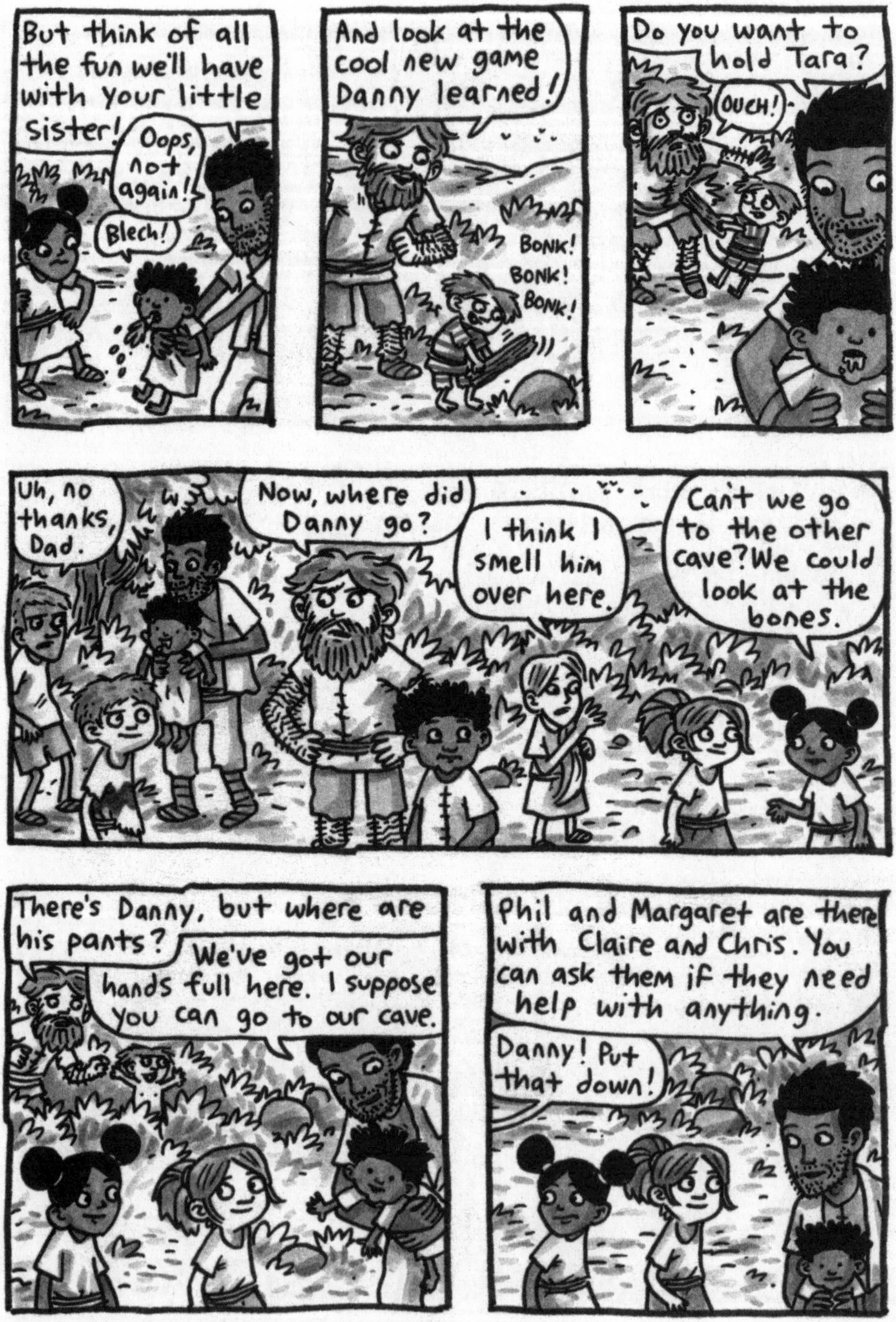

But think of all the fun we'll have with your little sister!
Oops, not again!
Blech!
And look at the cool new game Danny learned!
BONK! BONK! BONK!
Do you want to hold Tara?
OUCH!
Uh, no thanks, Dad.
Now, where did Danny go?
I think I smell him over here.
Can't we go to the other cave? We could look at the bones.
There's Danny, but where are his pants?
We've got our hands full here. I suppose you can go to our cave.
Phil and Margaret are there with Claire and Chris. You can ask them if they need help with anything.
Danny! Put that down!

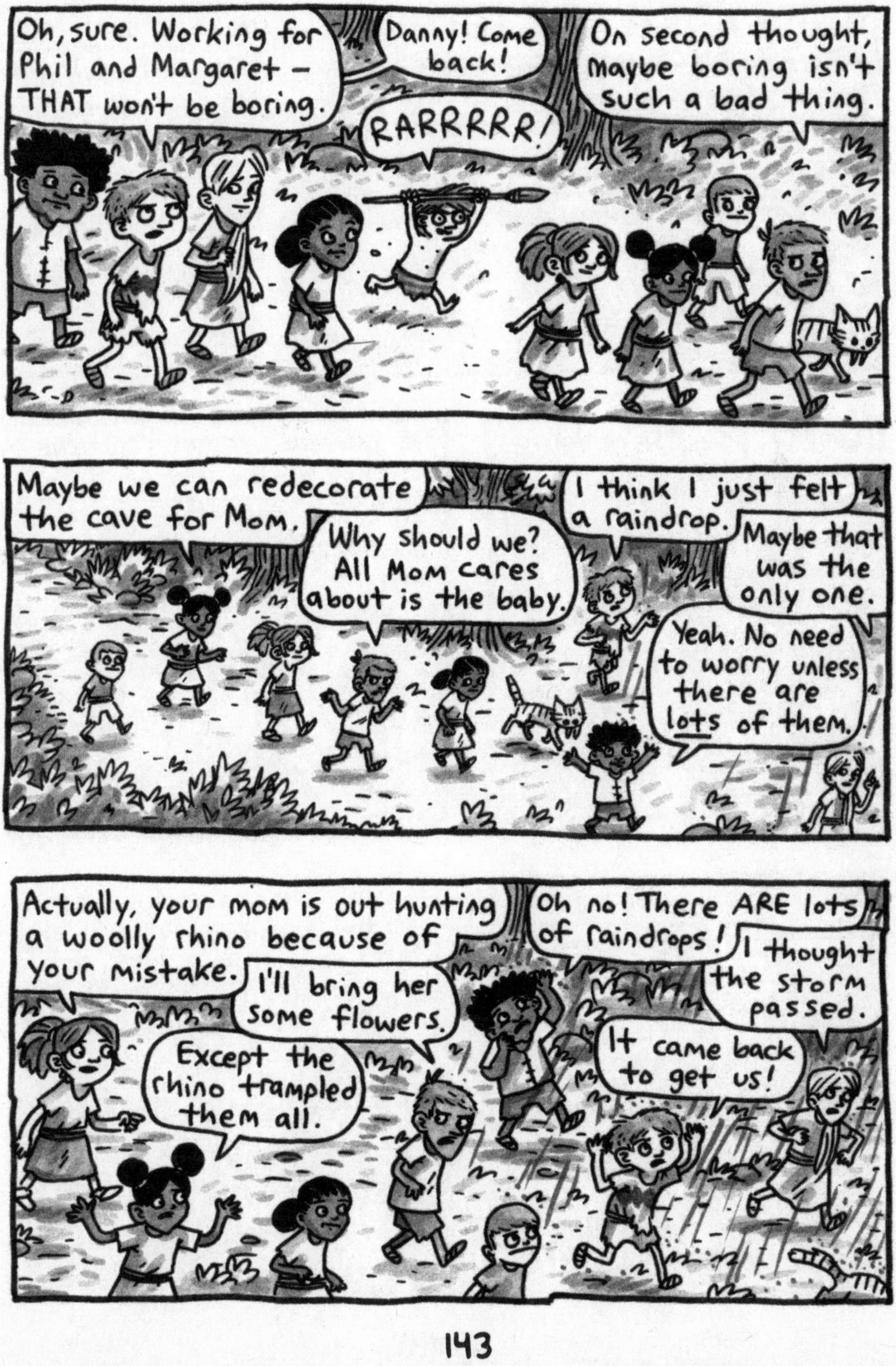
Oh, sure. Working for Phil and Margaret — THAT won't be boring.
Danny! Come back!
RARRRRR!
On second thought, maybe boring isn't such a bad thing.
Maybe we can redecorate the cave for Mom.
Why should we? All Mom cares about is the baby.
I think I just felt a raindrop.
Maybe that was the only one.
Yeah. No need to worry unless there are lots of them.
Actually, your mom is out hunting a woolly rhino because of your mistake.
I'll bring her some flowers.
Except the rhino trampled them all.
Oh no! There ARE lots of raindrops!
I thought the storm passed.
It came back to get us!

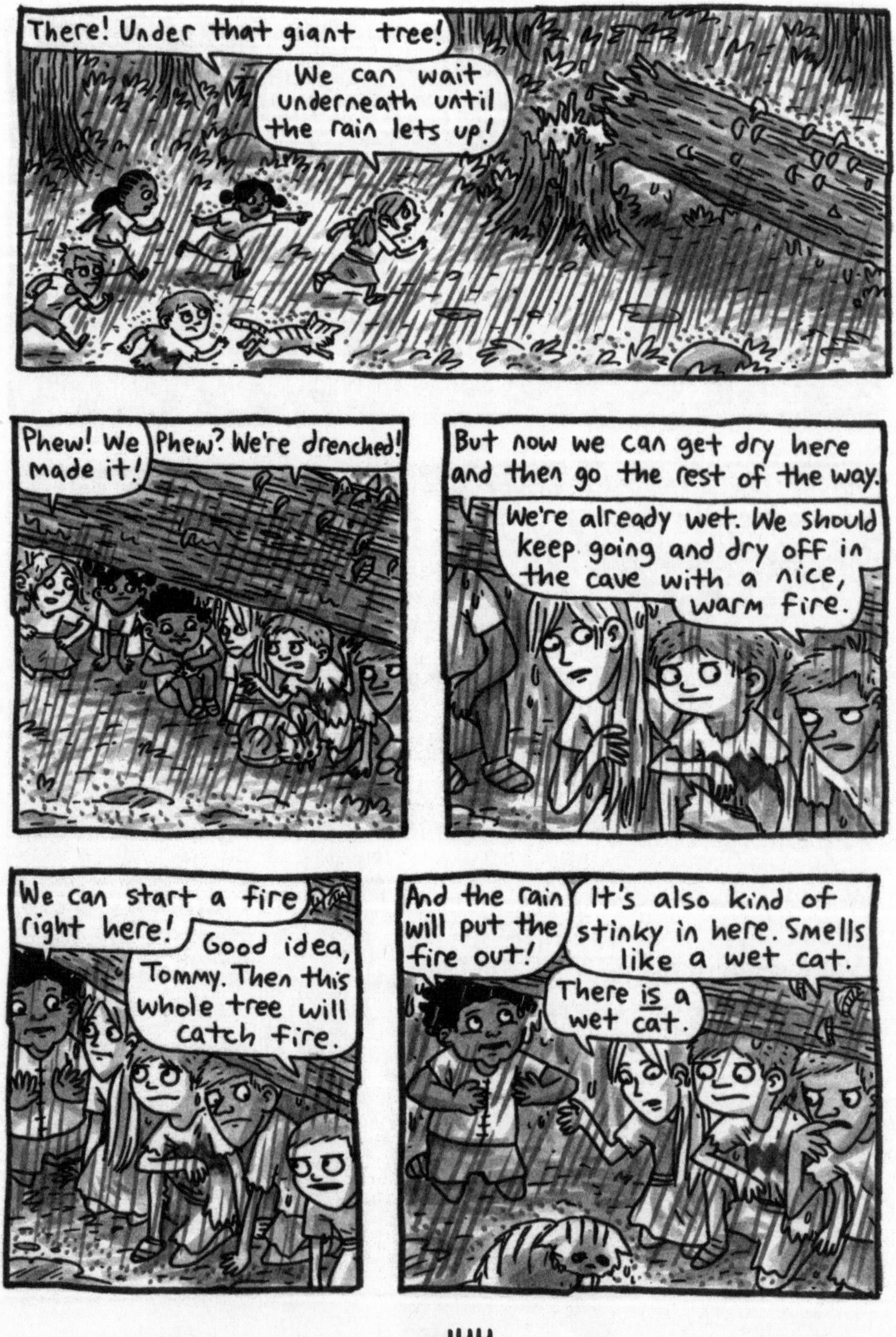
There! Under that giant tree!
We can wait underneath until the rain lets up!
Phew! We made it!
Phew? We're drenched!
But now we can get dry here and then go the rest of the way.
We're already wet. We should keep going and dry off in the cave with a nice, warm fire.
We can start a fire right here!
Good idea, Tommy. Then this whole tree will catch fire.
And the rain will put the fire out!
It's also kind of stinky in here. Smells like a wet cat.
There is a wet cat.

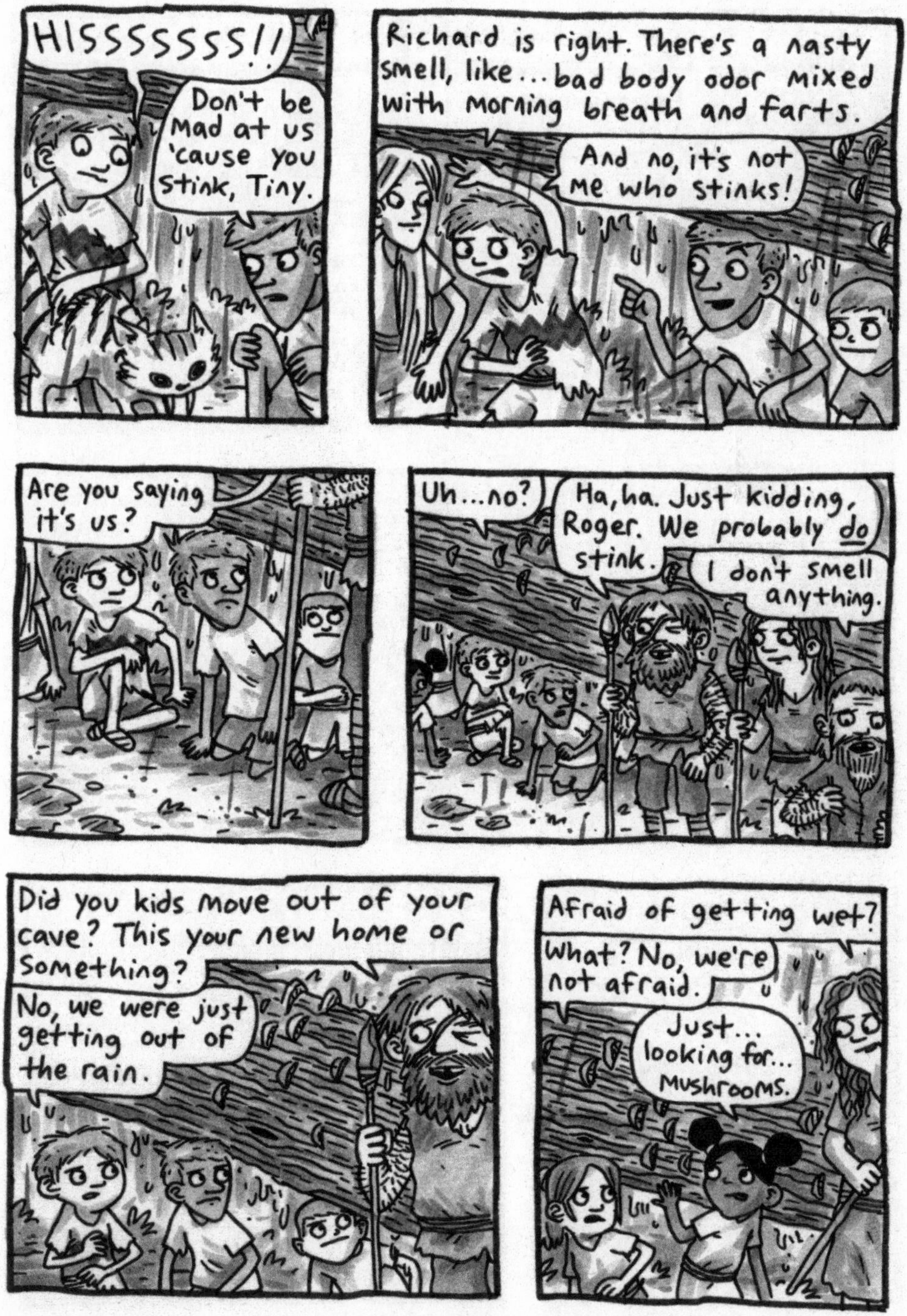
HISSSSSSS!!
Don't be mad at us 'cause you stink, Tiny.
Richard is right. There's a nasty smell, like... bad body odor mixed with morning breath and farts.
And no, it's not me who stinks!
Are you saying it's us?
Uh...no?
Ha, ha. Just kidding, Roger. We probably do stink.
I don't smell anything.
Did you kids move out of your cave? This your new home or something?
No, we were just getting out of the rain.
Afraid of getting wet?
What? No, we're not afraid.
Just... looking for... mushrooms.

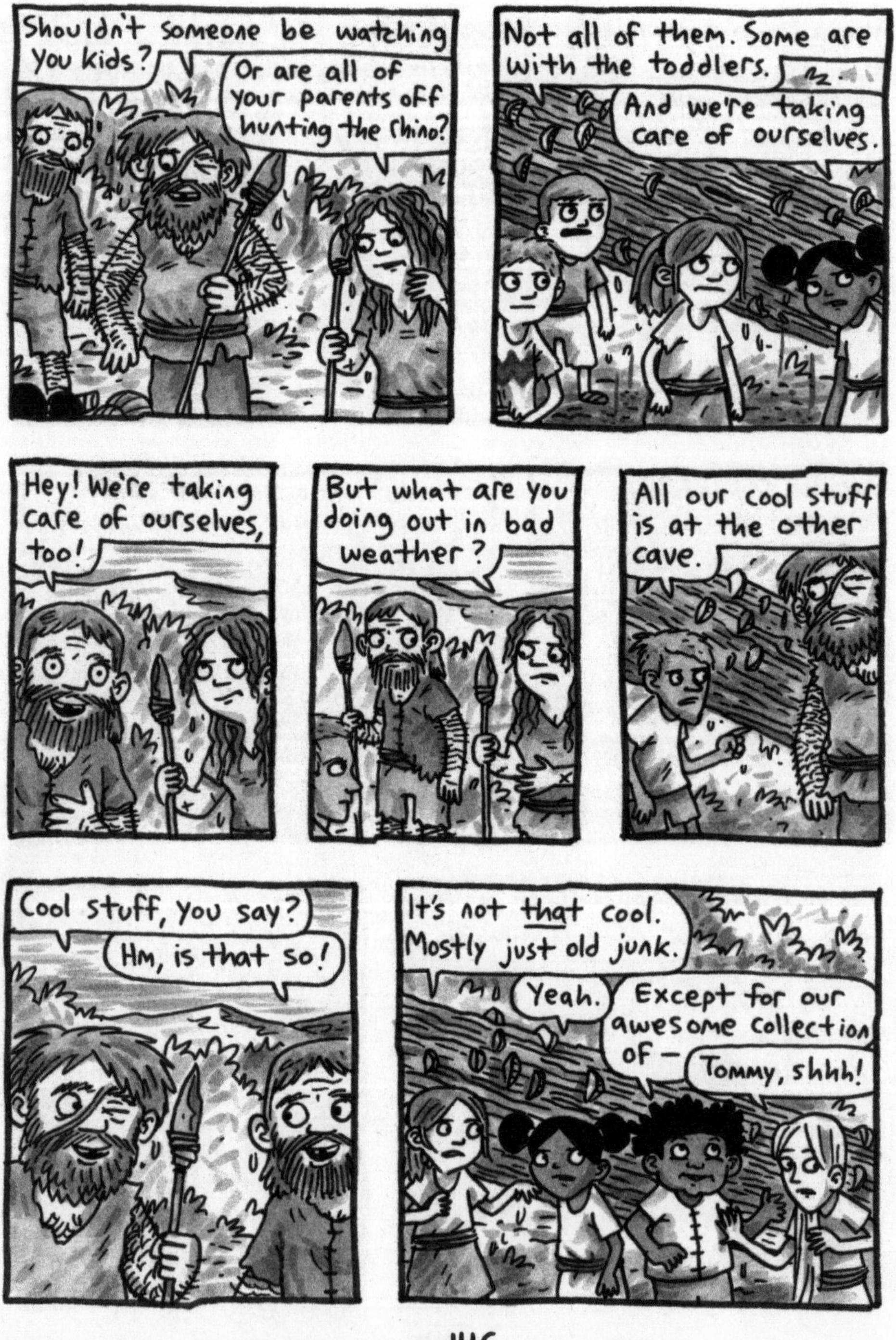
Shouldn't someone be watching you kids?
Or are all of your parents off hunting the rhino?
Not all of them. Some are with the toddlers.
And we're taking care of ourselves.
Hey! We're taking care of ourselves, too!
But what are you doing out in bad weather?
All our cool stuff is at the other cave.
Cool stuff, you say?
Hm, is that so!
It's not that cool. Mostly just old junk.
Yeah.
Except for our awesome collection of –
Tommy, shhh!

Maybe someday soon we can get a tour of that cave, too. It sounds really great!

Keep taking care of yourselves!

Those guys are up to no good. Definitely. Just because they're strangers doesn't mean they're bad people.

Yeah. You guys were okay! Then why do they want to see the other cave? They like cave tours!

And why were they out in the rain? We were out in the rain, too.

And they gave each other that sneaky "we've got an idea" look. You two make that look all the time. Exactly!

But why would they say "take care" when they left? Did you not see the devious smile when he said that?!

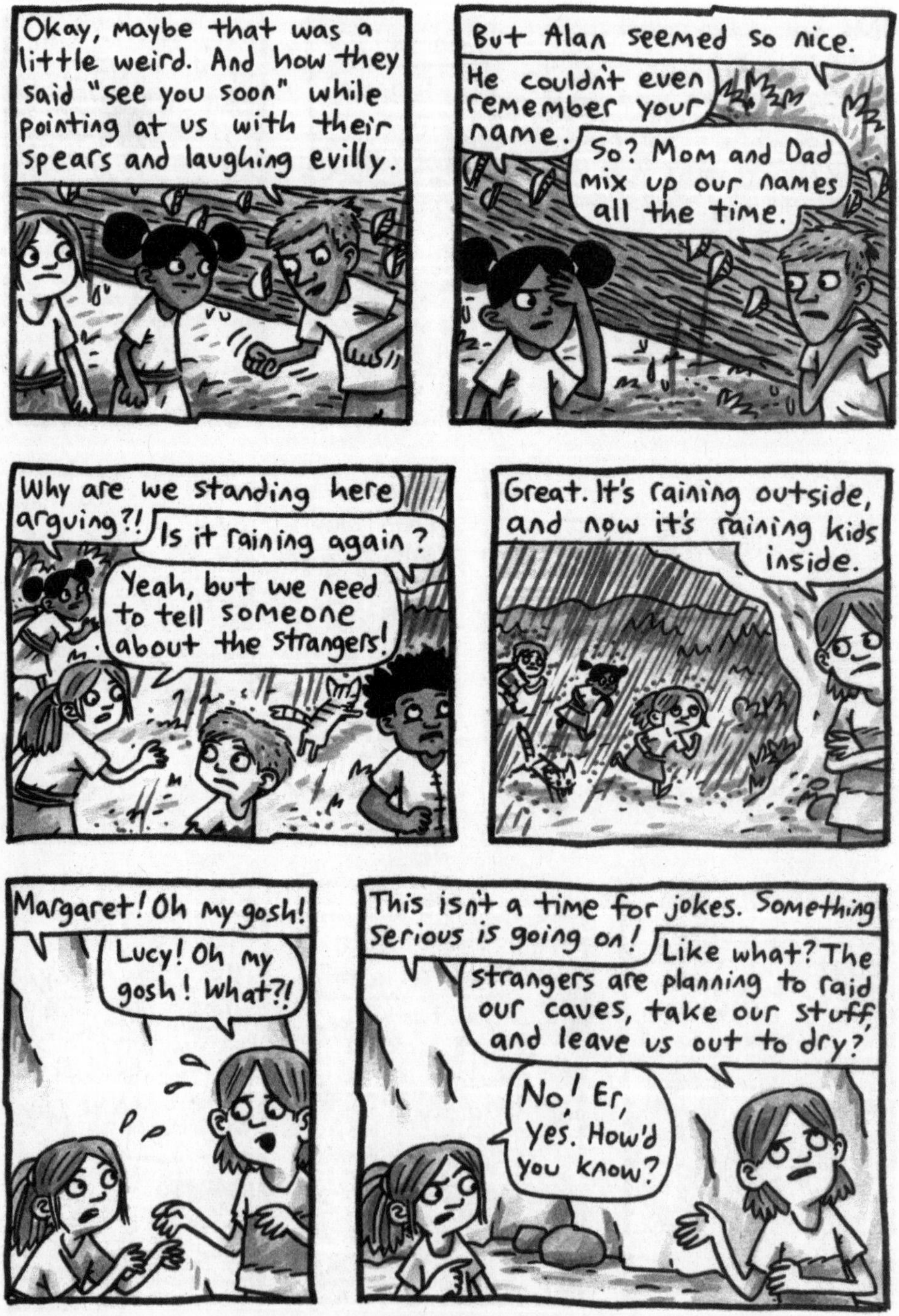

Okay, maybe that was a little weird. And how they said "see you soon" while pointing at us with their spears and laughing evilly.
But Alan seemed so nice.
He couldn't even remember your name.
So? Mom and Dad mix up our names all the time.
Why are we standing here arguing?!
Is it raining again?
Yeah, but we need to tell someone about the strangers!
Great. It's raining outside, and now it's raining kids inside.
Margaret! Oh my gosh!
Lucy! Oh my gosh! What?!
This isn't a time for jokes. Something serious is going on!
Like what? The strangers are planning to raid our caves, take our stuff, and leave us out to dry?
No! Er, yes. How'd you know?

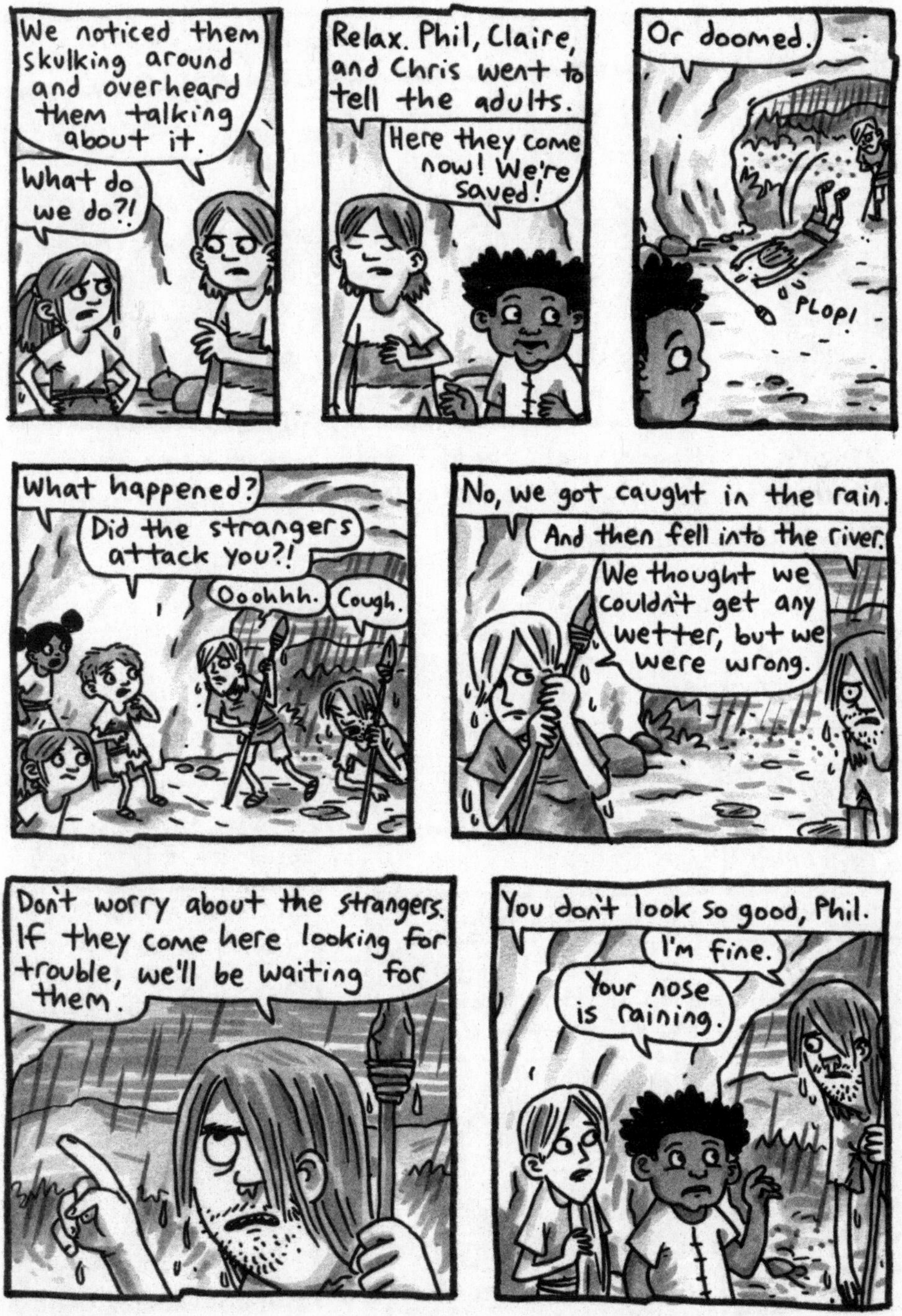
We noticed them skulking around and overheard them talking about it.
What do we do?!
Relax. Phil, Claire, and Chris went to tell the adults.
Here they come now! We're saved!
Or doomed.
PLOP!
What happened?
Did the strangers attack you?!
Ooohhh.
Cough.
No, we got caught in the rain.
And then fell into the river.
We thought we couldn't get any wetter, but we were wrong.
Don't worry about the strangers. If they come here looking for trouble, we'll be waiting for them.
You don't look so good, Phil.
I'm fine.
Your nose is raining.

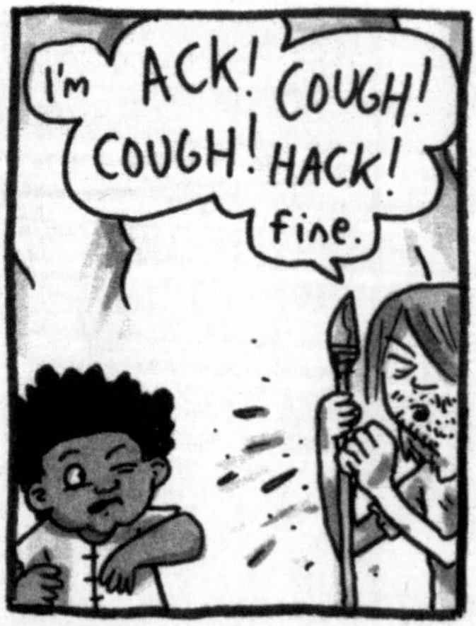
I'm ACK! COUGH! COUGH! HACK! fine.

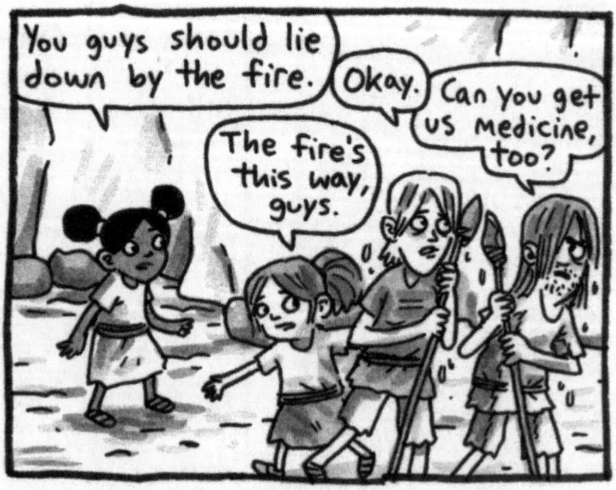
You guys should lie down by the fire.
Okay.
Can you get us medicine, too?
The fire's this way, guys.

Studies of Neanderthal teeth tell scientists that Neanderthals ate their veggies - but also that they used medicines!

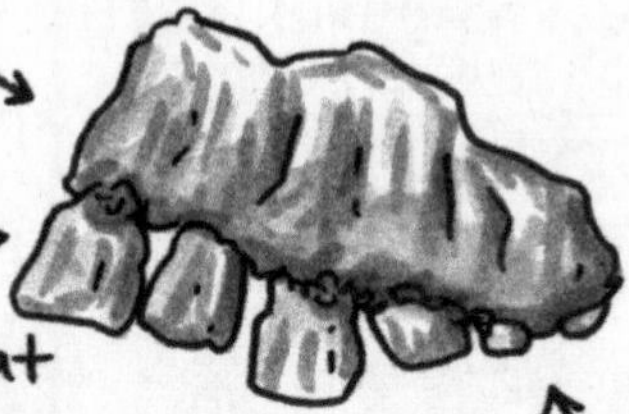

Plaque on teeth shows that some Neanderthals may have used plants that make aspirin and molds that make penicillin to treat illness.

Studies also indicate that Neanderthals weren't good at flossing!

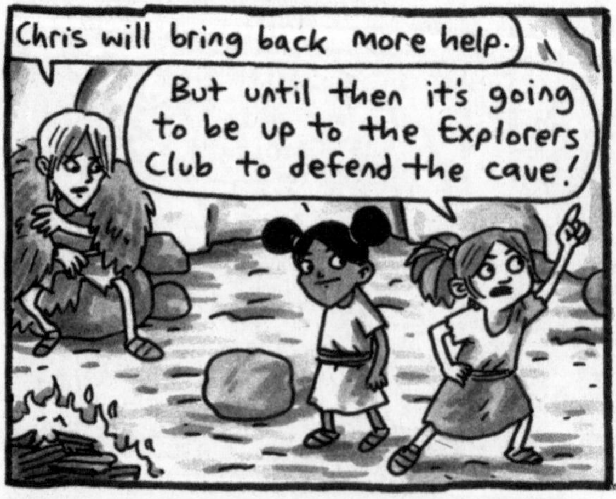
Chris will bring back more help.
But until then it's going to be up to the Explorers Club to defend the cave!

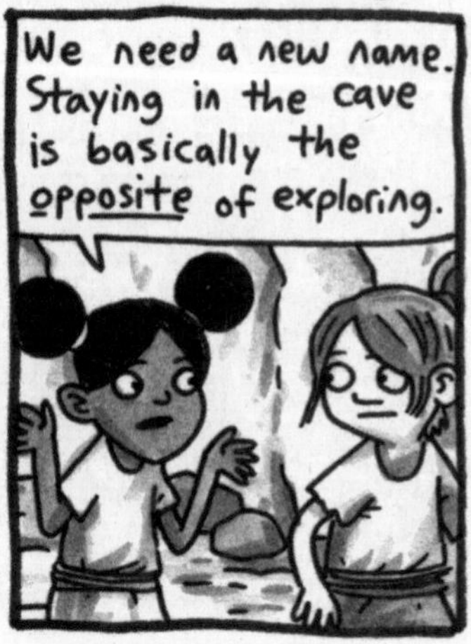
We need a new name. Staying in the cave is basically the opposite of exploring.

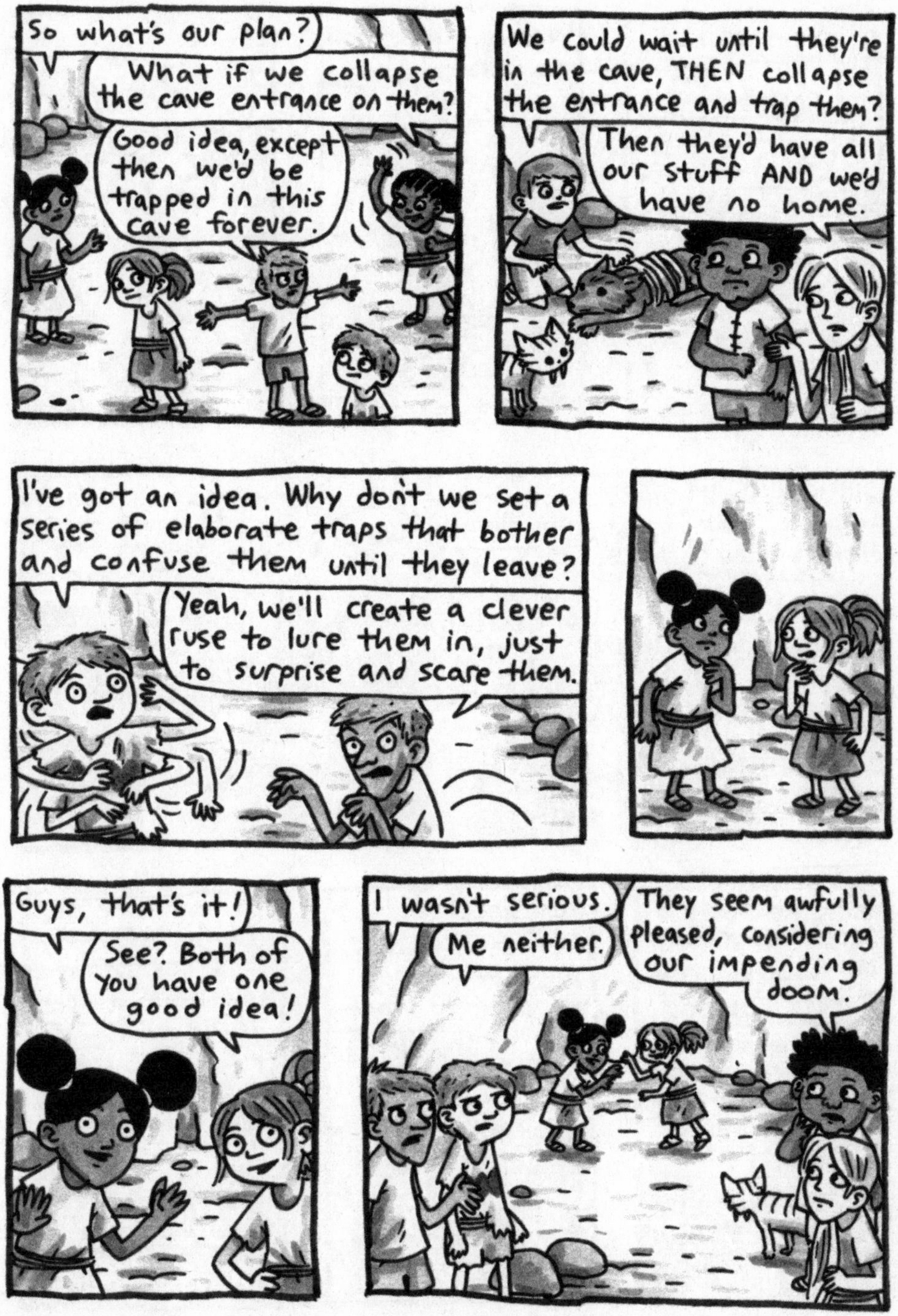
So what's our plan?
What if we collapse the cave entrance on them?
Good idea, except then we'd be trapped in this cave forever.
We could wait until they're in the cave, THEN collapse the entrance and trap them?
Then they'd have all our stuff AND we'd have no home.
I've got an idea. Why don't we set a series of elaborate traps that bother and confuse them until they leave?
Yeah, we'll create a clever ruse to lure them in, just to surprise and scare them.
Guys, that's it!
See? Both of you have one good idea!
I wasn't serious.
Me neither.
They seem awfully pleased, considering our impending doom.

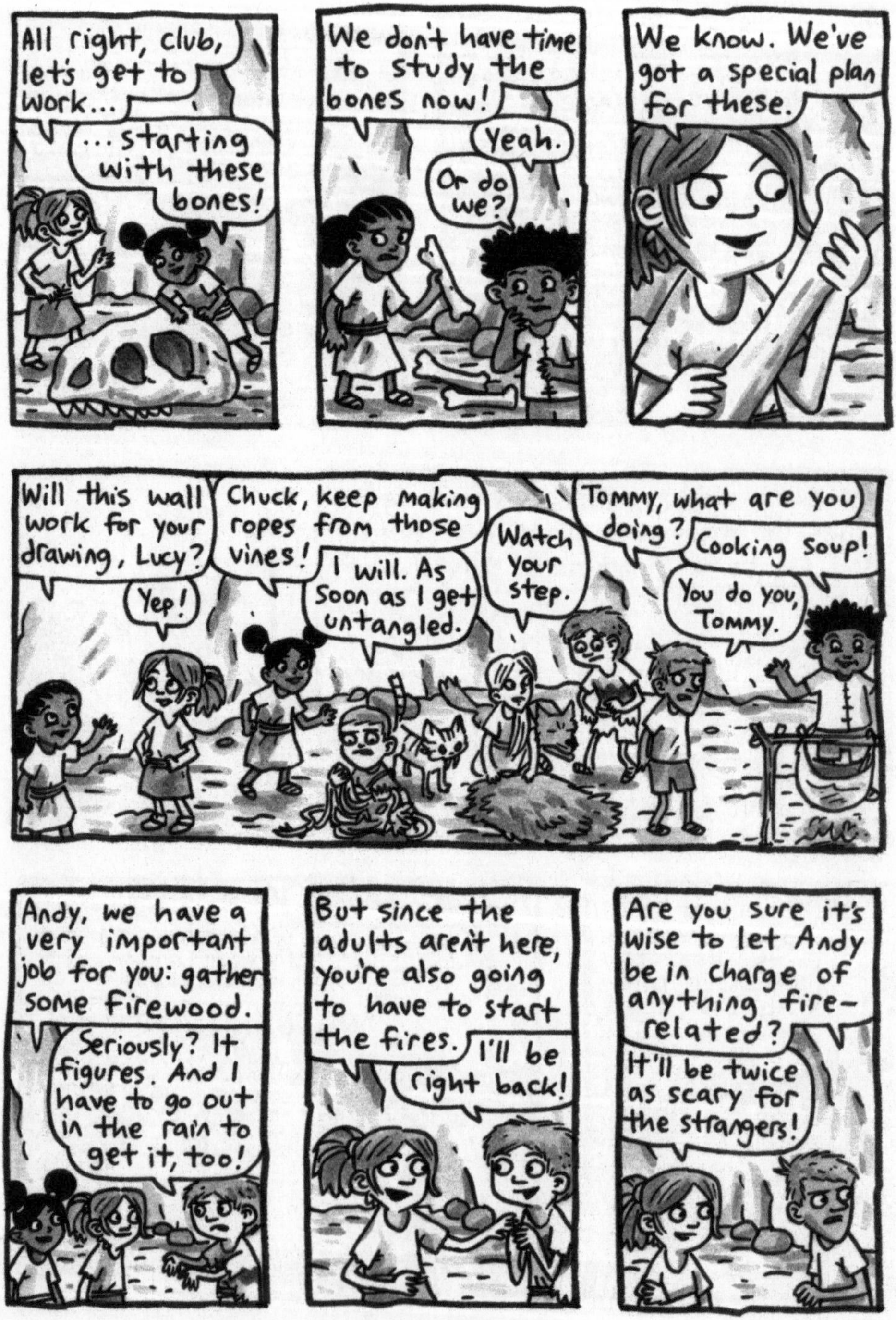
All right, club, let's get to work...
...starting with these bones!
We don't have time to study the bones now!
Yeah.
Or do we?
We know. We've got a special plan for these.
Will this wall work for your drawing, Lucy?
Yep!
Chuck, keep making ropes from those vines!
I will. As soon as I get untangled.
Watch your step.
Tommy, what are you doing?
Cooking soup!
You do you, Tommy.
Andy, we have a very important job for you: gather some firewood.
Seriously? It figures. And I have to go out in the rain to get it, too!
But since the adults aren't here, you're also going to have to start the fires.
I'll be right back!
Are you sure it's wise to let Andy be in charge of anything fire-related?
It'll be twice as scary for the strangers!

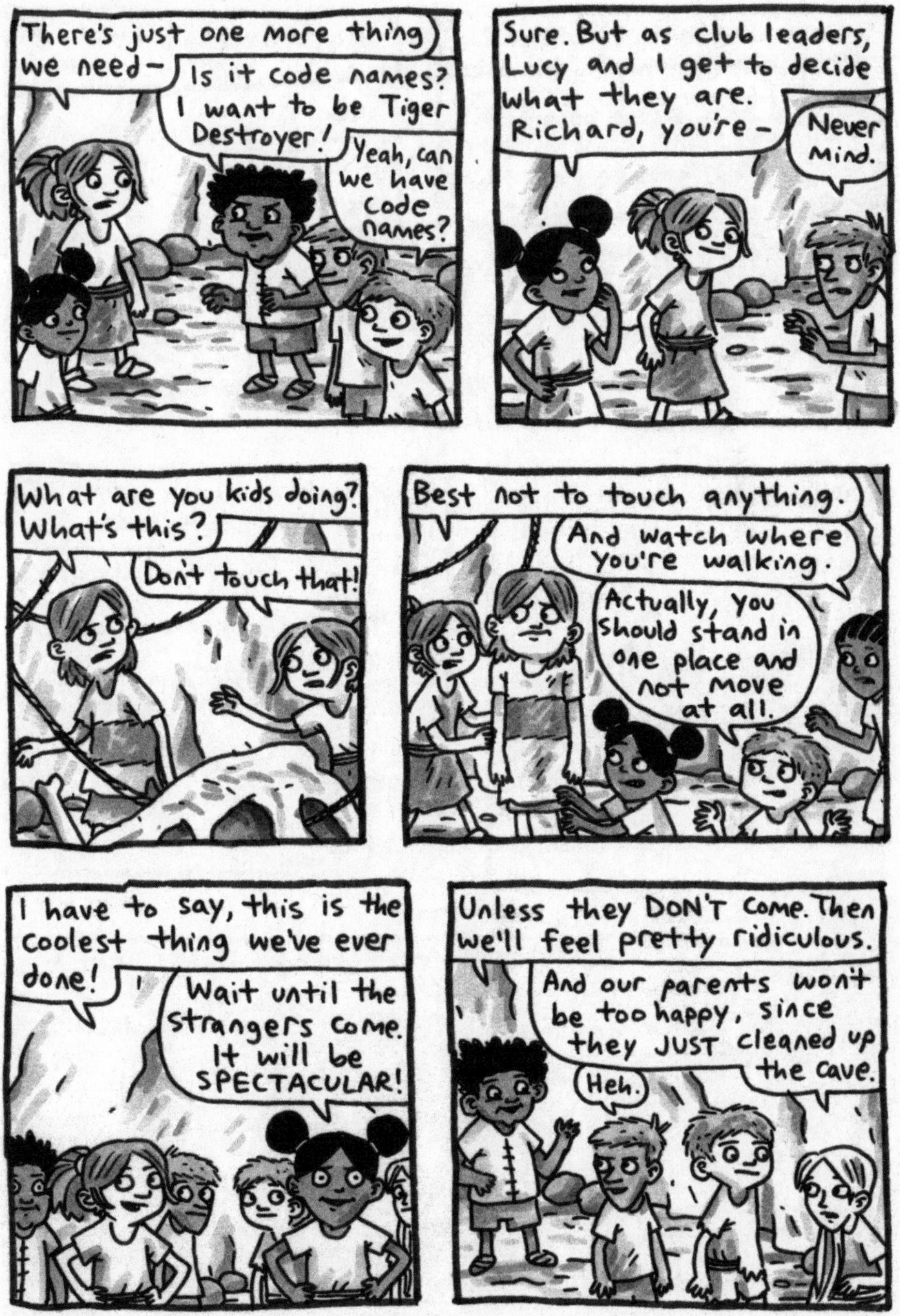
There's just one more thing we need–
Is it code names? I want to be Tiger Destroyer!
Yeah, can we have code names?
Sure. But as club leaders, Lucy and I get to decide what they are. Richard, you're–
Never mind.
What are you kids doing? What's this?
Don't touch that!
Best not to touch anything.
And watch where you're walking.
Actually, you should stand in one place and not move at all.
I have to say, this is the coolest thing we've ever done!
Wait until the strangers come. It will be SPECTACULAR!
Unless they DON'T come. Then we'll feel pretty ridiculous.
And our parents won't be too happy, since they JUST cleaned up the cave.
Heh.

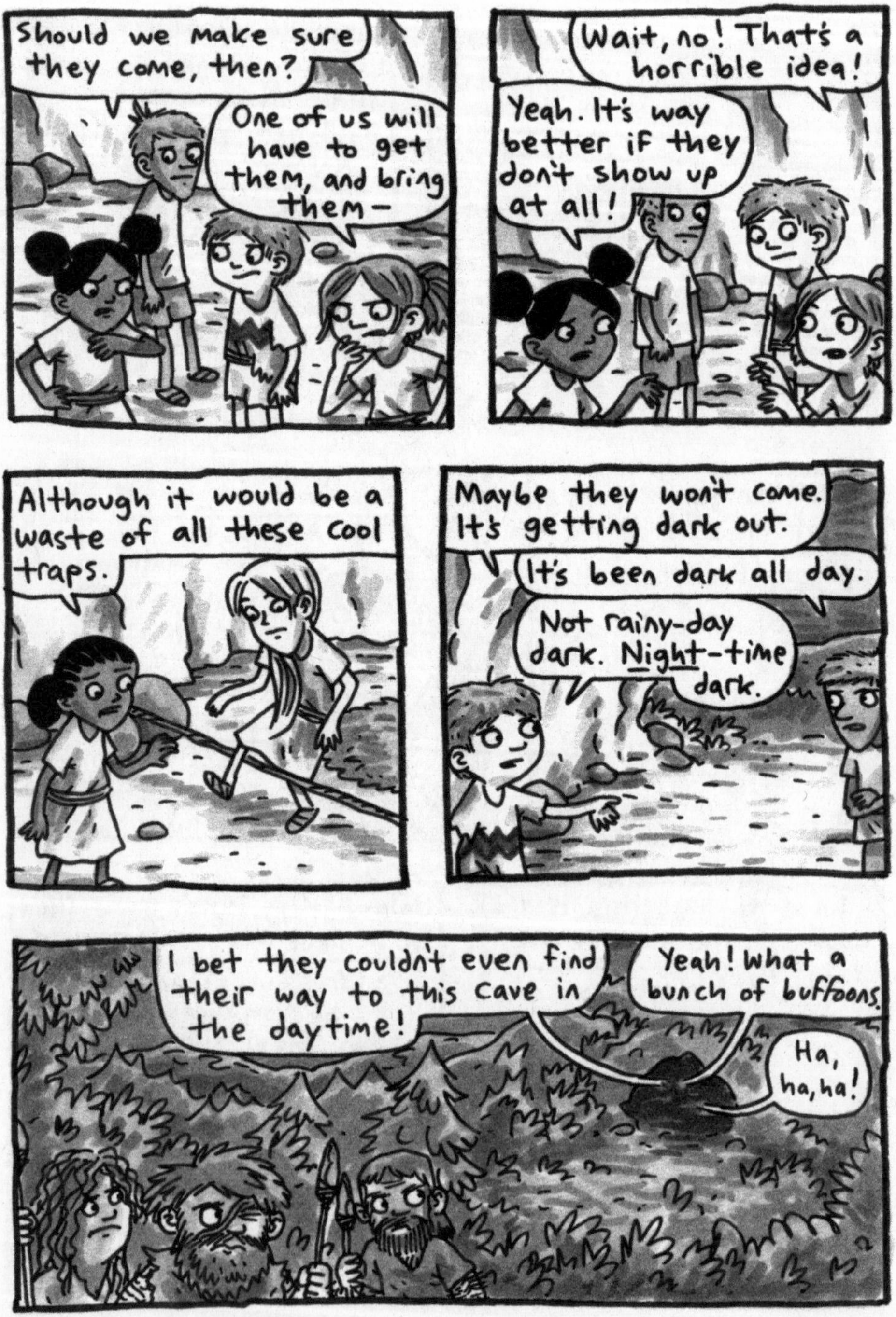
Should we make sure they come, then?
One of us will have to get them, and bring them—
Wait, no! That's a horrible idea!
Yeah. It's way better if they don't show up at all!
Although it would be a waste of all these cool traps.
Maybe they won't come. It's getting dark out.
It's been dark all day.
Not rainy-day dark. Night-time dark.
I bet they couldn't even find their way to this cave in the daytime!
Yeah! What a bunch of buffoons.
Ha, ha, ha!

THE OLDEST TRICK IN THE CAVE

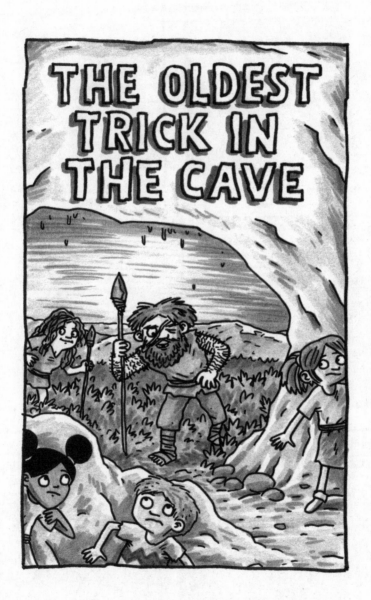

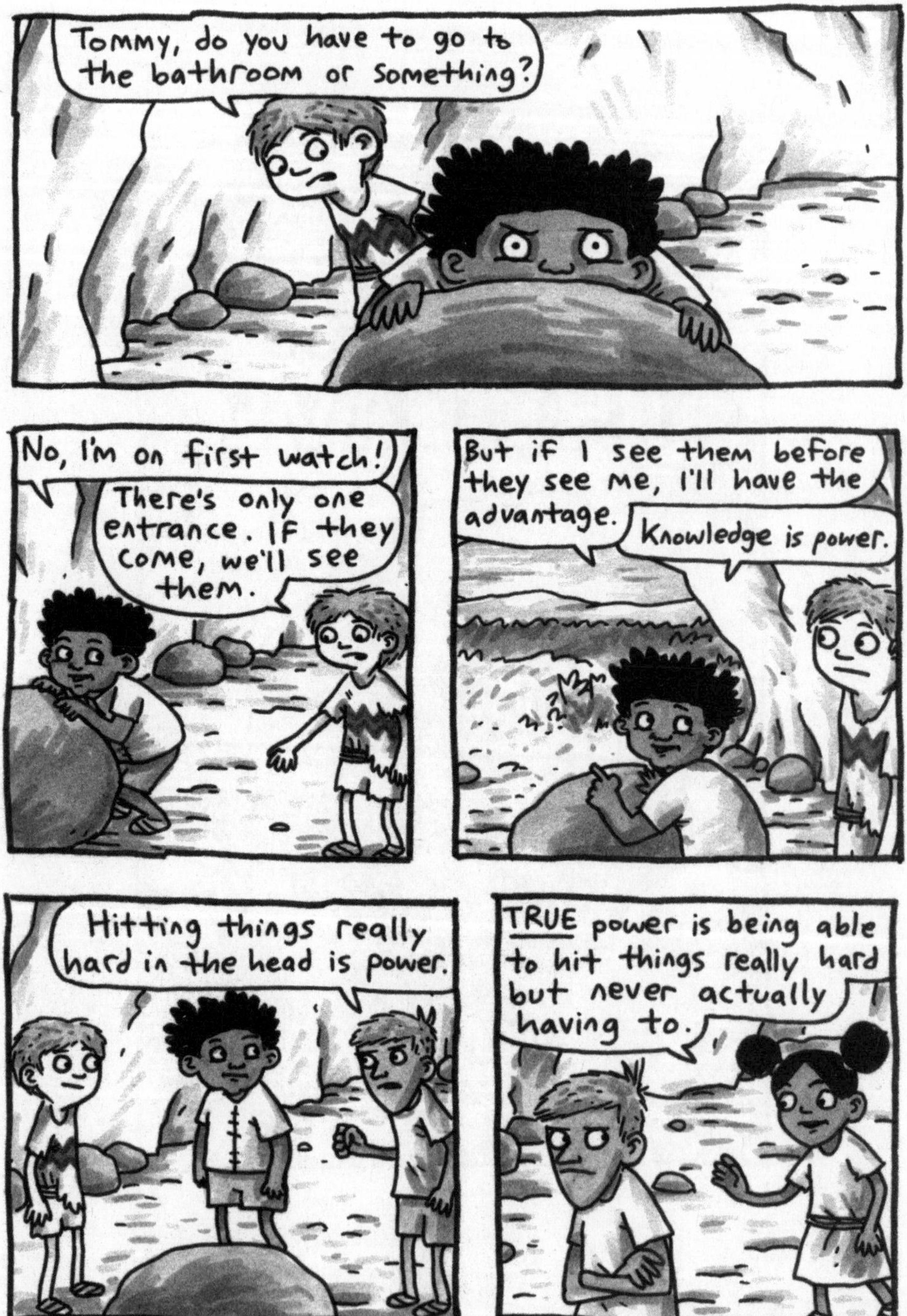

Tommy, do you have to go to the bathroom or something?
No, I'm on first watch!
There's only one entrance. If they come, we'll see them.
But if I see them before they see me, I'll have the advantage.
Knowledge is power.
Hitting things really hard in the head is power.
TRUE power is being able to hit things really hard but never actually having to.

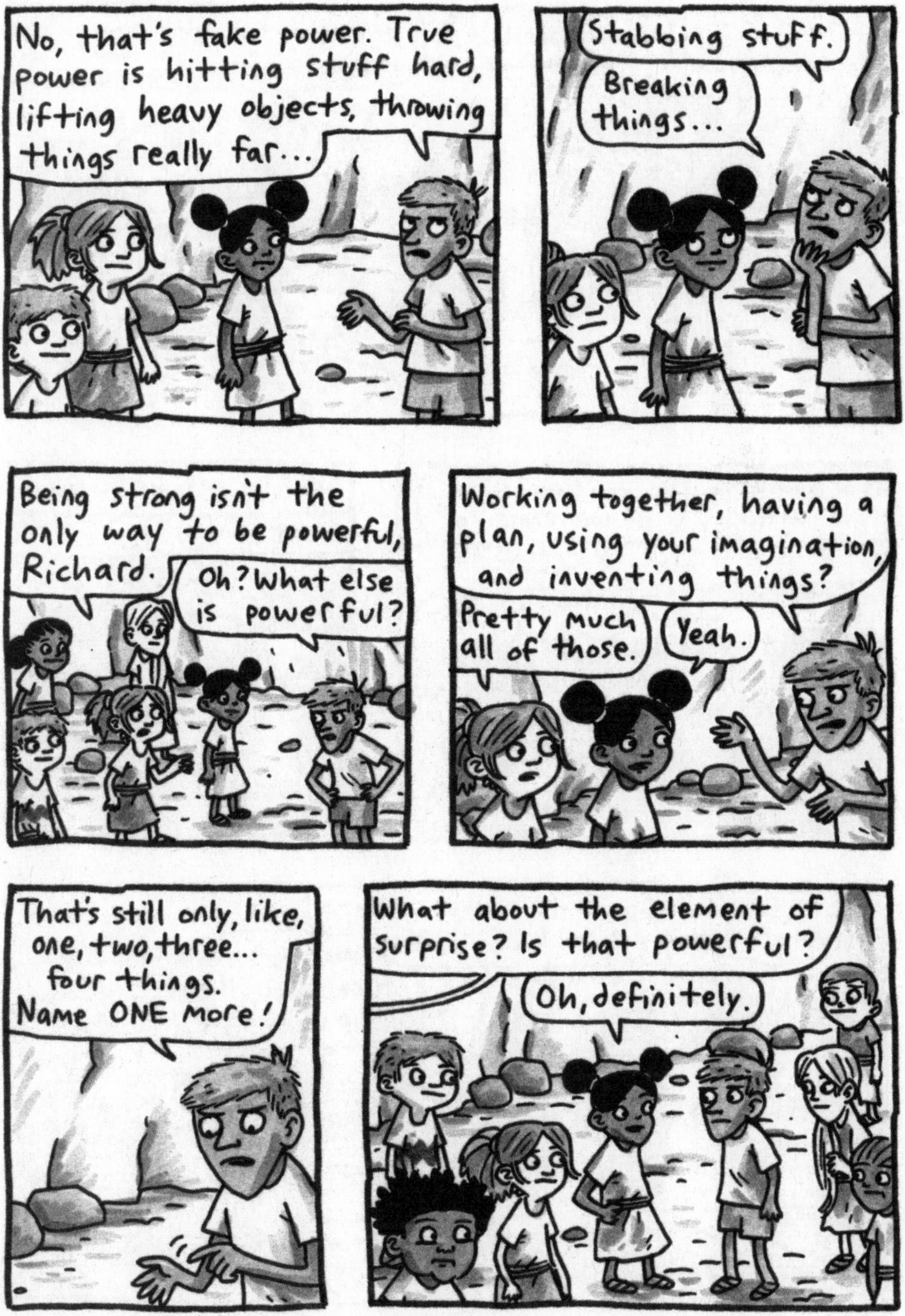
No, that's fake power. True power is hitting stuff hard, lifting heavy objects, throwing things really far...
Stabbing stuff.
Breaking things...
Being strong isn't the only way to be powerful, Richard.
Oh? What else is powerful?
Working together, having a plan, using your imagination, and inventing things?
Pretty much all of those.
Yeah.
That's still only, like, one, two, three... four things. Name ONE more!
What about the element of surprise? Is that powerful?
Oh, definitely.

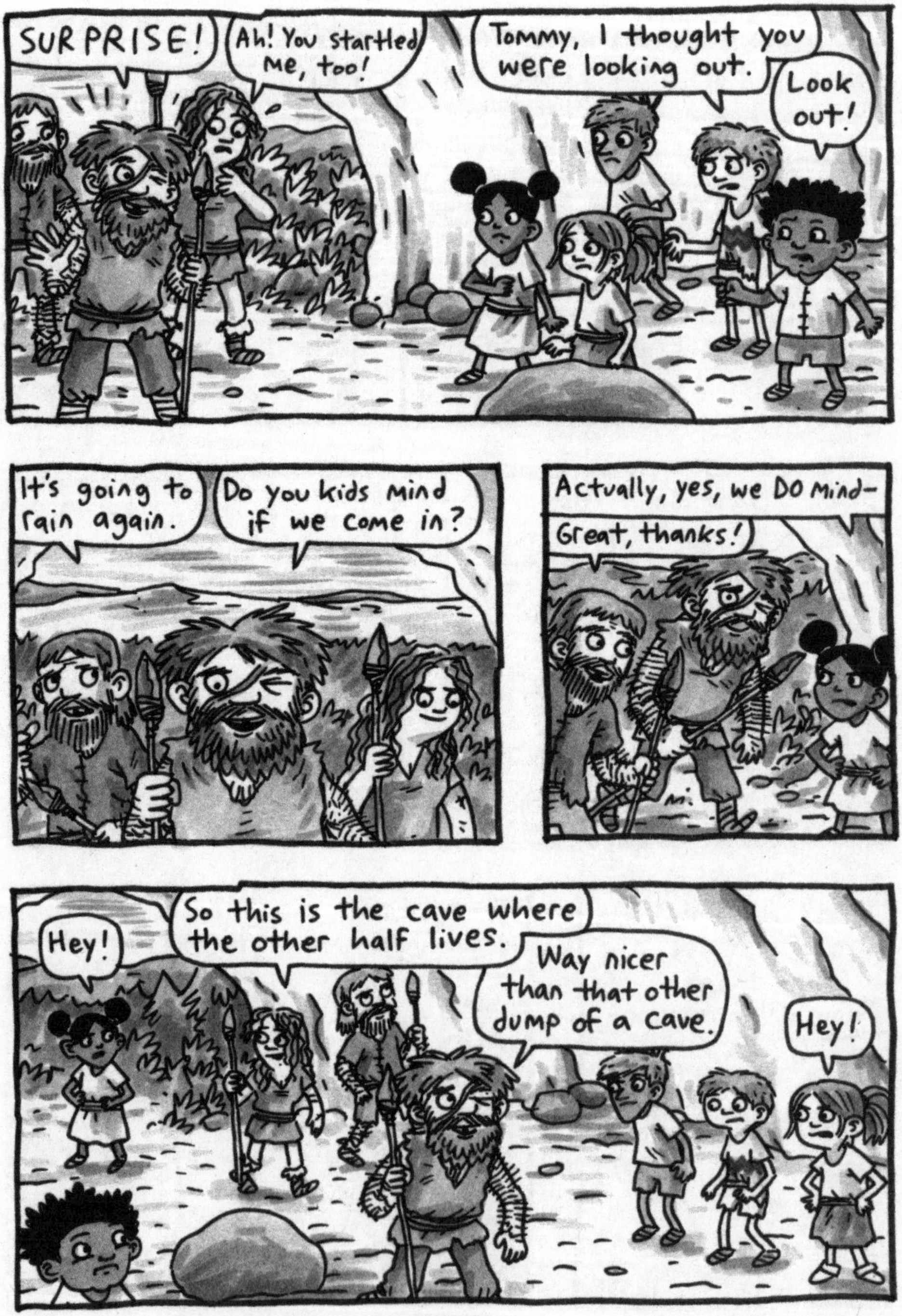
SURPRISE!
Ah! You startled me, too!
Tommy, I thought you were looking out.
Look out!
It's going to rain again.
Do you kids mind if we come in?
Actually, yes, we DO mind-
Great, thanks!
Hey!
So this is the cave where the other half lives.
Way nicer than that other dump of a cave.
Hey!

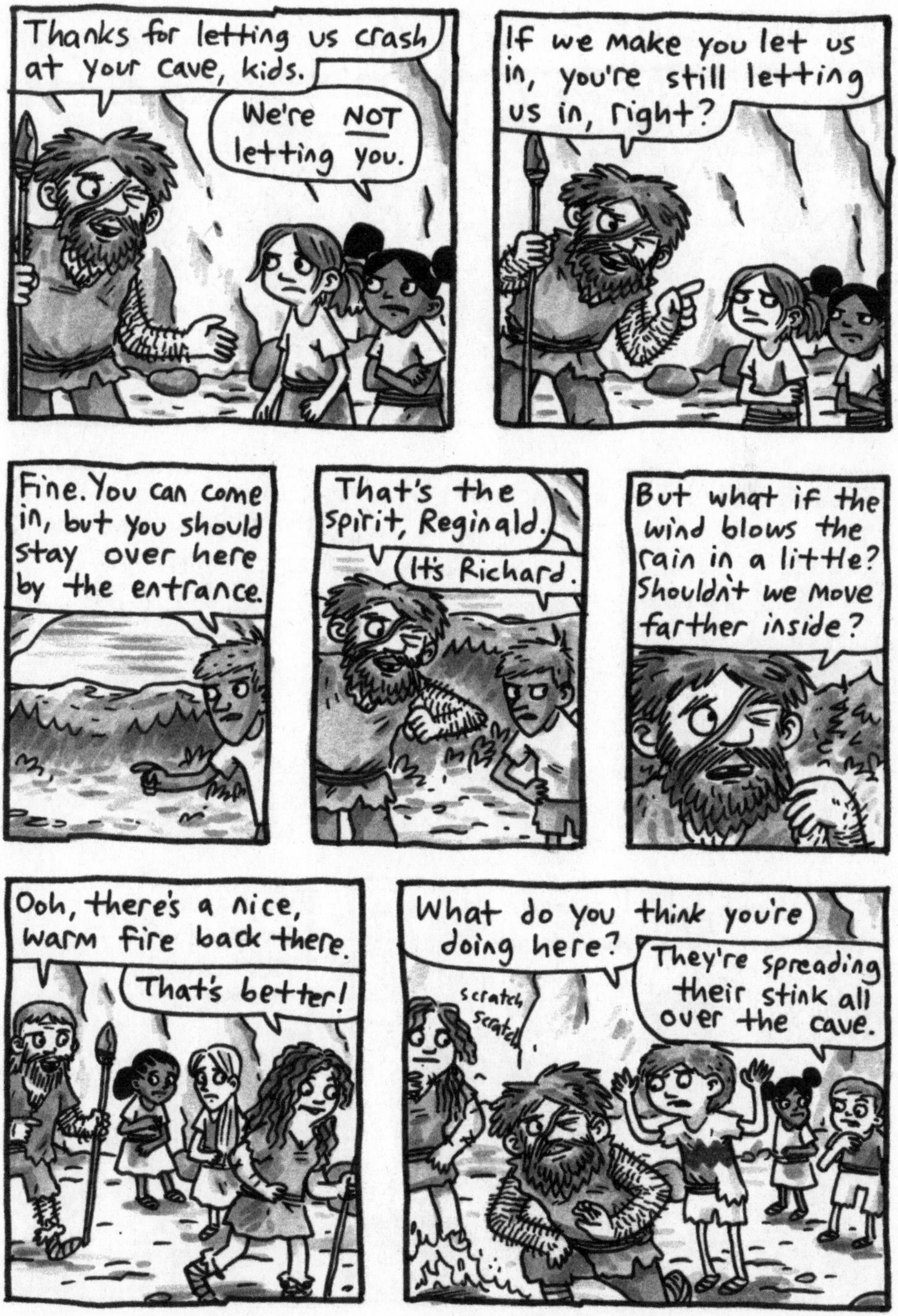
Thanks for letting us crash at your cave, kids.
We're NOT letting you.
If we make you let us in, you're still letting us in, right?
Fine. You can come in, but you should stay over here by the entrance.
That's the spirit, Reginald.
It's Richard.
But what if the wind blows the rain in a little? Shouldn't we move farther inside?
Ooh, there's a nice, warm fire back there.
That's better!
What do you think you're doing here?
scratch scratch
They're spreading their stink all over the cave.

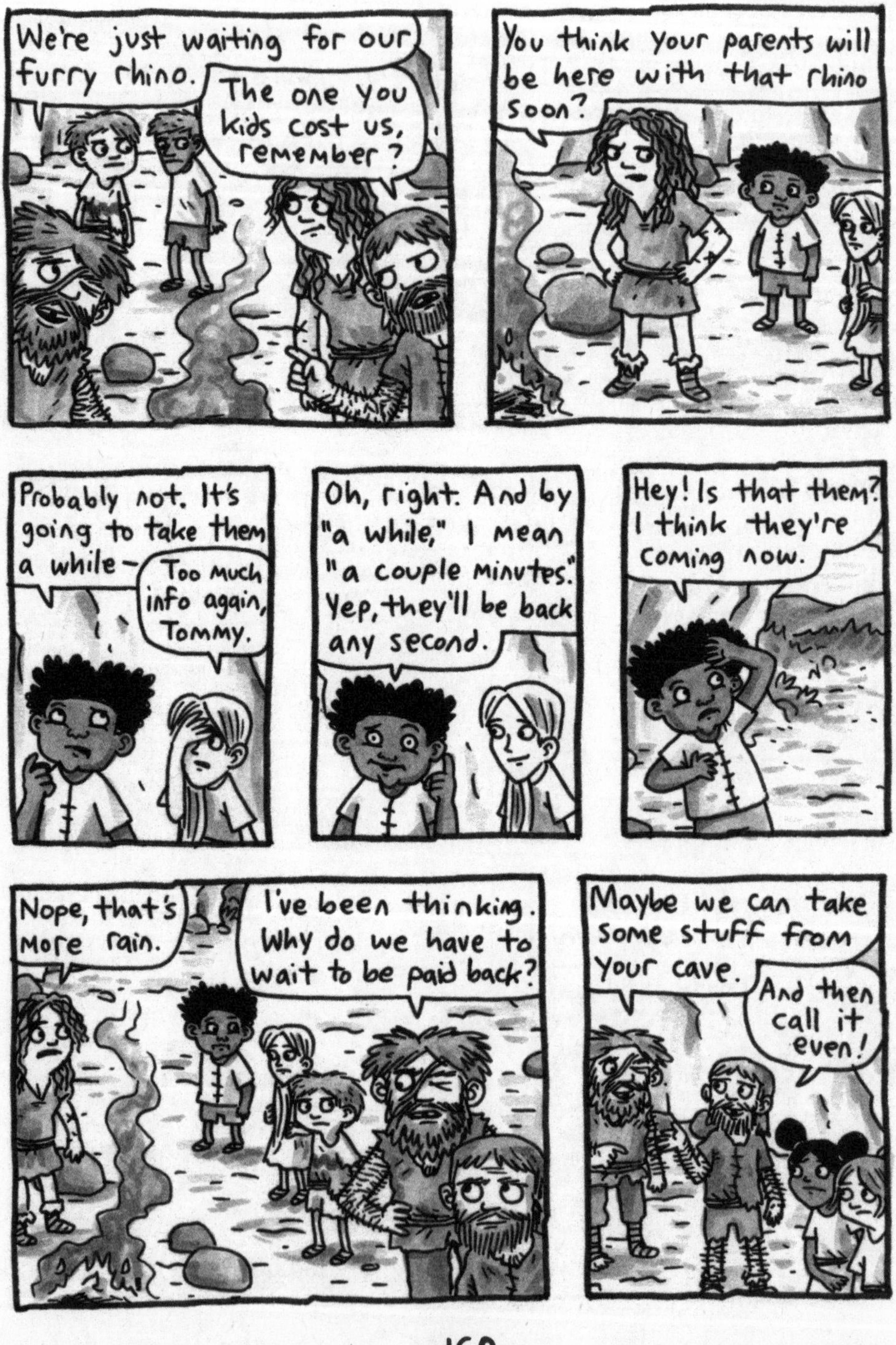

We're just waiting for our furry rhino.
The one you kids cost us, remember?
You think your parents will be here with that rhino soon?
Probably not. It's going to take them a while—
Too much info again, Tommy.
Oh, right. And by "a while," I mean "a couple minutes." Yep, they'll be back any second.
Hey! Is that them? I think they're coming now.
Nope, that's more rain.
I've been thinking. Why do we have to wait to be paid back?
Maybe we can take some stuff from your cave.
And then call it even!

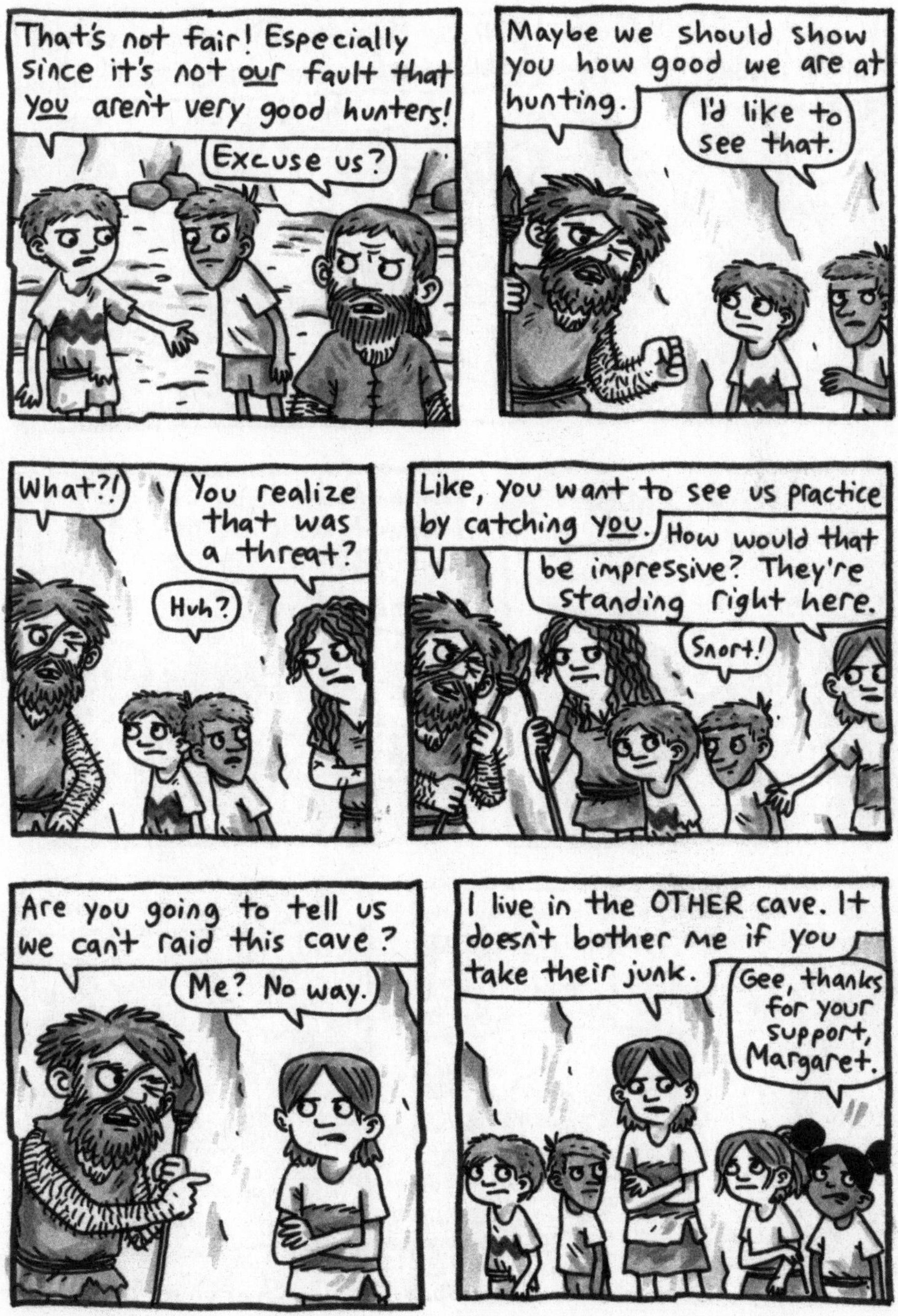
That's not fair! Especially since it's not our fault that you aren't very good hunters!
Excuse us?
Maybe we should show you how good we are at hunting.
I'd like to see that.
What?!
You realize that was a threat?
Huh?
Like, you want to see us practice by catching you.
How would that be impressive? They're standing right here.
Snort!
Are you going to tell us we can't raid this cave?
Me? No way.
I live in the OTHER cave. It doesn't bother me if you take their junk.
Gee, thanks for your support, Margaret.

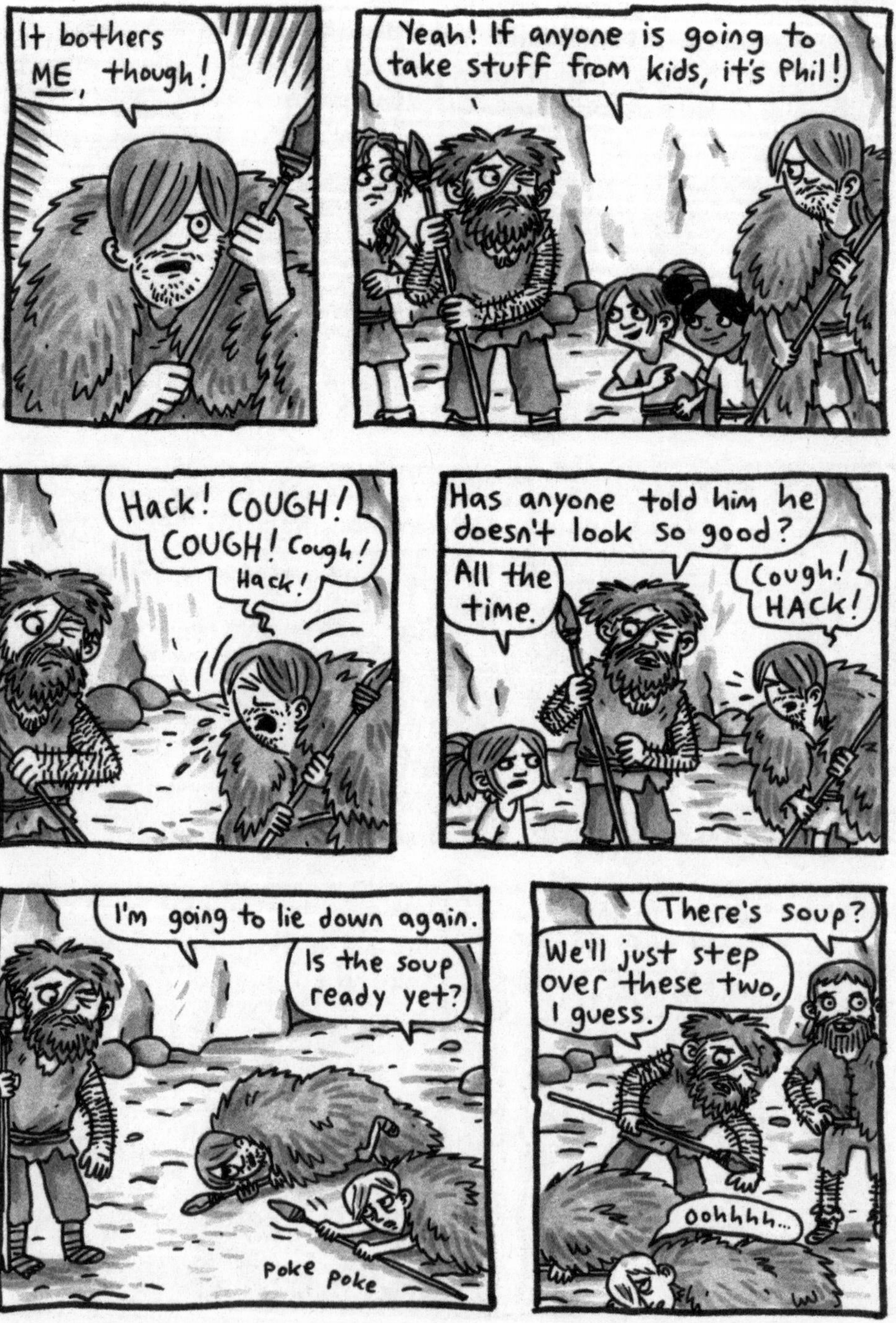
It bothers ME, though!
Yeah! If anyone is going to take stuff from kids, it's Phil!
Hack! COUGH! COUGH! Cough! Hack!
Has anyone told him he doesn't look so good?
All the time.
Cough! HACK!
I'm going to lie down again.
Is the soup ready yet?
Poke poke
There's soup?
We'll just step over these two, I guess.
Oohhhh...

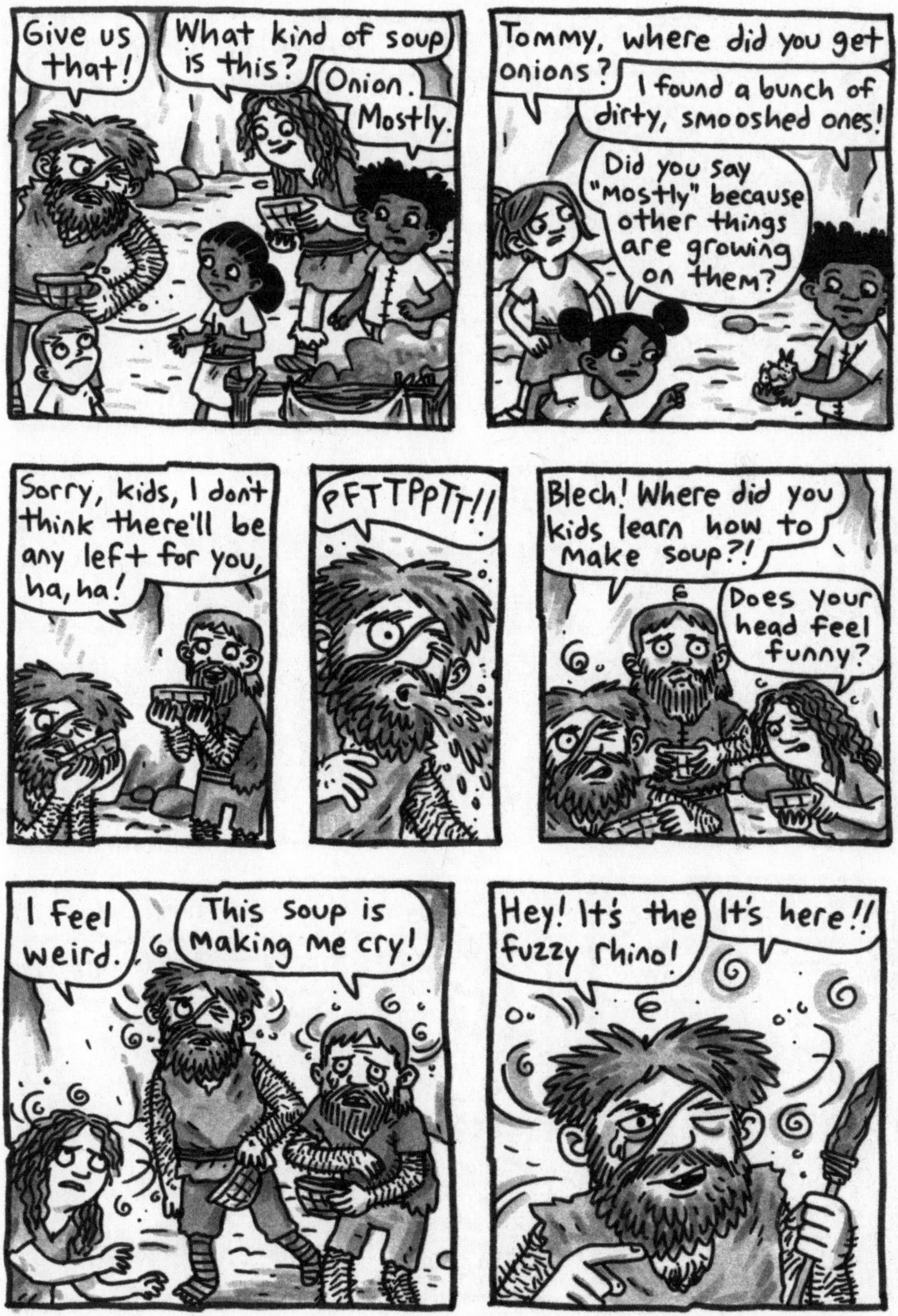
Give us that!
What kind of soup is this?
Onion. Mostly.
Tommy, where did you get onions?
I found a bunch of dirty, smooshed ones!
Did you say "mostly" because other things are growing on them?
Sorry, kids, I don't think there'll be any left for you, ha, ha!
PFTTPPTT!!
Blech! Where did you kids learn how to make soup?!
Does your head feel funny?
I feel weird.
This soup is making me cry!
Hey! It's the fuzzy rhino!
It's here!!

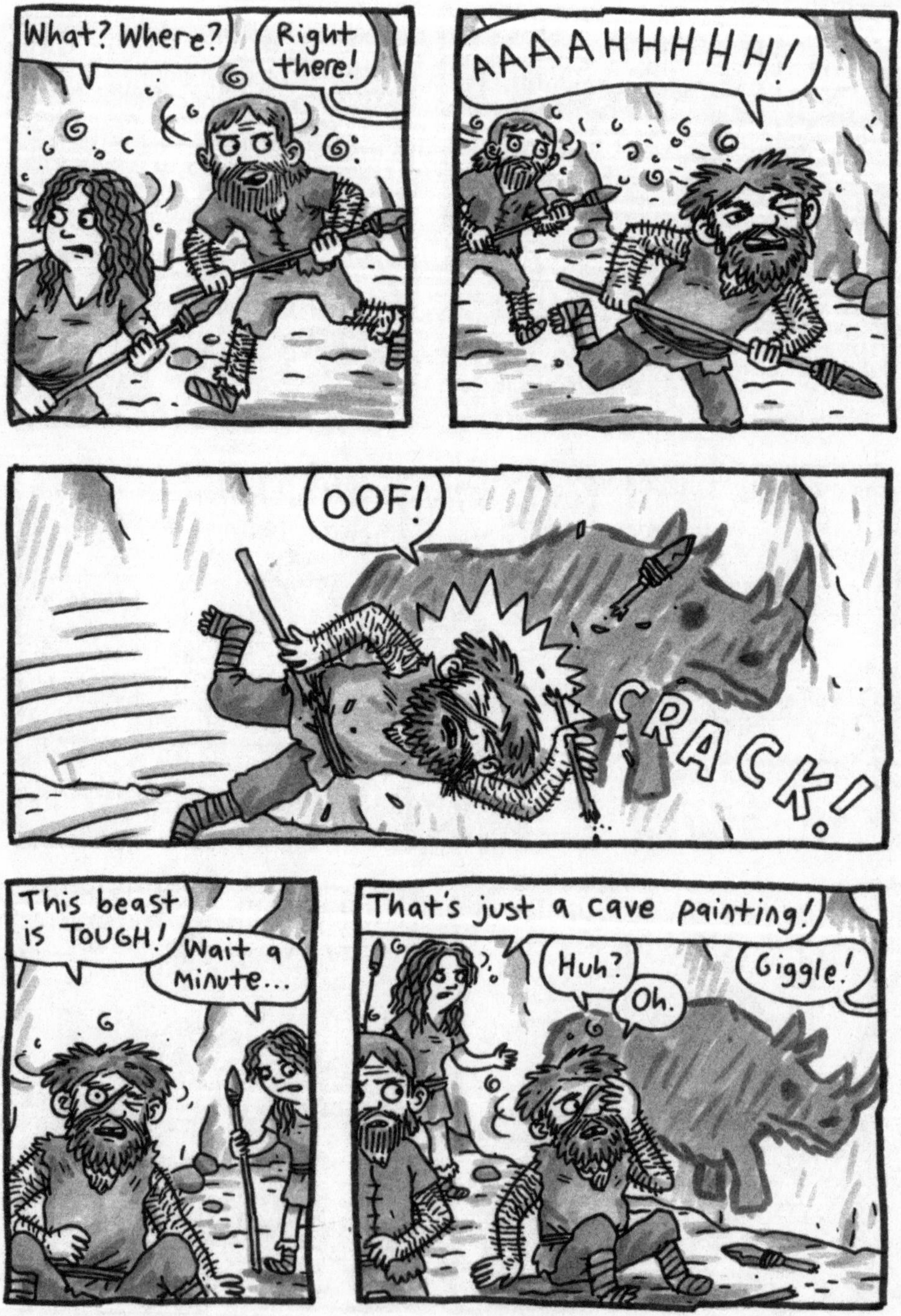

What? Where?
Right there!
AAAAHHHHHH!
OOF!
CRACK!
This beast is TOUGH!
Wait a minute...
That's just a cave painting!
Huh?
Oh.
Giggle!

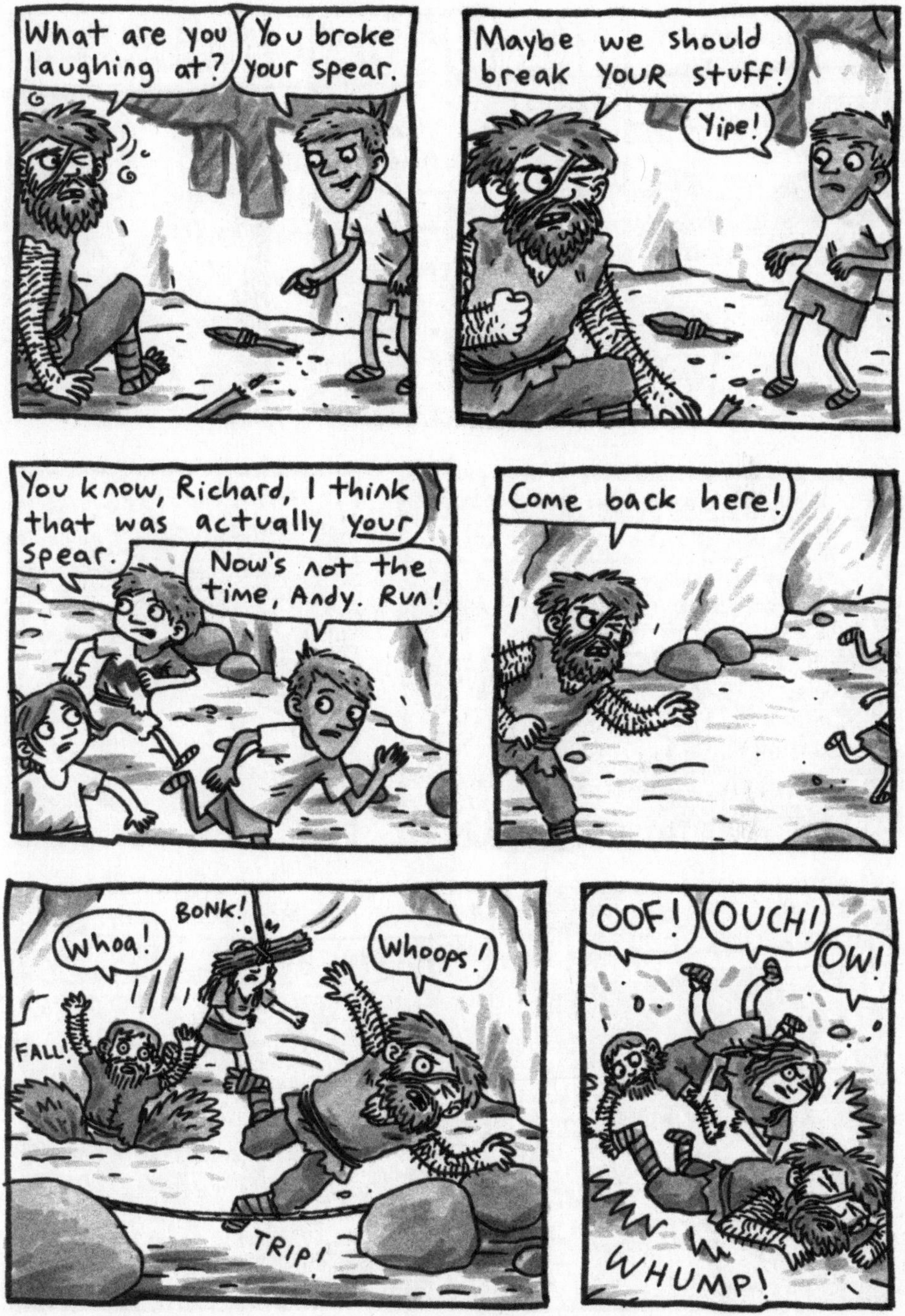
What are you laughing at?
You broke your spear.
Maybe we should break YOUR stuff!
Yipe!
You know, Richard, I think that was actually your spear.
Now's not the time, Andy. Run!
Come back here!
BONK!
Whoa!
Whoops!
FALL!
TRIP!
OOF!
OUCH!
OW!
WHUMP!

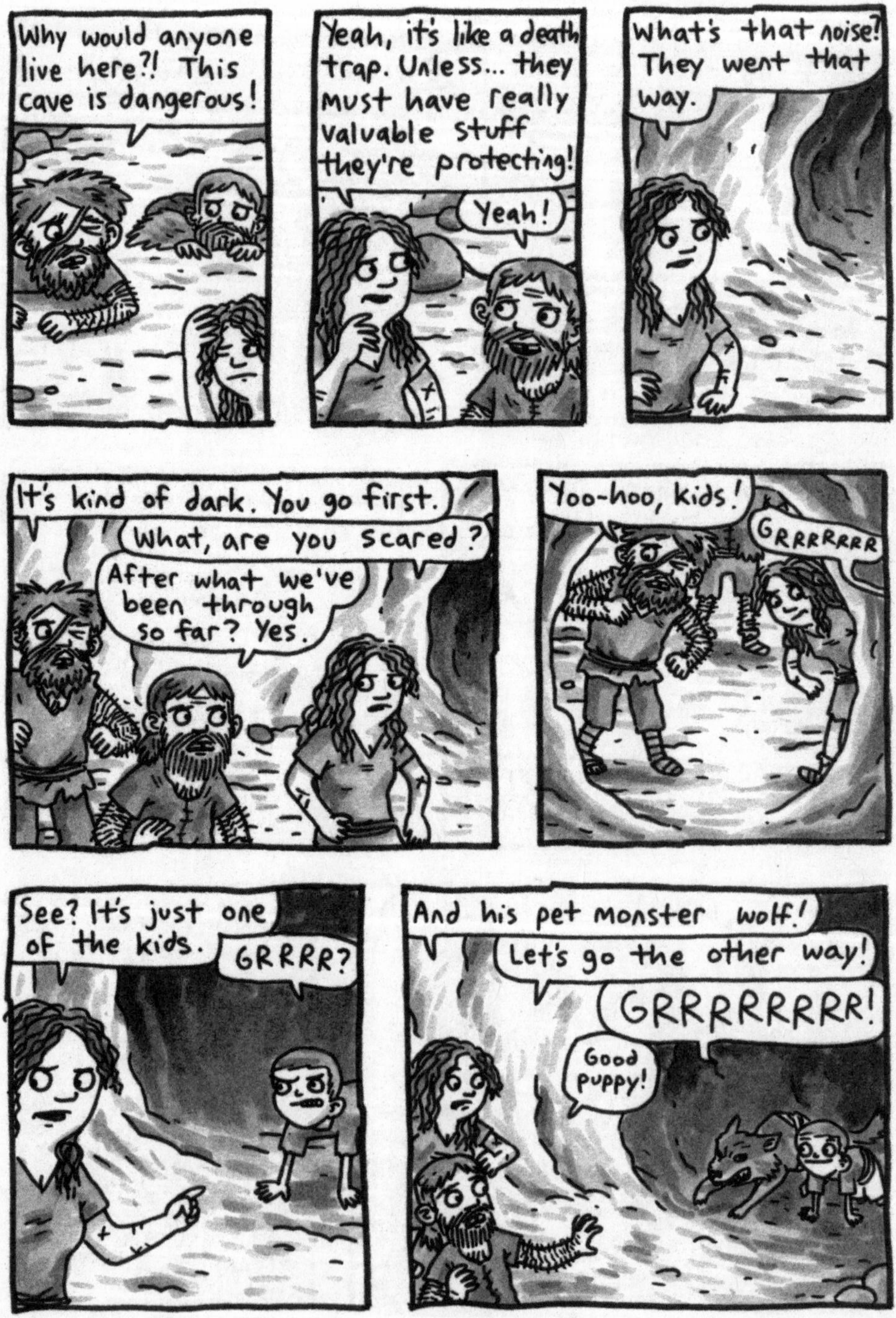
Why would anyone live here?! This cave is dangerous!
Yeah, it's like a death trap. Unless... they must have really valuable stuff they're protecting!
Yeah!
What's that noise? They went that way.
It's kind of dark. You go first.
What, are you scared?
After what we've been through so far? Yes.
Yoo-hoo, kids!
GRRRRRRR
See? It's just one of the kids.
GRRRR?
And his pet monster wolf!
Let's go the other way!
GRRRRRRRR!
Good puppy!

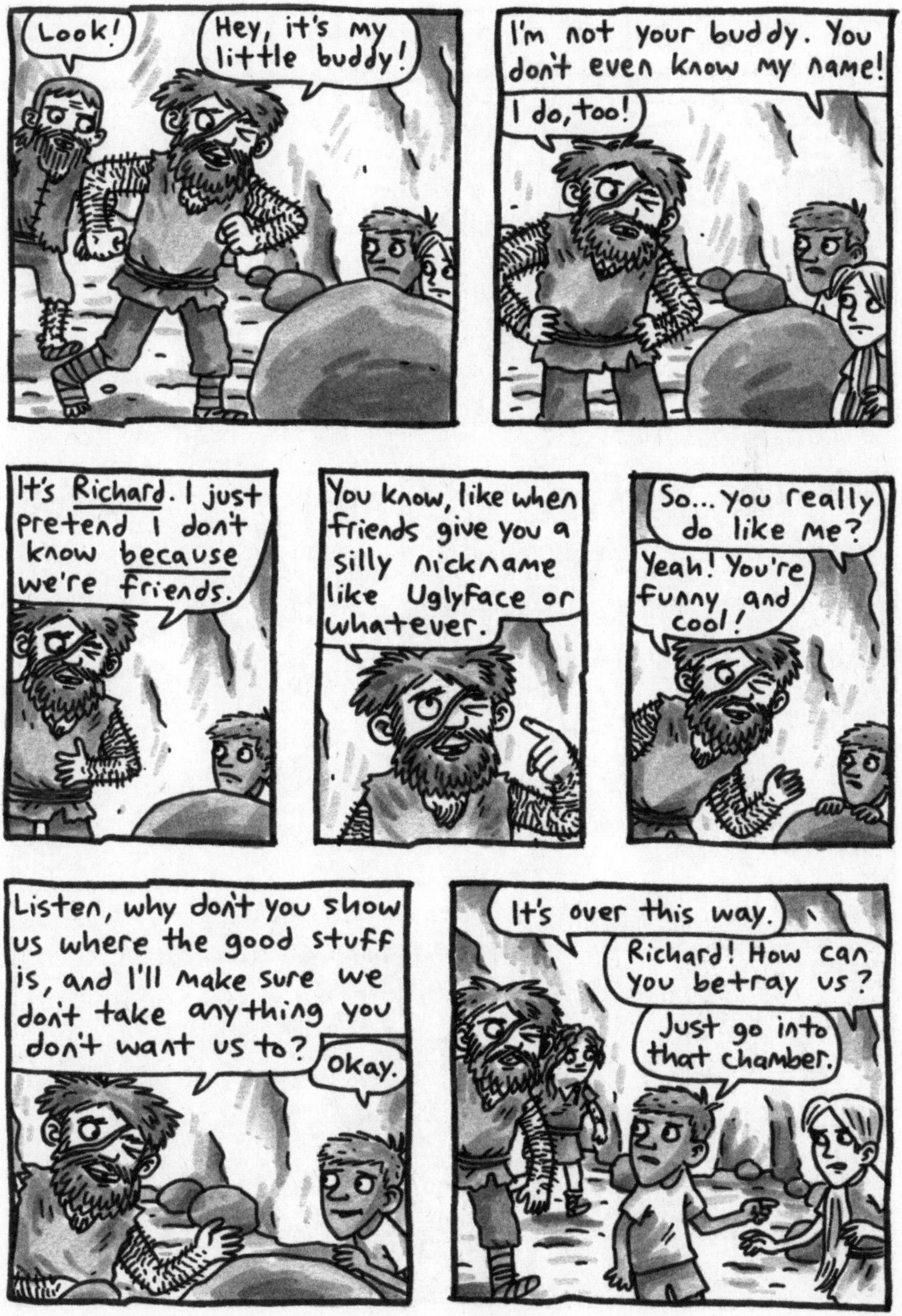
Look!
Hey, it's my little buddy!
I'm not your buddy. You don't even know my name!
I do, too!
It's Richard. I just pretend I don't know because we're friends.
You know, like when friends give you a silly nickname like Uglyface or whatever.
So... you really do like me?
Yeah! You're funny and cool!
Listen, why don't you show us where the good stuff is, and I'll make sure we don't take anything you don't want us to?
Okay.
It's over this way.
Richard! How can you betray us?
Just go into that chamber.

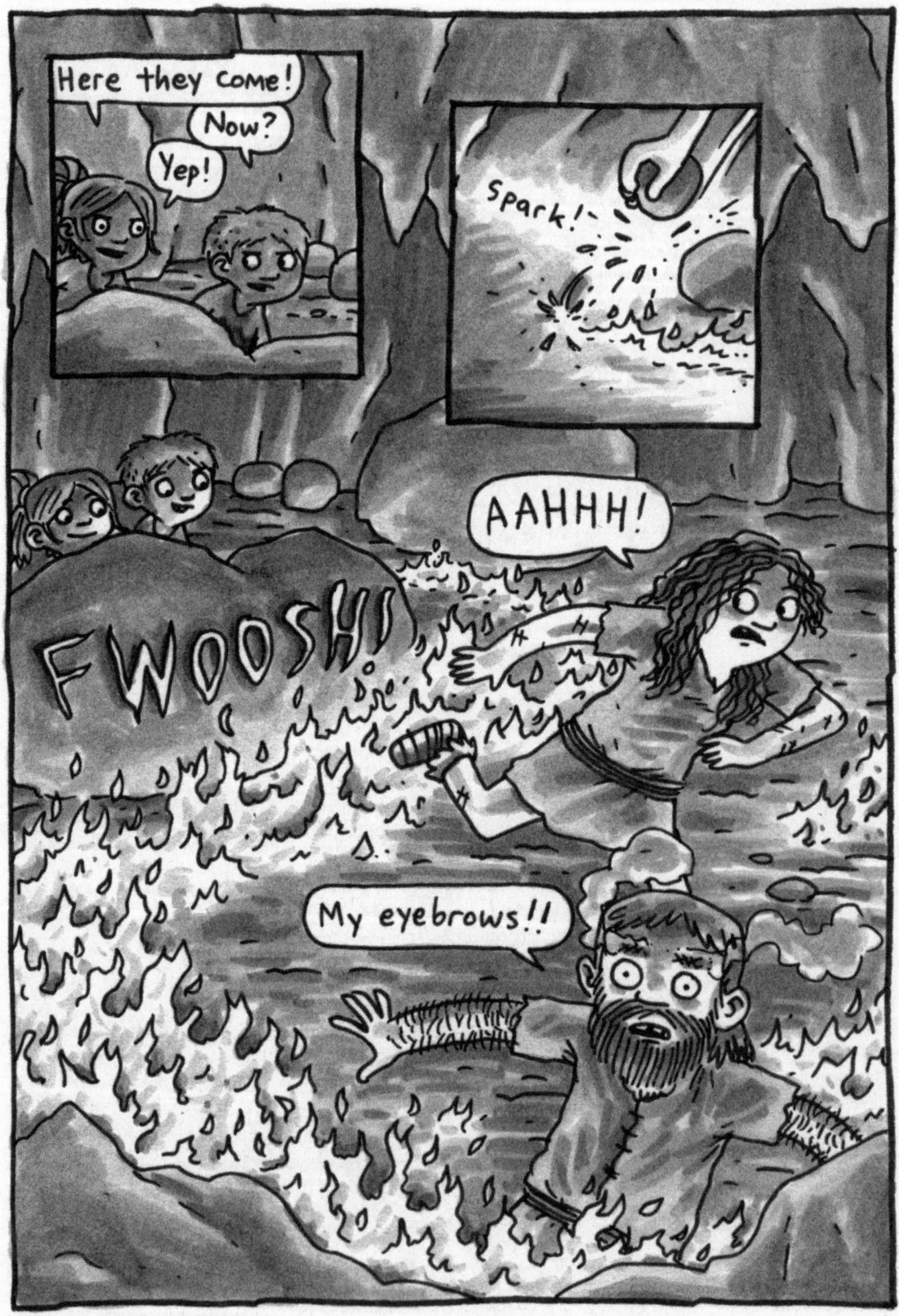
Here they come!
Now?
Yep!
Spark!
AAHHH!
FWOOSH!
My eyebrows!!

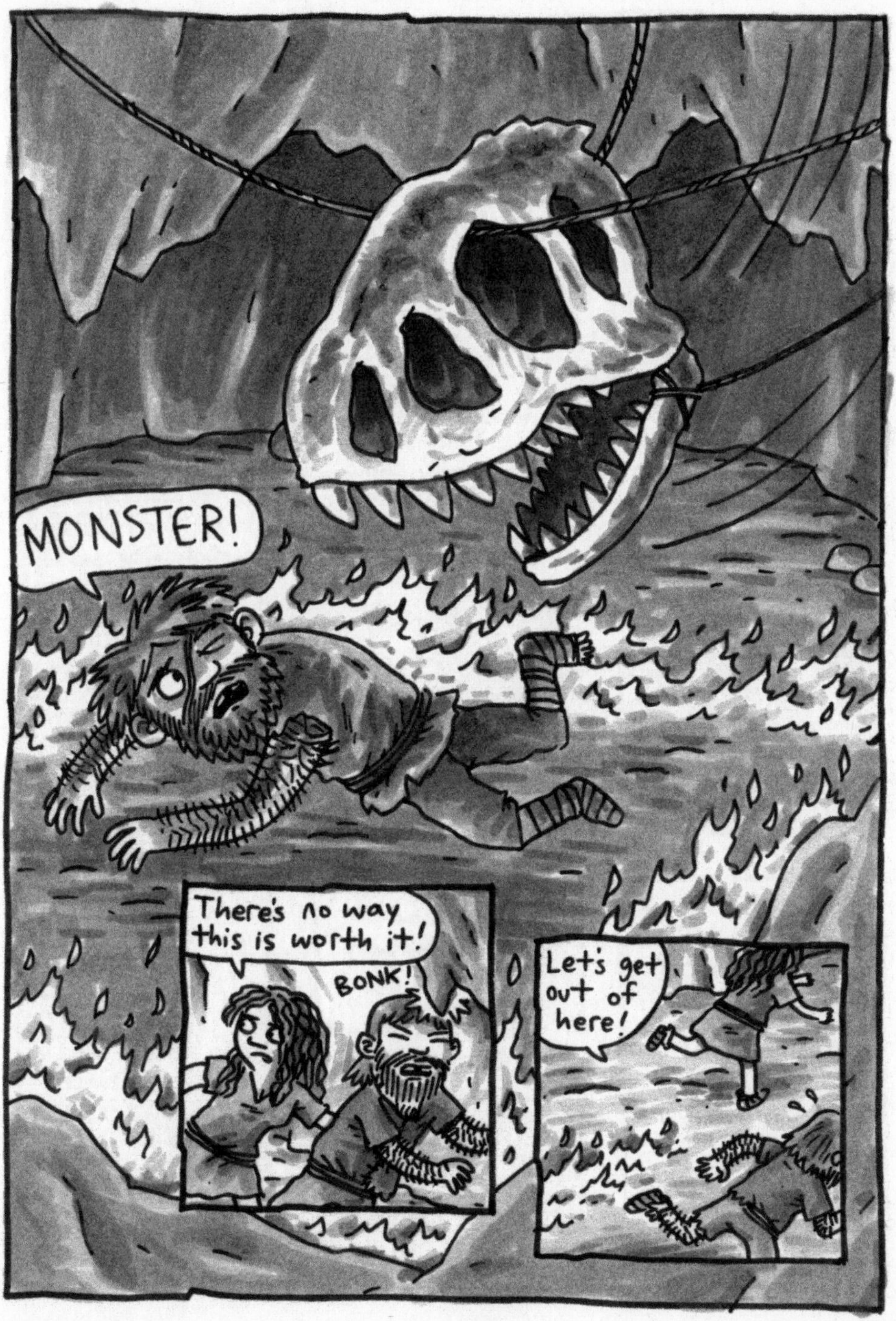
MONSTER!
There's no way this is worth it!
BONK!
Let's get out of here!

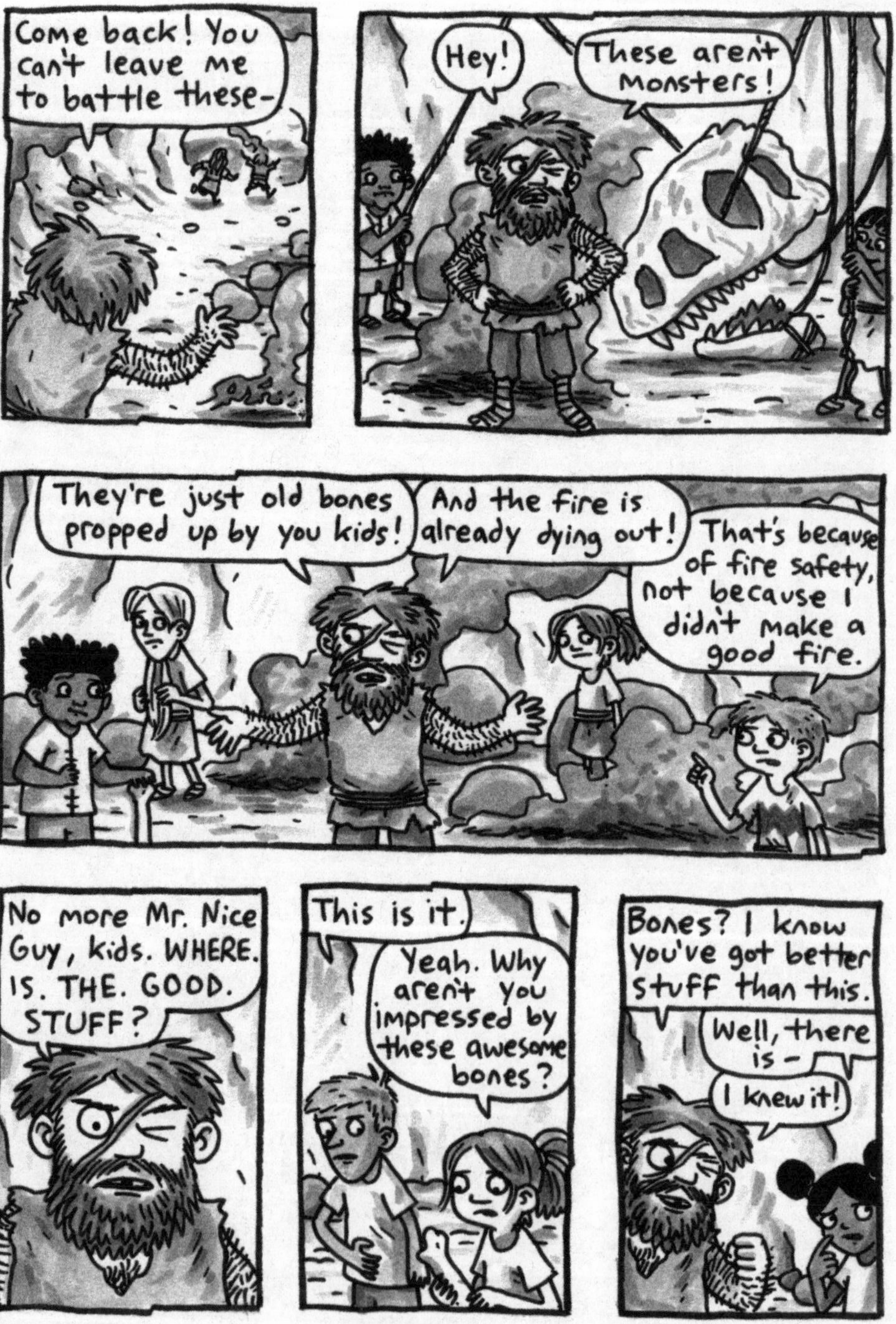
Come back! You can't leave me to battle these-
Hey!
These aren't Monsters!
They're just old bones propped up by you kids!
And the fire is already dying out!
That's because of fire safety, not because I didn't make a good fire.
No more Mr. Nice Guy, kids. WHERE. IS. THE. GOOD. STUFF?
This is it.
Yeah. Why aren't you impressed by these awesome bones?
Bones? I know you've got better stuff than this.
Well, there is -
I knew it!

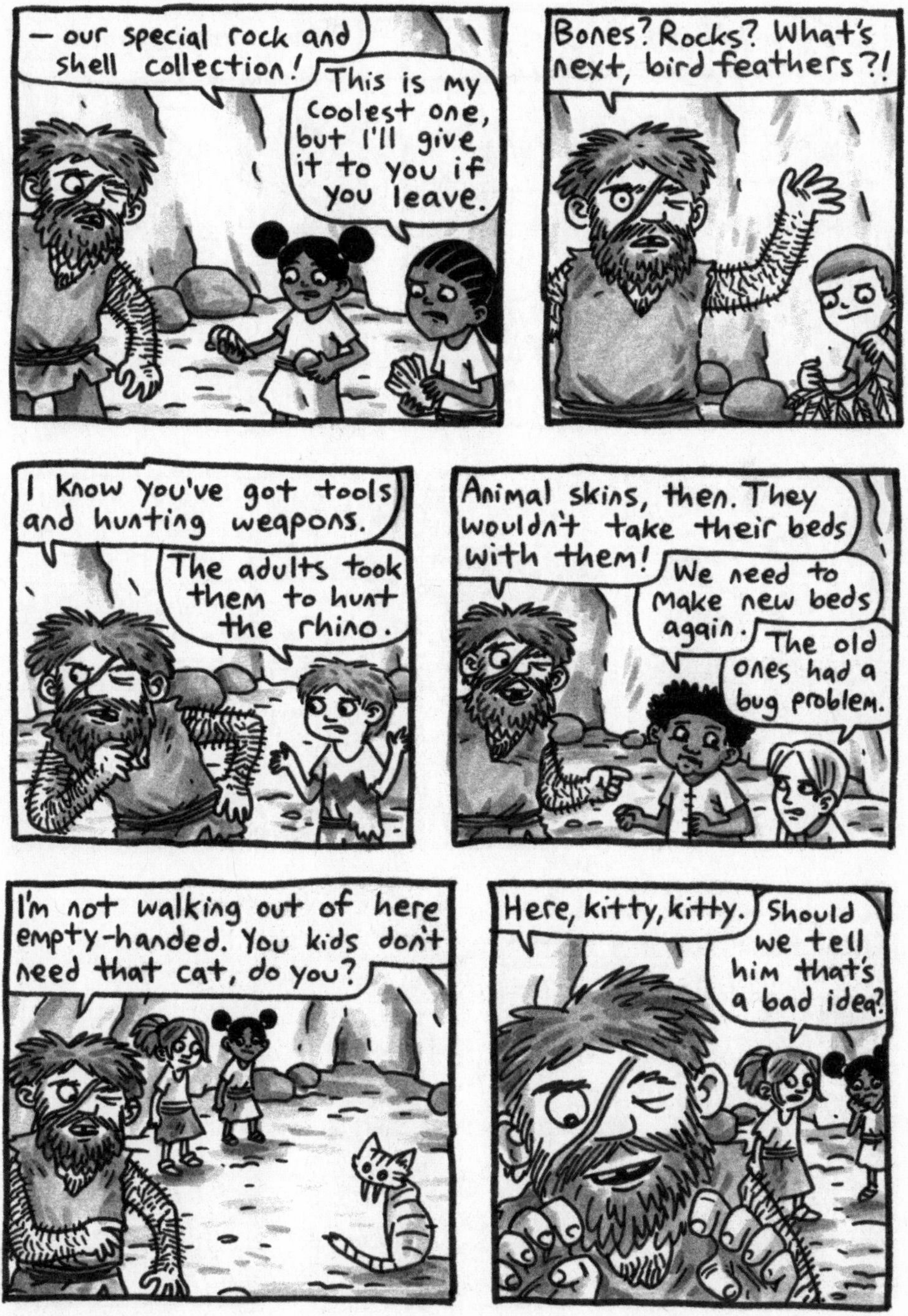
—our special rock and shell collection!
This is my coolest one, but I'll give it to you if you leave.
Bones? Rocks? What's next, bird feathers?!
I know you've got tools and hunting weapons.
The adults took them to hunt the rhino.
Animal skins, then. They wouldn't take their beds with them!
We need to make new beds again.
The old ones had a bug problem.
I'm not walking out of here empty-handed. You kids don't need that cat, do you?
Here, kitty, kitty.
Should we tell him that's a bad idea?

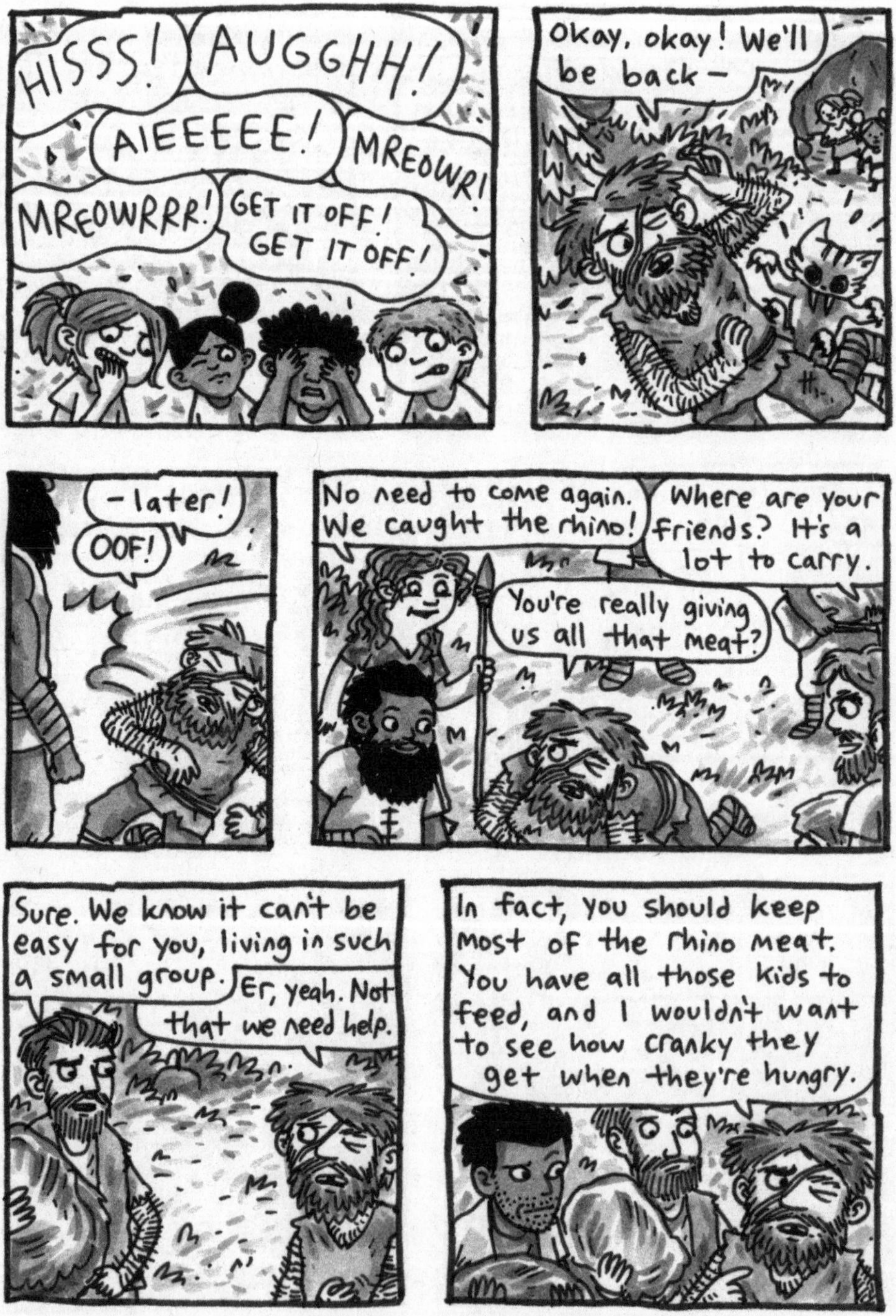
HISSS!
AUGGHH!
AIEEEEE!
MREOWR!
MREOWRRR!
GET IT OFF! GET IT OFF!
Okay, okay! We'll be back—
—later!
OOF!
No need to come again. We caught the rhino!
Where are your friends? It's a lot to carry.
You're really giving us all that meat?
Sure. We know it can't be easy for you, living in such a small group.
Er, yeah. Not that we need help.
In fact, you should keep most of the rhino meat. You have all those kids to feed, and I wouldn't want to see how cranky they get when they're hungry.

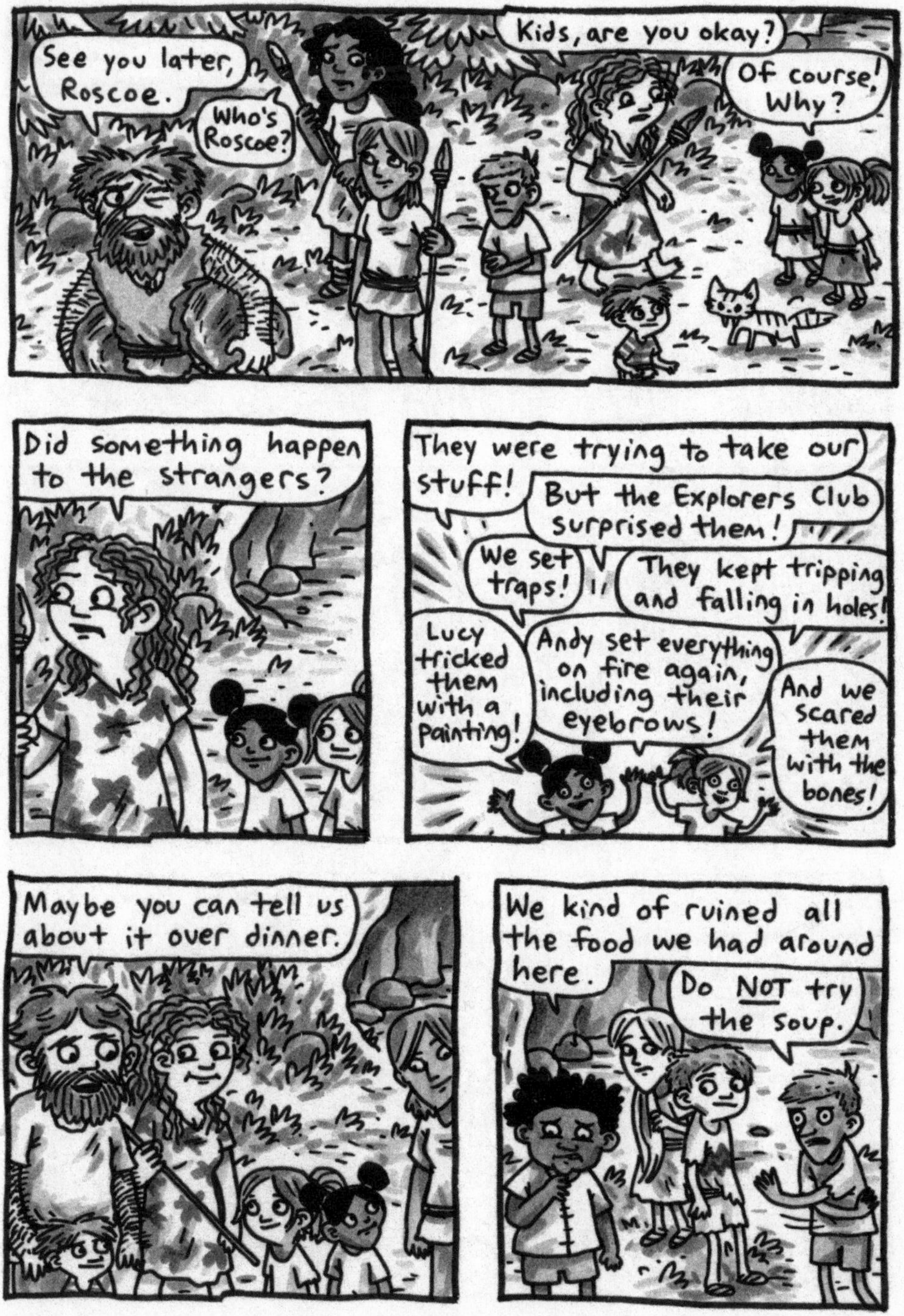
See you later, Roscoe.
Who's Roscoe?
Kids, are you okay?
Of course! Why?
Did something happen to the strangers?
They were trying to take our stuff!
But the Explorers Club surprised them!
We set traps!
They kept tripping and falling in holes!
Lucy tricked them with a painting!
Andy set everything on fire again, including their eyebrows!
And we scared them with the bones!
Maybe you can tell us about it over dinner.
We kind of ruined all the food we had around here.
Do NOT try the soup.

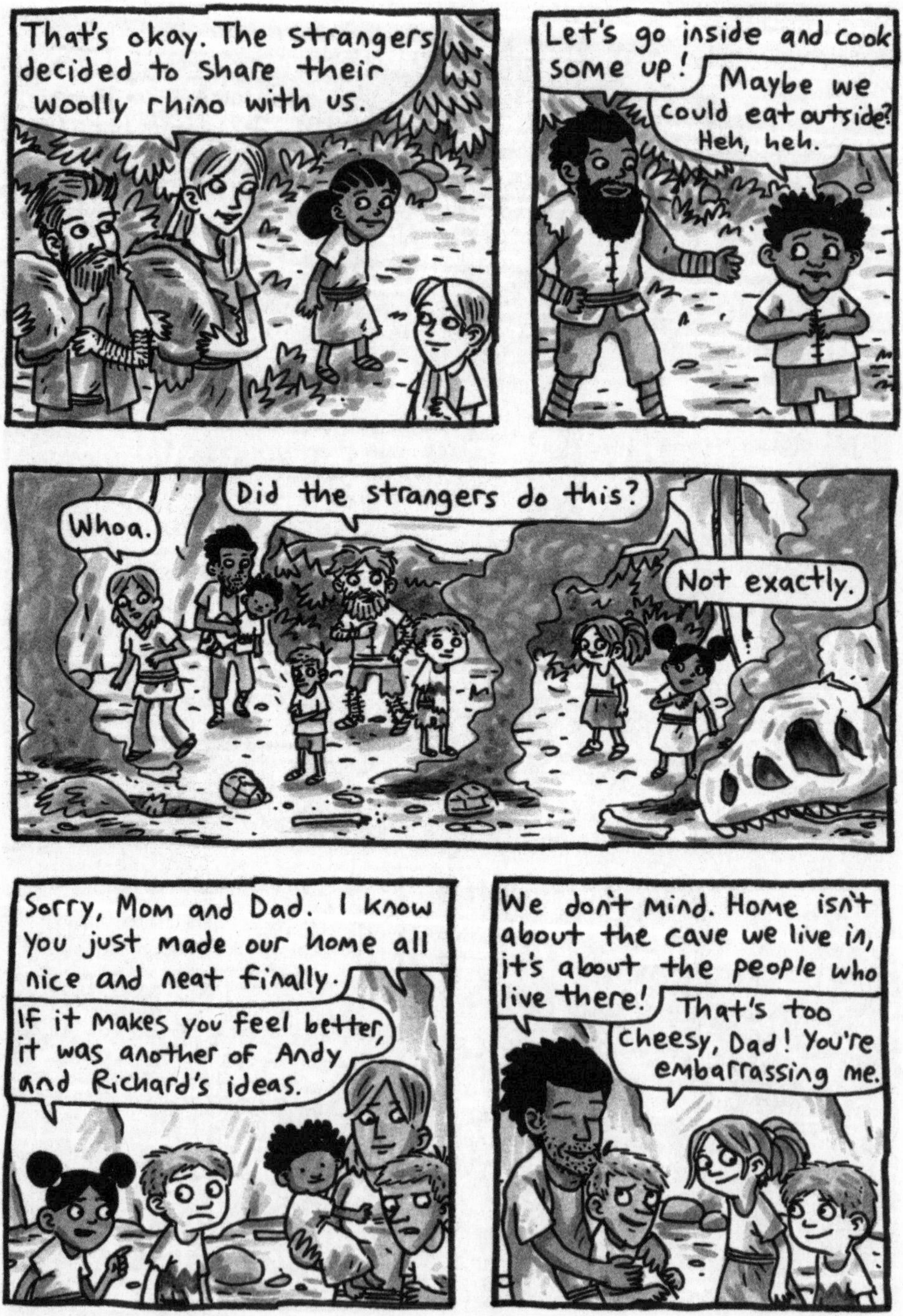
That's okay. The strangers decided to share their woolly rhino with us.
Let's go inside and cook some up!
Maybe we could eat outside? Heh, heh.
Whoa.
Did the strangers do this?
Not exactly.
Sorry, Mom and Dad. I know you just made our home all nice and neat finally.
If it makes you feel better, it was another of Andy and Richard's ideas.
We don't mind. Home isn't about the cave we live in, it's about the people who live there!
That's too cheesy, Dad! You're embarrassing me.

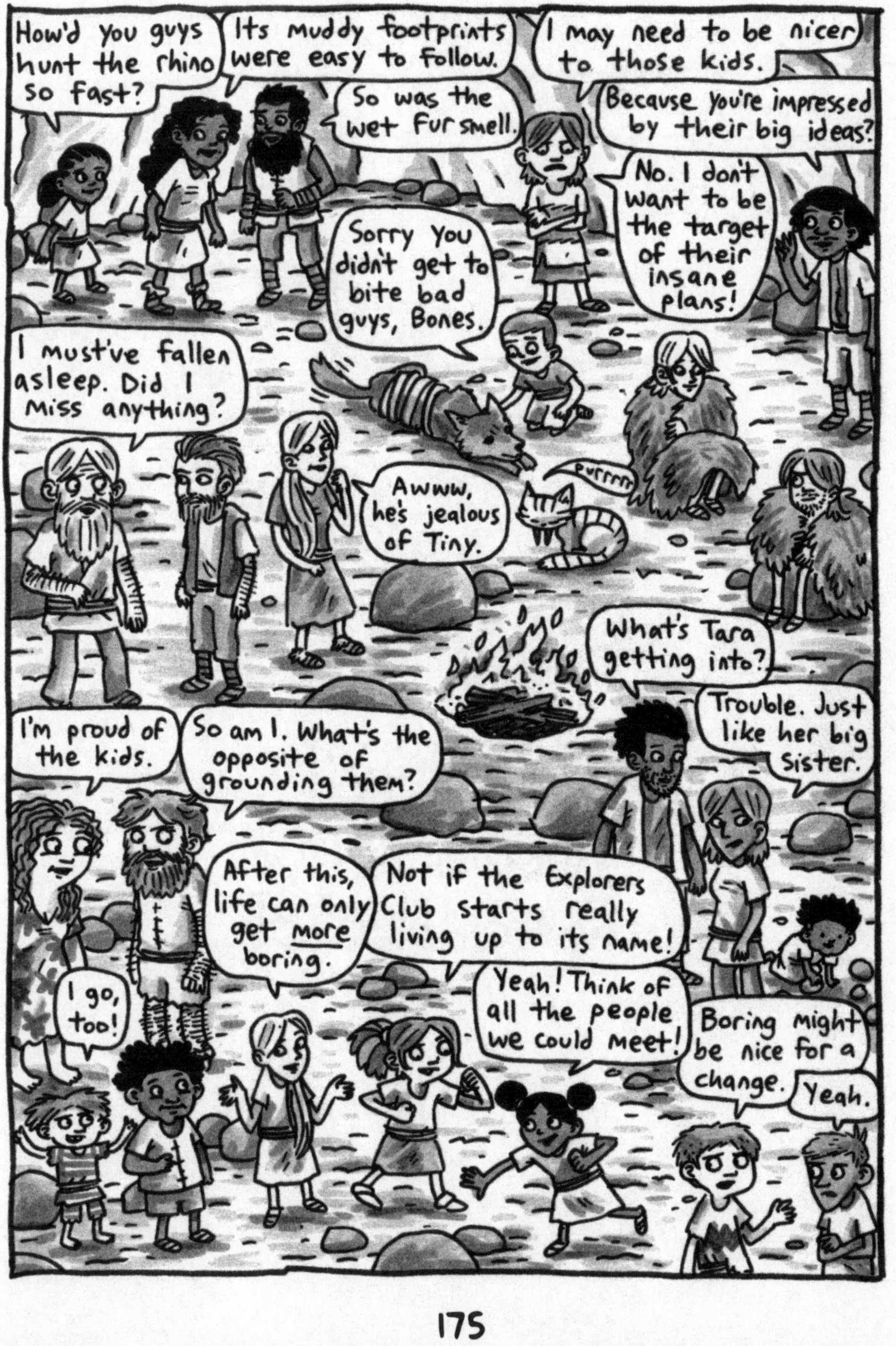
How'd you guys hunt the rhino so fast?
Its muddy footprints were easy to follow.
So was the wet fur smell.
I may need to be nicer to those kids.
Because you're impressed by their big ideas?
No. I don't want to be the target of their insane plans!
Sorry you didn't get to bite bad guys, Bones.
I must've fallen asleep. Did I miss anything?
Awww, he's jealous of Tiny.
Purrrrr
What's Tara getting into?
Trouble. Just like her big sister.
I'm proud of the kids.
So am I. What's the opposite of grounding them?
After this, life can only get more boring.
Not if the Explorers Club starts really living up to its name!
I go, too!
Yeah! Think of all the people we could meet!
Boring might be nice for a change.
Yeah.

THE END...
AND A NEW
BEGINNING!

FORTY THOUSAND YEARS LATER... (TODAY)

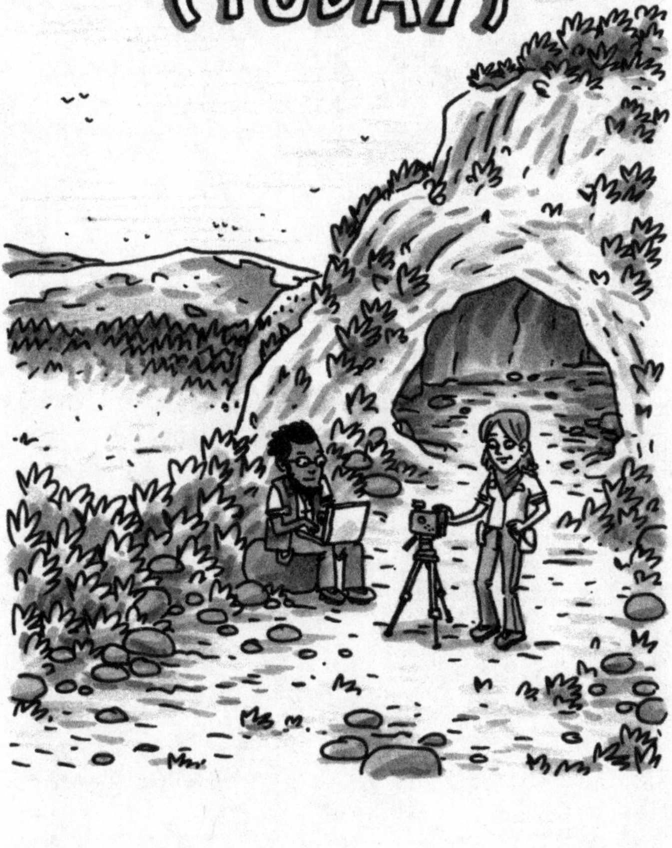

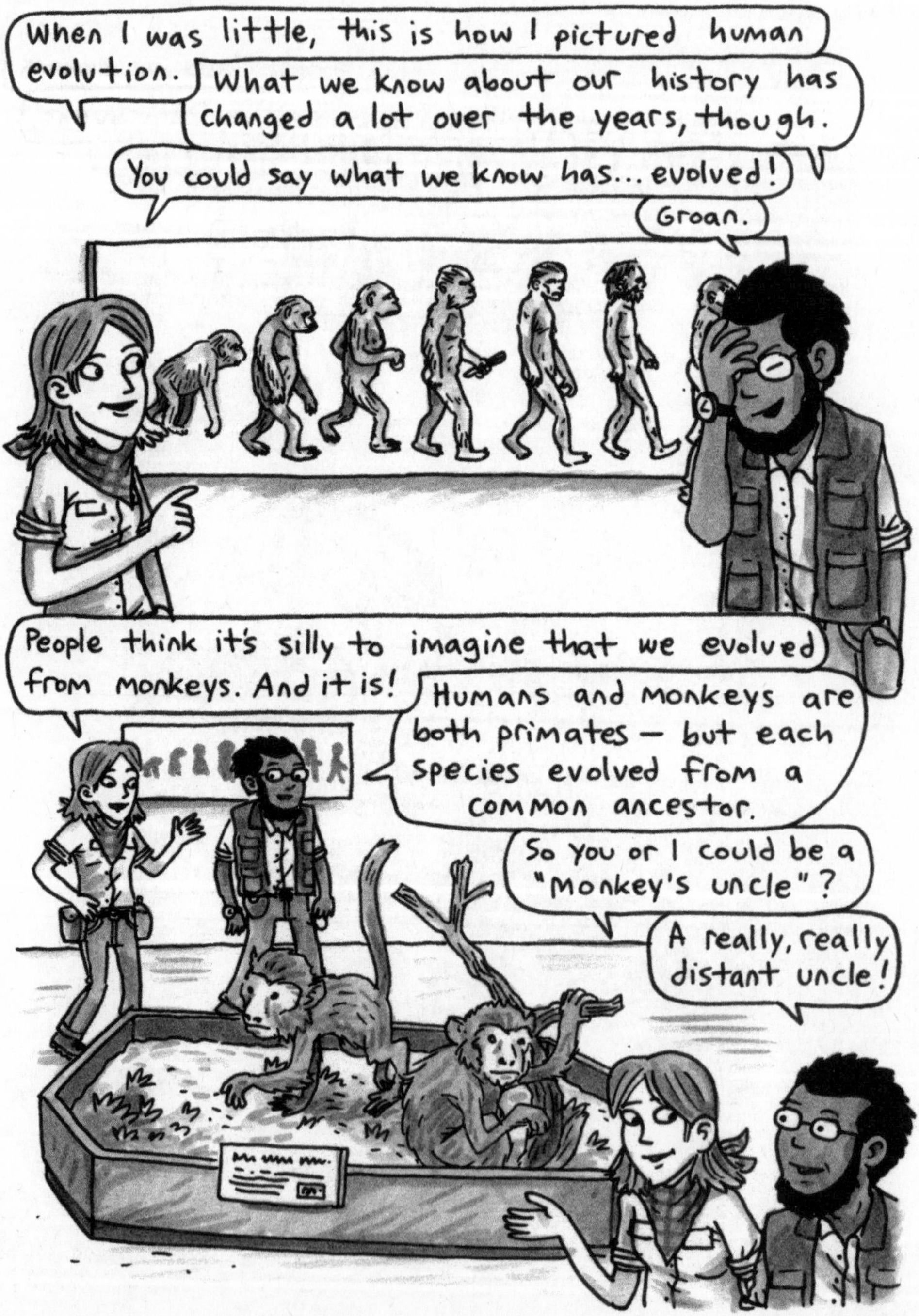

When I was little, this is how I pictured human evolution.
What we know about our history has changed a lot over the years, though.
You could say what we know has... evolved!
Groan.
People think it's silly to imagine that we evolved from monkeys. And it is!
Humans and monkeys are both primates — but each species evolved from a common ancestor.
So you or I could be a "monkey's uncle"?
A really, really distant uncle!

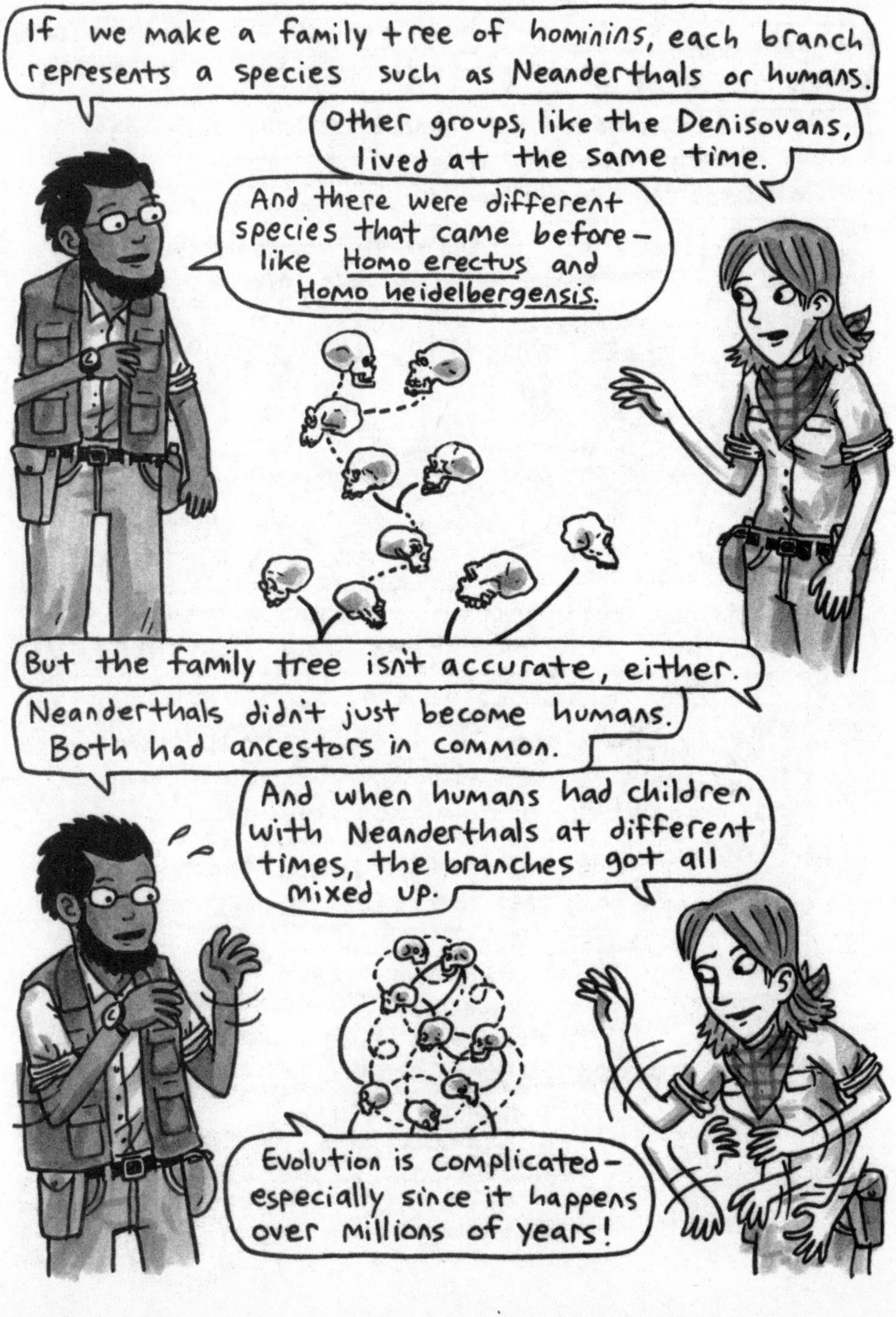
If we make a family tree of hominins, each branch represents a species such as Neanderthals or humans.
Other groups, like the Denisovans, lived at the same time.
And there were different species that came before— like Homo erectus and Homo heidelbergensis.
But the family tree isn't accurate, either.
Neanderthals didn't just become humans. Both had ancestors in common.
And when humans had children with Neanderthals at different times, the branches got all mixed up.
Evolution is complicated— especially since it happens over millions of years!

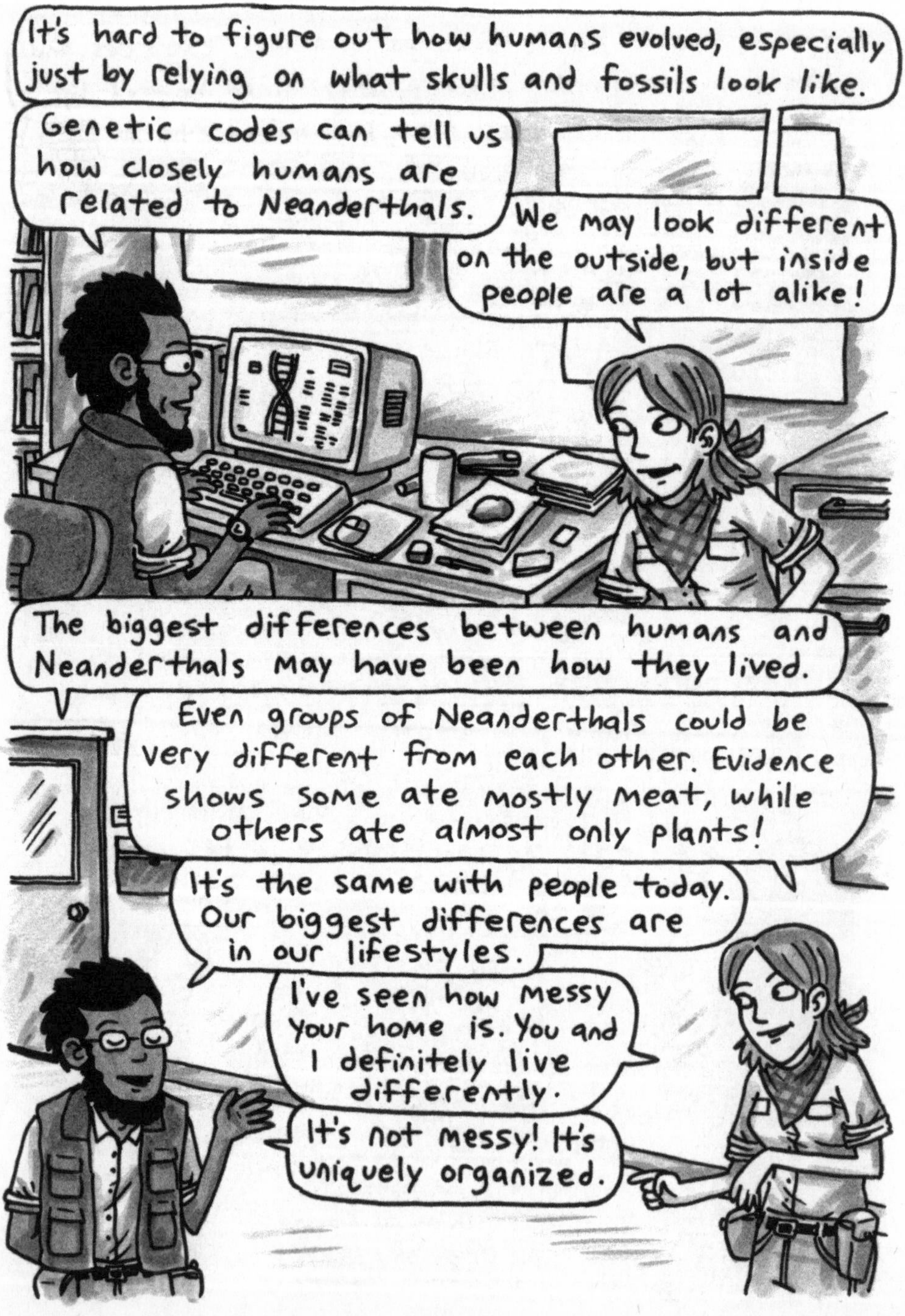
It's hard to figure out how humans evolved, especially just by relying on what skulls and fossils look like.
Genetic codes can tell us how closely humans are related to Neanderthals.
We may look different on the outside, but inside people are a lot alike!
The biggest differences between humans and Neanderthals may have been how they lived.
Even groups of Neanderthals could be very different from each other. Evidence shows some ate mostly meat, while others ate almost only plants!
It's the same with people today. Our biggest differences are in our lifestyles.
I've seen how messy your home is. You and I definitely live differently.
It's not messy! It's uniquely organized.

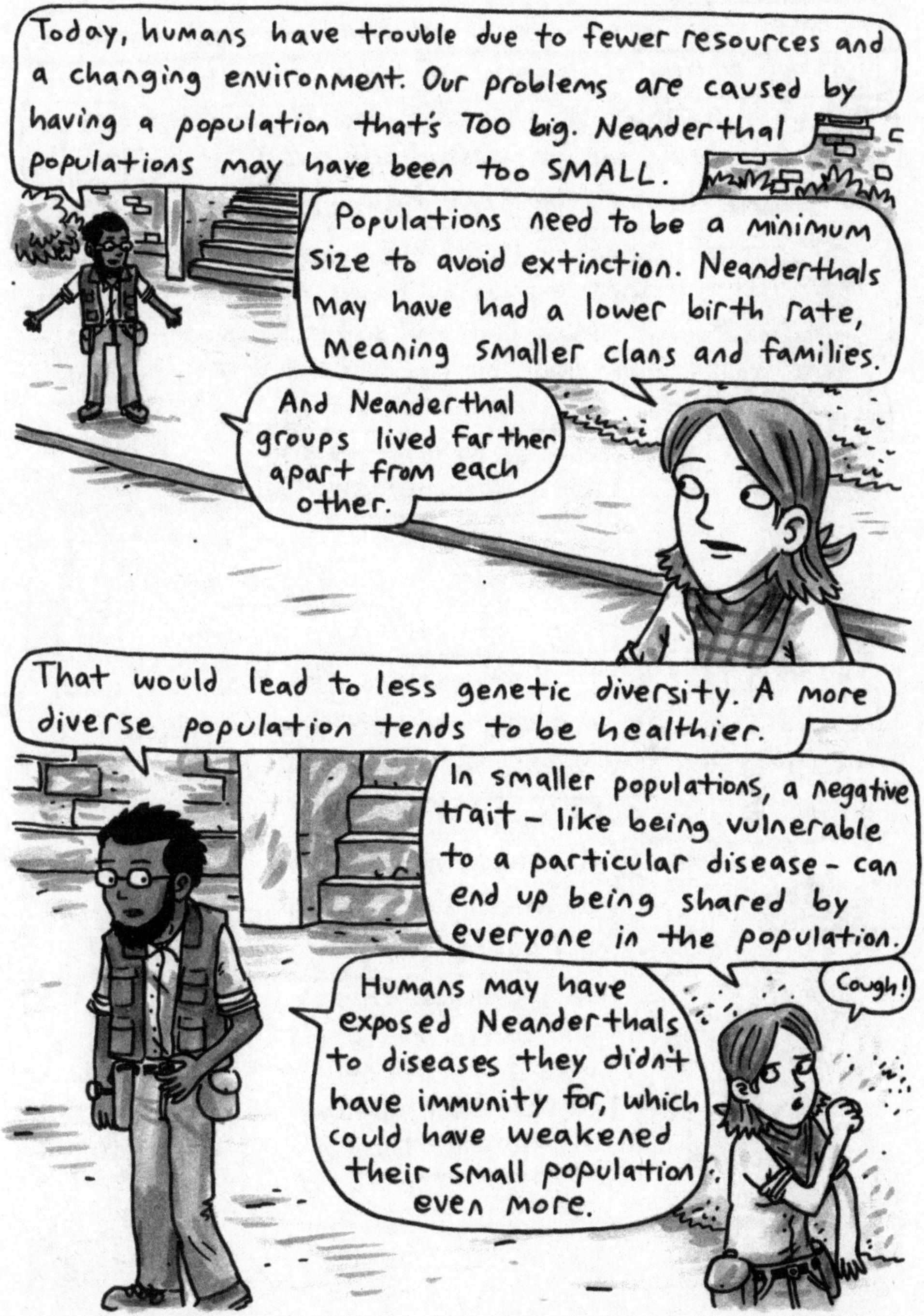
Today, humans have trouble due to fewer resources and a changing environment. Our problems are caused by having a population that's TOO big. Neanderthal populations may have been too SMALL.
Populations need to be a minimum size to avoid extinction. Neanderthals may have had a lower birth rate, meaning smaller clans and families.
And Neanderthal groups lived farther apart from each other.
That would lead to less genetic diversity. A more diverse population tends to be healthier.
In smaller populations, a negative trait - like being vulnerable to a particular disease - can end up being shared by everyone in the population.
Cough!
Humans may have exposed Neanderthals to diseases they didn't have immunity for, which could have weakened their small population even more.

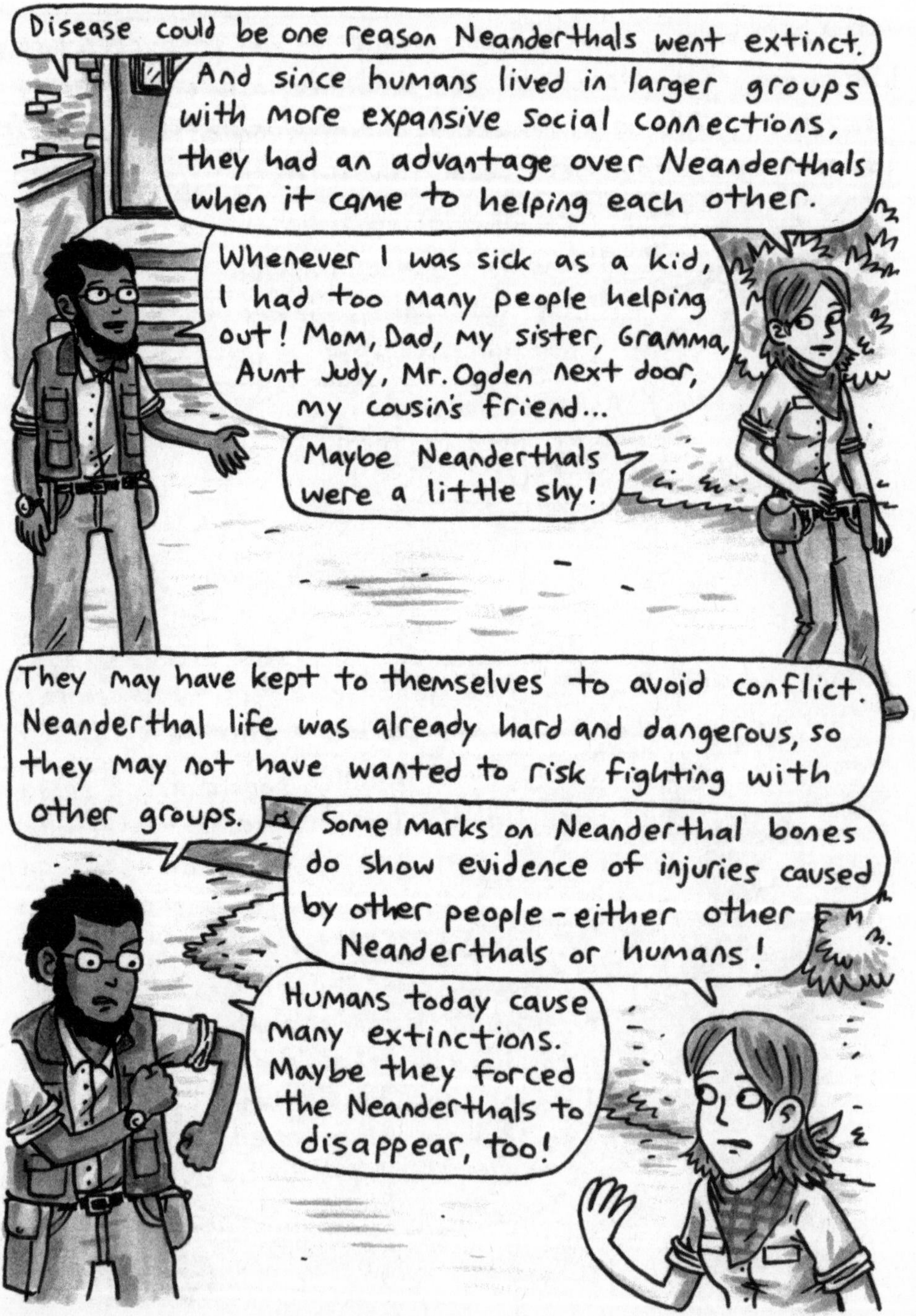

Disease could be one reason Neanderthals went extinct.
And since humans lived in larger groups with more expansive social connections, they had an advantage over Neanderthals when it came to helping each other.
Whenever I was sick as a kid, I had too many people helping out! Mom, Dad, my sister, Gramma, Aunt Judy, Mr. Ogden next door, my cousin's friend...
Maybe Neanderthals were a little shy!
They may have kept to themselves to avoid conflict. Neanderthal life was already hard and dangerous, so they may not have wanted to risk fighting with other groups.
Some marks on Neanderthal bones do show evidence of injuries caused by other people - either other Neanderthals or humans!
Humans today cause many extinctions. Maybe they forced the Neanderthals to disappear, too!

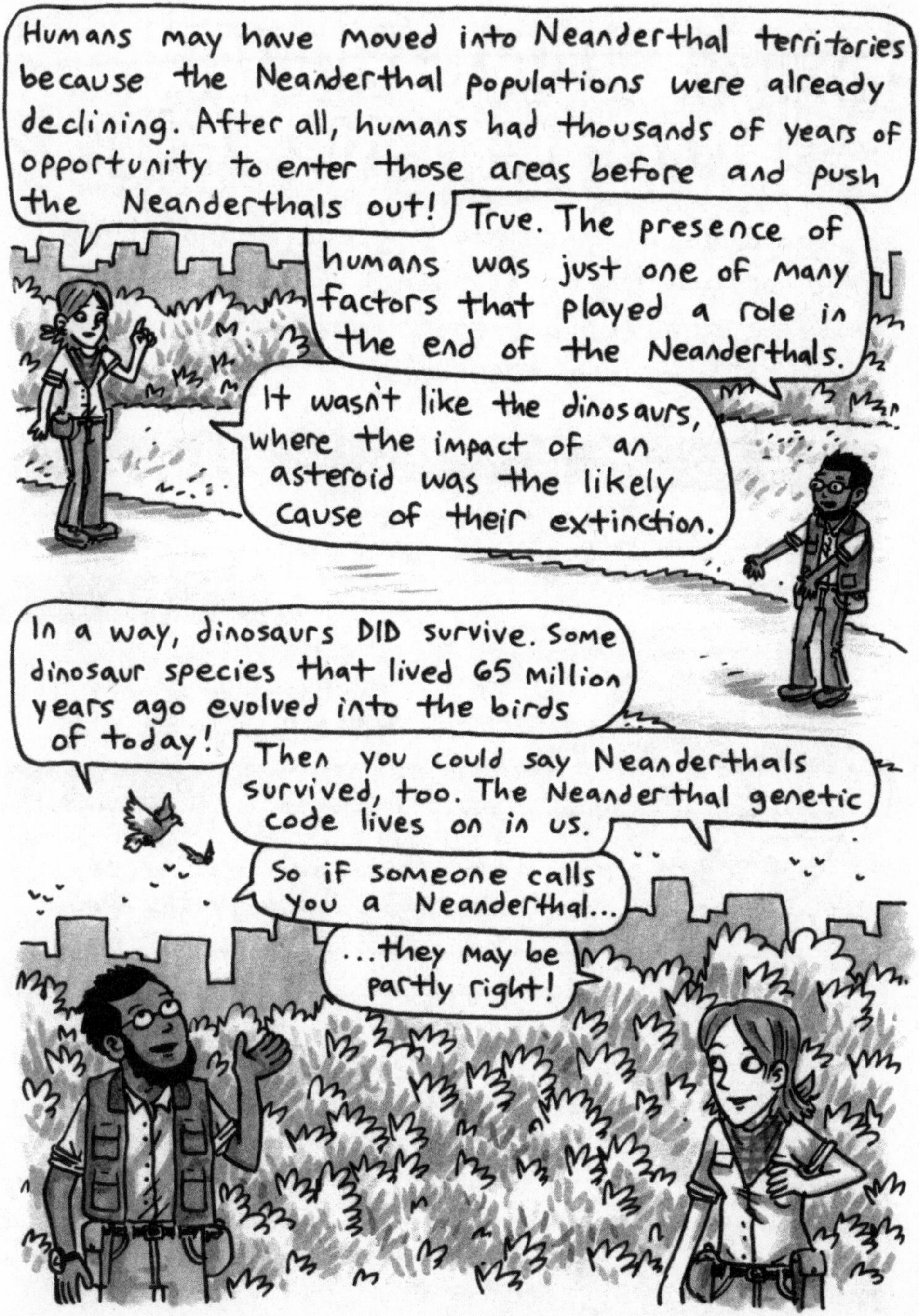
Humans may have moved into Neanderthal territories because the Neanderthal populations were already declining. After all, humans had thousands of years of opportunity to enter those areas before and push the Neanderthals out!
True. The presence of humans was just one of many factors that played a role in the end of the Neanderthals.
It wasn't like the dinosaurs, where the impact of an asteroid was the likely cause of their extinction.
In a way, dinosaurs DID survive. Some dinosaur species that lived 65 million years ago evolved into the birds of today!
Then you could say Neanderthals survived, too. The Neanderthal genetic code lives on in us.
So if someone calls you a Neanderthal...
...they may be partly right!

HOW LONG HAVE WE BEEN HERE?

It's hard to imagine how long ago Neanderthals lived, or how long ago humans first appeared, or how long ago our ancestors first walked upright. It was a long, long time ago!

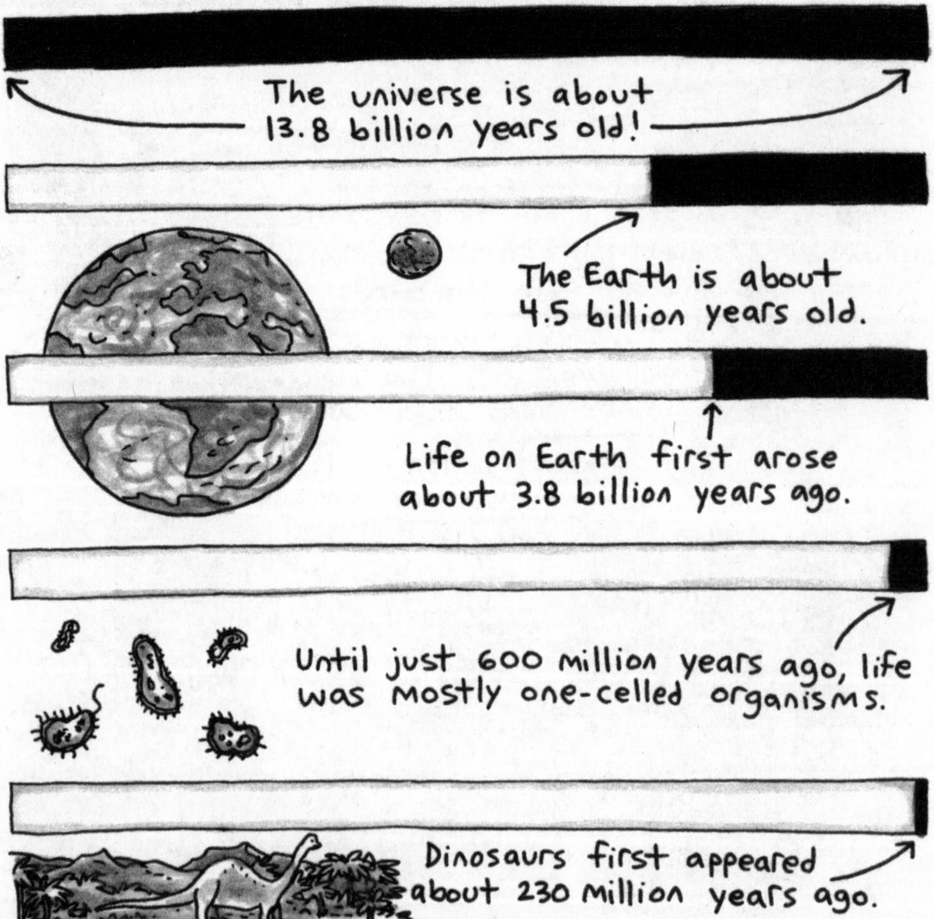

The universe is about 13.8 billion years old!

The Earth is about 4.5 billion years old.

Life on Earth first arose about 3.8 billion years ago.

Until just 600 million years ago, life was mostly one-celled organisms.

Dinosaurs first appeared about 230 million years ago.

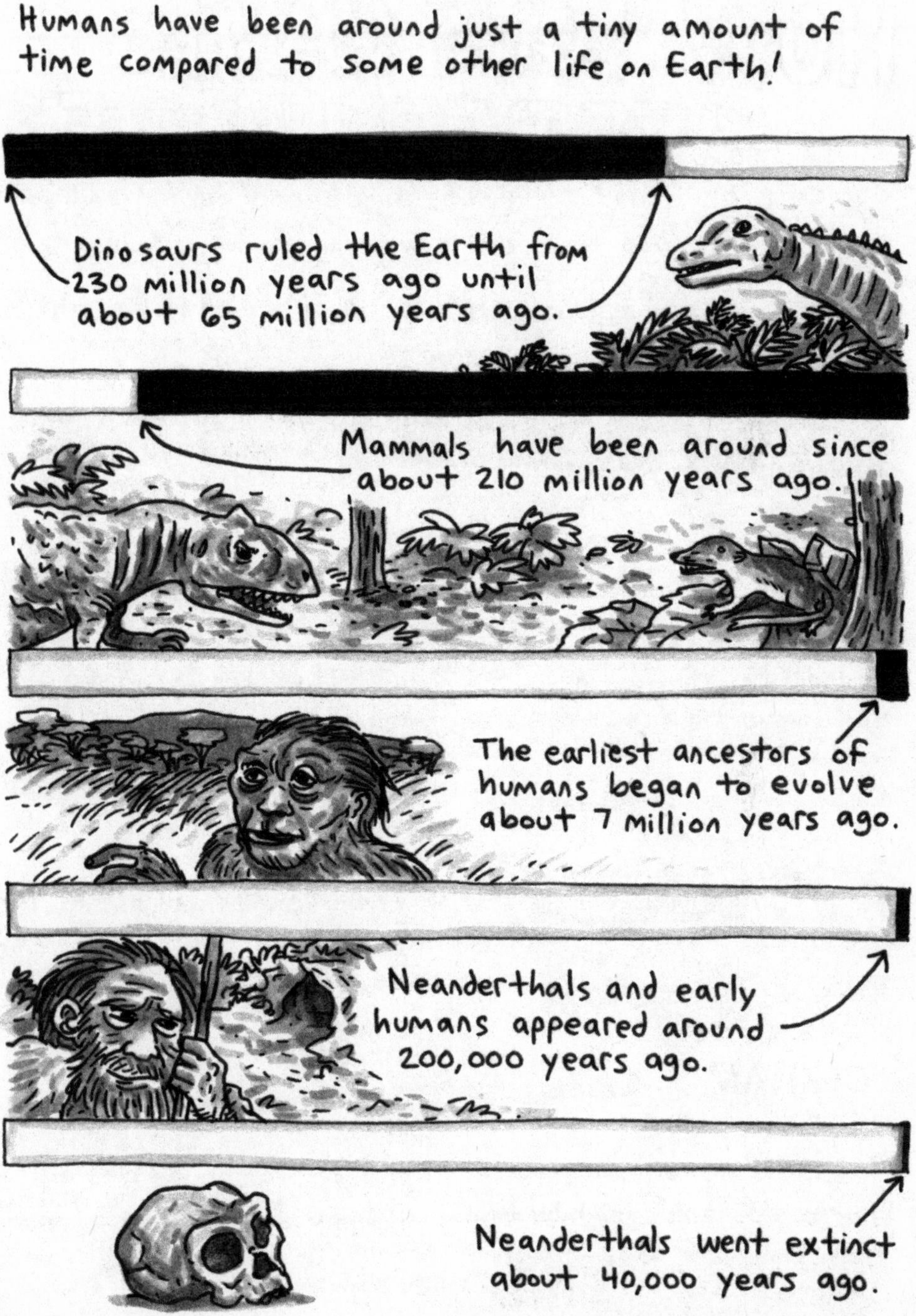
Humans have been around just a tiny amount of time compared to some other life on Earth!
Dinosaurs ruled the Earth from 230 million years ago until about 65 million years ago.
Mammals have been around since about 210 million years ago.
The earliest ancestors of humans began to evolve about 7 million years ago.
Neanderthals and early humans appeared around 200,000 years ago.
Neanderthals went extinct about 40,000 years ago.

FAMOUS CAVES

These are some of the best-known caves where evidence of Neanderthal life has been found - and no doubt there are more caves waiting to be discovered!

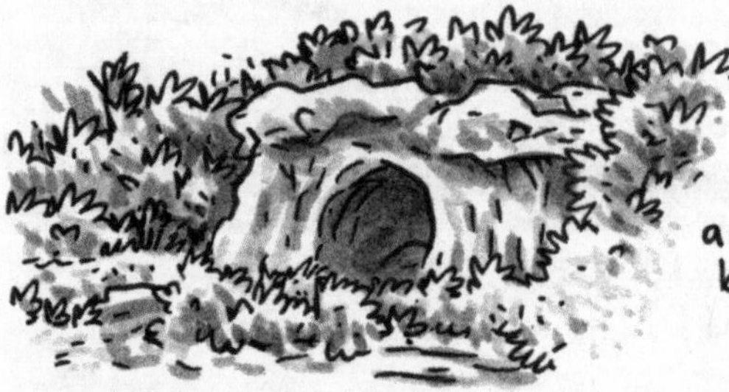

LE MOUSTIER CAVE

Dordogne, France

Contained Neanderthal bones and flint tools, which have been named moustierien after the site

VINDIJA CAVE

Donja Voća, Croatia

Some of the best-preserved Neanderthal fossils in the world have been found at this site.

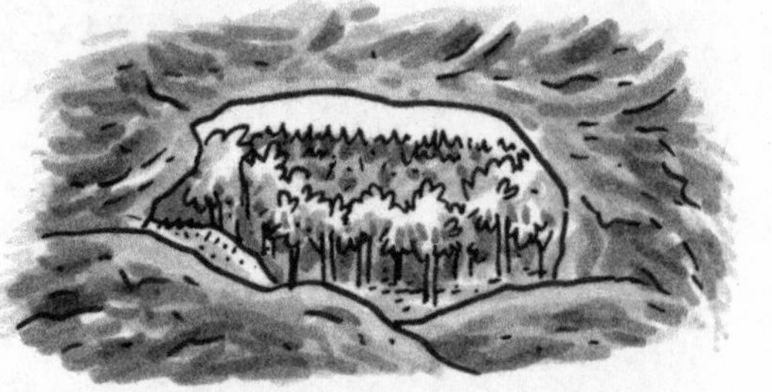

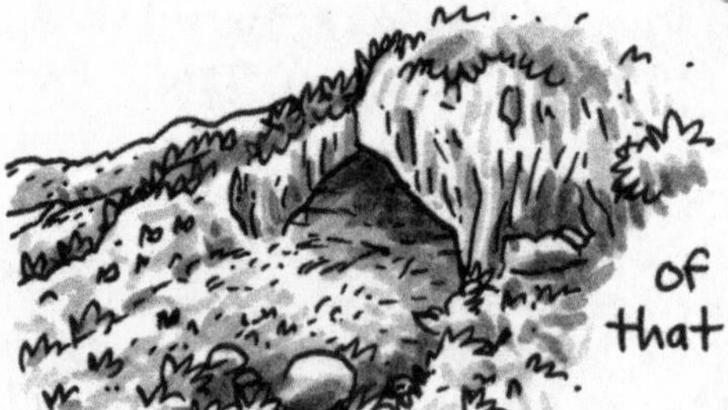

SHANIDAR CAVE

Kurdistan, Iraq

Held remains and artifacts of many Neanderthals, and evidence that they buried their dead

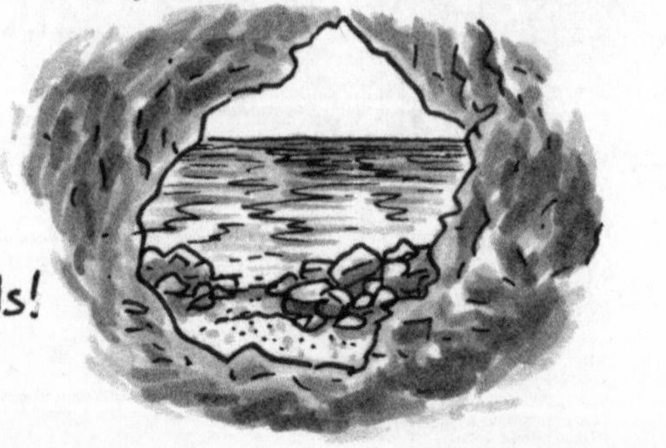

GORHAM'S CAVE

Gibraltar

One of the last known living spaces of Neanderthals!

REAL PALEONTOLOGISTS

Pam and Eric are book characters, but the paleontologists who have researched Neanderthals are actual people! These are just a few whose work helped me in writing the Lucy & Andy Neanderthal series!

 **RALPH AND ROSE SOLECKI** investigated Neanderthal burials and helped change the concept of Neanderthals as primitive brutes.

  **SVANTE PÄÄBO** decoded the Neanderthal genome and helped improve the science of paleogenetics.

CLIVE FINLAYSON has extensively studied the last-known sites of Neanderthals and their interactions with humans.

 **KATERINA HARVATI'S** research has included theories on modern human origins and the use of 3-D modeling in paleoanthropology.

 **FRANÇOIS BORDES** refined the study of stone toolmaking.

 **PAT SHIPMAN** wrote about how early humans may have been helped by domesticating wolves.

MARY C. STINER investigated how Neanderthals interacted with animals and plants.

You might think you need to be a scientist to see real fossils, but even if you're not a paleontologist (yet), you can visit museums to start your training as an expert on Neanderthals and evolution!

MUSEO DE LA EVOLUCIÓN HUMANA

MUSEUM OF HUMAN EVOLUTION

Burgos, Spain

Has an extensive collection of fossils and re-creations of hominin ancestors to tell the story of our human past

NATURAL HISTORY MUSEUM OF LOS ANGELES COUNTY

California, USA

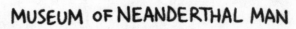

Permanent exhibits include the story of evolution in the Age of Mammals and the massive Dinosaur Hall

MUSEUM OF NEANDERTHAL MAN

La Chapelle aux Saints, France

Exhibits related to the first discovery of a Neanderthal burial plus workshops and programs on Neanderthals and prehistory

FACT OR FICTION?

Lots of things in Lucy and Andy's story really happened thousands of years ago, but maybe not quite everything. What did scientists find out, and what was made up?

DID NEANDERTHAL CAVES HAVE ROOMS?
From studying artifacts found in different areas of caves, scientists have learned that Neanderthals had separate spaces for sleeping, eating, and making tools. They didn't have TV rooms, though!

DID NEANDERTHALS COLLECT FOSSILS?
Dinosaur fossils haven't been found alongside Neanderthal fossils, so it's highly unlikely. But paleontologists know that Neanderthals collected interesting rocks occasionally.

DID NEANDERTHALS EAT A PALEO DIET?
While the popular "paleo diet" of today includes eating a lot of meat, Neanderthals definitely ate their vegetables. They couldn't import organic kale from far away, though! Many vegetables and plants we eat today, like tomatoes, peppers, and broccoli, didn't grow in Europe and Asia when Neanderthals lived.

DID NEANDERTHALS PLANT CROPS?

Neanderthals ate plants, but didn't grow them. Humans first cultivated specific plants around 10,000 years ago. So Neanderthal kids never had the chore of weeding their vegetable garden!

DID DIFFERENT KINDS OF EARLY PEOPLE LIVE TOGETHER?

There's evidence that at least three groups— humans, Neanderthals, and Denisovans — lived together. There may have been more, but we're still learning the extent of their interaction.

DID NEANDERTHALS ALWAYS LIVE IN CAVES?

It may seem that Neanderthals always lived in caves, but that's because most of the evidence we've found is in caves, where artifacts are better preserved. Artifacts from some open-air camps may mean Neanderthals slept under the stars more than we thought!

COULD NEANDERTHAL KIDS ACTUALLY OUTRUN A CHARGING WOOLLY RHINO?

No!

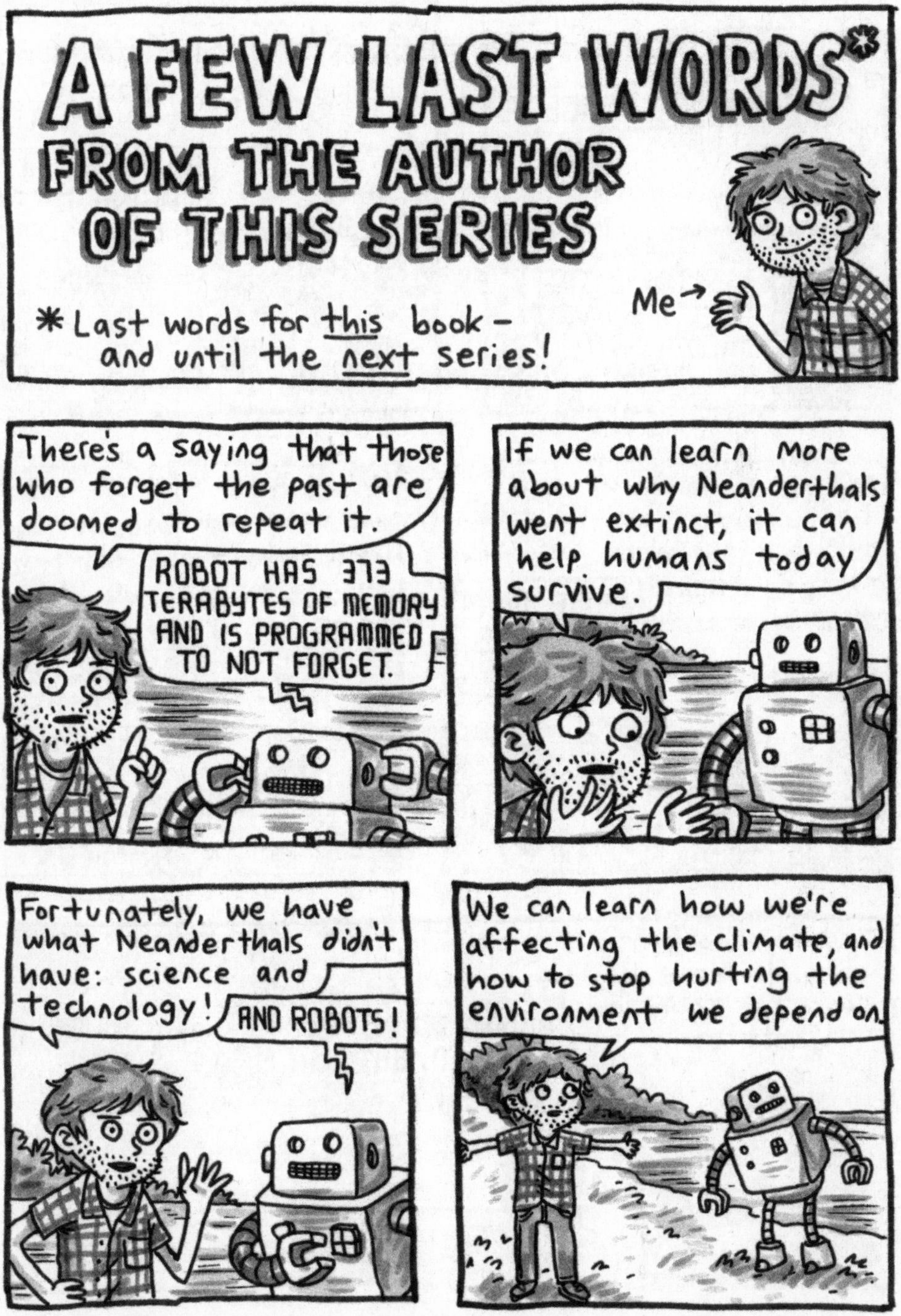
A FEW LAST WORDS*
FROM THE AUTHOR OF THIS SERIES
Me→
* Last words for this book – and until the next series!
There's a saying that those who forget the past are doomed to repeat it.
ROBOT HAS 373 TERABYTES OF MEMORY AND IS PROGRAMMED TO NOT FORGET.
If we can learn more about why Neanderthals went extinct, it can help humans today survive.
Fortunately, we have what Neanderthals didn't have: science and technology!
AND ROBOTS!
We can learn how we're affecting the climate, and how to stop hurting the environment we depend on.

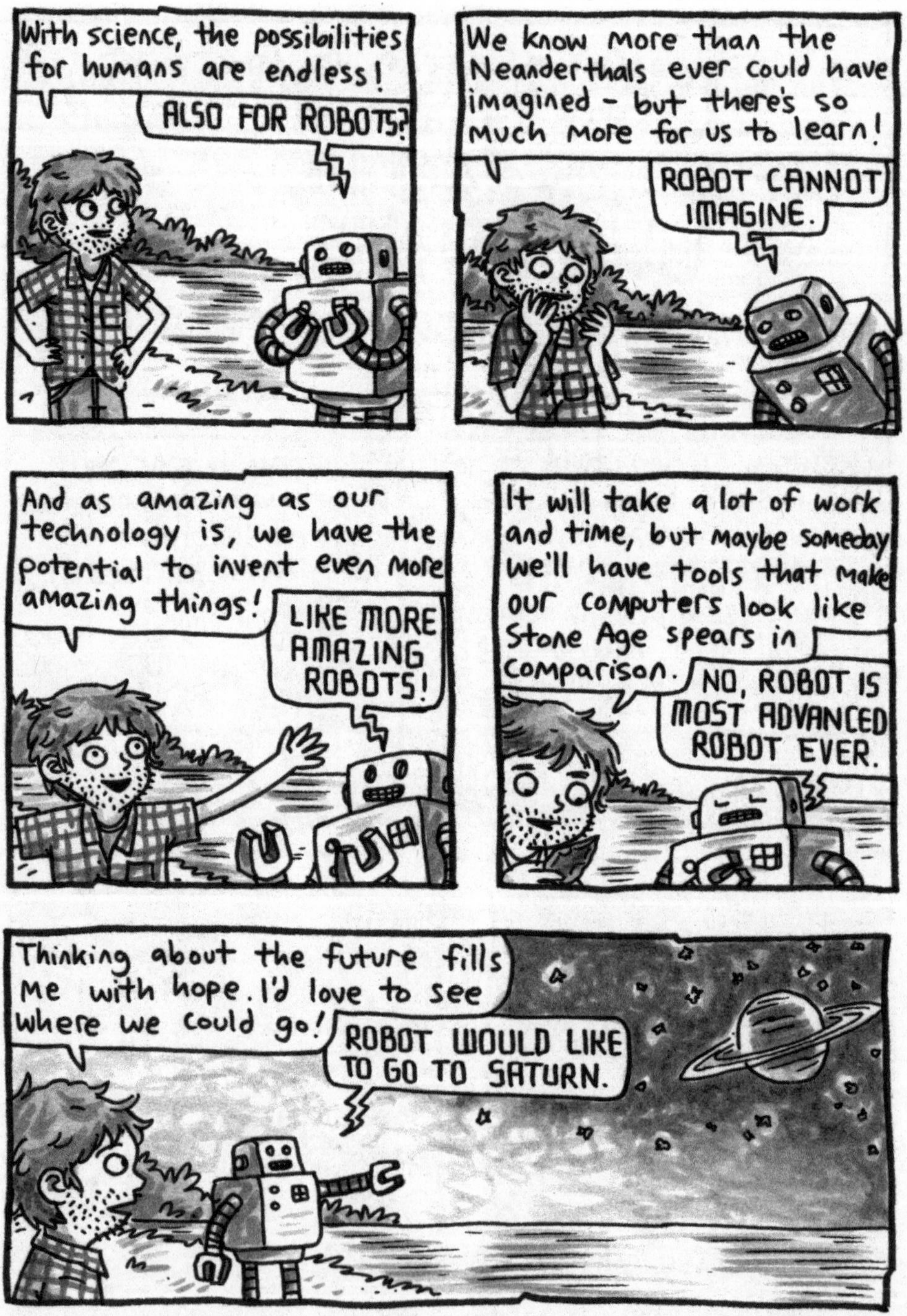
With science, the possibilities for humans are endless!
ALSO FOR ROBOTS?
We know more than the Neanderthals ever could have imagined - but there's so much more for us to learn!
ROBOT CANNOT IMAGINE.
And as amazing as our technology is, we have the potential to invent even more amazing things!
LIKE MORE AMAZING ROBOTS!
It will take a lot of work and time, but maybe someday we'll have tools that make our computers look like Stone Age spears in comparison.
NO, ROBOT IS MOST ADVANCED ROBOT EVER.
Thinking about the future fills me with hope. I'd love to see where we could go!
ROBOT WOULD LIKE TO GO TO SATURN.

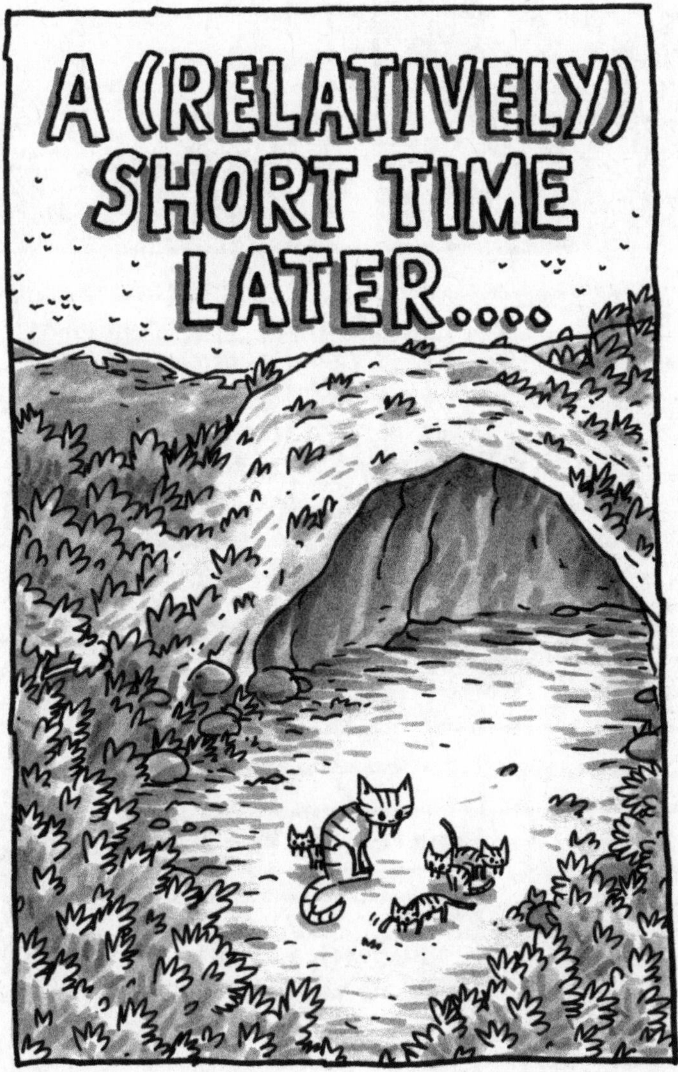
A (RELATIVELY) SHORT TIME LATER....

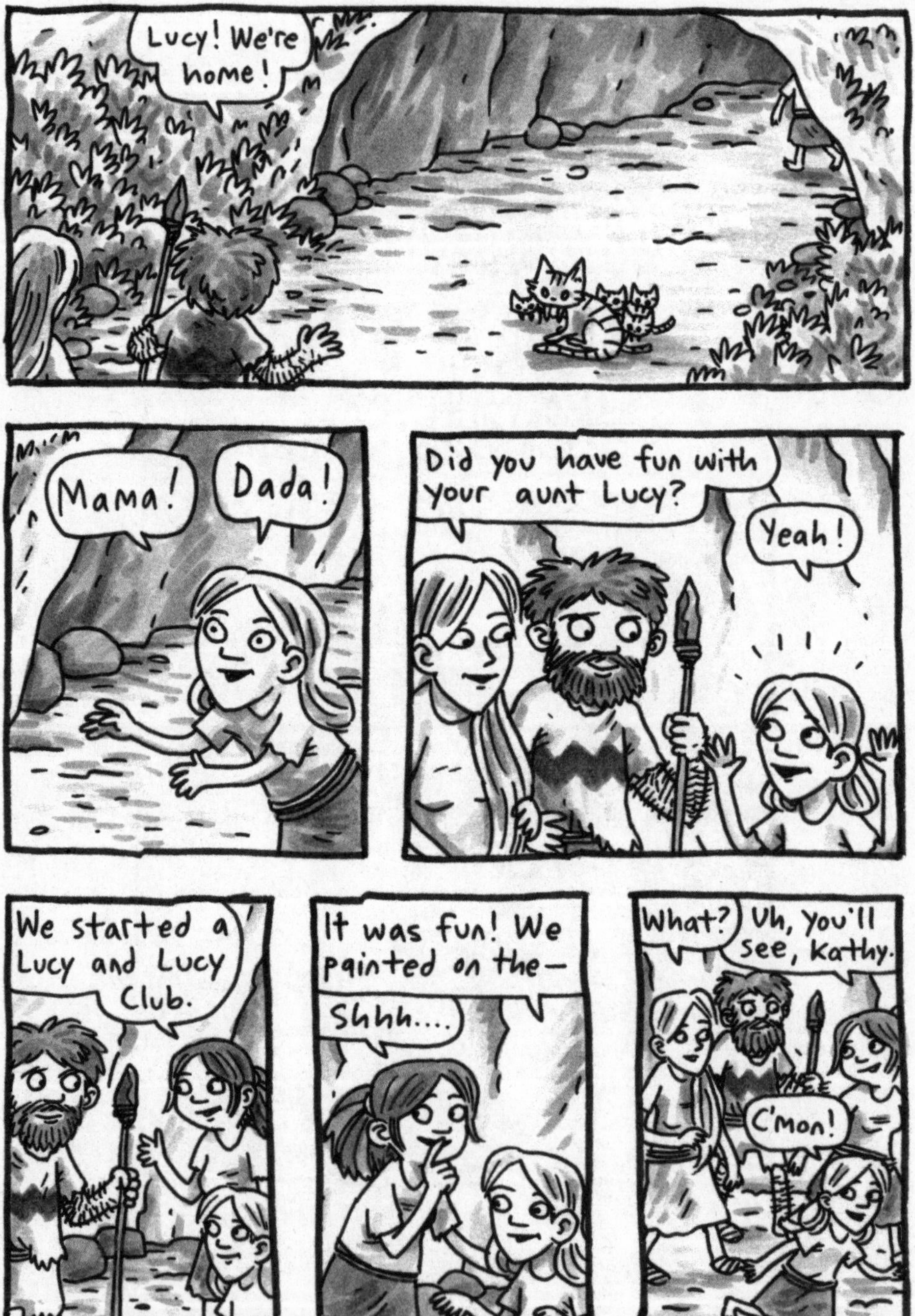
Lucy! We're home!
Mama!
Dada!
Did you have fun with your aunt Lucy?
Yeah!
We started a Lucy and Lucy Club.
It was fun! We painted on the—
Shhh....
What?
Uh, you'll see, Kathy.
C'mon!

Look, Andy. They did some... redecorating.

We painted all kinds of stories on the walls!

Nice! What's that one?

That's the time you fell in the river. And here's when you thought the mammoth poo was mud. And this is when you got scared by —

Giggle!

Are all these stories about me when I was a kid?!

Yeah! Mr. Richard and Mr. Tommy and Aunt Lucy told me ALL kinds of funny stories!

You know, maybe tomorrow I can tell you some stories about your aunt Lucy....

LOOK FOR THE STORY OF LUCY & ANDY'S GREAT-GRANDKIDS SOMETIME IN THE FUTURE!

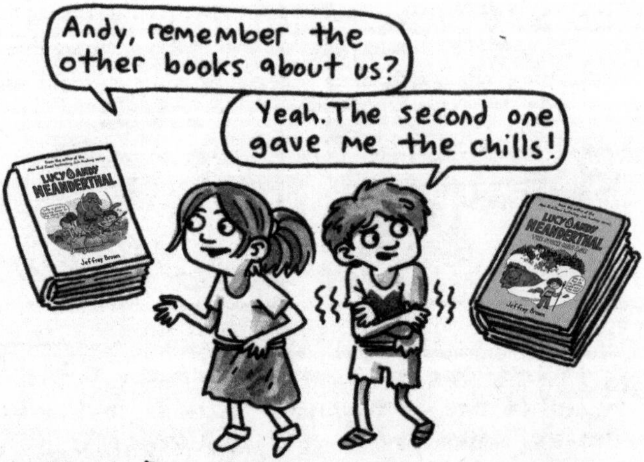
Andy, remember the other books about us?
Yeah. The second one gave me the chills!
LUCY & ANDY NEANDERTHAL
Jeffrey Brown
LUCY & ANDY NEANDERTHAL
Jeffrey Brown

Jeffrey Brown is the author of numerous bestselling Star Wars books, including *Darth Vader and Son*, and the Jedi Academy and Lucy & Andy Neanderthal series for middle graders. Fortunately, his cat is not scimitar-toothed.

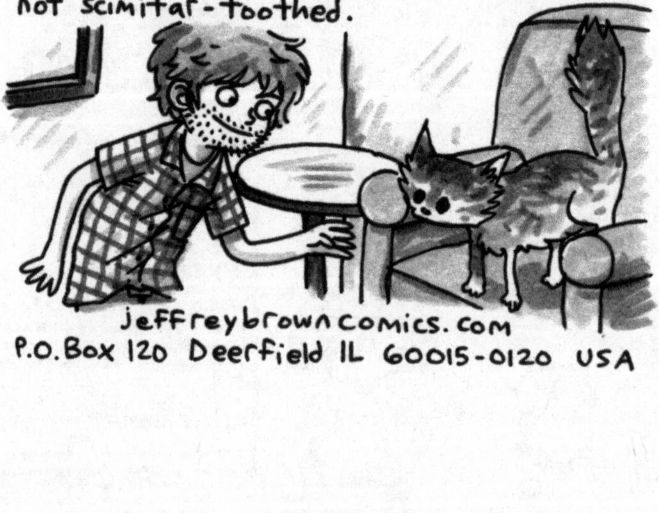

jeffreybrowncomics.com
P.O. Box 120 Deerfield IL 60015-0120 USA

Go back (WAY BACK!) to THE STONE AGE and see how it all began. . . .

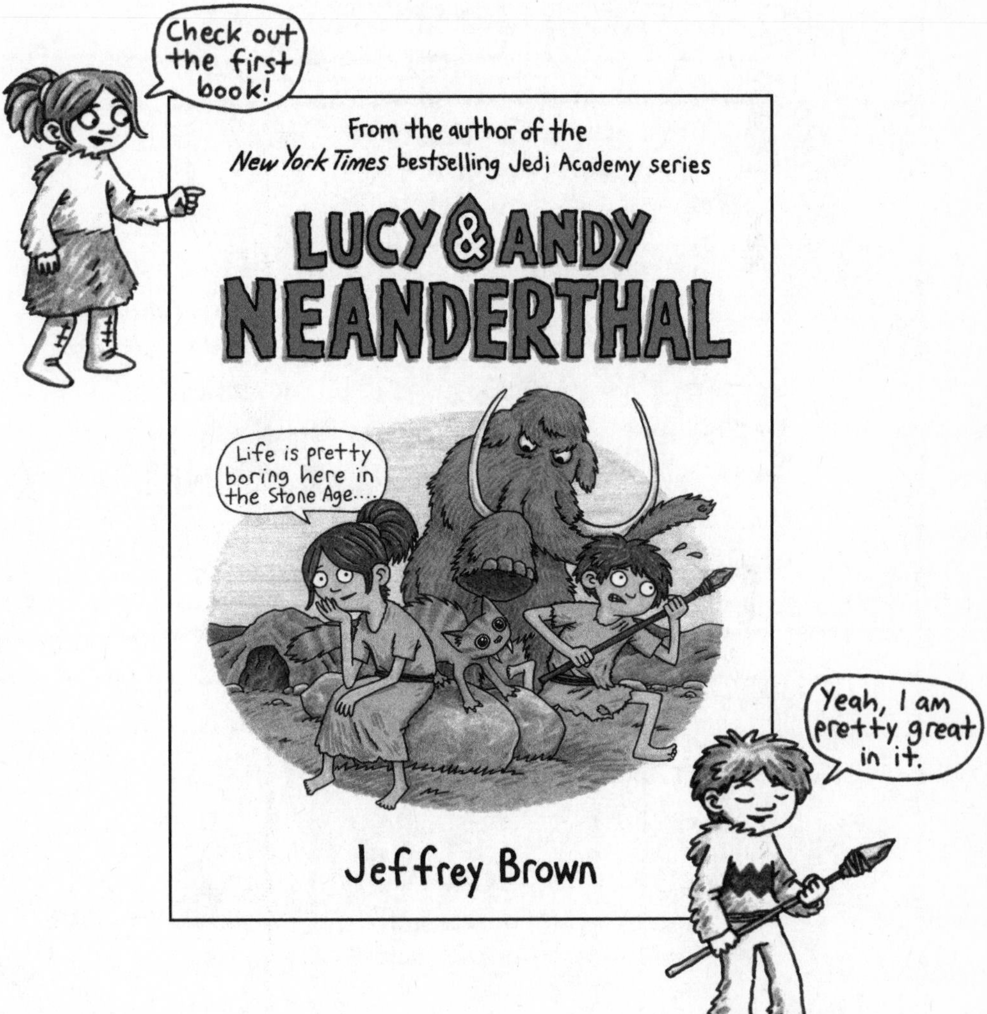
Check out the first book!
From the author of the New York Times bestselling Jedi Academy series
LUCY & ANDY NEANDERTHAL
Life is pretty boring here in the Stone Age....
Jeffrey Brown
Yeah, I am pretty great in it.

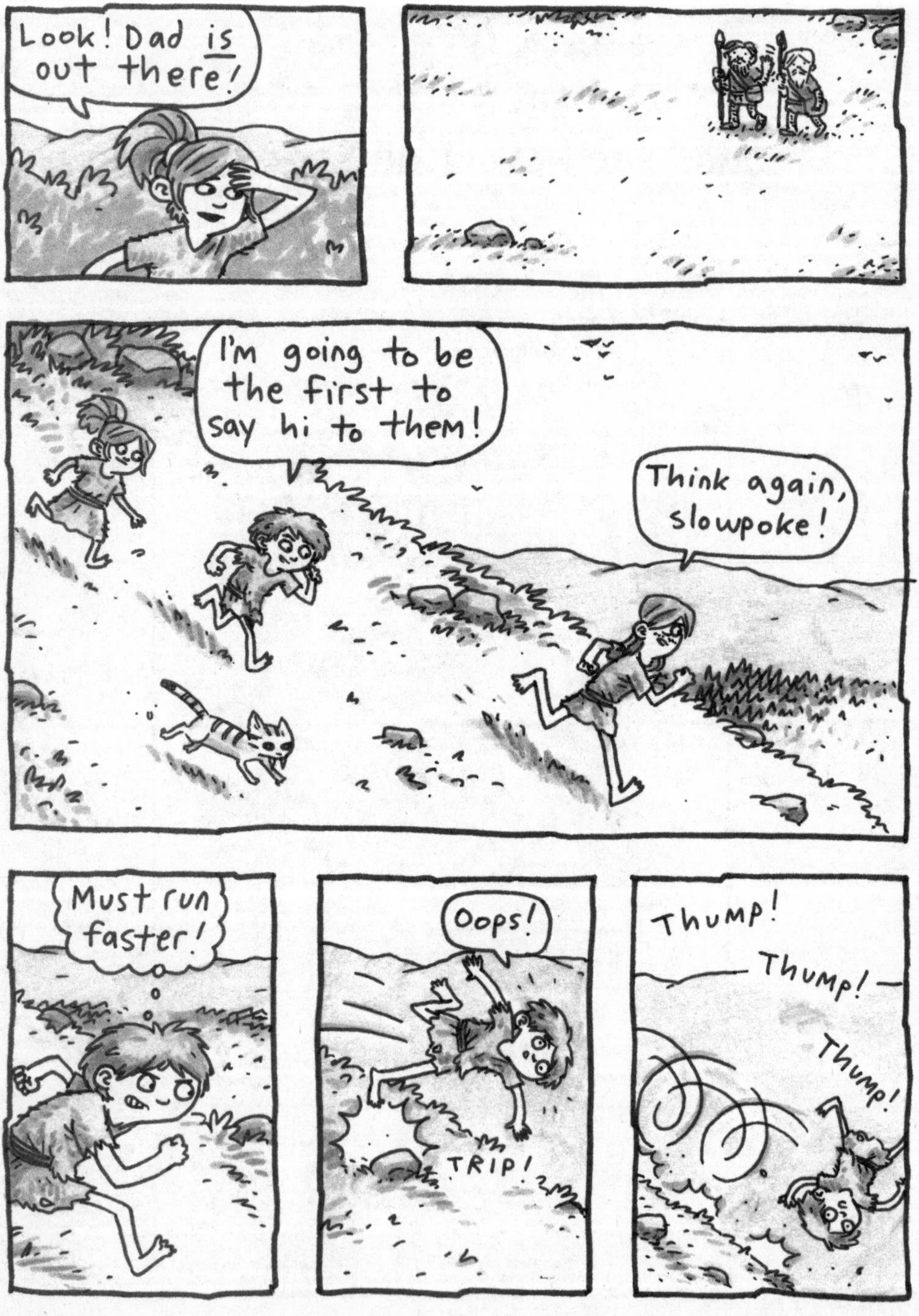
Look! Dad is out there!
I'm going to be the first to say hi to them!
Think again, slowpoke!
Must run faster!
Oops!
TRIP!
THUMP!
THUMP!
THUMP!

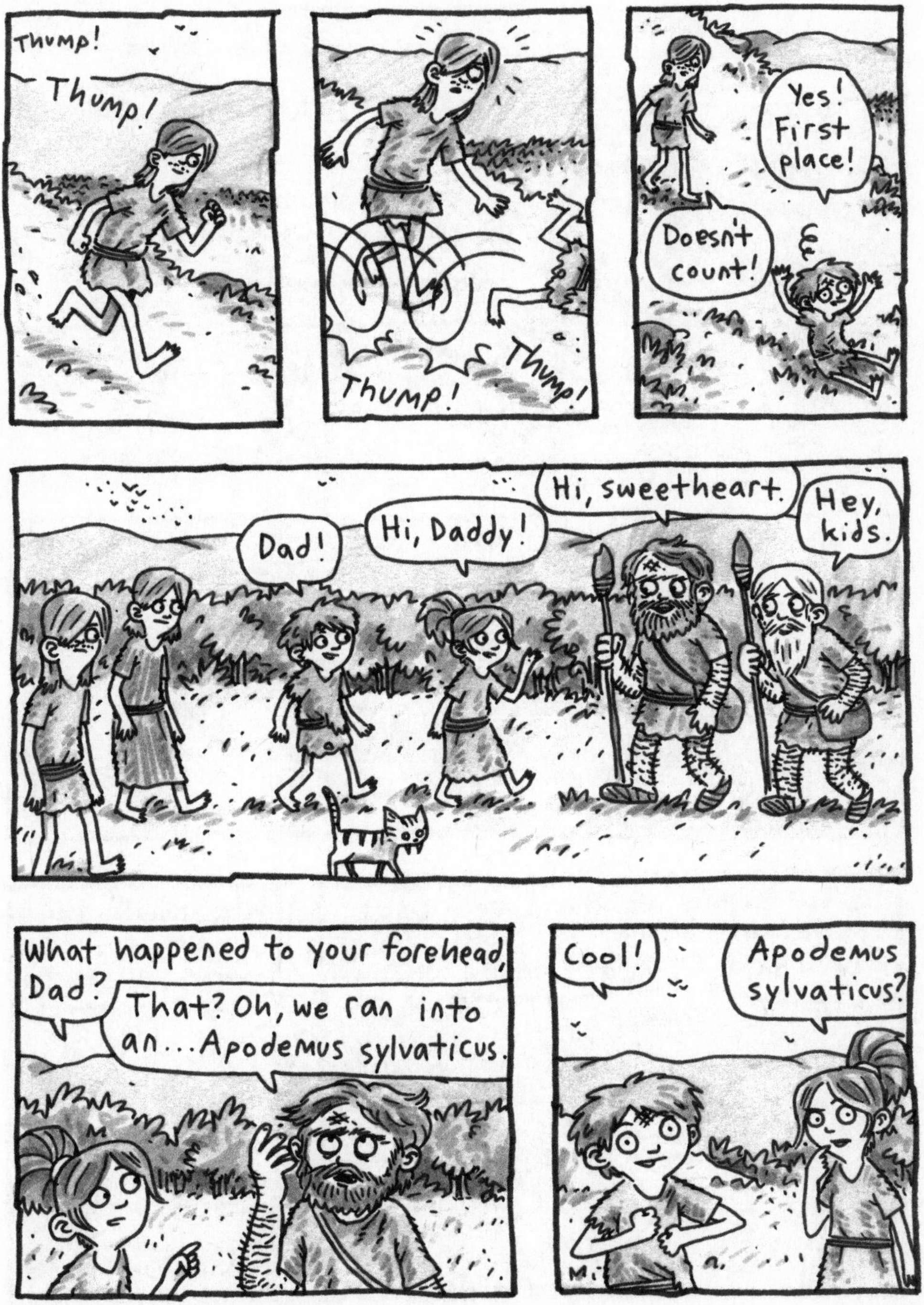
THUMP!
Thump!
Thump!
Thump!
Yes! First place!
Doesn't count!
Dad!
Hi, Daddy!
Hi, sweetheart.
Hey, kids.
What happened to your forehead, Dad?
That? Oh, we ran into an...Apodemus sylvaticus.
Cool!
Apodemus sylvaticus?

Apodemus sylvaticus (common name: wood mouse)

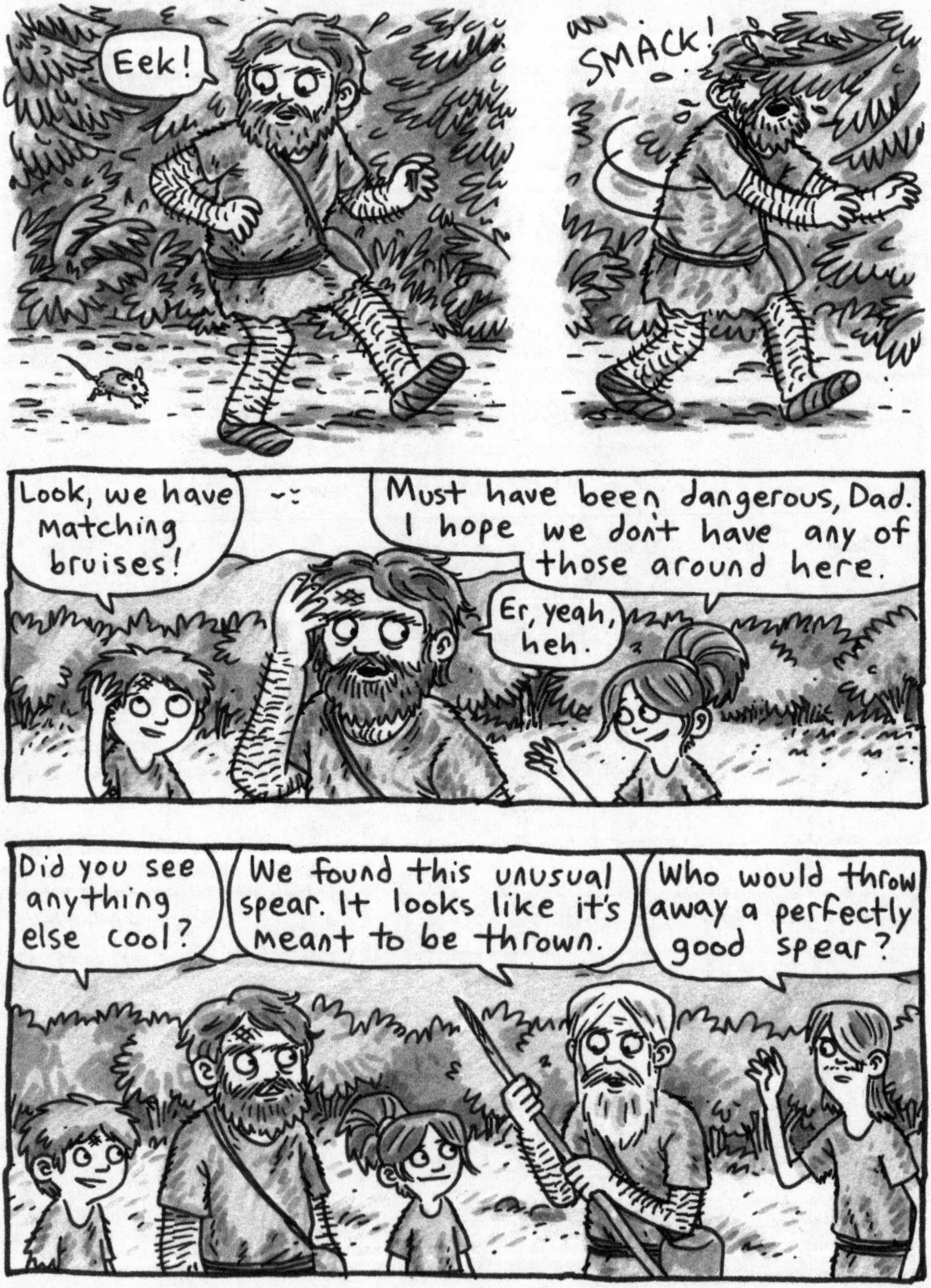
Eek!
SMACK!
Look, we have matching bruises!
Must have been dangerous, Dad. I hope we don't have any of those around here.
Er, yeah, heh.
Did you see anything else cool?
We found this unusual spear. It looks like it's meant to be thrown.
Who would throw away a perfectly good spear?

Chill out with another Lucy & Andy adventure!

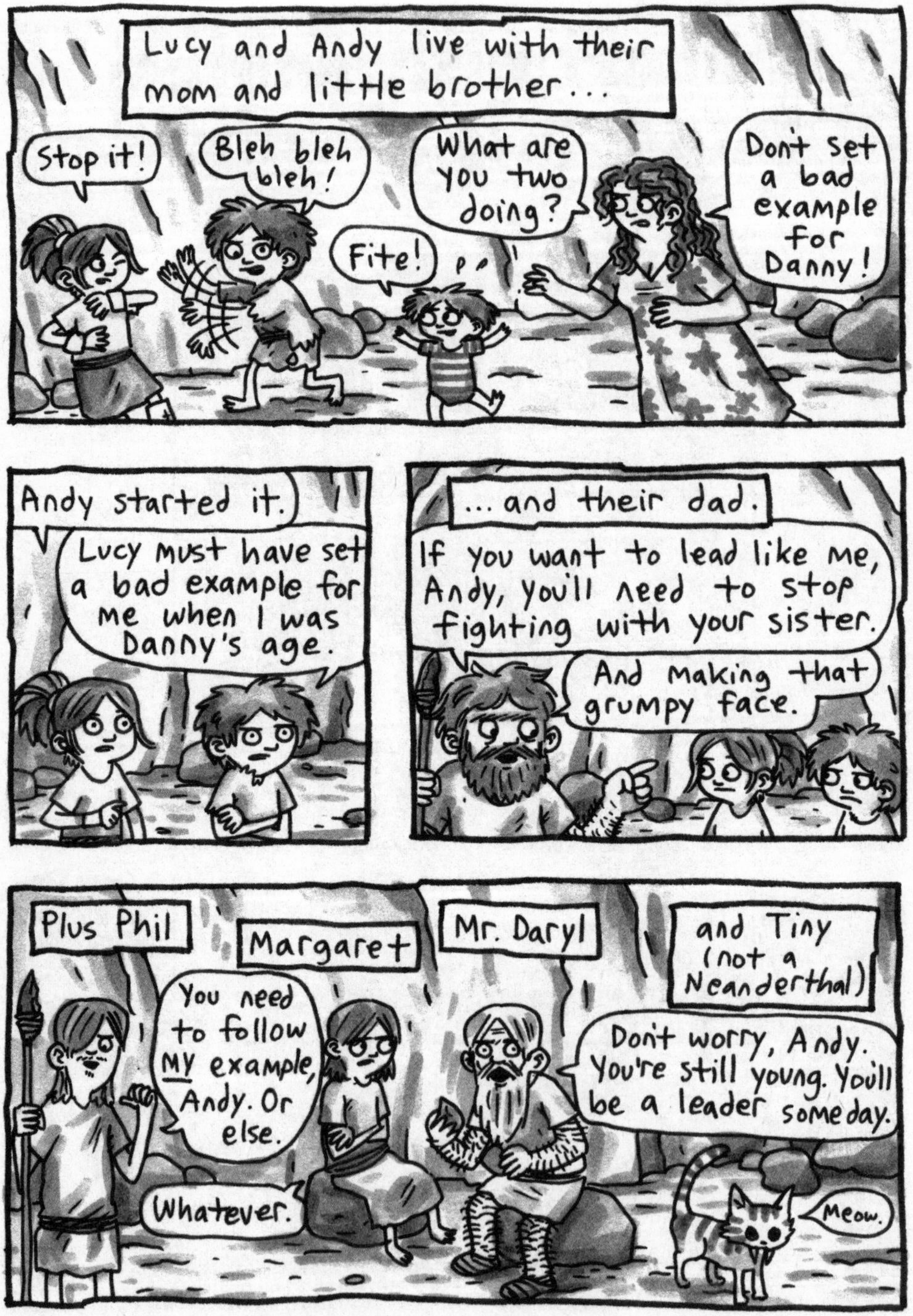

Lucy and Andy live with their mom and little brother...
Stop it!
Bleh bleh bleh!
Fite!
What are you two doing?
Don't set a bad example for Danny!
Andy started it.
Lucy must have set a bad example for me when I was Danny's age.
...and their dad.
If you want to lead like me, Andy, you'll need to stop fighting with your sister.
And making that grumpy face.
Plus Phil
Margaret
Mr. Daryl
and Tiny (not a Neanderthal)
You need to follow MY example, Andy. Or else.
Whatever.
Don't worry, Andy. You're still young. You'll be a leader someday.
Meow.

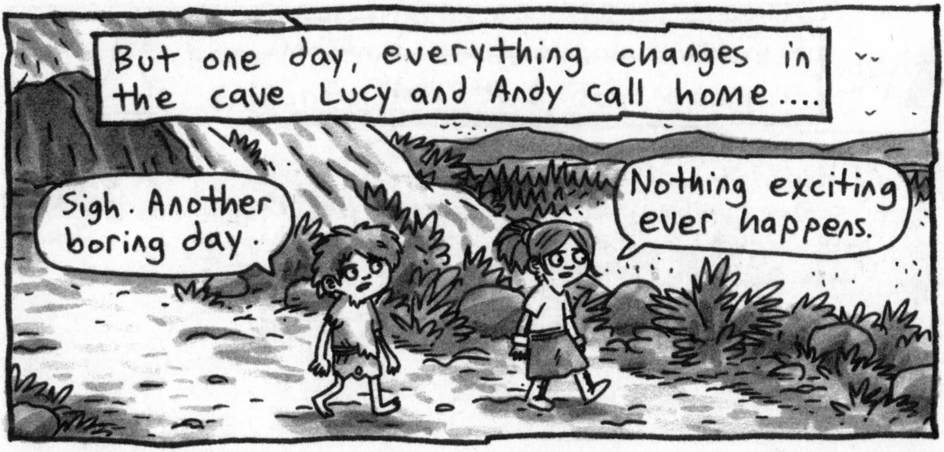
But one day, everything changes in the cave Lucy and Andy call home....
Sigh. Another boring day.
Nothing exciting ever happens.

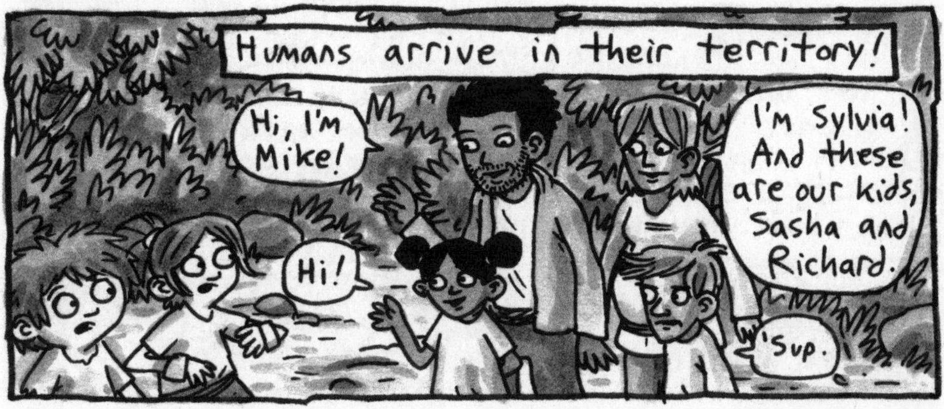
Humans arrive in their territory!
Hi, I'm Mike!
I'm Sylvia! And these are our kids, Sasha and Richard.
Hi!
'Sup.

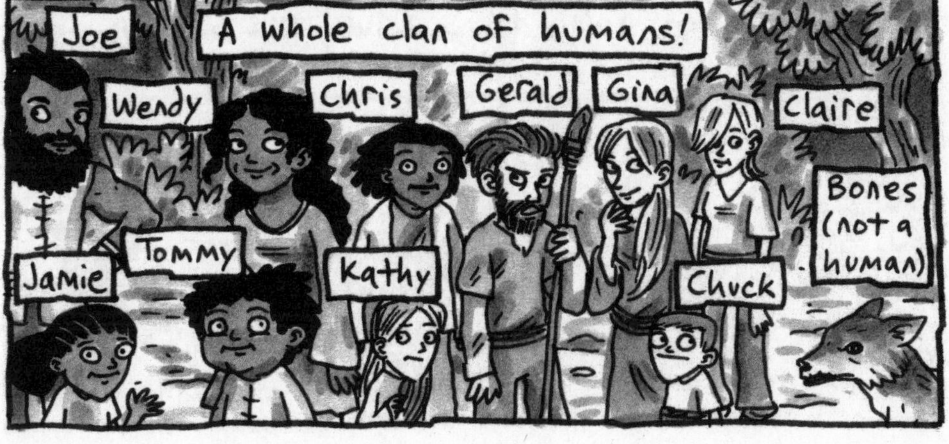
Joe
A whole clan of humans!
Wendy
Chris
Gerald
Gina
Claire
Bones (not a human)
Tommy
Jamie
Kathy
Chuck

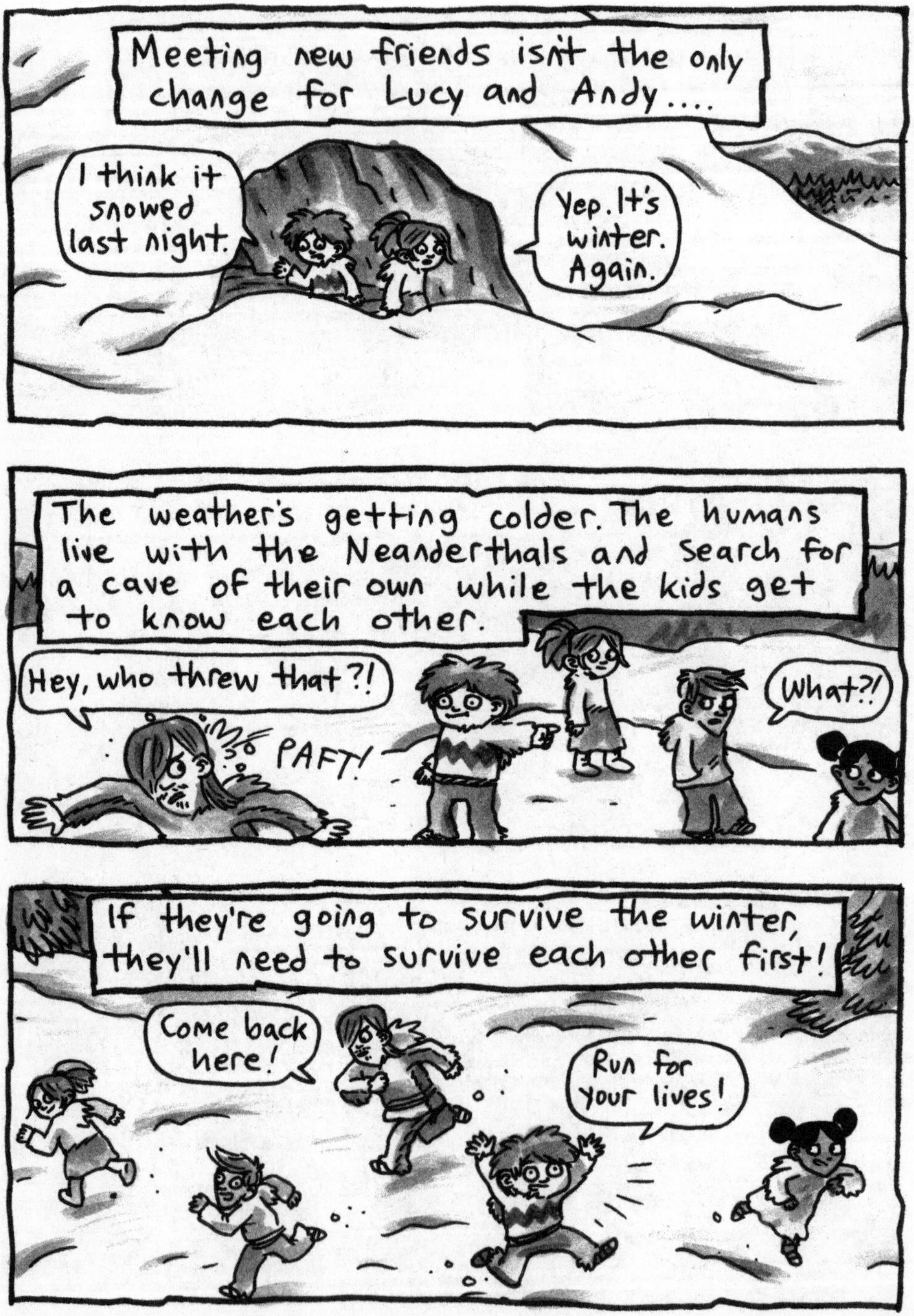
Meeting new friends isn't the only change for Lucy and Andy....
I think it snowed last night.
Yep. It's winter. Again.
The weather's getting colder. The humans live with the Neanderthals and search for a cave of their own while the kids get to know each other.
Hey, who threw that?!
PAFT!
What?!
If they're going to survive the winter, they'll need to survive each other first!
Come back here!
Run for your lives!